Praise for *The Teacher*:

'A terrific story, originally told. All hail the new queen of crime!' *Heat*

'A web of a plot that twists and turns and keeps the reader on the edge of their seat. This formidable debut is a page-turner, but don't read it before bed if you're easily spooked!' *Sun*

'A page-turner with a keep-you-guessing plot.' *Sunday Times Crime Club*

'Diamond neatly handles a string of interlocking strands.' *Daily Mail*

What the reviewers said:

'This is a story that immediately pulls you in and doesn't let go until the last page . . . The story flowed so brilliantly and made me keep turning the pages; a thriller from beginning to end. Each scene was rich and vivid; highly recommended.'

'It stands out a mile with its poisonous cover and the story within refused to let go of me.'

'A truly page-turning, somewhat gruesome read. Well written, pacy and with great characters.'

'*The Teacher* is a fast-paced grisly page-turner and an extraordinary debut from Katerina Diamond.'

KATERINA DIAMOND is the author of the *Sunday Times* and Amazon bestselling novel *The Teacher*, which was longlisted for the CWA John Creasey Debut Dagger Award and the Hotel Chocolat Award for 'darkest moment'. She has lived in various glamorous locations such as Weston-super-Mare, Thessaloniki, Larnaca, Exeter, Derby and Forest Gate. Katerina now resides in East Kent with her husband and children. She was born on Friday the 13th.

By the same author:

The Teacher

The
Secret

KATERINA DIAMOND

avon

AVON

A division of HarperCollins*Publishers*
1 London Bridge Street,
London SE1 9GF
www.harpercollins.co.uk

A Paperback Original 2016
2

Copyright © Katerina Diamond 2016

Katerina Diamond asserts the moral right to
be identified as the author of this work

A catalogue record for this book is
available from the British Library

ISBN 978-0-00-817221-3

Typeset in Sabon LT Std by Palimpsest Book Production Ltd,
Falkirk, Stirlingshire

Printed and bound in Great Britain by
Clays Ltd, St Ives plc

MIX
Paper from

For my husband, without whom I would think about murder a lot less.

Chapter 1: The Pro

The present

Bridget could hear cars passing on the wet roadside below the windows of the listed Victorian building where she worked. The traffic around Exeter's Quadrangle started to change at this time of night, from people making their way back from work, to people seeking something a little more interesting than what they had going on at home. She looked down from her window. The rain had abated for a few moments and the streets were empty, aside from the occasional vehicle. The only other sound she could hear was her flatmate, Estelle, in the room next door, 'entertaining' her client, headboard banging against the wall. She stared at the illuminated face of the clock tower a few hundred yards from her house and waited. Her visitor was late. He was never late.

There was a knock on the door and before Bridget

had a chance to answer, Estelle burst in, half-naked and out of breath.

'I need a solid.'

'Sounded like you were getting one.'

'Good one.' She adjusted her bra and flicked her hair extensions back. 'I mean I need a favour.'

'What kind of favour?' Bridget didn't want to know; Estelle's favours were always a little extreme.

'I've got Hitchcock with me and he wants extra time. I need you to take the Baby.'

'No way, Estelle, he's your problem, not mine. Besides, I'm waiting for someone.'

'Come on, please, Bridge! He doesn't even do anything, he just needs a cuddle and he sleeps the whole time. I'll be ten minutes – tops!'

Bridget looked at her watch.

'Fine, but just this once, Estelle, you know I'm not into all that.'

'I'll owe you one, big time.'

'You will.'

Estelle blew her a kiss and disappeared. Bridget couldn't help but keep looking out of the window, waiting for Sam. He would usually let her know if he couldn't come, and the silence was making her nervous. The city of Exeter was strangely quiet tonight. Generally, everyone went to bed early during the week, preparing for another hard day at work, but on a Friday it was usually busier than this. Tonight definitely had more of a Wednesday feel. She watched a car approaching. It was slowing as it got near. The rain made it hard to discern the make, so she held on to the hope that it might be Sam. But as the black four-by-four pulled on to the battered forecourt, her hope faded. Through the rain, she saw a man step out of the car and rush to the front door. The buzzer rang, Estelle's buzzer; they had one each, so each girl could tend to her own clients. Two girls per floor over two floors, with a communal kitchen and lounge at ground level. The sound went off again. It was frowned upon to open the door to someone else's bell, but Bridget went downstairs through the communal hallway and looked out of the spy hole in the shared front door. It was too dark to see the man, and his face was shielded from the rain by the collar of his trench coat. She took one last look through the spy hole and opened the door. The man kept his face covered and walked in, shaking off his umbrella.

'Where's Estelle?' the Baby asked.

'Come in, Estelle asked me to take care of you today,' Bridget said nervously, stepping out in front of the man. The Baby must have come straight from the office – she hoped he had his own nappy on underneath that bespoke Savile Row suit because there were some lines she just would not cross, even in the line of duty. As she led him up the stairs and to her room, she got the feeling he didn't much care who was looking after him, just as long as someone was. He was one of the less perverted of Estelle's clients, and that was saying something.

Bridget slowly undressed him, hanging each item carefully on a mahogany clothes horse. She pushed him on to the bed and sat down next to him, pulling him close to her and wrapping her arms around him.

'I'm hungry, I need milk.' He nuzzled into her.

'Oh, um . . . I don't . . .'

'Estelle usually keeps it in a bottle in the fridge. You need to warm it up though.' He seemed annoyed at having to tell her these things.

'OK, sorry, just wait there.' She rushed out of the room, silently cursing Estelle. This was not the deal.

She found the milk in the fridge and put it in the microwave. She pushed the button and stared at the red digital clock counting down. When it got to zero, the clock went back to the actual time and looking at it, she realised with a pang that she ought to be with Sam right now. All week she looked forward to her Friday visits with Sam. They would drive out to the Double Locks pub and huddle together in the corner. She began to worry again; it wasn't like him to be late, he was never late. That feeling was creeping under her skin, the feeling that if she didn't hear from him soon she may never hear from him again.

She took the bottle and shook it to disperse the heat. As she walked back to the bedroom, the door to Estelle's room opened and out walked the man they all referred to as Hitchcock. Bridget had never seen him up close before; he was fiercely private. She could only just see Hitchcock's eyes, very dark, staring at her with a mixture of disdain and scrutiny. There was something familiar about him. She had always assumed that he was called Hitchcock because he looked like the famous director – no one used real names in this game – but he was tall and slim, his dark hair peeking out from under his fedora. He looked nothing like the original Hitchcock.

He turned away quickly and Bridget ducked into her room to find the Baby curled up on the bed in a babygro, sucking his thumb. She rolled her eyes and walked towards him. She could hear Estelle and Hitchcock arguing at the front door before it slammed shut. A moment later, her bedroom door opened and Estelle walked in. Flustered, she took the bottle from Bridget and sat down next to the Baby, beginning to stroke his hair.

'I can take over now; he had to go.'

'What were you fighting about?'

'He wasn't happy about bumping into you, that's all. I told him earlier I had the place to myself. I thought you would be out. Come on, Baby.' She lifted the Baby's head on to her lap and put the bottle in his mouth – he suckled away. Bridget supposed as kinks went, it was a pretty harmless one.

'I'm going to take a shower, then,' Bridget said, before quickly exiting the room.

Their hot water wasn't working again so Bridget gathered her things and went to ask Dee, who lived upstairs, if she could use her shower.

'Are you sure you don't mind?'

'No, it's cool. I was just getting ready to go out. What do you think of this?' Dee did a twirl in what was obviously a stolen dress: blue sequins with a low neckline. She was a notorious shoplifter; some of the gifts she had given Bridget in the past attested to that. Dee was in between flatmates – previous tenants always looked for another house share after spending a few weeks with Dee and her sticky fingers.

'You know those earrings of mine you like, the vintage blue crystal ones? They would look really nice with that dress. They're in our bathroom downstairs, if you want them.' Bridget smiled at Dee. It was always better to offer her things before she took them anyway.

'You're a star. Maybe tonight I'll meet my millionaire,' Dee said, blowing Bridget a kiss as she made her way down the stairs to the floor below.

Bridget loved the feeling of hot water. Living in this house felt dirty, everything felt wrong. She wished she could be back home with her family, or even call her mother, but that wasn't an option at the moment. She washed her hair for the first time in a week, feeling the filth and grime hidden underneath the layers of hair-spray. Dirty hair held a style better. Estelle would make her hair pretty again with rollers and a curling iron. Bridget was never any good with that stuff. Luckily she was naturally quite appealing, in fact she looked better without make-up on, but the men here weren't interested in natural beauty. They wanted the hot plastic on their arm, with the push-up bras and the fake tans; they wanted the glamour-model look, not the girl next door. Mostly Bridget just provided dates, unlike Estelle, who was all about the extra-curriculars – that's where the real money got made, that's where you got to meet the important men. Bridget hadn't proved she could be trusted yet.

She turned off the water and ran her fingers through her hair, it squeaked between her hands as she worked through the tangles. It felt so good to get all that shit off her. She threw a towel around herself and headed into Dee's lounge, where she spotted several things of her own that had gone missing in the last few days. She didn't begrudge Dee; she knew it was something she had no control over, and none of those stolen things meant anything to her anyway. Nothing in this life meant anything to her, except Sam.

She walked down the stairs back to her flat, wearing just her towel. The door was ajar. Something was off. She pressed her back against the wall and peered through the gap. She could see Dee's foot, her blue patent shoe hanging off at the heel. Bridget crouched down and peered in further, she could hear a noise coming from inside. *Don't panic*, she thought to herself. *You know what to do*. Still, her stomach twisted as she saw what was inside the room.

Dee was laid out on the ground, eyes wide open, her face frozen in an expression of surprise. Bridget could see her body moving as she struggled for breath. Blood pooled beneath her, and her legs were wet with red. Bridget could see a five-inch slash mark high up on the inside of her thigh. Her femoral artery had been cut; she would be dead within minutes. One thought entered Bridget's head.

Shit. They know who I am.

Bridget started to move forward into the flat, knowing she had to get her phone. It was barely six feet away. Dee's eyes moved towards her, flashing her a foreboding look, a warning. She saw a tear falling from the side of Dee's head on to the floor as her eyes filled with an emptiness Bridget was all too familiar with. This wasn't the first dead body she had seen, but it was the first time she had actually witnessed someone die. She couldn't think about that right now. *Remember. What do you do now?* Whoever had done this was still in the flat. She couldn't risk it. *You need to warn Sam.* Bridget needed to get to a phone. Sam would know what to do.

Chapter 2: The Survivor

The present

First of all, Bridget needed some clothes. She backed up the stairs, trying to make sure she didn't make any noise; she knew whoever had hurt Dee was still in the building, probably hurting Estelle.

She looked through Dee's clothes hurriedly, grabbing a black velour Hooch tracksuit. It was the only thing that went down further than the thighs and higher than the nipples. She crept down the stairs again. She could hear a man talking on the phone, with an accent she couldn't quite place.

'What do you mean it's not her? There're two women here and one bloke dressed as a fucking baby . . . Yeah, one of them has black hair and the other is blonde. I sent you the pictures . . . Well, she's not here then, is she . . . All right, all right, I'm sorry. I didn't mean to disrespect you. I'll find her . . . Don't worry, they're all

9

dead . . . No, no one saw me . . . There's definitely no one else here . . . OK.'

She peered through the crack in the door again. The man was in her bedroom, his shadowy figure facing away from her. She could see her mobile phone on the side table, right above where all her shoes were kept, but she couldn't go in. Slowly, she backed away from the bedroom, back into the communal hallway. Her breathing was fast and erratic but she tried to be quiet, tried not to disturb anything as she walked.

She opened the sash window in the hallway, wincing at the slight sound, and ran quickly down the fire escape. The cold, wet metal was a shock to her feet. She was trying hard not to make noise on the rickety iron staircase; in places the metal had completely eroded, so she had to be careful not to cut herself or put her foot through the steps. She ran down the side alley that was parallel to the back of the building, stopping at a yellow road-gritting salt box. The weather had been mild enough lately that she hadn't needed to worry about it being disturbed for a while.

Bridget opened the box and reached inside. She dug around, the sound of the dirty chunks of rock salt scraping against each other setting her teeth on edge. She felt the leather strap of her backpack between her fingers and tugged hard. The salt displaced with a *crunch*, making more noise than she'd anticipated. She shot a look behind her to make sure no one was there. She was alone. She opened the bag and checked the contents. A roll of bank notes, a phone, a Leatherman multi-tool, an emergency power pack and a spare phone battery. The battery in the phone was dead so she switched it to the spare. There wasn't a lot of battery left on the emergency one either. If this didn't qualify as an emergency, she didn't know what did. The only number on the phone was Sam's. She pressed the screen.

Straight to answerphone.

'Sam? It's Bridge. Where the hell are you? Are you in trouble? A man came to the house while I was using the shower upstairs, but when I came back down they were all dead.' She tried to keep the panic out of her voice, whispering furiously so as not to attract any attention. 'I only saw Dee's body. I didn't see the others, but I heard him talking. It was me they were after . . . I didn't see who it was though. He had a slight accent, I think, and he didn't sound young, but that's all I can tell you for now. I'm going to go to our meeting spot. Please be there.' She checked over her shoulder, paused and took a deep breath. There was a feeling in the pit of her stomach that told her she wouldn't be speaking to him for a while. 'I love you, Sam.'

Bridget hung up, swinging the bag on to her back. She began walking towards the town centre, keeping one eye on a few drunks on the corner of the street. She wondered if they were who they appeared to be. Were they watching her? She surveyed the cars along the road, searching for a model more than twenty years old, as they were easier to get into. It was a long way to her usual meeting place with Sam. She needed a car.

Her eyes landed on a J-reg Vauxhall Cavalier. She dropped behind it and got to work, removing a paracord bow from the bag. Bridget kept one eye on the road as she worked, and ducked further down behind the car as she saw a man, walking in her direction. She didn't have long. Her heart skipped a beat when she saw another, younger man emerge from the building behind him. The two men paused in the street, a few cars down from where she crouched. She could hear the rumble of raised voices as they began to argue.

Now was her chance.

She made a slipknot in the cord. She leveraged the door a fraction with the Leatherman and slid the string through the space, moving it slowly from side to side with one hand either end of the string until the loop connected with the bobble on the plastic door lock. She pulled each end of the string until the knot was tight around the lock then yanked the ends quickly upwards, unlocking the door.

The men both turned at the clunk, their faces hidden in the darkness. There was a beat of silence. Bridget waited a few seconds until they turned back to face one another, then carefully opened the car door. She reached under the steering column and unscrewed the cover, telling herself to keep calm. *You've done this a million times before.* She pulled out the wire bundle and stripped the two red battery wires of their casing, exposing an inch of copper with the knife on her Leatherman, then twisted them together. She stripped the brown ignition wire before getting in the car to crank the starter over. The moment that exposed ignition wire hit the battery the two men would know where she was; she had only seconds to get away. She took a deep breath and touched the wires together. As soon as the engine started, Bridget glanced through the window to see the two men moving, running to get to the car before she could drive away. She threw the backpack on to the seat beside her and pulled out into the road, turning the wheel so hard her hands hurt. If they had any doubts before they heard the wheelspin, they certainly didn't now. Looking through the rear-view mirror, she was just in time to see the pair jumping into a car, ready to follow her.

Chapter 3: The Hunted

The present

Bridget took the road to St David's station, wishing she had told Sam that she would meet him there, where there were people and places to hide in plain sight. She carried on driving, aware that the men were not far behind her. She saw them turn each corner as she reached the other end of the street, their car jolting on to the kerbs as they chased her. Bridget thought briefly about Estelle, and what must have happened to her. *I should have called an ambulance.* She couldn't think about what she should have done, all she could think about was getting away from these men. Her eyes flitted between the rear-view mirror and the road ahead. As she drove down Bonhay Road she felt so exposed; there wasn't enough traffic to get lost in.

They were gaining on her. She drove across the bridge towards Cowick. She would have to get rid of the car.

It was good for distance but they were past that now. She just needed to make sure they didn't get hold of her and she stood a better chance of that on foot. There were some smaller streets coming up, with lots of red brick housing set back from the main road. Glancing behind, she couldn't see their car, and she quickly turned the steering wheel and drove through an entrance into a private car park behind a small row of houses, immediately killing the engine. They wouldn't be able to see the car from the road – not yet, anyway. Bridget jumped out and ran as fast as she could towards the river. As she sprinted, she heard the sound of a car coming. It was them. She ducked behind a large council wheelie bin and waited for them to pass her. They had slowed right down, obviously searching for her. Her breathing felt as though it had stopped as she crouched on the ground next to the bin. She waited for the sound of the car to die, and when she was sure they had gone, she emerged, keeping close to the buildings as she ran down to the river, taking the underpass to the lower walkway that ran alongside the bank. Hopefully they wouldn't see her down here from the road. She had completely forgotten that she wasn't wearing anything on her feet; ignoring the pain of the tarmac, she made her way towards the Cricklepit Bridge. Everything was lit up, but she stuck to the shadows when she could and moved faster when she couldn't.

Bridget looked behind her, sure that she was not alone. Even the pubs along the bank looked derelict. She longed for a crowd to lose herself in, wanting to bury her presence like a needle in a haystack. She felt as though she was standing on a stage with a spotlight pointed right at her face. Looking to the left, she caught sight of the children's play area, and felt a stab of relief. She ran to it, clambered over the fence and squeezed her body into the adventure castle, grateful that she had grabbed something warm to wear. *Stay out of sight, at least until you catch your breath.*

As she watched the riverbank, a man emerged from the path she had just scrambled away from. He was scanning the area – was he the man who'd killed Estelle and Dee? Was the Baby dead, too? Was he still in his romper? Bridget remembered his wedding ring and wondered how his family would feel when they were notified that he was found dead, dressed as a baby with a prostitute on either side of him.

It was drawing close to the hour. Bridget felt a thud of realisation: *the backpack*. She had left the backpack in the car. There was no way she would make it to the rendezvous on time, and she had to find a way to let Sam know.

Judging by the intense way the man was surveying the bank, Bridget couldn't shake the fact that it was definitely him: the one who had killed her friends. He was a big man, thick set with a beard but no hair on his head; he almost looked like a caricature of a strong man from an old circus poster. He was out of place in the picturesque setting of the river. He walked with sinister purpose, getting closer and closer to the play area. She was trapped in the wooden castle. If he thought to look in there, he'd find her immediately. Her heart stopped when he paused at the entrance to the play area, but then he carried on to the bridge and walked across, stopping again on the other side. She breathed out. She was going to have to make a break for it before he retraced his steps. *It's now or never*. She slowly climbed out of the wooden structure and, with one eye on the man, she quickly moved back across the playground to the railings and slung one leg over, followed by the other. Losing her balance, Bridget fell, straight on to a broken bottle. The area was a popular spot with disaffected teens from the estates; she'd seen them guzzling their miniature ciders before returning home after school. There were discarded bottles everywhere.

'Fuck!' she said, louder than she should have.

The man's head whipped around; he turned back towards her and sprinted towards the park. Bridget pulled herself to her feet using the fence as leverage; she could feel broken glass digging into her kneecap but she knew she had to shake the pain off. If he got hold of her, it was the last thing she would need to worry about. She could feel the blood draining from her face; she limped as fast as she could towards the Haven Banks housing complex but then thought better of it – she was bleeding and would leave a trail. At this time of night, the silence was so deafening that even the smallest intake of breath would be heard inside that complex – it was a nicer part of town, there would be no late-night parties, no drunks littered in the hallways or dealers pushing their gear. She should have run to one of the rougher estates where it was easier to disappear. She should have gone to a hotel and hidden. What the hell had she been thinking?

Bridget looked around and quickly assessed her surroundings, deciding where the safest place to hide would be. *Where would he be least likely to venture?* Suddenly it became obvious to her as she stared at the black water of the river. A few miles down the river was her meeting place with Sam, if he would just hold on she could make it there, in the water, if she didn't pass out on the bank first. The man was getting closer and she needed to make her move now. She swiftly edged over the side into the water, being careful not to make a noise as her body became immersed in the icy cold. *Breathe.* If he knew where she'd gone he would follow her. She was completely in shadow as she moved through the water, hidden under some overgrowth that hung over from the bank. She was grateful that she couldn't see any swans. That was the last thing she needed. She could hear the man on his phone approaching.

'She was here, I just saw her. Yes. I know how important this is . . . Are you sure? OK, I'll meet you there.'

He was out of earshot again. She would have to stay put for a few minutes, make sure he was gone, because as soon as she ventured out from this spot she would be in full view again. It was cold in the water, so cold; she reached down to her knee and felt the glass poking out of it. She didn't know whether to pull it out or leave it in. Her mind buzzed with stories, thinking of reports she'd read where stab victims were fine until the weapon was removed, at which point they bled to death. She couldn't remember if any major veins or arteries ran through the knee. Sam would know what to do. The adrenaline was pumping so fast that she couldn't think clearly; was she afraid or just really fucking cold? For now she just needed to concentrate on getting to Sam. She had to get to their place. It was her only chance.

She edged along the side of the river towards the back of the pub where she hoped Sam would be waiting. It'd be shut now, but it was secluded enough that they wouldn't need to worry about being seen together. She was out of breath from the cold. She hadn't heard the man for a long time. Maybe it was safe to get out? She wanted to let go of the edge and just let her head fall beneath the surface. Moving slowly was even more exhausting. She was so tired. *Is this hypothermia?* Drowning wasn't even something that she cared about; she just wanted to fall asleep for a bit. Just a little sleep, then she could start moving again. She tried not to think about what was in the water. Since she had been small and seen a documentary about a giant deep-sea squid Bridget had had a fear of dark water. She could see it now as she blinked. Each blink seemed to last a little longer than the one before. The only thing propelling her to open her eyes again was the thought of that squid with its enormous red head and the tentacles that swept through the water like wet velvet, heavy but effortless. Always just about to touch her as she moved forward beyond its grasp.

Bridget reached the Double Locks pub and dug her frozen fingers into the grass on the embankment, dragging herself out of the water. She had made it. The upside of the extreme cold was that she no longer had any pain in her knee, or any feeling in her legs at all, for that matter. She was so exhausted; she had to rest for a moment. The damp grass was warm and soft compared to the sharpness of the water. She could barely move and it was so dark that she just lay there, looking up at the moon with the clouds rolling over it. *Don't fall asleep.* Her eyelids became heavy and as much as she wanted to fight it, her body was taking over. It was time to close her eyes.

Chapter 4: The Traitor

The present

DS Adrian Miles sat at his desk in Exeter Police Station, making origami mandarin ducks out of report forms. It was the best possible use he could imagine for them at the moment, as he certainly wasn't going to be filling any of them out.

He looked over at his partner's desk. DS Imogen Grey was due back to work today. Adrian had offered to swing by and pick her up but she had been determined in her refusal. She was an obstinate one all right, rejecting help of any kind. They hadn't really spoken while she'd been off, just the odd phone call here and there to tell her about the less exciting proceedings going on, like DI Fraser becoming the new acting DCI, and the shake-up within the department. A shake-up which included an investigation into every officer there. That had been fun.

Imogen Grey walked into the room, a slight smirk appearing on her face when she saw her desk, which was completely littered with origami animals.

'Busy then?'

'I made you a welcoming committee.'

'You've got quite the talent there, Miley. I hope each one doesn't represent someone you've killed, like in that Chinese movie about the baby.'

As the seconds passed, Imogen's smirk turned into an uncomfortable smile, the kind of smile that says, *I don't want to talk about it*. Her eyes were flat and Adrian knew that walking through those doors had taken her all kinds of courage. He really wanted to get up and give her a hug, but he also didn't want her to thrust her knee into his genitals, so he just stood up and shook her hand. He stroked the back of her wrist with his thumb, his way of saying 'I'm glad to see you back.' She pulled away and took a deep breath before taking her jacket off and sitting down.

'Can I get you a coffee?'

'Don't, Miley.'

'Don't what?'

'Don't . . . be nice to me, I can't handle it.'

'What?' He put his most affronted face on. 'I'm always nice to you! You're the mean one!'

She considered this for a moment.

'OK, fine, black with two sugars then, please.'

He stood up and walked over to the machine; within seconds he had a steaming hot cup of what looked like watered-down mud. After smelling it, he decided against getting himself one. He put the sugars in and took it back over to Imogen, who was just taking a file from Denise Ferguson, the desk sergeant.

'We have a case!' she said, taking the coffee from him and sniffing it, before putting it on the desk as though it was a urine sample. 'I'll get us some coffee on the way.'

'What's the case?'

'Triple homicide.'

'Whoa! Do you think that's a good idea?'

'They can't hurt me, Miley, they're dead.'

'I know, but wouldn't you rather start out with something a little less gruesome?'

'It's sweet of you to be concerned,' she said sarcastically. 'But I want to work, I want to catch the bad guys before they catch up to us.'

'As long as you're OK.'

'I will be. Believe it or not, I've been through worse.'

'I know you have. I wish you'd talk to me about it, Imogen. That stuff you said . . . About what happened before you transferred from Plymouth – I'm here for you, if you want to talk.'

'Miley, drop it, please. Fraser is waiting for us at the crime scene.'

'OK, I'm dropping it. Let's go.'

The road was cordoned off outside the house when they arrived. Adrian parked a few streets away, nearer to Exeter prison. He was glad it wasn't night time. The darkness carried the sounds from inside the jail and left them whispering in the air. At least in the daylight you could pretend you weren't standing so close to all that scum. Imogen was looking up at the prison windows, almost in a trance. Adrian thought he could see tears as she stared at the formidable red brick structure.

'You OK?' he said, putting his hand on her shoulder. She snapped her head round and looked at him; he moved his hand immediately and they set off for the crime scene.

As Adrian walked into the flat, he could tell it was some kind of brothel. He saw the blonde girl first; she was translucent and her skin looked almost wet. It must have been some kind of body glitter designed to make her glow, but on the dead skin it looked like the silvery sheen found on rotten meat. With her short, sparkly blue dress and her white legs covered in red, it was like some kind of horrific superhero costume. He thought of his battle-ready, limited-edition boxed Wonder Woman toy and his throat constricted.

He stepped over her and into the bedroom. There was a man in what appeared to be an adult babygro with a ladies' comb sticking out of his neck, the long metal spike at the end jammed firmly into his jugular with several other puncture marks surrounding it. A vision was thrust upon Adrian: someone rapidly stabbing the man in the neck with great force. He had seen enough to know there were no hesitation marks: whoever had done this had killed before.

'Are there any IDs on the bodies?' Adrian asked DCI Fraser.

'They took the man's car already. We managed to trace him through the registration; he didn't have any

ID on him. His name is Edward Walker. As for the girls, we think the one out there lives in the flat upstairs.'

'There's another girl?'

'Yeah, Estelle Jackson. She's in the other room. It's not pretty.'

Adrian followed DCI Fraser back past the blonde and into the bathroom. His hand immediately went up to his mouth.

'What the hell?'

'Jesus Christ.' Imogen was standing beside him.

Adrian wanted to step in front of her to block her view but he knew it wasn't his place. He just looked to see if she was OK. If she was shaken, she was hiding it well, but she couldn't quite disguise the shallowness of her breath.

The girl lay in the bathtub, her face caked in blood, her stomach open and her guts piled up in her lap. Her eyes were wide open, which was probably the most disturbing part. Like one of those paintings where the eyes follow you around the room. She had obviously tried to stand up at some point; the shower curtain was on the floor and the tiles were covered in desperate handprints.

'According to the coroner she was still alive when . . . this . . . happened. She bled out in the night. She probably tried to get up which is why . . . those bits have fallen out.' Fraser gagged as he said it and turned away so that he could no longer see the girl. In all the time Adrian had known Fraser, he had never reacted like that to a crime scene.

'Why would they do this to her specifically, and not

to the others?' Adrian peeled his eyes away from Imogen, who hadn't once taken hers off the body.

'Well, she was obviously the main target of the attack, or at least the closest thing. Judging by the nature of her injuries, she was tortured, my guess is they were after information on something, or someone. There's another girl who lives here, her name is Bridget Ford, apparently. She isn't anywhere as far as we can tell,' DCI Fraser said eagerly.

'Do we know what she looks like?' Imogen piped up, her eyes firmly fixed on Estelle's body.

'Yeah, there are some photos of them together, and the Ford girl's handbag is still in the bedroom. The guys are looking upstairs, apparently the hot water wasn't working down here so we think Ford went upstairs to take a shower and when she came back she found all this.'

'And we have no idea what happened to her after that?' Adrian asked.

'No.'

'You think she got away?' Imogen said.

'Or she was involved. I mean, why hasn't she called the police?' Fraser said.

'Or she could be dead some place else?' Imogen offered.

'Well, until we know differently, she's a suspect, I guess,' Fraser said.

'Innocent until proven guilty? Do we not do that any more?' Imogen seemed to be annoyed. She stomped out of the flat.

Adrian sighed. Even he found it hard to look at the

girl in the bathtub. He stepped outside after Imogen, and smiled at the familiar sight of her sucking on a cigarette.

'Hey,' he said.

'Hey.' She pulled out her packet of cigarettes and offered him one.

'I've given up.'

'Sure you have.' She continued to hold the packet and he took one. Today didn't feel like the right time to argue.

'Are you OK?'

'I thought we talked about this, Miley? Ask me if I'm OK one more time, I dare you.'

'I'm not OK,' he said, lighting the cigarette, 'so I was just guessing that you probably aren't either.'

She turned to him with a consolatory smile and put her hand on his shoulder.

'Miley, I am OK, but I really don't want to look at that poor woman in the bathtub again. We should talk to the neighbours.'

'Fine with me.'

After hours of no useful responses from the neighbours, Imogen drove Adrian back to the station. She was happy to have his familiar presence in the passenger seat again. It had been a long time since Imogen had felt that level of trust with someone – she didn't think she'd ever have it again after the way she'd left her old force in Plymouth. She swallowed hard, touched her stomach surreptitiously. She could still feel the scar. Adrian looked over and smiled at her; in spite of herself, she grinned back. Adrian was one of the good ones; she looked forward to getting into more morally ambiguous situations with him, as crazy as that sounded.

Talking of moral ambiguity – as they walked into the station, Imogen was met with a bad taste in her mouth as she saw who was sitting in her chair, no doubt waiting to speak to her. The one person she thought she'd left behind.

Chapter 5: The Case

The present

Imogen's old police partner, DI Sam Brown, was persistent if nothing else. Before being transferred to Exeter, Imogen had been partnered with him in Plymouth. She had moved to the other side of the county just to get away from him, had had to leave Plymouth after everything that had happened. How could he be here now? On her first day back at work she was being confronted by the duplicitous shit-bag who had sent her into one of the most horrific situations she had ever encountered. He was the reason for her trust issues. They had been friends, real friends, but then he had betrayed her. He was at least partially responsible for the giant scar on her torso. Coupled with the bullet mark she'd sustained in the Exeter schoolteacher case, she was building up quite a nice collection.

'Are you . . .' Adrian said. He trailed off before finishing the sentence, obviously thinking better of it.

'I'm glad you didn't finish that thought, Miley,' she said, just about ready to punch anyone who asked her if she was 'all right'.

'What are you doing here?' Adrian called across the room to Sam.

'I need to talk to you both.'

'This is not happening right now, come back some other time.' Imogen slammed her bag down on the desk and pointed at the man who had the effrontery to sit in her chair.

DCI Fraser walked over with a big smile on his face. He always had been hopeless at reading social indicators.

'I just realised you guys are called Brown and Grey and you were partners. That's pretty funny.' Fraser laughed.

'Can we talk in private?' Sam asked.

'No, you absolutely cannot,' Adrian interjected.

'Keep your knickers on, I need to speak to you too, Detective.' He turned to Adrian.

'You should go with him. It pertains to the murder case,' Fraser said.

'A woman turns up with her insides hanging out . . . should've guessed you would have something to do with it.' Imogen sneered.

'Please,' Sam implored. 'I have some important information about your triple homicide.'

'Fine,' Imogen said.

She walked to the family liaison office, followed by

30

both Adrian and Sam. Adrian slammed the door and Imogen stood with her arms folded. She was aware of the prying eyes from around the office, all staring at the large glass window, clearly trying to discern what the conversation was about.

'Come on, guys, sit down, please.'

'I'm just dandy standing up.'

'Look, I'm not going to bring out all of the excuses but there are a few things you aren't privy to here. I was given clearance to tell you this morning when all this shit went down.'

'Clearance? What are you talking about?'

'Imogen, I was undercover in Plymouth. I was investigating the department. You've got it all wrong.'

'I repeat: what are you talking about?'

'I know you're angry with me about what happened. But there's so much you don't know. I'm sure after everything else that's happened here lately, you can appreciate what I'm talking about.' He glanced from Imogen to Adrian. 'I heard about Harry Morris. The schoolteacher case.'

Adrian shook his head. 'We're not talking about that now, DI Brown. That case is closed. Finished. Get to the point.'

Sam held his hands up, a gesture of mock-surrender.

'There were things happening in Plymouth, Imogen. Things you weren't aware of, things that went on back then which are still going on. A whole world we didn't uncover at the time. I had to get on the inside and see who was a part of it. I've been working on it for the last year.'

'Were you investigating me? While I was there?'

'A little, yeah. We had to know who was involved.'

'Involved in what?'

'At any one time in the UK, there are four thousand trafficked human beings in the country. We had it on good intel that there were members of the Plymouth police force who were not only complicit in these dealings, but actively running some of the operations.'

'Are you serious?'

'Women and kids, brought into the country illegally, sold into slavery, prostitution, pornography, we still don't know all the details. This investigation has been pretty hard to get a hold on without blowing our cover and getting a bunch of innocent people killed. It's a delicate situation.'

'What's that got to do with our homicide case?' Adrian asked.

'The girls you found dead. The girl that's missing is an undercover, her real name is DS Bridget Reid. Ford is a pseudonym. She's been working as a pro for the last six months in that brothel.'

'She's been working as a pro?'

'Not a real one, her clients were all set up. Anyway, she was there the night the other girls were killed, she was on the scene but she managed to get out. She left me a message. I gave it to DCI Fraser already and he's looking into it.'

'Did she see the killer?'

'She said she didn't. I lost contact with her. I was supposed to meet her down at the pub by the locks but she never showed.'

'Do you think she's dead?'

A look passed across Sam's face. 'I don't know. I need you to find her, please. I can't look, it would blow my cover.'

'Wouldn't want to do that, now would we?' Adrian was staring Sam down. 'We're going to need everything you have on her operation.'

'It's all here.' Sam looked more concerned than Imogen had ever seen him before.

'Is she smart?' Imogen asked.

'She is. She's important, OK? This isn't like her. If she hasn't been in contact, it's because she can't.'

'She's your girl?' Adrian raised his eyebrows at Sam, who nodded.

'She is. She's a good officer, too.'

'Why me? After what you did, what makes you think I would help you?' Imogen asked, stepping forward, facing up to her former partner.

'Because what you think you know is not what happened, Imogen! I tried to warn you over and over to keep away from certain things, but you just couldn't help yourself, could you?'

'Well, I'm a detective, that's kind of my job.'

'You have no idea how big this is, Imogen. Every name leads to another name, and it takes time to find out who exactly is doing what. We just didn't know if it was a genuine lead or not; it's taken us this long to find out.'

'You could have told me at the time!' Imogen pushed back the tears. 'You could have told me when I was still in Plymouth!'

'I tried to tell you. That's why I got myself assigned to this place when they made the call for extra cops. I wanted to look out for you, but you wouldn't let me. We were friends once – I thought you might hear me out.'

'Can you blame her?' Miles butted in.

'It wasn't clear who I could trust, Imogen, I swear, until you got attacked that night I wasn't sure if you were part of it or not.'

'You didn't know if I was involved in the trafficking of women and kids? I think that says everything about how close we were. You and Stanton were the only people who knew where I was going that night.' She was seething. 'And stop saying my fucking name!'

'Look, we will find DS Reid,' Miles said.

'Bridget, her name is Bridget.'

'OK, we're already looking for her. We'll take extra care when we pick her up, and we will let you know straight away,' Miles said. 'But you can't be a part of this investigation. You have to trust that we are doing the best we can.'

'Let me ask you something.' Imogen turned to Sam.

'OK, but I may not be able to answer you; this is an ongoing investigation.'

'Are you still investigating the police?'

'Yes.'

'People from the Plymouth station? The Exeter station too?'

'It's a big operation; it would be naive to think they could pull all of this off without any inside help. At the very least it's happening under your noses and nothing is being done. Either everyone in your precinct is stupid, or someone knows something and is covering it up.'

'And you have no idea who?'

'I'm sorry, no.' He moved closer to Imogen, she felt Adrian step in too, like a guard dog. 'For the moment it would be good if we carried on like you hate me. That's been pretty good for my cover, believe it or not.'

'I do still hate you, Sam, this changes nothing. You can say what you want but you were the only person who could have betrayed me in that way.' She paused and glanced at Adrian before continuing, uneasy about exposing herself. She lowered her voice. 'You were the only person I told I was pregnant, and they knew, Sam, they knew before they cut me. That's how I knew it was you.'

Sam's face changed, he looked genuinely confused; she couldn't tell if he was being sincere or not. Imogen slapped him across the face. She could feel Adrian silently cheering her on. Sam grabbed his cheek and his face flushed with anger.

'Find Bridget, that's all I care about.'

'We will.'

DI Brown left the office, still rubbing his face. When he was well out of earshot and view, Imogen turned to Adrian.

'I believe him,' Adrian said as he rested on the edge of the table, folding his arms across his chest. 'I know you hate him, Imogen, and I still don't know what the hell happened to you back in Plymouth, but if DI Brown knows something about this investigation we owe it to ourselves to look into it. After what happened a few weeks ago . . . We need to be on it.'

'I know. I agree.' Imogen kicked the chair.

Chapter 6: Just a Boy

Age 10

I'm trying really hard to concentrate on the face in the wallpaper. When I stare at it long enough I see the face of a grumpy old man. He is staring at me, frowning. The pattern is really girly but it's always the old man I see. Sometimes I pretend the old man is God and I pray to him. I say pray, but really I just give him a list of questions and wait for his expression to change. Naturally his expression never changes and my questions remain unanswered, loitering in my head.

This is my sister's room but she's not here any more. My mum keeps it the same in case she comes back, but she's not coming back. You don't come back from there. I don't know if I believe in heaven, really, or hell for that matter. I like to pretend heaven is real though, and that she is there, stuffing her face with ice creams and chocolates. Pistachio ice cream was her favourite, some-

times Baba would buy a whole big tub of it, just for her.

Since my sister died, my mum cries a lot. Understandable, I suppose, but when I walk into the room she dries her eyes and smiles at me, as if her smile could disguise the despair. I may be young but I'm not stupid. She doesn't talk about my sister and we aren't meant to either, but I do. I come here and talk to God about her.

My mum's cooking lamb for dinner; she must have upset Dad in some way because lamb is usually reserved for Sundays. Today is Tuesday. In four days I'm going to be eleven years old, so maybe this is an early birthday dinner. My stomach is rumbling. I can feel the hollow pit; I haven't eaten since breakfast yesterday. I should go back to my room before I get caught in here. I'm not supposed to be here, if my father catches me I will likely have to do without dinner. On an ordinary day I might risk it, because I like being in this room more than the food my mum usually prepares. The smell of that lamb though – it's made my mouth water.

Back in my own room, I feel more alone and the smell of the food isn't nearly as strong as it was in my sister's room, which is just a few steps down from the kitchen. I can't feel my sister in here. I pick up the book that sits by my bed. It's my father's favourite book so I've been instructed to read it. Apparently it will prepare me for when I am older. It's important to him that I am not weak. Every day he gives me a passage to learn and I must recite it for him before dinner, before I'm allowed to eat. Yesterday I wasn't in the mood but the

38

smell of the lamb has made me not want to take another stand. My father likes it when I stand up to him, to a point. I see his lips curl upwards when he thinks I am not looking, so sometimes even if I'm starving I make the sacrifice in order to make him like me. I like it when he likes me.

At dinner, I recite the passage he has asked me to remember. He seems disappointed that I couldn't hold out even longer, he's disappointed that I learned the words. It seems that no matter what I do I am the disappointment. Some days I think it is all about the words I'm asked to remember, some days I think he wants me to defy him and other days I think he wants me to starve to death. I gave up trying to figure my father out a long time ago. Soon he will think of an alternative punishment for learning the words, as I seem to have got better at memorising them. I guess that comes with getting older. He can't trick me any more. I wonder what I will have to do next.

My mother is silent throughout dinner; she is often silent. Her face has changed since my sister died, I don't know whether it's just because she has cried so much that she has changed her face forever. She is thin, too; sometimes she's not allowed to eat either.

The lamb is delicious and I want more as soon as I'm finished. When I am older I want to be a chef so that I can cook for myself. My father doesn't think there is any money in that profession, though; he wants me to be a businessman. I never really understood the term 'businessman' – surely any work is business and so anyone with a job is also a businessman. I don't *really understand a lot of things like that. My father is a businessman, he wears a suit and he makes money. Sometimes I will open a drawer at home and there will be a big bundle of notes held together with an elastic band. I once found twenty thousand pounds in the bottom of my parents' wardrobe. My father doesn't talk about his business much in front of my mother; occasionally he might say he has a good or a bad day but never any more detail than that. He has promised me that when I am older he will take me to work with him and I can see how to earn good money, because nobody wants to be poor.*

My dad usually goes out again after dinner. Sometimes when he comes home he smells funny. I don't know what the smell is exactly but it's a mixture of smoke and whisky. I don't know how people can drink whisky; I think it tastes horrible. One time my father left the drinks cupboard open, he has a lot of whisky from all over the world. He is a collector of whiskies, he told me that one of his bottles of whisky cost as much as our house. He wouldn't tell me which one though. I look through the collection and try to figure out which one it might be, but they all look the same, and when I unscrew the cap and sniff, none of them smell very nice. I took a few swigs though and it was like that horrible washing-up-liquid taste, like your mouth just wants it gone. It burned my throat, too.

After dinner I make a start on my next passage in my room. I tend to go up as soon as possible in case my parents argue, because they like to bounce insults off me: your mother wraps you up in cotton wool, how will you ever become a man? If I'm not there the arguments are usually over much faster. If they're not arguing about each other's shortcomings then they're arguing about my sister and whose fault it was that she died. The general consensus in my family is that it was my fault.

Before I have read through the passage even once, my bedroom door opens and my father's head appears. He tells me to get my shoes on and go with him. I am excited and nervous. Sometimes when my father comes home from his night-time expeditions his knuckles are bloodied. I've seen him hit my mother with some force before, but never enough to make his own hands bleed. So it must be from something else.

In the car we don't talk. He puts loud music on. We pull up to a restaurant of some kind but when we get out of the car we don't go inside, we go through an alley down the side of it instead, and into a house that's nestled behind it. My father has the keys. The house is smoky and smells strange. There are two women whose faces instantly change when my father enters the room; they look scared and they sit up straight. I feel somewhat better now that I know it's not just at home that my father makes people uncomfortable. There are lots of weird things on the coffee table. Strange-shaped jars and containers, white powder, bags of pills and green leafy stuff and razor blades strewn about.

Mindy is the blonde girl's name. She has black smudges under her eyes, she doesn't look very clean and her hair is dark in places where it's greasy. She has bruises on her legs although she doesn't seem to notice them. I see her eyes travel to my dad's hands and she relaxes when she sees they are empty. The other girl is called Margot. Margot seems like a posh girl's name, or I always thought it was, it reminds me of that old TV show with the lady who wears the long wafty dresses. Margot doesn't look anything like that though, she has blue hair and so much eye make-up I can barely tell what colour her eyes are. Margot's head is shaved up one side and she has a tattoo on her neck. It's a word, but I can't read it.

The girls refer to my dad as 'Daddy', which is confusing to me because they obviously aren't related to us in any way. Margot jumps up and comes over to my dad, she kisses him on the lips but he pulls away and pushes her hard, so that she knocks into the table and some of the beer falls to the ground. Mindy rushes to pick it up. It occurs to me that Mindy is also a name from an old TV show my dad likes to watch sometimes. I wonder what the girls' real names are.

Dad tells me to sit on the sofa while he does some work and he tells Mindy to look after me. He takes Margot by the wrist. I can see he's grabbing her hard but she doesn't pull away or cry or anything, she just follows as he leads her out of the room. Mindy puts the television on a music channel; it's all rap music which I don't really like. She takes the bag of green leafy stuff and rolls it into a cigarette. I watch as she lights it and draws in, sucking hard, so that almost half burns away before she pulls it from between her lips. She exhales straight into my face. The smoke smells strong and musky, not like my dad's cigarettes. Her lips *are cracked and sore looking but she gives me a nervous smile. She looks so much prettier with it. Her hand is on my leg and I act as though it were not my leg at all, even as she circles her fingers around my knee. I watch the TV instead.*

By the time my dad comes back, my head hurts a bit, not like a headache, like a foggy soup inside my mind. Margot is nowhere to be seen and Mindy looks somewhat panicked for a moment until music starts upstairs, obviously reassuring her that Margot is OK. I know that feeling; sometimes my dad goes into a room with someone and they don't come back out. I've waited outside my mother's room for hours before, waiting to see if she reappears. She always does.

My dad speaks to Mindy in whispers and I can see her biting her lip, trying to look pretty but she looks so tired and scared. I didn't notice it before but now I can see that she's shaking, a barely noticeable shudder every time my father reaches for her. She's afraid to flinch but her body desperately wants to. She obviously knows the penalty well. I can hear her making quiet excuses as her breathing grows shallow. She's telling my dad that I'm only a kid and she couldn't do it. Couldn't do what? Apparently I have to grow up some time and she should do what she's told. I still feel woozy and guilty for not helping Mindy. My dad is going to hit her, we all know it and so there is nothing more to say. I just sit and watch the spectacle.

As expected, Dad grabs a fistful of Mindy's hair and smashes her face into the wall. Blood spurts from her nose but she barely whimpers. To my surprise, my father calls me over and pushes Mindy's face towards mine. She kisses me gently on the lips and I can taste the metal in her blood as it drips from her nose. She also tastes a bit like liquorice, which I don't really like. My father lets go of Mindy and she takes my hand. My father tells me he will be back for me in a little while and then Mindy leads me upstairs to her bedroom.

Later, as we drive home, I go over in my mind the passage I am to recite for my father tomorrow. The words take on a new significance.

> *Just as I have come from afar, creating pain for many*
> *men and women across the good green earth,*
> *so let his name be Odysseus . . .*
> *the Son of Pain, a name he'll earn in full.*

Chapter 7: The Fixer

Plymouth, two years earlier

The girl was lying on the ground, her skirt hitched up around her thighs, exposing needle marks and soiled underpants. Imogen looked at the room: cold, stark and empty. What a place to die. The former girls' school had certainly lost its charm quickly after its closure. Obscenities were scribbled on the blackboard and the windows were thick with dirt. She wanted to cover the girl with a blanket, to keep her warm, to lie with her and stroke her hair, tell her everything was going to be OK. She looked so lonely and forsaken. Imogen had to look away for a moment, and force those feelings down.

'Jesus!' she exclaimed, slipping back into her role as someone who wasn't bothered by things like dead bodies. She held her nose for effect. The smell of the week-old corpse left festering on the floor of the unventilated room was overwhelming. Imogen had to maintain the guise of a hardened exterior, everyone in the Plymouth Police Force did. It was important that they all kept up the bravado, the illusion of morale. If they expressed their true response when they saw these things, these hideous things that occurred, then it would be easy to fall apart, inevitable even. It wasn't always the big things that got you, it was the things like the girl's hair being stuck to her face, or that it was winter and she had summer clothes on.

'Any ID on her?' her partner DI Brown asked. He'd been her partner ever since she'd started at Plymouth a few years ago, and the pair of them got on well. Most of the time.

'You look if you want, I'm not touching her.'

'We'll let the techs look, I'm not touching her either. She looks about ready to pop.'

Imogen noted the distended and discoloured skin. Her body had reacted the way we all do when we die; it started destroying itself, digesting itself. The bacteria in the poor girl's body were trying to make their way out, the gases under the skin causing it to swell until even the slightest touch could cause it to burst.

'You ever touch a popper, Sam? It's not cool,' she muttered, subconsciously smoothing her own skirt down because she couldn't adjust the girl's.

'No, I guess it isn't,' Sam said, distracted. 'Come on, let's get out of here, I'm starving. I'll buy you lunch.'

'You're hungry?' She couldn't imagine anything worse than eating at this particular moment in time.

'A nice mixed grill or something extra greasy, that's what I fancy.' Sam smiled.

46

'You're going to have a heart attack if you keep eating like that.'

'I've got to take care of my figure, Grey, takes a lot of work to maintain this fine physique.' He rubbed his belly. Samuel Brown was a short man with a thick-set body and more hair poking out of his shirt than was actually on his head. You couldn't accuse him of being vain, that was for sure.

'I'll pass, thanks. I'm off shift in an hour so I thought I might go get this paperwork filed.'

'Suit yourself. You can cover for me then, I need to eat. You seeing your mother tonight?'

'Yep, same as yesterday. Probably same as tomorrow.'

'You can't keep this shit up, Grey, you need to get a life of some sort. She needs to accept help from someone other than you.'

'Everyone we try just ends up walking out on her. She's a nightmare, but she's my nightmare. Anyway, she gets worried when she doesn't see me.'

'No wonder you're single, you won't even give yourself a chance at a normal bloody life.'

'You've supposedly got a life, Brown, and yet you're still single, what does that say?'

'I'm a lone wolf. It's a choice, you can't harness this beast. It wouldn't be fair to all the others. Besides, me being single isn't a consolation prize, this is how I choose to live my life.'

'Yeah, well, this is how I choose to live mine.'

'I think I saw a burger van up at the intersection, I'm going to grab something on the go then talk to some of the charming residents of this street, see if they

47

saw anything. You sure you don't want a nice fat juicy burger all dripping with fat and cheese?'

'As appetising as that sounds, no thanks.' She smiled and walked out.

As Imogen turned the key in the lock to her mother's place, she could smell burning. She rushed into the kitchen and saw smoke. There was a blackened pan on the stove, full of four burst boiled eggs and no water. Her mother must have put them on well over an hour ago. Imogen looked up at the fire alarm; it was smashed to pieces where her mother had obviously attacked it with the broom. That was the second one this month. Imogen would have to get on to their handyman about fixing it.

'Hey, Mum, I brought you some fish and chips.'

'You're abandoning me, aren't you? You're always banging on at me about my cholesterol levels but today you bring me fish and chips,' Irene said.

'You should have been a detective,' Imogen replied as she threw the greasy parcel on the only available part of the kitchen counter and searched the cupboards for a clean plate. She should stay and wash up; the stagnant water in the sink was overflowing with almost every item of crockery her mother owned. Flies hovered over the surface. She made a mental note to get her mother paper plates from now on.

'Where are you going?'

'I have a date,' Imogen lied, looking around the room. It was filthy; she could feel her skin crawling. God only knew what bacteria were in the air. Imogen almost wished she was back at the crime scene. She'd have to phone a cleaner at the same time as the handyman.

'A date?' Irene's eyes lit up. 'With a man?'

'No, with a buffalo.'

'Thank God, I was starting to think you were . . .'

'Yes, I know what you thought.'

'Is he a criminal? You haven't gone and fallen for someone you arrested?'

'No, he's not a criminal.' Imogen tipped the fish and chips out on to a plate. She hastily squirted ketchup on to the side and then handed the plate to her mother.

'I don't like tomato sauce.'

'Then why do you buy it?' Imogen walked away, wiping her greasy hands on an even greasier kitchen towel. Irene was stalling, but Imogen didn't care. She wasn't going to be emotionally blackmailed into staying for her mother's own personal amusement; she did have a life, despite what Sam thought. She knew it was only a matter of time before the name-calling began, before Irene tried to make her feel like shit as per usual. She was going to make sure that she was out the door before her mother got the chance.

A little while later, away from the chaos of her mother's house, Imogen pulled up outside Plymouth Police Station and looked at herself in the rear-view mirror. She pulled out her mascara and reapplied it.

She walked in and sat at her desk, before pulling out the relevant forms for her report about the dead girl. She looked over at Sam's desk. He was long gone already, a discoloured apple core lying on top of the crime scene photos. It can't have been his, she was

49

pretty sure he was allergic to anything that wasn't processed or dripping in trans-fats. She leaned over and picked up the photos, tossing the core in the bin. Something about apple cores made her feel sick, maybe it was the myriad of tooth marks and the knowledge of all the saliva and forensics that put her off. Since spending a weekend on a forensics seminar she had been put off a lot of things. Apple cores, hotel rooms, the backs of taxis. They were all very evidence heavy, in the form of bodily fluids.

She looked at the images of the girl. As she stared, the phrase 'There but for the grace of God,' sprang into her head. She wasn't a religious person, but she appreciated that particular sentiment. It could have easily been her who was lying face down in her own excrement and vomit. These things happen gradually. You make one bad decision, then another, each one slightly more fucked up and soul destroying than the last. Then *bam*, before you know it you're an addict; willing to do absolutely anything to get that next fix. It wasn't lost on Imogen; if she thought about it she could probably pinpoint the exact moments in her life where she had fought with herself to make the right decision. Where, thanks to God or whoever else was in charge that day, she hadn't had the overwhelming urge to self-sabotage. She'd had the opportunities, she just knew that there were some decisions you couldn't come back from. She was grateful, because it was in her DNA to mess up; it was genetic, hereditary. At least that's what it felt like. Not for the first time, she wondered about her father – what had he been like? Had he too had the same streak as her mother, that awful capacity to self-destruct? She'd never known him. She never would.

'Detective Grey?' DCI David Stanton's voice snapped her out of her trance; she put the photos down and turned around. He stood in the doorway to his office, looking sullen and stern like he always did. Sullen and stern, but undoubtedly attractive. Imogen felt her stomach flip slightly.

'Sir?'

'My office!'

She walked across the room, aware that the sound of her heels carried, hoping no one would look up. The day was coming to an end; only the brown-nosers would be around now. The brown-nosers and her. She stood to attention as Stanton closed the door behind her. Her boss was a tall man, a good few inches over six foot. He had medium-brown hair with flashes of grey at the temples and he was never completely clean-shaven, almost, but not completely.

'Is there a problem, sir?'

'I thought you were gone for the day?'

'Just wanted to get my paperwork done tonight, sir. You know, while it was fresh in my mind.'

'I admire that work ethic, Grey.' He walked back around and released the shutter on the blind. 'It couldn't wait till tomorrow?'

'It could have, yes.'

He was a foot taller than her. She could feel his warm breath brush the top of her ear as he stood behind her, close but not touching.

'So, why are you really here?' he whispered. The hairs

on the back of her neck stood on end, her skin prickled as he said the words. She could feel his body heat, he was right there, right behind her. She wanted him to throw her down on to the desk.

'I'm not sure, sir,' said Imogen at last.

'Stop calling me sir, Imogen.'

He was really close now, as close as it was possible to be without contact. She could feel the desire in him, feel his temperature rising. They were touching without touching, longing to put skin on skin. To feel fingers tracing the lines of each other's body, to kiss, to lick, to bite. Their flirtation had almost reached breaking point. How much longer could they play this game?

'What should I call you, then?' she asked quietly, suggestively. Every part of him was leaning towards her. She was delirious with excitement and anticipation. As he leaned closer still, there was a sudden knock at the door and she felt Stanton take an abrupt step backwards. The spell was broken.

'Come in,' he said, clearing his throat, moving away from her. Imogen swallowed hard, trying to slow her heart rate back down.

The door opened as Stanton smoothed his tie and sat down behind his desk, in an obvious attempt to hide his stimulated body. He didn't look at Imogen.

Jamie, the desk sergeant, entered and handed a file to Stanton.

'Thanks, Jamie. Detective Grey—' He looked up at her. She could feel the heat in her cheeks. 'You can go home now; finish your paperwork tomorrow. You're done for tonight.'

Imogen nodded. Without making eye contact with him, she walked out of his office and grabbed her stuff from her desk. Looking back once, she saw Stanton putting his jacket on, shrugging his arms into the sleeves. She forced herself to look away. She needed to get home, and she needed a cold shower.

Chapter 8: The Goddess

Plymouth, two years earlier

Imogen and Sam walked into the pathologist's office. The dead girl was laid out on the slab. She was cleaner, her hair was brushed and she looked almost peaceful. Imogen was glad that she had finally been treated with some respect.

'So what's the verdict, doc? Do we know who she is or what killed her?' Sam asked the pathologist.

'Overdose of epic proportions; she took something pretty horrific. There's no hits in the database for her DNA. I sent her pics over to missing persons already. You'll have to check with them,' Dr Carol Foster said.

'Did you do a rape kit?' Imogen asked.

'No obvious signs of sexual assault,' Foster said. 'But there is something. She has some scarring that indicates that she's given birth, at least once, but possibly multiple times.'

'How old do you think she is?' Imogen asked.

'Twenty if she's a day. God only knows. She's been through a hell of a lot. She could be younger.' They all stood over the body staring, each lost in their own ruminations.

'What about the toxicology report?' Brown interrupted.

'Well, it seems to be a crystal meth-like compound, but it's got something else in it, I've not seen anything like it before. The full report will take a while,' Foster said, obviously grateful for the return to science. Anything to avoid getting emotional over a case.

'Is there anything else?' Imogen asked.

'Actually, yes.' Foster walked over to the girl and lifted her hand. 'She has the remnants of a UV stamp on her hand; I think it's entry to some sort of nightclub.'

'Let me see,' Imogen said, leaning forward as the doctor shone the light on the girl's left hand.

'I know that stamp! It's for Aphrodite's, that club down town,' Sam said immediately.

'Aphrodite's?'

'Yeah, it's owned by that Greek family. Bit of a dive.'

'Never heard of it.' Imogen shrugged.

'Not being funny, Grey, but that's kind of an endorsement in itself. When was the last time you went to a nightclub?'

'Aphrodite? The Goddess of Love – is it a strip club?' She wouldn't be surprised if Sam knew all about the local strip clubs – some of the comments he made on a daily basis had her working hard to resist punching him in the face.

'No, but I've heard rumours about the things that go on behind the scenes there – you know, bung the manager a few quid and he'll arrange for some extra entertainment out back.' Sam let out a big cheesy smile as he spoke.

'Underage?' Imogen asked.

'Nah, just the usual skanks.'

'That's really nice, Brown. Skanks are people too.' Imogen shook her head.

'Whatever you say.' Sam was indifferent as usual, lifting the blanket and checking out the rest of the girl's body.

Imogen shook her head. She could never quite discern if this was all part of her partner's bravado act, or if he really was just a misogynistic pig.

'Is that where they got the drugs do you think? The nightclub?'

'I don't know, but let's check it out.'

Aphrodite's was a pink and red monstrosity, a stone's throw from the infamous Union Street in Plymouth. The club was clearly trying to cash in on the vintage retro mania that was taking over the town, and yet somehow it missed the mark entirely. It was a clash of red leather booths and deep pink walls, mosaic mirror tiles almost wall to wall, and everything else was made of shiny black surfaces. There was an overriding theme of pink flamingos, and the male bar staff wore Hawaiian shirts while the women wore fifties-inspired dresses that looked more like swimsuits, and left very little to the imagination. There were poles dotted around the room, but maybe they were just for show. There was definitely an undertone of sleaze about the place. Imogen didn't even want to think about what was going on behind the scenes.

'We're not open yet!' a man called out from behind the bar.

'I'm Detective Brown and this is Detective Grey.' Sam pulled out his badge as they walked across the room and leaned against the bar.

'Really? Those are your real names? Or are you just Tarantino fans?' the barman asked, looking Imogen up and down.

Imogen looked at Sam and he shrugged.

'*Reservoir Dogs*, you know, Mr Pink and Mr Orange, stuck in the middle, the world's smallest violin?' Another voice came from the end of the bar. There was a man sitting there holding a scotch, one eyebrow raised at them. He wasn't wearing the bar staff uniform.

Imogen shrugged. 'We need to show you a picture. We have a body in our morgue that needs identifying, and the victim had a stamp on her hand from this place.' She walked over to the man with the scotch; he seemed comfortable, like he spent a lot of time there.

Sam wandered off in the opposite direction, looking around the club.

'OK, let me see your ID first, please. Can never be too careful around here.' He smiled and held his hand out. He had toffee-coloured hair and a natural tan. His eyes were amber and green with a sort of Clint Eastwood squint that was incredibly distracting. She imagined he spent a lot of time staring menacingly into the distance.

Imogen reached into her pocket and pulled out her wallet, holding it up for the man to see her ID. He took the card from her hand.

'Imogen. That's a pretty name.' He tilted his head and looked at her; unlike the barman, he didn't break eye contact. He stood up slowly, keeping his eyes fixed firmly on hers, and moved closer to place the ID back in her hand. 'How can I help you, Imogen?'

She wasn't sure if he was trying to intimidate her or flirt with her. His eyes were dancing and he had the most confident smirk she'd ever seen. Imogen cleared her throat.

'You can start by telling me your name.'

'My name is Dean. Do you want my number, too?' He grinned, the furrow in his brow relaxing.

'I want you to look at this picture and tell me if you recognise the girl.'

She pulled the photo out of her pocket and handed it to him. He briefly shifted his gaze from her to the photo before handing it back.

'Sorry, I don't know her.'

'Are you sure? Are you the manager here, Dean?'

'I'm afraid not, just passing through.' He looked at her and smiled, softer this time. When she looked into his eyes she could see the hardness behind the smile. She blinked and looked away, unsure what his pull was. She decided it was best to avoid eye contact with him for now. Something about him was deeply unsettling.

'Do you know the proprietor, Elias Papas?' She saw him flinch.

'I know him, yeah; he's not here much though. He's more of a silent manager.'

'What about his brother, Antonis Papas?' She was almost certain he was trying to hide a sneer as he drank from his glass, avoiding the question entirely. From what she'd guess, he knew him all right, and he didn't like him.

'You're sure you don't know the girl?' Sam appeared by Imogen's side, his eyes fixed on Dean. Imogen hadn't even noticed him approaching. Dean's eyes were still on hers; she wasn't looking at him but she could feel him grinning at her discomfort.

'Best I can tell you is we have a ladies night here on Thursdays, it's more than likely she was here then.'

'We? I thought you were just passing through?' Imogen said.

'It's a figure of speech.'

'Sure it is.'

'Do these cameras work? Wait, don't answer that, I'm going to use my special psychic powers and say they don't,' Sam scoffed.

'I believe they're out of order at the moment, but you'd have to check that with George over there. He works here. George! Come here!' The uniformed barman walked over to them and smiled. Dean held out his hand for the photograph again, and passed it to his colleague. 'George, you seen this girl?'

'No, sir, I haven't.' The barman shook his head.

'Sir?' Imogen smiled. Passing through my ass, she thought to herself. 'Is that a figure of speech, too?'

'Would you believe me if I said yes?' Dean said.

'My instinct is telling me you're pretty liberal with the truth,' she said. He was leaning towards her, dangerously close.

'Do they teach you how to read people in detective school?' Dean smiled at her and moved backwards, returning to his drink. Imogen took the photo from George, and returned it to her wallet.

'George, are the cameras in here working at the moment?'

'I'm sorry, Detective, they aren't.'

'Well,' she shook her head. 'Thanks for nothing, guys.'

Dean pulled out a business card and handed it to Imogen. She glanced down at his name: *Dean Kinkaid*.

'Shouldn't you give me one of yours, you know, in case I think of anything?'

Reluctantly, Imogen pulled out one of her cards and handed it to him. She was already certain that this was not the last she'd see of him. She couldn't figure out how important he was. Generally speaking, people stick to their own and there was nothing Greek about Dean Kinkaid, not with his green eyes and dark sandy hair. His name suggested Irish origins. Maybe he would be useful in the future; it was easier to flip someone who wasn't blood loyal.

Chapter 9: The Lover

The present

The first thing Bridget could feel was her leg. It was throbbing, beats of pain working their way through her body. She opened her palm and touched the surface underneath her; it wasn't the muddy riverbank that she'd fallen asleep on. It was a bed.

My head is killing me. She opened her eyes. As they adjusted to the light, she saw a sliver of sunshine peeking from the far corner of the room. From her surroundings she discerned that she was in a basement or cellar of some kind, below street level, that was for sure. She could see where the grate led up to the road; she could also see the shadows of people's feet as they occasionally walked over the glass bricks. *Where the hell am I?* She looked down and saw that her leg had been bandaged. She no longer had the tracksuit bottoms on, just her underwear and a hooded jacket, the one she'd taken from the brothel. It gaped open; instinctively she pulled it closed. She felt groggy, as though she was hungover, but she hadn't been drinking the night before so it was probably just from the swim and the water. The room smelled of damp, with torn, filthy wallpaper falling away from the walls. There was a wrought-iron bed and a Persian rug. There was also a large standard lamp with a pink lampshade, almost exactly like one her grandmother used to have. In the corner sat a yellowing kidney-shaped dressing table with a brush and a hand-held mirror laid out on the surface. There was even a picture hanging above the bed. It looked like someone's bedroom.

She swung her legs over the side and stood up. Dizziness forced her back down and she stared at her hands for a moment. They didn't look like her hands. She ran to the metal door on the far wall, her leg protesting as she moved. Bridget tried in vain to push it, pull it, anything, but it wouldn't open. The window was the same, frosted and thick, there was no way out. There was a piece of fabric hanging in the corner, she walked over and saw a dirty old toilet behind the curtain. This room felt as though it had been made just for her. She tried to think. Surely whoever had put her here wouldn't have gone to all this trouble if they were going to kill her straight away.

Her head was thumping now, the air was stale and she could feel the damp coating the walls of her throat as she breathed in. There was a vent in the corner above the door, she raised her hand to it but couldn't feel any airflow at all. *Where were the rest of her clothes?* She glanced around, spotting her tracksuit bottoms folded at the end of the bed. She rushed over and pulled them on. They were clean, and smelled of washing powder. It was warm down here, wherever here was. There was a half-empty bottle of mineral water by the bedside table; she grabbed it and drank thirstily. *What's that funny taste?* Perhaps the man who'd been chasing her had caught up to her at the riverbank. Could he have carried her to a car and then taken her back into the city? She felt the foundations of the place vibrate, and wondered if she was near a train station. Was she even still in Exeter?

There was no way out. Bridget banged on the door, but it was thick and made barely any noise. She moved her fingers along the walls to see if any of the exposed bricks were loose, but they all held tight. She looked at her hands again. When she was a child, Bridget would often get put in her room as punishment. Her current surroundings were strangely reminiscent of that room, right down to the bad seventies painting hanging over the bed. When she was grounded by her father, Bridget's brother would sneak treats in to her and she would stay there with no television, no contact with the family. Her father's strictness had been reflected in his own police work; he was part of the reason she'd joined the force in the first place. She could deal with this. She would find a way out eventually. She knew she would.

Bridget suddenly heard the sound of a key turning in the lock. She hobbled back over to the bed and lay down, closing her eyes almost fully. She needed to get some information; she needed to see what she was dealing with. The blurred image of a man walked into the room. She wasn't sure why, but she wasn't scared. Immediately and without reason, she felt that she could trust him. It was the strangest feeling, going against all her police training. She sat up.

'You're awake?' The man had a tray of food with him. He put it on the chair next to the bed and sat down next to her. A thought popped into Bridget's head: *you're not Sam*. The stranger brushed the hair out of her face and kissed her on the cheek.

'Why am I here?' Her voice sounded strange to her ears.

'I'm sorry Bridget, I'm just trying to keep you safe. Remember, I am always on your side.'

'I need to get in touch with Sam.'

'I spoke to Sam. He's going to come for you when he can, for now he told me to tell you to stay put.'

'He did?' She was confused. 'Can I call him?'

'I can't let you use a phone, I've told you, they're always watching us.' He pointed to a camera she hadn't noticed in the darkened corner near the window. 'When I can, I will get you out of here to safety. I'm sorry, my beautiful girl.' He put his hand on her shoulder; to her surprise it felt good, comforting. 'You should eat. Keep your strength up.'

She looked at the plate of food on the tray. Whoever this man was, he knew what she liked. Lucozade was her comfort drink, her brother used to buy a bottle of it on his way home from school and smuggle it in to her if she was grounded. There was a red apple too; she loved red apples, as a child she would take out the pips and make pictures with them. She and her brother had invented their own secret language using the pips, leaving each other hidden messages around the room. There was also a yogurt with a spoon, and a chicken salad sandwich with mayonnaise and mustard on granary bread: perfect. *How could he know these things?*

The man smiled at her. He moved his hand around her back and pulled her closer to him, lowering his lips to hers. Her thoughts blurred: *I can't remember your name.* She kissed him back, his lips were so soft and he tasted of cigarettes. Hazily, Bridget put her hand up to his face and stroked his cheek. He kissed her hard, pushing her on to the bed. She clawed at his clothes, desperate for the feeling of security she somehow knew she would get from being in his arms. She pulled her underpants off and they slipped under the covers together. Bridget climbed on top of him; the weight of his body was making her leg ache. Quickly, she unzipped her top and he put his hands on her, moving them up and down her body. God, this felt good.

As they moved together, Bridget was overcome by a wish for the man to stay with her, but somehow she knew that this was just a stolen moment, that they didn't have much time. This man was protecting her, he couldn't be her captor. Her whole body felt as though it was on fire. She had never felt like this with Sam. *Had she?*

When he was done, the man stood up and pulled his trousers back on, doing up his flies as he stared down at her on the bed. He handed her the hooded sweatshirt back and Bridget wrapped it around herself. He smiled at her and went behind the curtain to use the bathroom; Bridget picked up the sandwich, and ate the whole thing in a few bites. Leaving the yogurt, she picked up the spoon, put it in her pocket and thirstily drank the Lucozade. The man came back to the bed. He grabbed a bag from the side of the room, rummaged inside it and handed her a bottle of water. She took it gratefully.

'I'll come back soon. I promise.' He went to the door and then turned back. 'I forgot, you need to take your antibiotics, you don't want your leg to get infected.'

He pulled a tub of pills out of his pocket and handed her two. She placed the pills on her tongue and washed them down with the water. She immediately needed the toilet. When she emerged from behind the curtain, the man was gone, along with the empty tray. He'd taken the apple back too.

Bridget ran to the door and pulled on the handle. It was locked. She sat back on the bed as a wave of dizziness washed over her. She shouldn't have taken those pills. What was the matter with her? She had an overwhelming urge to sleep again; she lifted her knee on to the bed and started to undo the bandage. The wound wasn't as bad as she thought it would be, it was scabbing over already. It had felt so deep when it had happened. The memory of cutting it by the river seemed distant now, as though it was slipping further and further away from her.

There was a sudden scratching noise in the room. Bridget turned her head. It was coming from the corner behind her, it sounded as though someone was clawing at the wall. But it wasn't a person; to her surprise there was a dog sitting there. It looked strangely familiar; with its brown and white markings, it looked like her old dog, Wilberforce. He was scratching at the concrete floor in the corner, trying to dig his way out. The sound of his panting was comforting to her, like an old friend, a reminder that she wasn't alone.

'Hey, doggy!' she called out.

How did he get in here?

The dog turned around and dashed over, sitting obediently at the side of the bed and breathing excitedly in her face. She didn't know how it was possible, but this *was* Wilberforce, it had to be – he had a bone-shaped brass tag on his collar with a big W engraved on it. Wilberforce had died when Bridget was just thirteen years old. She was dreaming. She must be. As Bridget stared, the dog lay down on the ground and started to wheeze. She watched him struggle for breath, remembering the day they had found him dead – knocked over by a car in the street. To her horror, she realised that it was happening again, before her eyes – the blood was oozing out from underneath him. The puddle of blood was spreading, carpeting the floor, beginning to rise. Bridget began to panic. *What was in those pills?* She lay down, trying to steady herself, trying to keep a hold of her thoughts.

'It's not real, it's not real,' she repeated over and over to herself.

Bridget lay on the bed, red water now lapping at her sides. It was splashing on to the throw. She could taste it in her mouth as the waves got more and more aggressive. Her hands, her hands were red. Was this some form of latent guilt for what had happened to Dee? If only she had been watching, then Dee would still be alive. *I'm so sorry, Dee. It's not real, it's not real.*

The bed rocked. Bridget lay as still as she could. The sensation reminded her of when she was a child, when she used to play hide and seek with her mother. She would lie under the duvet, keeping totally still as her mother frantically searched the house for her; to this day she didn't know if she really couldn't see her under there or if her mother had just been playing along. The first explanation was more likely. Finally, the rocking stopped. Time seemed to stretch. Bridget cautiously opened her eyes; sure enough, the red water was gone, taking Wilberforce with it. The room had returned to normal, and apart from a banging headache, Bridget felt calm again.

She re-wrapped the gash on her leg and lowered herself off the bed, grabbing the stool from under the dressing table and taking it over to the camera, trying to stay out of its view. She got on to the stool and reached for the camera, pulling at the wire that snaked from the side. It came loose. It wasn't attached to anything, it had already been cut. It was just for show. *Why did he tell me they were watching?*

Safe in the knowledge that she wasn't being watched, Bridget grabbed the baseboard of the bed and pulled it towards her. It was heavy but she was determined. Her leg throbbed. Her brain began to feel patchy, as though her memory was slipping away. She felt in her pocket for the spoon she'd taken from the tray. She would use it to scratch a message into the floor, in case she forgot everything again. She couldn't put it anywhere too obvious. She walked to the end of the bed and then she saw it. Her blood ran cold.

There was a message there already. Lying next to the words was a metal spoon, the end of it worn down to almost nothing. Her name was carved into the floor, again and again, the handwriting growing more and more manic as the words stacked up. She had been here for a while. She had done this before. *What was wrong with her memory?*

Bridget got down on her knees and started to scribble her name once more. Over and over. Her hand began to ache. Her head hurt and she felt nauseated. Who the hell was that man? The man that had made her feel so good, who she had wanted to stay with her. Who she had wanted to sleep with? She searched her mind for a name. Nothing happened. She couldn't find it. Was he another hallucination? What the hell were those pills? She hoped to God she would remember. She didn't want to go to sleep again for fear of forgetting everything. God knew how many times she had forgotten all this before. She lay down and clutched at her head, hoping to stop the spinning. Her eyes grew heavy and sleep drew closer. It was pulling her down, down into the darkness . . .

Chapter 10: The Scarred

The present

Imogen stumbled around the bathroom in the morning half-light. She thought about running herself a hot bath, but she didn't want to lie in the water looking at the remnants of her stomach wound. Since leaving Plymouth, she'd found baths harder, preferring to shower so that she couldn't see her body. Although the scar was pink and faded she liked to pretend it wasn't there. The scar wasn't the only thing: if she looked down, she could just see the bullet wound she'd sustained in the schoolteacher case too. It had healed in the last few weeks, forming a neat plum circle. Somehow, that one hurt less; it didn't give her the same amount of trauma as the injury she'd sustained in Plymouth. She closed her eyes, the memory of what had happened rushing back. Leaving Plymouth. Transferring to Exeter. Sam. *The scar.*

Imogen turned on the shower. She had to keep going. These days, she spent hours every morning smacking the shit out of the punching bag she'd installed in her garden. Rain or shine, she was out there kicking and punching her way back to work. Still, she couldn't look at herself until the towel was securely around her, hiding her embarrassment. Twice now she had almost been killed. Twice she had failed at her job. Twice she had needed rescuing. Never again. She picked up her baggy combat trousers and loose-fitting raglan t-shirt and got ready for work.

When Imogen arrived at Adrian's house there was no answer. She knew he was home; his bike was still chained up to the front railings. She banged on the door again and saw the blinds upstairs twitch before hearing thumping on the stairs. The door swung open and he appeared, shielding his eyes from the sunlight that poured through the door.

'Have a good night?' She smiled. Adrian groaned.

'What time is it?'

'Time to go, Miley, get dressed.' She looked down at his trousers, pulled up but not done up, socks and shirt in his hand.

'How's my car?' Adrian had given Imogen his car after crashing in her own at the end of the last case they'd worked on together. The sort of thing Sam would never have done. Adrian was a better partner in so many ways.

'Hideous, Miley, but I do appreciate it. I need to get something a little less middle-aged-travelling-salesman though.'

'You leave her alone.' He pulled his shirt over his head, still buttoned up from the day before.

'I'm going car shopping this weekend; you're welcome to help me out.' Imogen heard the toilet flush upstairs and Miles looked away sheepishly. Imogen raised an eyebrow. She knew exactly what had made him sleep in late this morning. He pulled on his boots and grabbed his keys.

'I think I've got Tom this weekend.'

'Bring him along, he probably knows more about cars than you.'

'Hey! I've taught my son everything he knows.'

'If you say so.' She walked over to his car and got in.

'Didn't you lock it?' Miles asked.

'Trust me, I could leave the engine running and the door open and no one would steal this piece of crap, Miley. No offence.'

Adrian and Imogen walked into the station to find DCI Fraser trying to catch their attention without anyone else noticing, raising his eyebrows at them across the room. He looked so shifty that they couldn't help smirking at each other. Fraser was one of the few people that Adrian trusted, as much as he trusted anyone. Not quite unconditionally, but there was an innocence about him, with his constantly raised eyebrows as if he had just been told something very surprising indeed and he just couldn't wait to tell the next person he bumped into, confidentiality be damned. Upon entering his office they closed the door.

'Forensics are down by the river at the moment scouring the place. There's a lot of pressure from above to find this Bridget girl in one piece. Apart from anything else, we have a lot of questions for her.'

'What's with all the subterfuge?'

'I know your ex-partner has a vested interest in this, Imogen . . . I mean, Grey . . . and I know he thinks he's heading the investigation, but he isn't. For starters, her being his girlfriend means that he's way too close to this, and secondly, we don't know his involvement at this point. The fact is, we have to treat him as a suspect in her disappearance.'

'I think that's wise, sir,' Imogen snorted.

'I don't know exactly what happened at your old station, Grey . . .' He looked at Adrian.

'It's OK. You can talk in front of him.'

'I know you claimed that DS Brown was instrumental in an attack you sustained and I know about the restraining order. If you don't want him in this office, I can arrange for him to come for briefings when you're out. I wish I could keep him away altogether but we need to keep him close, at least for the time being. We need to find DS Reid.'

'No, it's fine. I can deal with it.' She looked embarrassed at this concession. 'But thank you.'

'So what's the plan then, Fraser?' Adrian asked, trying to divert the attention away from Imogen.

'The plan is we find her. They've gone over the riverbank near the pub where she was supposed to meet Brown, but they can't see anything. A car was reported stolen near her place and found near the river – we're

73

just confirming the forensics but it looks as though it was definitely her. We're looking a bit nearer to the bank now as she was most likely on foot the rest of the way.'

'What about us? What do we do?'

'The usual. Go over her phone records. Request any private CCTV footage from the area. Sam said she had a camera set up in her room to record stuff going on, in case she had a run in with anyone important. I will liaise with Brown, so any information you get comes to me first, OK?'

'I thought all her Johns were fake? Informants and plants.'

'We're a bit blind at the moment. All we have are second-hand accounts of what went on. The tech guys have her laptop, so you can go see Gary Tunney if you want.'

'Thank you, sir.'

'Oh, and just to let you know, Tunney's transfer is official as of next week. He will be our very own computer forensic nerd. With us full time.' He gave them a thumbs up.

'Good to know,' Adrian said as they left, heading straight for the laptop.

Chapter 11: The Boat

The present

'What have you found?' Adrian asked Tunney, who was fiddling around with Bridget Reid's computer.

'Well, she had a motion-activated camera in the brothel, so every time she, or anyone else, came into the room the camera switched on, recorded what happened, and sent the info straight back to this hard drive, which is time and date stamped. It's more sophisticated than a lot of surveillance equipment, and from looking around on her laptop I can see that she knew her way around technology. Which obviously helps us out.'

'Did you know her?' Imogen asked.

'She came to my lab once, yeah, she was a smart cookie.'

'Let's not use past tense just yet,' Adrian interjected.

'So did you watch any of the footage?'

'I did, and it's a lot of her on her own in her room; when a guy visits she locks the door and they just sit around with loud music on.'

'Anything else?'

'Well the girl from upstairs comes in and takes clothes, goes through her stuff when she's out, bit of a magpie, I think. Don't see much of her actual flatmate except when they're in there together.'

'What about Sam?' Imogen asked.

'Friday night regular. Under the covers stuff. Obviously they both know the camera's there and so . . .'

'So they're in bed together?'

'Yeah, a lot of whispering and stuff. I don't know about anything else. Seemed kinda wrong to watch any of the sexy stuff. So I just forwarded through it, nothing of much interest there. I mean . . . well you know what I mean.'

'Someone's going to have to watch it.' Imogen pulled a face.

'I'll watch it. I don't know him so I can be more objective,' Adrian offered.

'So she doesn't talk about any information she might have gained in these Friday night meetings?'

'Nope, all her communications are via encrypted email, like seriously encrypted. She had some skills. I mean has,' Tunney corrected himself as Adrian shot him a look.

'Anything else on the drive we should know about? Footage of the murders'd be a hell of a bonus.'

'Well, there is an anomaly in the metadata; I think there are some videos missing from the file.'

'Can you find those videos?'

'Short answer is yes.'

'What's the long answer?'

'It's going to take me some time. Like I said, she has skills.'

'And it's not possible these videos are just clips of her and Sam?' Imogen asked, a slight grimace on her face.

'Well, she left those in, so it seems unlikely it's just that.'

'But she's the one who will have deleted the files?'

'Yeah, but this isn't as simple as just clicking delete, she'll have had to work to get rid of that data. After a point the information gets sent to whichever tech is dealing with her stuff, my guess is she didn't want them seeing it.'

'You'd better find that data then.'

Adrian's phone beeped and he looked at the message. Fraser.

'Fraser has the CCTV from all the cameras at the riverbank, all the ones that are working at least. He says they've found something.'

Thanking Tunney, Imogen and Adrian set off back to Fraser's office. On the way up, Imogen looked around the corridor to make sure they were alone. She put a hand on Adrian's arm, clearly agitated.

'I know what Sam's been saying, Miley, but I don't trust him. There are a lot of things he isn't telling us. Believe me, he was my partner, I know. He isn't – he isn't a good person. He's hiding things.'

'Well, it's a classified operation. There must be things he can't tell us.'

'I worked with him, Miley, and I know when he's lying. I wouldn't be surprised if it was him who deleted those files, whatever they are.'

'Does he have those kinds of computer skills?' Adrian asked her, surprised.

'He could have had help.'

'Well, Tunney is on the case.'

'I'm just letting you know that you can't believe a word that comes out of Sam's mouth.'

'Are you OK, Grey?'

'Really?' She looked as though he had just spat on her face.

'I mean . . . you seem really upset. I don't know this guy as well as you do, but look – he's still working, he can't be as bent as you're thinking. Are you sure this isn't paranoia getting the better of you?'

'Fuck you!' She pushed him hard and he slammed against the wall. It didn't take a detective to realise she was upset.

Adrian knew that feeling and made a deal with himself not to be such a prick in the future. He remembered how people called him paranoid at times when he started spiralling out of control, and it did nothing but make him worse. He wouldn't do that to Imogen. She had just got back to work; he should give her a break.

In Fraser's office, the three of them gathered around the CCTV. They saw Bridget running terrified into the park and hiding inside a children's adventure castle. They saw a man coming down to the river and looking for her, getting close and then going the wrong way.

'Why doesn't she go to one of the flats or something?'

Imogen asked, leaning in to look closer at the screen. Adrian had already tried that and it was no use, the faces were a blur. As they watched, a car pulled into the shot and the fuzzy figure of Bridget slipped into the water, clinging to the side of the river and moving along the bank.

'She must be fucking freezing.' Adrian felt cold just watching it.

'Yeah but she's alive, that's something,' Fraser offered.

'What's that?' Imogen pointed to the screen.

'What?'

'Look, the boat, that one there, it's moving.'

They watched as Bridget disappeared down the river, a few moments later the boat Imogen was pointing to started to follow her, moving in the same direction.

'Can you read the name on that boat?' Fraser asked hopefully. 'It would be great if I can tell the press something.'

'No, but it's got those distinctive stripes on it. We'll go down and have a look, see what's what.'

'What do you think they're doing? Do you think this is an opportunistic attack?'

'I don't know, maybe it's a coincidence that this boat is travelling in the same direction as she is.'

'I don't believe in coincidences,' Adrian said, moving towards the door.

'Well, whatever's going on here, there's a good chance the guy in the boat saw something.'

'I know how much you like the water, Grey. Let's go,' Adrian said, trying to crack the frosty atmosphere. He knew Imogen didn't have any sea legs.

'I'll get on to the company that handles the boats down there, see if I can get a list of the owners,' Fraser said.

The boat was surprisingly easy to find. *Glitterbug* was a small blue ship with two stripes of different thicknesses; Imogen and Adrian found it moored near the spot where it had been in the video footage. Adrian watched as Imogen approached the boat first, peering inside.

'I think there's someone in there,' she said finally. 'I think I hear a radio or something.'

Adrian stepped aboard and offered his hand to Imogen. He banged on the cabin door and heard shuffling coming from inside. The door opened and a man peered out. Adrian held his badge up.

'I'm DS Miles and this is my partner, DS Grey of the Exeter Police Force. We're making inquiries about something that may have happened here on Friday night. CCTV in the area saw that you were on your boat. A police officer went missing.'

'Oh, do you mean the girl in the water?' The man stepped out on to the deck.

'You saw her?' Imogen asked.

'Yeah, I did, I dunno what she was doing. I thought she was hammered. I was going to call someone but I didn't want to get involved, you know?'

'So what did you do?'

'Well, I followed her a bit in the boat, but it got too dark to see and I didn't want to hit her. I called out a few times but no one answered. It's not very well lit the further down you go.'

'You still didn't call the police?'

'You see all kinds of crazy shit down here, kids mucking about, pissheads and stuff. I just figured she was fine.'

Imogen was shaking her head furiously. She pulled out her phone and started texting someone, her fingers flying over the keys.

'What were you doing on your boat so late anyway?' Adrian asked, resting a hand against the door of the cabin.

'I just like it at night, it's usually quiet and no one bothers me down here.'

'Did you see anyone besides the girl?'

'Not at first, no, but I did see a silver car come and look around.'

'Did you see anyone in the car?'

'There was only one bloke in it, I think.'

The detectives exchanged looks. If there was only one person in the car then it couldn't have been the men from earlier, unless one of them had come back on his own. Or maybe it was Sam Brown. Imogen's phone beeped.

'Do you know what kind of car it was?' she asked the man, her eyes on the phone screen.

'A saloon, that's about all I can tell you; like I say, it was really dark and I wasn't exactly close.'

'Anything else you remember about the car? Anything at all?'

'No, I'm sorry. Nothing.'

A phone started to ring on the boat and Imogen looked past the man into the darkness of the cabin. The ringtone was coming from inside.

'Hmm,' Imogen said, holding up her mobile, 'I just dialled DS Bridget Reid's phone. That's interesting. You want to tell me why you have it?'

Adrian immediately pushed past the man before he had a chance to react. He went into the cabin and found the vibrating phone resting on a little table to the left of the door. The man raised his hands up.

'Look, look, OK, I found it in the park. I had no idea it belonged to the girl in the water. How could I?'

'We're going to need you to come in and make a statement.'

For a moment, the man looked as though he might be going to resist, but then he nodded. 'No problem, anything to help the police.'

The detectives watched closely as he locked the cabin door, and followed Imogen and Adrian willingly off the boat.

Imogen watched the man from the boat through the glass window of the interrogation room. He seemed very calm, but there was something about him that made her skin crawl.

'His name is Ben Vickers and he's got previous.' Miles burst in with a file.

'What kind of previous?'

'Well, he's on the sex offenders' register, for a start.'

'You're kidding?'

'I wish I was. No, he's been cautioned three times for stalking and he lost his job after he sexually assaulted one of the women he worked with. It wasn't a violent assault, but still. He was a security guard up at the shopping centre.'

'Any connection to Bridget Reid?'

'None that we can see. No connection to that house either. There's a note here that says he was arrested for soliciting a prostitute, but he got out of it.'

'It's tenuous, Miley, but I guess he might have known Bridget through her flatmate or something.'

'So why aren't you in there?'

'He's waiting for his lawyer. But we can go in now, if you like.'

They stepped into the room and sat opposite Ben Vickers, who had a disconcerting smirk on his weather-beaten face.

'I don't expect my lawyer to be much longer,' Vickers said. 'I hate to keep you waiting like this. I just know how these things work, and I'm not talking to you without representation. I been stung before, you see. But I expect you know that by now.'

'Yes, we are aware of your record. It's not a problem, we don't mind waiting.' Adrian folded his arms and settled in, staring down Vickers. Vickers stared straight back.

Eventually, the door opened and in walked the lawyer, a tall man in a sharp black suit. He sat next to his client and addressed Adrian directly.

'My name's Jonathan Clark and I'm here to represent Mr Vickers. Can I get a moment alone with my client?'

'It's all right son, I got nothing to hide,' Vickers exclaimed.

'Mr Vickers, you are not under arrest. We just need

you to tell us exactly where you got that phone that was found in your boat,' Adrian said.

'I told you, I got it in the park.'

'When?'

'Well, I saw the girl come out of the park, the kids' play area bit, and I saw her get into the water, so after I tried to follow her I went to the park and the phone was there. I was going to bring it in but I forgot.'

'So the last time you saw her was in the water?'

'Not exactly.'

'But you said you couldn't follow her in the boat and so you went back.'

'Yeah, that night, that's right.'

'OK, so you saw her after that night?'

'First light I went down to the river and I saw her lying on the grass. I slept in my boat, woke up with the sun.'

'And you didn't call the police then either?'

'Not my business, is it?'

'What state was she in?' Imogen said through gritted teeth. What was wrong with people?

'I'm pretty sure she was asleep.'

'So did you approach her?'

'No, I'm not stupid, probably get done for something or other if I did.'

'Did you even check if she was alive?'

'Some bloke in a black car came along and lifted her up, she was out of it but she was definitely alive, moaning and stuff she was.'

'What bloke? What did he do with her?'

'Put her in the passenger seat of his car, that's why

I thought he probably knew her, didn't shove her in the boot or nothing.'

'Jesus Christ,' Imogen muttered. What upset her most was that this kind of thing wasn't unusual, people watched crimes take place all the time but didn't want to get involved. It made her job so much harder.

'Was this the saloon you told us about before?' Adrian leaned forward as he spoke to Vickers.

'No, it wasn't a saloon, it was like one of them poncy cars'

'A sports car?'

'No, no, like a Jeep thing, you know, a four-by-four. One of them what's got the big wheel on the door of the boot.'

'Like a Land Rover or something?'

'Yeah, that kind of thing.'

The door opened and Fraser stuck his head in, nodding for them both to come out. Imogen looked up at the clock before turning to the tape recorder.

'Interview suspended at 13:41.' She switched the tape off and then looked at the lawyer. 'We'll be back in a bit.'

'They found the other videos on the laptop,' Fraser whispered to Imogen once they were outside the room. 'I think maybe we need to have another word with your ex-partner.'

Chapter 12: The Video

The present

Adrian, Imogen and DCI Fraser walked into the tech lab to find Gary Tunney concentrating grimly on the laptop.

'What did you find?'

'Well, it looks like she set up a cloud account that all her videos were automatically sent to. It wasn't easy to find. She used layer upon layer of encryption, but anyway, I've got them.'

'I've always suspected that you're a wizard,' Imogen said, patting Tunney affectionately on the head.

'So . . .? Don't leave us hanging!' Adrian interjected.

'Right, well, one of the guys who visits her is an undercover, and they definitely seem like more than just friends. She puts the music on and then he gets a bit fresh, just a kiss, instigated by him. She pushes him away.'

'So that's it? Do we know who that is?'

'I've put in a request to find out the name, we can't blow his cover and we might not even be able to interview him,' Fraser said.

'Well, that's bullshit.'

'Do we think Sam knew about this guy and her?'

'It's possible,' Tunney said, clicking on another one of the entries. 'We know he wasn't happy about something.'

Cue Sam bursting into her room and literally pulling Bridget out of the bed by her throat and pinning her against the wall. Tunney paused the tape and looked at them both.

'Woah!' Imogen exclaimed.

'I should warn you, what happens next is not cool.'

'Play it.' Adrian braced himself.

Tunney turned the machine back on and they saw Sam Brown repeatedly hitting Bridget Reid in the face and stomach. Adrian felt himself getting light-headed just looking at the screen. It was a horrible reminder that your first instincts about people are usually the right ones. The first time he had met Sam Brown he hadn't trusted him, but he'd allowed himself to be suckered in, had given him the benefit of the doubt. He felt guilty for what he'd said to Imogen earlier. The scene reminded him of being a child, of the awful times that he'd seen his father smacking his mother around, usually high on something or other.

'So maybe it was Sam who made her delete the files.'

'I think that's a fair assumption.' Tunney nodded.

'Does this happen at any other time? Does he do it again?'

'Yeah, none quite like this one, but he definitely hits her one or two other times.'

'So maybe she knew something was going to happen to her, and she was collecting evidence,' Adrian said, almost to himself.

'That's a hell of a leap, Detective,' Fraser responded.

'Desperate times.'

'Undercover is very isolating, I doubt she felt like she could do much from where she was. Probably fewer than a handful of people knew what she was doing.'

'Is it possible that she just ran away? We need to speak to that UC, he looked pretty friendly with her.'

'I'm working on it,' Fraser said apologetically.

'What do we do about Sam?'

'What do we do with any suspect? Bring him in,' Fraser said.

'Do we cut Vickers loose?'

'Let's just wait for forensics to go over the boat, the weather's on the turn again so they're doing their best to get it done before the rain starts. Find out what car Brown has and I'll find out what this other fella drives.' Fraser paused for a moment. 'I shouldn't need to say this out loud, but if any of the press approach you, don't say anything. Only the people in this room know about this tape. Let's keep it that way.'

'Turn it off,' Adrian said to Tunney, who still had the footage from the room showing: Bridget slumped against the wall with Sam consoling her. The disturbing familiarity made it impossible for Adrian to look away.

Chapter 13: A Boy Alone

Age 14

My dad's really upset. I've never seen him like this, in fact I didn't even think it was possible. Mum has been in hospital for a few days now; they don't know when she's coming out. Last week after I got home from school I found her on the floor of the kitchen. She's had a stroke, apparently. Her face looks weird, weirder than usual. It's kind of droopy but stiff at the same time. Like she was left for too long in front of an open fire and started to melt, but was snatched away just in time.

We go to the hospital every day, my dad goes when I'm at school too. I can't be bothered with school at all, I just want to be free of it. I don't feel like I'm learning anything and most of the time the teachers don't treat me with any respect. I have this one teacher who talks to me like I'm scum; I don't know what his fucking problem is but one day he's going to regret it.

There's a girl I like too, her name is Claire Hastings. She's almost one of the popular girls, but she is like the quietest of all of them. She doesn't parade around with her skirt rolled up at the waist like a total skank. Sometimes she talks to me, when no one is looking. I think she likes me but she would never let any of her friends see; she hasn't quite made it to the inner circle, and being seen with me would put a stop to that. Part of me likes the secret friendship we have, but part of me is angry that she's ashamed of it. None of the other girls at school look at me. I'm invisible. I'm not on the rugby team, I'm not one of the blonde-haired, blue-eyed boys who follow them around ready to burst, the girls prick-teasing them with their shirts that are a size too small, pulling at the buttons across their chests. Skanks.

On Friday nights my dad takes me to the club. I feel better about it now that I'm taller – it was awkward for a while. I had a growth spurt when I was thirteen and now I'm almost six feet tall. The girls are used to me now. I like the girls in the club better than the girls at school. They make a fuss over me and generally do whatever they're told. At school no one knows who I am, but at the club I'm important. I'm not the foreign scum who gets treated like a second-class citizen – I was born in this country, but that doesn't seem to make a difference anywhere else.

Mum has been given a date to come home, finally. Dad actually seems a little better, back to his normal self. Dad being back to his normal self isn't actually such a great thing, but at least I can predict his behaviour, rather than living with his weird outbursts. I know he feels guilty about Mum's stroke; I think he thinks it's because he hits her. But he doesn't even hit her that much any more, not really, not compared to how it used to be. Surely it would have happened before now if it was to do with that.

I find it weird that Dad loves Mum. He isn't even remotely faithful to her. I've seen him with loads of other women. I never really knew what he was doing before, but now that I have done it too, I understand. Sex is weird, it's like a game or something, it's all about pretending to be in love with someone for a little while and then when it's over you can go back to being strangers. The girls I have been with so far change into different people when I have sex with them. The girls at the club, I mean. I think all of the girls at school like to act like they've done it, but I know they haven't. They hold it over the boys like some big prize. I'm still not sure what the big deal is, to be honest with you. The girls at school are nothing like the ones my dad knows. Most of the girls he knows are all hooked on 'shit', as he calls it. He says it keeps them in line.

Dad tells me we need to get ready for Mum's return; he has brought some of the junkie girls back to our family home, which feels weird. I don't like them touching my mum's stuff. Dad is making them clean the place, although I don't think they know how to clean. He says he has an errand for us, a surprise for Mum. We get in the car when the junkies have left, but

I want to stay and clean the place again – I know where those sluts have been.

We drive all the way across the city to a part of town I haven't been in before. We're parked under a tree and my dad is watching the street. It's very quiet, not that there's silence, but there's an eerie lull in the air. I can hear children playing and car stereos, but still it feels quiet. It's a warm day and there's a man washing his car further down the road. I wonder what we could possibly be here for. Then I see her. I feel like I have been punched in the gut when I look at her properly. It's like looking at my sister, except it can't be her because she's dead. But there she is, playing with a bucket of mud in her front yard. My dad tells me to go and speak to her, to ask her for help to find my lost dog and to get her to come to the car. This is the present for my mum, the little girl. A replacement girl.

I can't say no to my dad, but I know this is a bad thing to do. It's strange being on this side. When I was little, my mum would always warn me about wandering off and some stranger taking me home with them so that I could never see my family again. Sometimes that would be the point of wandering off, hoping to be taken by another family, to get away from my fucked-up parents, but no one ever wanted me.

I approach the girl. The front door to her house is open and I look inside to check no one is around. I can hear the distant sound of a radio somewhere inside, upstairs most likely. I tell the girl about my lost dog and ask her if she will help me. She's reluctant to leave the front yard but I show her a picture of my beloved old dog, the one that my father drowned in the bathtub as one of my punishments. We look under cars on the street and call out the name. I don't use my dog's real name in case anyone hears. We get close to my dad's car and I feel sick. I'm amazed that no one is watching us. I look over at the girl's house again, but there's still no sign of life. The overconfidence of a summer's day, as if the bad guys only come out on dark stormy nights. My dad is waiting near the car, and when we get close enough he grabs her and wraps her in a blanket. I look around but no one has noticed. He puts her in the boot and we drive away.

We put the girl in my sister's bedroom downstairs and close the door. Her cheeks are streaked where she's been crying but she must have passed out in the boot. I wonder how long it will be before anyone notices she is gone. I want to stay in the room and watch over her while she is sleeping, but Dad says we have to go and attend to some business.

We go to the house where Mindy lives. Mindy is still there but Margot hasn't been there for a while. No one talks about her any more and I know better than to ask. I liked Margot. Mindy doesn't look like herself these days, her cheeks are sunken and she has scabs all over her face. Her eyes are lighter, they have a white glaze, and sometimes she zones out completely when we are in bed. I might have to switch girls because she's not much fun any more. She has a new housemate now, her name is Carla but she doesn't speak any English. I *don't know where she's from but she isn't as pretty as Mindy, even the way Mindy looks now. Carla cries a lot, which pisses my dad off; he wants me to teach her a lesson. He said it's important that I learn how to deal with these girls because one day I will be in charge of the business. He makes me inject something into her arm, I have to tie it off so the vein pops up before I can put the needle in. I do it, but I don't really like needles. When I take over the business I don't think I'll use them.*

After I inject her, Carla stops crying and just stares into space. She looks more peaceful now. Mindy looks at my dad hopefully but instead of giving her what she wants he pulls her off the sofa and takes her upstairs. I sit there and watch Carla; her eyes move towards me but she doesn't really seem to care what I'm doing so I just keep watching her. People don't generally like it when you watch them, but I like to watch them more than anything else.

It's been a few days now and Dad has told the little girl we took that her parents gave her to us and that she will be well looked after here. He told her some bad people wanted to hurt her, so her parents asked us to look after her for a while. We all have to pretend that she is my sister so the bad people can't find her. We even pretend to my mum.

The stolen girl lives in my sister's room, which is annoying because sometimes I still like to go in there. She cries a lot but she seems to believe that we are what we say we are. All girls cry a lot, I think. My dad assures me that it won't be long before she forgets her parents entirely. It's been on the local news, but no one saw anything, nothing at all. I've seen a few missing posters stapled to lamp posts, and the newspapers are going crazy for it too. I keep waiting for a knock at the door but it hasn't happened yet. Only Dad and I know she is here. Mum can't really talk yet and it's not as if she has any friends who would visit her. No one comes to this house unless my dad makes them.

I knock on my new sister's door and go into the room. I talk to her about school and how much I like Claire Hastings. She asks me if Claire is pretty. She asks me why my mum just stares at the TV all day and I explain that she isn't very well. She also asks about my dad; she hasn't really had much to do with him yet apart from one or two meetings. She mostly has to deal with me. I bring my sister treats and milkshakes, I use my pocket money to buy her sweets and a new doll all of her own. I read my new sister a story every night until she falls asleep. Sometimes that takes hours, but I like the company. It's nice having someone to talk to again and I always did like this room the best. It's peaceful, away from the main bit of the house. I think she will like it here, I know how to make her laugh and she doesn't cry when I'm around. It's nice to be a big brother again.

It's almost the end of term at school and I'm looking forward to the break from all the other kids. I don't get them and they don't get me. I do wonder sometimes how many other people feel like I do, so completely out of touch with the rest of the world, like an outsider looking in. Is everyone else just playing the game, too? Copying other people so that no one will realise what it is they really think about, what they dream about?

I'm stuck in my form room on my own during lunch because I didn't do my homework again. I just don't see the point. Claire Hastings comes in to get something from her bag and she smiles at me and looks around to check no one is looking before coming and sitting on the edge of my table. I hate her for that but I like that she wants to talk to me. She plays with her fingers nervously when she speaks. She even helps me with the homework that I haven't finished and says we can sneak out of the fire exit; the teachers won't come back for a little while longer. The fire exit leads to the back of the school where some of the kids go to huff Tippex and drink cider. It's quiet today, because even though it's June it's threatening to rain. Claire asks if I want to play a game of mercy and I say sure.

She looks nervous, and I like watching her look nervous so I just stand with my back to the wall, facing the long hedgerow that runs the length of the building. She puts her finger on my neck and starts to move it downwards. Her nerves seem to be getting worse because I don't even flinch, I just stare her in the eyes, her fingers travelling down the front of my body. I think she thinks that just because I'm quiet at school I'm frigid or something, some scared little virgin. But I'm not. It's nice to have a girl touch me because she wants to and not because she's scared of my dad. Her fingers are trailing down my stomach now and she has a strange look on her face, like she doesn't want to do it, but she still keeps doing it as I continue to watch her.

She purses her lips together in concentration as she tries to undo my belt without looking down. I can feel my own face is more serious now too as I wonder how far she's willing to go, because I sure as hell won't be saying mercy at any point. I see her gulp and lick her lips as she manages to undo the belt and get to my fly. Normally this game is played with several boys lined up against the wall and several girls teasing them. Of course, I've never been invited to join in. She looks at me again, begging me with her eyes to stop this, but I don't. She undoes my button and zip and I feel my trousers hanging on my hips. She coughs and then puts her hands on the waist of my trousers pulling them down hard and fast, taking my underpants with them. At that moment she whispers the word sorry, almost inaudibly before staggering backwards, away from me. Then I see them.

Almost my entire class have burst round the corner. I can't really hear what's happening because I am dizzy with anger. I feel it rise up through me like a bolt of lightning. I look at Claire who is almost in tears, trying to catch my eye, searching for forgiveness, but that's not going to happen. My jaw is clenched as I bend down to pick up my trousers. I'm not crying but I am so fucking angry. I feel like fire could shoot from my eyes and burn them all to the ground as they point and laugh at me. Claire's friends surround her in a warm embrace filled with laughter and solidarity. She's one of the gang now.

97

When I get home, I get in the shower and scrub my skin raw until I draw blood. I try to think of a way to make that bitch Claire regret what she's done. I consider telling my father, but I think he'd be angry with me. He warned me that girls don't understand respect until you teach them. I know she has a dog that she loves. I could just kill it and nail it to the fucking telephone pole outside her house. I wouldn't do that though, because I like animals. It might take a while but I'll think of something else. Dad says revenge is even better when they don't know it's coming, so I'm going to wait for the perfect time, when she's forgotten about it completely, when she thinks I have forgiven her. Then I will make her sorry. Not only will she wish she'd never met me, she will wish that she'd never been born.

Chapter 14: The Good Girl

Plymouth, two years earlier

Imogen and Sam found themselves in Dr Carol Foster's domain for the second time in as many weeks, staring down at a sixteen-year-old girl laid out on the slab. The girl didn't have needle marks in her arm this time. She had beautiful long hair that was glossy and highlighted, her nails were manicured and her legs waxed. She wasn't one of the city's lost children; she was from a nice home, a good background.

'The parents are on their way in.'

'Great,' Imogen said. She wasn't looking forward to dealing with that level of emotion; it was much easier to remain detached and clear-headed when you could be objective about the case. In many ways she preferred the strays, the Jane Does. Grieving parents added an extra level of obligation, an extra level of guilt.

'What do we know about her?'

'We know she's not a habitual user. I would even go as far as to say this might have been her first time,' Foster said with her eyebrows raised.

'Unlucky, kid,' Sam said to the girl.

'But the big news is that it's the same drug as that other girl, the Jane Doe. That's why I called you in.'

'Thank you,' Imogen said.

'I'm going to hazard a guess that we will be seeing more bodies like this. It's nasty stuff,' Dr Foster said.

The door to the exterior office opened and the doctor's assistant nodded at them. The parents were here. Mr and Mrs Baggott. Carol covered the girl's face with the sheet. The door opened again and in walked a husband and wife, well groomed and well off, both looking petrified with that mixture of hope and fear on their faces. Imogen knew they were hoping it was someone else's little girl lying on that table. It was the same look you saw on everyone's face when they came to ID a body, those final few moments of hope before their worst fears were confirmed. It occurred to Imogen how hard this part of Carol Foster's job must be: constantly taking people's final hopes away. Or maybe it was the humane thing to do, putting a definitive end to the worry, replacing the clawing feeling of hope with grief. Grief was a much more civilised emotion; you could get counselling for that.

It felt like time stood still as they all sucked in a breath and waited for Carol to pull back the sheet. For a brief moment the parents stared at the face, confused, unsure if it was in fact that of their daughter. Imogen had seen this reaction before too. She could imagine their thoughts: *she looks kind of like our little girl, but not really, I mean, our baby has these bright sparkly eyes and a smile that lights up any room. This can't actually be her.* Then the realisation would set in: it was her, or what was left of her anyway. Seeing a loved one dead was like seeing the chrysalis after the butterfly has left, empty, missing something important.

'No! No! No!' the mother cried, breaking the silence so that everyone could breathe again. Imogen closed her eyes. The question had been answered and now a clear set of procedures could begin. The father comforted the mother, his face still ashen and his voice still unable to utter the words that they waited for.

'It's her, it's our Nancy,' he finally said, and his wife disappeared into his embrace, sobbing relentlessly into his chest.

Carol Foster covered Nancy's face, no longer a nameless teenage girl. Imogen couldn't help but think of the first girl, the one who had not been given an identity yet. Who would be missing her?

Sam put his hand on Mr Baggott's shoulder and led him through to Carol's office. Imogen followed, ready to tell them how their daughter had died. Steeling herself to ask the questions they wouldn't want to answer. Ready to hear the lies they would tell in order to protect their daughter's reputation. Knowing full well it wouldn't be easy to get to the truth.

Mrs Baggott continued to cry. Imogen handed her a box of tissues and sat next to her.

'I'm so sorry for your loss.'

'What happened? How did she . . .?'

'It was an overdose.'

'You're wrong, she didn't even drink. She definitely didn't do drugs.'

'We think it may have been her first time.'

'Can that happen? Can you die the first time?' Mr Baggott asked.

'Yes, unfortunately it can happen. It's entirely possible that someone lied to your daughter about the type of drug it was; they tell them it's just a harmless high and then they get them hooked.'

'That must be it,' he said, almost to himself.

'Do you know where she was last night?'

'She was at her friend's house. She stays there once a week after horse riding. That's why we never knew she was out all night. She's a good girl. She was . . .'

'We're going to need her friend's details.' Sam handed Mr Baggott a pen and paper.

Mrs Baggott grabbed hold of Imogen's hand and squeezed it hard. She moved in closer and stared at her. Her eyes were red and wide; she was in a state of shock.

'Promise me someone will pay for this!'

'I promise,' Imogen said helplessly. What else do you tell someone who has just had their whole world ripped apart, she wondered. You tell them what they want to hear; you give them something to hold on to. There is no other option.

Imogen and Sam stood outside the house of Lindsey Finlay, friend of Nancy. It was a pretty, beach-front cottage like something out of a fairy tale, set in a small fishing village close to the city of Plymouth. Gulls squawked above them. Imogen wished she could go and jump in the sea, wash off the dirty feeling that had crept over her the minute she saw Nancy's body. Another difficult interview, but hey, she was the one who wanted to join the police. These kinds of interactions had never entered her mind when she'd started training. She'd imagined herself dealing with the scum of society, not telling some picture-perfect family that their teenage daughter was possibly implicated in two deaths.

She glanced down at the address in her hand once more; they were at the right place. Lindsey Finlay was the girl Nancy had allegedly stayed with once a week. Sam rang the doorbell.

A pretty blonde girl with headphones on answered the front door. She smiled at them and Sam held his warrant card up. Instantly, her smile disappeared and she pulled off the headphones. Oh yeah, she knew she was in trouble.

'Hello?'

'Are your parents here?' Imogen asked.

'Mum! The door!' The girl's face cleared and she yelled backwards into the house. Obviously she assumed she was off the hook, that this was a matter for her parents not her. Imogen watched as she grabbed at her headphones again, ready to put them back on as her mother descended the stairs.

'Can I help you?' Mrs Finlay asked. She saw the badge and her face went white. 'Oh my God, is it Bill? Is he all right?'

'Actually, we need to speak to you and your daughter about Nancy Baggott.'

'Nancy? What's happened?' Lindsey asked.

'Can we talk inside?' Imogen asked.

'Sure, come in.'

Mrs Finlay led the way into the lounge, a blue and beige room that looked as though it was straight out of an interior design magazine, complete with driftwood and nauticalia. Lindsey followed dutifully and sat next to her mother. Imogen and Sam remained standing; the sofa seemed a little too clean to park their inner-city bottoms on.

'There's no easy way to say this. Nancy was found dead this morning, she died of an overdose.'

'Are you serious?' Mrs Finlay half laughed, as though the thought was so alien it was ridiculous. Lindsey remained quiet but her silence spoke volumes. 'My God! You are serious.'

'Apparently she stays here every week after you both go horse riding together,' Sam said to Lindsey.

'No, there must be a mistake; Nancy hasn't stayed with us for weeks.' Mrs Finlay looked at Lindsey, whose eyes shifted away.

'Lindsey, do you know why her parents thought she was here?' Sam asked.

The girl was trying her best not to squirm in her seat.

'Was she seeing someone? Is that it? Did she have a boyfriend her parents wouldn't approve of?' Imogen asked. She recognised that look on Lindsey's face, not to mention the fact that she had been a teenage girl once too.

'Come on, this is about finding out what happened

to your friend. She can't get in trouble for it, not any more.'

'She met this guy,' Lindsey whispered. 'I don't know his name; I just know he works in one of the nightclubs.'

'What? How old is he?' Mrs Finlay piped up, shutting Lindsey down.

'I told her not to, I swear, I told her that he was bad news.'

'Why didn't you tell anyone?'

'I promised her I wouldn't. But she stopped coming to horse riding weeks ago, she was too busy hanging out with him.'

'And you don't know his name?'

'No, sorry.'

'Did you ever meet him?' Imogen asked.

'No, but I saw him pick her up once, he had black hair and brown eyes, looked foreign, maybe Spanish or something. She didn't tell me much about him.'

'Was the nightclub called Aphrodite's, by any chance?'

'Yeah, maybe, I think so. I'm sorry, Mum.' Lindsey burst into tears.

'It's OK, baby.' Mrs Finlay pulled Lindsey in for a cuddle. Imogen knew that ultimately, she was glad that it had been Nancy who had died and not her baby.

Imogen and Sam left Lindsey Finlay to deal with her mother's barrage of questions. They could interview her again if needs be, but they'd got enough from her at this time.

They pulled up outside Aphrodite's again. Imogen set her jaw; she was determined not to be fobbed off this time. Nancy Baggott made it two connections to the club, and if there was one thing they taught you in detective school, it was that there is no such thing as a coincidence.

Dean Kinkaid was outside, smoking a cigarette. His face lit up when he saw Imogen; maybe he was like this with all the women, she thought, but damn, that smile made her feel special. Cross with herself, she tried to quash the thought.

'Imogen!' He beamed. 'I thought I'd never see you again.'

'That's Detective Grey to you,' Sam barked.

'Just passing through again, Dean? You spend a lot of time here for someone who doesn't work here.'

He ignored her question. 'How can I help you guys? Got another body for me to look at?'

'Actually, yes,' Imogen said. She noticed a fleeting look of concern in his eyes. Could she be imagining it? Dean Kinkaid was a hard person to read.

She pulled out the picture of Nancy and handed it to Dean, watching his face as he studied it.

'I've seen this one,' he said to Imogen's surprise.

'You have?'

'Yeah, she's been here before, in the day, not at night. What is she? Fifteen?'

'She's sixteen. Got a good eye for girls' ages, have you?'

'You have to have when you look like me, honey. Lots of girls come on to me, believe it or not. Last thing I need is some bullshit statutory rape charge.'

'Wow. That may be the most conceited thing I've ever heard,' Sam said.

'You jealous?' Dean smiled at him.

'Apparently she was seeing some guy who worked here. Was that you?' Imogen asked, hoping his answer would be no.

'I have a strictly over-eighteen policy. I'm no pervert.'

'What about your pal George, is he a pervert?' Sam asked.

'Come to think of it, I did see her talking to him,' Dean said.

'Is he inside? Can we talk to him?' Imogen put her hand on the door; Dean touched her arm as if to stop her.

'George no longer works here.' Dean smiled. 'He moved back to Greece. Or so I heard.'

'Well, that's convenient, isn't it?' Sam piped up again.

'Not really. Reliable staff are hard to come by.' Dean smiled again; this time it was more forced. 'Look if you want to, I won't stop you. The place is empty.'

'But you don't have a vested interest in the place at all, because you don't work here?' Sam pushed past Dean and into the club.

'He doesn't seem to like me much,' Dean said.

'Do you care?' Imogen smiled, knowing full well the answer to that question. 'What's your story, Dean Kinkaid?'

'There's no story. I'm just helping out a friend by watching over the place from time to time.'

'Do you work?'

'You mean you didn't look into me already? I'm offended.' He held his hand to his heart as though he'd been wounded, but his burning smile said otherwise.

She noticed a pendant around his neck, a tiny shell trapped in a resin ball. He saw her eyes focus on the pendant and he wrapped his hand around it protectively.

'Should we look into you?' she asked.

'I'm an open book; ask me anything and I'll be honest with you,' he said as he stuffed the pendant inside his button-down t-shirt. She saw the edges of a black tattoo on his pectoral muscle and blushed as the smile widened on his face.

'Where is George?' She looked up at him.

He leaned forward slightly, bringing his eyes to within inches of hers.

'I have absolutely no idea.' He spoke in a low voice, biting on his lip, obviously trying to draw her eye.

The doors of the club burst open and Sam came out, marching back in the direction of the car.

'We're wasting our time here, Grey! He's right, there's no one there.'

Imogen stepped backwards, away from Dean. 'Mr Kinkaid, you have my number. If you think of anything, call me . . . I mean . . . call the station, someone will take the call and pass on the information.' She walked away before he had a chance to respond, joining Sam in the car.

Back at the station, Imogen threw her keys on to the desk. She thought about the Baggotts and how they would be feeling right now. She shouldn't waste time feeling sorry for herself when there were people dealing with things like that. She chewed her lip. George's disappearance was almost a clear indicator that he was

108

involved. After asking around, it seemed as though he had a reputation both with the ladies and with a little side action drug dealing. She wondered if he had actually gone back to his own country or if he was lying in a hole somewhere in the UK.

Was Dean some kind of enforcer? That seemed the most likely scenario. Hiring in people who would do your dirty work wasn't unheard of. Was this just a case of one rogue barman who couldn't keep his dick in his pants, or was this about the club? Perhaps George had brought too much attention to their organisation. She couldn't help wondering if this wasn't just the tip of the iceberg. Had George run off to escape scrutiny? It gave Imogen a headache just thinking about it. To top it off, Sam had been in a foul mood all the way back from the club. She glanced over at him; he was drumming his fingers on his desk angrily, his face like thunder.

'Where are we on the Baggott girl?' DCI Stanton appeared next to them, his eyebrows raised. 'The press are going to be all over this, you two. I need something to tell them when I get bloody cornered.'

'Ask her,' Sam snapped.

'Grey? What's the word? Do we know what happened?'

'She was more than likely seeing one of the barmen at Aphrodite, that club in town,' Imogen said.

'Did you bring anyone in?'

'The guy we were after has supposedly left the country, sir. I'm requesting the flight manifests now.'

'Supposedly?'

'The man we spoke to at the club today was a little

109

less than forthcoming. He was too busy making eyes at Grey,' Sam said.

'He was pretty open, I thought, he told us he recognised the girl, said he had seen her with George, the barman. His name is Dean Kinkaid,' Imogen offered, ignoring Sam's comment.

'He was all over you and you were loving it,' Sam snipped.

'You let him get to you, Sam. You're imagining things. He was helpful.'

'Helpful, my eye!' he shouted.

'All right! Enough!' Stanton said, holding up his hands as though they were a pair of squabbling toddlers. 'First thing tomorrow, bring this Dean character in and interview him on tape. Then I can decide if he is being forthright or not.'

Stanton stormed back into his office and slammed the door shut.

'What's his problem?' Sam asked.

'Maybe it's you acting like a big baby, Sam. Sometimes you need to play nice with people in order to get the information you need, not that I would expect you to understand that. That's all that was going on with me and Dean. I was being nice.'

'Doesn't hurt that he's tall, dark and handsome, huh?'

'Are you jealous? Is that what this is about?' Imogen smiled. 'Aw, Sam, I didn't know you cared.'

'Jealous of you? With that scrote? He's bad news, Grey. Maybe you're stupid, I don't know. Are you that desperate for a boyfriend? What is it with women and bad boys anyway?'

'You're crazy, and my love life is none of your business.'

Sam sighed. 'OK, look, I'm sorry. I just hate the filth and scum that peddle drugs and if he's mixed up in that, which I guarantee he is, then you need to keep a wide berth. You're already on his radar and you're too good for that. You don't know what people like him are capable of.'

'I'm tired, I'm going home. Sam, let's just forget it. I need some alcohol and a hot bath.' Imogen picked up her things and left the station.

Her whole life she had fallen in with men who had deemed themselves to be her protectors; even Stanton had done it on cases in the past. Was Sam next? She hoped to God he didn't have a thing for her, because there was nothing there, no attraction, no nothing. Sam was a good friend and sure, she'd caught him looking at her sometimes when she was dressed in her tight jeans, but she figured that was just something men did. What she didn't appreciate was feeling like someone's property or, even worse, someone's project. She didn't need her life to be fixed or made better, and she didn't need to be protected from the world. She was a big girl and in her twenty-seven years she'd had to deal with a hell of a lot more crazy than most of the men she had ever met.

When she got home, Imogen ran herself a steaming hot bath; she liked the water so hot that it hurt to move. She lay there with the radio on, listening to reports of the dead girls and the media frenzy that was already starting, the panic over the supposed new killer drug that was taking kids out left, right and centre. Never let the facts get in the way of a good news story. Wasn't that the journalists' motto?

The next story was interesting; a piece about the upcoming appeal of a set of parents who had been found guilty of murdering their own child, just over a decade ago. Isabelle Hobbs. Imogen cast her mind back, trying to remember the ins and outs of the story. They'd claimed their little girl had been abducted and had never strayed from their story, even in all the years that had gone by since, even when they were jailed for it. The media had torn them a new one at the time, and as soon as anything like parole came up, the newspapers made sure to plaster poor Isabelle's face all over the front page again, next to a picture of the stony-faced parents, who were always portrayed as killers, never as grieving. It hadn't ever been about the little girl, though, not really – the press couldn't give a monkey's. But a pretty little face with 'new facts' sure as hell helped to sell copies. Imogen hated the media; she thought of them as vultures, picking at the carcasses of the weak, preying on the vulnerable. They would interview people and then pull out the one phrase that completely corroborated their cause and discard the rest. As far as Imogen could tell, journalists were only ever trying to further their own careers.

She turned the radio off and lay in silence, listening to herself breathing. She hadn't been flirting with Dean, had she? She was all about DCI Stanton, really, and yet here she was thinking about the both of them as she lay naked in the bathtub. She couldn't decide who the bigger lowlife was: Dean, for being whatever the hell he was, or Stanton, for making advances on her when he was married. It all depended on your sense of morality. She shook off the idea of them both and rinsed herself under the shower spray before unplugging the bath. She liked the way her skin felt when she finally stood up, smooth and fresh, as though all of her pores were open and the cold air was making its way underneath her skin. She slipped on some pants and a comfortable robe and went down to veg out in front of the TV.

Imogen was three glasses into her bottle of wine when she heard the thumping on the front door. She opened it to find DCI Stanton standing there, a mixture of anger and lust on his face. Before she'd had time to think, he lunged at her and pushed her against the wall.

Trying to catch her breath, Imogen dropped her glass, feeling the tepid splash of the spilled wine as it dashed against her calves. *This was finally happening*. She tried to reach for the door, to close it before anyone saw. She kicked at it with her leg and it slammed shut. Stanton grabbed at her thighs and pulled them up to his waist. He pushed hard against her, knocking the wind out of her, but she didn't care. She didn't care if she never breathed again. She let her robe slide to the floor as he undid his trousers.

She pulled urgently at his shirt. She had often wondered what he looked like under his suit. He looked good. Imogen reached for him; she worked with lots of young men who spent their lunch hours at the precinct gym, men who would ask her out, but she said no to them every time. Those men didn't have the power that Stanton had, the confidence, the arrogance, the knowledge that he was the best. She had never found arrogance attractive before, but there was something about the DCI that she just couldn't resist.

As he kissed her, Imogen couldn't help but think of Stanton's wife, the thoughts invading her mind even as her tongue explored his. She wondered if they made love like this. Had he cheated on her before? She wanted to believe that she was the only woman who could bring out this animal in him. That this was the first time. That she was the first woman.

With all the pushing and pulling, they didn't even make it to the bedroom. She was propped up against the bookcase in the hallway. She didn't care about the shelves digging into her back. She just wanted him to keep going. She pushed all thoughts of his wife out of her mind as he ripped at her underpants. The elastic snapped and they caught on her thighs, but Imogen didn't care. She could feel him bulging and she wanted to take that need away from him, to make him feel peace. He slowed right down and pushed his face into hers, staring at her. He was searching for the same thing she was, she knew it; the look in the eyes as he finally entered her told her so. It was as though he could see his soul through her eyes now that they were interlocked. They stayed focused on each other as he slowly moved, pushing her against the bookshelves, one leg hitched up around his waist. She pushed him back on to the floor and climbed on top; he wasn't deep enough.

She wanted it to hurt. She saw his eyes travel up her body, reading him and watching his every breath, moving forward on him, watching him moan. She was going to make him wait for the finish; she was going to decide when this ended. Maybe that's why she was attracted to power, because she knew she had the ability to take it away.

Chapter 15: The Detox

The present

Bridget held the spoon in her hand as the man entered the basement room with her tray of food. The man sat next to her as she ate her sandwich and gently stroked her thigh. She let out a small moan. *Why does it feel so good?*

When she had finished eating, she put the tray on the side table and the man kissed her. He had beautiful brown eyes and his kisses were so soft, he was everything she could have wished for, and yet she could not remember his name. Did she even know his name? Did she know where she was? All she knew in this moment was that he was everything, and his touch was electrifying. A thought floated through her brain: *why was she doing this to Sam?*

As they kissed, Bridget worried that they should stop, but at the same time she never wanted it to end. She

116

loved this man, this big man with his strong hands and his soft curls. She put her fingers on his face, feeling the coarse stubble. She pulled him towards her, on to her, into her and they made love again. Every part of her that touched him was screaming; she could barely stand how good he made her feel. When he was done, he climbed off her and they lay together, her back to him, cradled in the shape of his naked body, skin to skin. His arms were around her and she could feel his breath on the back of her neck. 'I love being with you,' he said.

'I love being with you, too,' she replied. She wasn't lying.

'I love you with all my heart. When this is all over I want us to go away together, somewhere far away from here.'

'That would be nice.' She nuzzled into his embrace.

'I wish I could stay longer, but I can't, they can't know about us.'

'It's OK, I understand.' *What do I understand?*

He stood up and pulled his clothes on hurriedly, grabbed a bottle of pills from his pocket and handed her two of them. He watched as she picked up her water bottle and went through the motions of swallowing the pills down before leaving the room, locking the door behind him. *He's not my Sam.*

The man hadn't noticed that Bridget had kept the pills in her hand. Her thoughts were muddled and confused, but one thought was overriding: she didn't want to take those tablets again. She wasn't going to swallow them. Instead, Bridget put them on the floor and bashed them with the base of the lamp, turning them to powder. She bent down and blew the dust across the room, disposing of the evidence.

Bridget felt dirty. Now that he was gone, her feelings were changing; she had a nagging sensation that the man, whoever he was, was not on her side. Was he the one doing this to her? Drugging her, keeping her here in this dream world of a basement? Was this Stockholm syndrome? Could she have fallen in love with her captor? It didn't feel natural, it felt chemical. She couldn't remember a damn thing before this day and yet as soon as he'd entered the room earlier she'd been overwhelmed by feelings of love towards him.

Bridget pulled back the bed and stared at the floor. Her name over and over again. A worn down spoon. She drank water from the dirty tap on the wall, knowing she needed to get the drugs out of her system. God knows how many of those pills she had taken up until now. *God knows how many times they had slept together.*

She threw up.

She hoped that the effects of the drugs would wear off soon. *Had she tried to stop taking them before? Had she fallen asleep and then woken up oblivious yet again?* She couldn't go to sleep, she needed to drink water and stay awake, she needed to flush her system and clear her mind. Maybe it was dangerous to come straight off the pills, but she didn't care. At this point, she felt like she would rather be dead than live like this forever. She wondered if Sam was out looking for her. She imagined that he probably thought she was already dead. Maybe he'd even stopped looking.

Bridget sat on the edge of the bed, occasionally getting up and walking around when she felt her head growing heavy. She needed a plan. She thought about the man; he would be coming back, she would have to sleep with him again. What upset her the most was that she got excited at the prospect. She tried not to cry as she thought of how much she wanted his hands on her again, how much she wanted to lie with him, to put her lips on his.

She couldn't understand how she could feel this way. Perhaps she could use her desire for him to her advantage: she could figure things out and he would never get a hint that she had stopped taking the drugs, because she wanted him, she really, really wanted him. She knew he liked her too: he was in love with her, wasn't he? Good. She could use that. Her mind felt as though it was beginning to clear; she was undercover again, back to being a cop. Now she was getting her wits back, she needed to find a way to manipulate and exploit this situation to her advantage. Bridget smiled, but her head felt weary. It's hard to make plans when you spend ninety per cent of your waking time trying to remember something that's been wiped from your mind.

Chapter 16: The Request

The present

Bridget Reid had been missing for two weeks now. Adrian was on hold, waiting to speak to the undercover cop who had been in her videos. They weren't allowed to know his name or meet him in person, but they'd been granted a telephone interview.

'Detective?' came the voice on the end of the line.

'Hi, I'm DS Miles. I need to talk to you about DS Bridget Reid. You've been a hard man to get hold of.'

'I have a rock-solid alibi for the night she went missing, if that's what you're after.'

'No, we've been told about that. This is about your relationship with DS Reid.'

'Undercover is a bitch, and we were both working two ends of a big operation. Sometimes it's nice to kick back with someone you don't have to pretend with. We kissed once, but she told me to back off and I did. I got the wrong end of the stick.'

'What about DS Brown, do you know him?'

'Vaguely. I know he has a temper on him. Bridget had some bruises and she wouldn't say, but I got the impression they were from him.'

'Yes, we saw video footage of them together. He knocked her about a bit.'

'I'm sorry to hear that. Bridget's a good woman.'

'When was the last time you saw DS Reid?'

'A few weeks ago, but nothing happened that time. Honestly, if I could think of anything that might help you I would tell you. This is every UC's worst nightmare. I don't know anything. We were just part of each other's cover, that's all.'

'OK, thanks. If I have any more questions I'll get word to someone.'

'As for Sam Brown, there are a lot of creeps with access to that house. I don't know if he'd be my first choice of suspect.'

'I'll bear that in mind,' Adrian said, and the phone went dead.

'Well?' Imogen asked. She was sitting beside him, anxiously jiggling her leg up and down as she waited to hear what he had to say.

'Nothing, he has no idea where she might be. He doesn't fancy Sam for it though.'

'There's a surprise.'

'I owe you an apology, Grey.'

'What for?'

'Lately I don't trust my own instincts. I second-guess

myself a lot. I can't tell who's being straight and who isn't any more.'

'What are you getting at?'

'I'm getting at the fact that I was a shit to you. You told me not to trust Brown and I was a knob about it.'

'Yes, you were, Miley.' She smiled.

'We need to get a lead from somewhere. This is ridiculous. She can't have just vanished! There must be some bloody evidence somewhere.'

'Talking of which, the forensics found nothing on the boat, nothing whatsoever. Every single bit of evidence has been processed now. Right down to the loo brush.'

'Are they sure he didn't just clean up after him?'

'Nah, Fraser said the boat was filthy, hadn't been cleaned in ages. The phone was literally the only thing that related to Bridget.'

'What a weirdo. Why wouldn't you call all that in?'

'Well, he has a history with us that isn't so shiny; maybe he just didn't want to be a suspect.'

'He fucked that up then, didn't he?' Adrian sighed. 'Where's Fraser now?'

'Talking to Sam.'

Adrian went in and sat next to DCI Fraser in the interrogation room. Imogen was watching from behind the two-way mirror. They'd agreed it would be better if she stayed out of this one, given her history with Sam. As a courtesy to Sam, the tape machine wasn't on, but Fraser had obviously decided he wanted to make him as uncomfortable as possible anyway.

'You're interrogating me? Really?' Sam said.

'You've left us no choice,' Fraser responded.

'What are you talking about?'

'You haven't been straight with us. We found the videos.'

'The videos of me and Bridget?'

'I'm talking about the deleted videos.'

'OK, you've lost me.' Sam shifted uncomfortably in his seat.

'You know Gary Tunney, right? You know how good he is at finding stuff that no one else can find?' Adrian said. 'Stop fucking around! You're either helping or obstructing. If she's alive – and at the moment that's a big if – you need to be completely straight with us. You *know* what we're talking about.'

'What are you saying?' Sam's voice changed, lowered. His face clouded over and he sighed, looking resigned. 'It's not what it looks like.'

'You know what it looks like? It looks like you beating seven shades out of a fellow police officer at least half the size of you.' Adrian fought to keep his voice under control.

'It wasn't real.'

'Looks pretty real to me.'

'Well, that was kind of the point. When we find Bridget she'll tell you.'

'*If* we find her. How do I know I can even trust you any more? There are at least five separate occasions where you backhand her.'

'Look, Miles, watch those videos again and you'll see that her flatmate was there in the room, every time it happened.'

123

From what Adrian had seen Sam was telling the truth here, the flatmate had indeed been present in the clips, standing in the edge of the frame.

'Go on.'

'Bridget was new to the house and she thought Estelle was suspicious of her. She had to get her on side. Estelle's former boss had put her in hospital a few times; Bridget thought taking a few hits might endear her to Estelle.'

'So did it work?'

'Look, she thought I was a dirty cop, as such I needed to act like one. It was part of my cover, too.'

'What about the other UC? Did you know about him and Bridget?'

'Know what?'

'There's some video of her and him being intimate.'

'I don't know anything about that.' Sam's face had gone pale. Adrian stared at him; he looked like he was telling the truth.

'Was she like that, then? Did she get around? Who else should we be questioning?' Adrian added, leaning forward to look Sam in the eye. Sam's expression turned black; he was staring at Adrian as though he wanted to cut his throat.

'So you deleted the videos?' Fraser said, when Sam didn't answer.

'That was Bridget's idea. The whole thing was her idea. She didn't want the plug to be pulled. She didn't want me getting in trouble. Just ask Imogen . . . I'm not like that.' He looked at the mirror. 'Tell them, Imogen!'

There was no response.

'All sounds very convenient, Brown, without Bridget to back up your story.'

'Then fucking find her and she can!' Sam shouted, slamming his hand on the table.

Adrian knew that undercover work was tricky, and that it took a special kind of person to do it. Sometimes it was hard to remember who you were. You couldn't ask people too many questions without raising suspicions, so you had to make them trust you enough to spill of their own accord. Sam's story was plausible, he supposed – if Bridget was trying to gain traction with Estelle then it was possible she'd engineered the beatings in order to gain her trust.

'What sort of car do you drive, Sam?'

'I've got a silver Volvo, why?'

'We found a witness who saw a man putting Bridget into his car.'

'What? When? Why the fuck didn't you tell me?'

'Some guy on a boat saw her being put in a black four-by-four at about seven in the morning.'

'Well, it wasn't me. I was here talking to you.' Sam was looking directly at Fraser.

'Fine,' Adrian said and stood up. Real or not, Sam wasn't pulling his punches in those videos. He walked out to find Imogen standing by the door.

'Believe him?' she asked.

Adrian shrugged and shook his head.

'How the fuck did you put up with him as your partner?'

She ignored the question, touching a hand to her stomach. It was a gesture he'd noticed her doing a lot lately whenever Sam's name was mentioned. Almost as though it was a nervous tic. 'So what now, Miley? Do you think she's still alive?'

'We have to work on the assumption that she is. There's more footage of the riverside, tapes from private residences. It's going to be a good few hours' work, and then there's the traffic cams. We need to find this four-by-four.'

'Let's do it.'

Chapter 17: The Intruder

The present

Several hours of watching CCTV footage was enough to send anyone to sleep. Adrian and Imogen were on their fifth cup of coffee each and their third soggy cheese and tomato sandwich from the canteen. There was a surprising amount of traffic at seven in the morning, and it seemed that everyone and his wife owned a black four-by-four. So far, they'd ruled out eight of the vehicles because the insides were clearly visible, and they'd managed to follow a few cars to their destinations, usually schools or office blocks. They were just about to take a break when Adrian noticed a four-by-four coming from the right direction at 7:20 in the morning. There was a man in a baseball cap in the driver's seat and what seemed to be a sleeping girl in the passenger seat. He sat forward, feeling a rush of adrenaline. She could be Bridget; she looked about the right age. He wrote down the licence plate and handed it to Imogen, who typed it quickly into the database.

'Bingo,' she said.

'Who is it?'

'Well, it's registered to a Maeve Wilson and it's apparently a Megane. Except that's an old RAV4, so someone's swapped out the plates,' Imogen said.

'Right then, I guess we follow it through the tapes, if we can. Thank God for the stupid one-way system.' Adrian clapped his hands together in feigned enthusiasm.

They searched for each street camera individually, trying to find the vehicle and then map out a direction. Each road had at least two options; the driver could have taken either route. After finding the same car on several of the recordings, there was then nothing, presumably as the car got closer to the industrial estate on the outskirts of town.

'You think he's got her at a warehouse or something?'

'He could just be swapping vehicles. I think we need to go drive round there and check it out. See if anything jumps out at us.'

'You think anything will?'

Adrian shrugged. 'It's worth giving it a shot. If there's nothing, we can get back on the videos in the morning. I need out of this room.'

The industrial estate was a bust and so Imogen went home to shower and change. She needed to freshen up before going to her mother's house for her weekly barrage of insinuations. The shower took less than five minutes; as always, she kept her eyes on the wall in front of her, avoiding looking down at the scars on her torso. After washing her hair, she jumped out and wrapped herself quickly in a towel before entering her bedroom to throw on her usual combats and tee.

Sam Brown was sitting on her bed. Imogen leapt backwards, her heart pounding with shock. She stared at him.

'Imogen, you're wasting time looking at me,' he said calmly, his eyes travelling up and down her body. She wished she'd used a bigger towel.

'Sam! How did you get in here?' She stopped in her tracks. She knew how he'd got in; he had done it before in her old place, several times. 'How did you know where I live?'

'Oh come on, I know you have a problem with me, but Imogen, it's completely unjustified!'

'Really? And you think breaking into my place is "justified"?'

'You're being dramatic. I knocked and there was no answer so I came in through the back.'

'The back was locked, Sam. Get out before I fucking report you!'

He stood up and walked over to her. She backed away as much as she could but he kept coming forward.

'You need to convince your partner Miles to let this thing with me go. God knows what they're doing to Bridget, and you two are pissing about looking at me.'

'You beat the shit out of her, Sam!'

'It was her idea!' he hissed.

'At this point, I don't know if you've ever been straight with me. You need to get out right now.'

'If something happens to her, it's on you!' he shouted, grabbing her by the shoulders.

'I'm not the one who put the person I love in that position. Undercover in a fucking brothel that you think may have been a cover for human trafficking? What were you thinking?'

'I needed someone I could trust.'

'Trust? What do you even know about it? I trusted you in Plymouth, Sam, I trusted you when you were my partner!' She could feel her scar throbbing. 'Look what happened then!'

He gripped her shoulders harder; she felt his nails cutting into her skin as he stared her down. She had never responded well to being threatened. Instinctively she thrust her knee into his crotch, almost losing her towel; Sam recoiled and she lunged forward, grabbing the marble Buddha from her bedside table. She held it over her head, her other hand holding her towel in place.

'Get the fuck out before I paint the fucking walls with your brain!' Her heart was thumping. She had seen that video. She knew that Sam would have no qualms about beating the absolute crap out of her. Regardless of what Bridget had or hadn't asked him to do, he had done a pretty convincing job of it. She saw his eyes look at the Buddha and then a smile spread across his face.

'Fine, but one of these days you're going to feel pretty stupid. You're wrong about what happened in Plymouth, Imogen. It isn't my fault that you've got that scar.'

He stood up and walked down the stairs. Imogen stood there in her towel, breathing hard. She didn't move until she heard the front door shut. Quickly, she went over to the window to watch Sam get in his car and drive away. As soon as she was sure he was gone, she threw on her clothes and rushed out of the house. She jumped in the Granada and made the hasty decision to go to Adrian's house. It was dark and the chances of him being home were slim; the chances of him being alone were even slimmer, but she couldn't face seeing her mother right now and she didn't want to be by herself. She found herself driving the long way round, along New North Road. She passed Bury Meadows, the park that she'd learned had been originally donated to the city as a burial ground for cholera victims – like everything, a grim hidden history that people sat and ate lunch on without a clue. Unaware of the thousands of bodies buried beneath their Marks and Spencer's avocado sandwiches. Then came Exeter prison, ticking away in its own little world, most of its inhabitants unconcerned with what was happening outside those walls, unencumbered with the daily grind but no doubt with their own battles to fight. The lights in the windows were slowly going out, one by one. She thought of the men inside, all adjusted to the routine, ready for bed whether they were tired or not, the simple choice of bedtime taken away from you. Did the worst of the worst cry at night when they thought no one was watching, or were they just so jaded that nothing mattered to them any more? Part of her hoped it was the latter.

Imogen followed the road around and across the city until she pulled into Adrian's street. The song on the radio had somehow brought her to tears, an eighties pop ballad whose words suddenly held the key to everything she felt was missing in her life. She wiped her face and tried to compose herself. The light was on inside Adrian's house.

She got out and knocked on the door. Adrian opened it, his eyes widening when he saw her on the doorstep. She obviously didn't look as normal as she'd hoped because his expression swiftly changed from surprise to concern.

'What's happened?'

'Oh God, it's nothing really, I'm just being stupid,' she said, pushing past him and heading straight for the cupboard where she knew he kept his alcohol stash. 'Can I crash on your sofa tonight?'

'It's nothing and you want to crash on my sofa? What the hell's going on, tell me! Are you all right?'

'I feel so pathetic, Miley, I don't even want to say.'

'Come off it. Talk to me!'

'OK, but don't go all nuts or alpha male on me, I really can't handle it, all right?'

'I promise, now spill.'

'Sam just kind of broke into my house.'

'He did *what*?'

'I was in the shower and then when I got out he was sitting there on my bed. He came in through the back; he said he'd knocked first. He told me we have to stop looking at him or we won't find Bridget.'

'Did he hurt you?'

'No, no, nothing like that. I did kick him in the balls though.'

'Well, that's something.' Adrian began to pace, his face dark and his fists clenched at his sides.

'I just didn't want to stay home alone, that's all.'

'Of course, look, you can have Tom's bed, you don't have to sleep on the sofa.' Adrian grabbed the whisky that was already on the table and poured her a glass; Imogen necked it and flopped on to the sofa, dragging her nails across her forehead. 'We need to tell Fraser.'

'No way, Miley. I'm not going to be the helpless female,' she said, ignoring the fact that she had just driven across town in order to avoid being a helpless female in her own home.

'He's done this before, right?'

'Yeah, back in Plymouth. After I left, before I got transferred here, I stopped taking his calls and blocked his emails. I changed my numbers and everything, but he was just determined to speak to me. To explain his side of things.'

'He says he was investigating your department.'

'He may well have been; doesn't mean he's not bent, does it? There are a lot of ways to be bad, Miley. You saw him on that video.' She had noticed Adrian's face the first time the video played, and she recognised that look. It was the look of someone remembering.

'When he broke into your house before, did he do anything . . . untoward?' His fists were white.

'No. Apart from scare the shit out of me, he never touched me.' She knew if she told Adrian about him

133

grabbing her, all bets would be off, so she kept it to herself.

'Am I allowed to hit him?'

'No, I don't want to make a big deal out of it. I'm just going to head off up to bed, if that's OK?'

Adrian's phone rang. He showed her the screen. It was his son Tom.

'I have to take this, I'm sorry.'

She waved his apology away. 'No worries. I'm just going to crash. Thanks, Miley.' He put the phone to his ear and she headed for the stairs, desperate to lie down and sleep.

The next afternoon, Adrian pulled up outside Tom's school. His son had asked him specifically to come, a rare request and one that Adrian would never pass up. He spotted Tom pacing up and down, biting his fingernails unashamedly in the way that teenagers do. Their relationship had been better lately, but it still wasn't like him to talk to Adrian rather than his mother. There hadn't been any urgency in Tom's voice on the phone last night, though, and so Adrian decided not to panic. Seeing Adrian pull up, Tom jumped in the car and they drove out to a café on the Countess Weir roundabout. It was busy, but Tom insisted they got a table in the corner.

'Are you going to tell me what's up?' Adrian finally asked.

'I had work experience last week.'

'I know, your mother said you went to work in one of your stepdad's companies. I wish I'd known; I could have found you something with us. I do have my uses.'

134

'I did say I wanted to do something with you rather than Dominic. But she didn't want me to.'

'I thought you guys got on OK?' Adrian said, trying to suppress the smile that wanted to materialise after Tom's last statement.

'We do, we do.'

'So yeah, carry on, work experience. What happened?'

'Well, I was just doing crap stuff like filing and sending out memos and stuff, just forwarding mail on, general admin, nothing major.'

'OK. Sounds pretty normal.'

'Yeah.'

Adrian took a big gulp of his coffee. He knew when someone was beating around the bush, but he didn't want to stop Tom from what he was trying to say. Sometimes you needed to let people ramble. Tom had stopped speaking though; instead he was staring out of the window, watching the cars as they pulled in and out of the forecourt.

'Go on.'

'Well, I was filing some stuff and it wasn't making much sense, so I looked some things up and now I think maybe Dominic's doing something dodgy.' The words came out in a rush.

'Dodgy how?' Adrian leaned in. This was the first time Tom had ever mentioned his stepfather to Adrian in a way that was anything other than messianic worship. Somewhere in the back of Adrian's mind he felt incredibly smug.

'I think he's having an affair or something. He goes away for weekends. He's like never home. I looked at his expenses and they're crazy, Dad, and they don't match up with what he's telling Mum.'

'Does he know you did any of this? Have you spoken to your mother about it?'

'I can't tell her.'

'I don't know what to say, mate. Are you sure?'

'I think so.' Tom reached into his bag and pulled out a folder full of a huge pile of papers. He put them on the table. 'I took photocopies of all the stuff.'

Adrian took a deep breath. 'Tom, what do you want me to do with this? If you're right then your mum's going to be devastated.'

'I know you and Mum hate each other, but she deserves better than this. She's not a bad person.'

'First of all, we don't hate each other, not in the slightest. It's just complicated, that's all.' Adrian couldn't tell his son that all the hate thrown his way was fully deserved. When he'd found out that Andrea was pregnant, he wasn't even old enough to drink. He'd felt completely unprepared, yet whereas Andrea had tried her best from the moment she found out, Adrian had just gone off the rails and done all kinds of crazy things – that is until he joined the police force.

'Will you have a look at it?' Tom started chewing his fingernails again. 'Please, Dad.'

'I shouldn't be looking at this stuff. If your mother ever found out . . .'

'I highlighted all the bits that don't make sense. I know I get my maths head from Mum but if you could just have a look, see what you think?'

'Thanks.' Adrian picked up the file and looked

through briefly. Tom had written underneath each weekend entry what Dominic had told Andrea he was doing. 'You've got a good memory.'

'Most of those coincide with my rugby matches. I don't remember over half of the dates there, but the money he spends is the same.' Tom grabbed a page from the stack in Adrian's hand and held it up. 'I mean, that weekend was his birthday and he told her he had some New York thing going on that he couldn't get out of, but all his bills were paid in Edinburgh. It doesn't make sense.'

'OK, look, I'll get someone who knows about this stuff to look into it. You did the right thing by showing me. Now,' he picked up a menu, 'do you want some food?'

Adrian put the files on the seat next to him and called the waitress over. Tom never asked him for anything, so he couldn't not help out. He was right though, if Andrea found out that Adrian had helped Tom look into Dominic there would be hell to pay. It wasn't long until Tom could legally decide who to spend his time with, though, and so Adrian decided the risk was worth it. Even though Andrea's behaviour had been reasonable lately, he knew better than to bank on that; she had been known to flip out over the smallest of things. If he could forge a better relationship with his son through this, it would all be worth it.

Chapter 18: The Child

The present

The mail dropped on to the mat as Beth Ackerman walked down the stairs, holding her daughter Cassandra. She was getting heavier. Almost four times her birth weight now. The phone rang and Beth arranged herself with the baby so she could answer it; since becoming a mother, she'd realised that you actually did need six pairs of hands to get everything done.

'Hello?' Beth said into the phone, praying it was someone offering to come over and give her some kind of reprieve from motherhood.

'Is Doctor Ackerman there?'

'One moment, please.' She cradled the phone in the only spare part of her shoulder and turned back to the staircase, calling out to her husband. 'Jeremy! Phone!'

Jeremy came pounding down the stairs, handed Beth a pair of cufflinks and held up his arm before taking the phone off her. Cassandra was fast asleep so Beth placed her in the car seat carrier that lived at the bottom of the stairs.

'What is it?' Jeremy said into the phone. 'Yes, I'm just leaving now.'

Beth put the first cufflink in for him, smiling. He kissed her on the cheek before resuming his angry phone face. She put the other cufflink in. He always had that face when he took calls from his assistant; she would phone with inane questions and he would bark at her down the phone. Beth could hear the voice of the girl operating at breakneck speed on the other end of the phone, then the sound of a dial tone. Jeremy hung up.

'Problem?' Beth asked.

'Oh no, they delivered the wrong something or other to the surgery, apparently it's my job to sort it out. Bloody morons.'

'Would you like some breakfast?'

'No, I best be going.' He kissed her again and grabbed his jacket before heading out the door. Leaving her alone with the baby.

As the door slammed, Cassandra started to cry. Deep breaths, Beth thought to herself as she picked the eighteen-month-old up and held her close. She looked at the clock; she had twenty minutes to get ready before Cassandra's check-up. She guessed she would just have to go without a shower again, but that's what happens when you have babies, you put yourself last. That's what she'd read, anyway. She smiled as she looked at Cassandra; she'd wanted a baby for so long and now she had her. Cassandra continued to scream.

'And how are you and your husband coping, Mrs Ackerman?' the healthcare assistant asked.

'Great, it's great.' Beth beamed. She didn't want to give away how hard it had been, so much harder than she'd expected.

'It's not unusual for people to struggle in the first few months. Post-natal depression is a very real thing.'

'Oh, no, I don't have post-natal depression.'

'You're not failing if you admit it, you know.'

'No, that's not what I mean. I don't have it because Cassie is adopted.'

'Oh gosh! I'm so sorry.'

'It's OK, it's fine.'

'Well, she certainly is a beautiful little girl. Aren't you lucky?' They both stared down at Cassandra, lying on the little bed, smiling and gurgling.

'Is she OK, though?' Beth said. 'I mean, if she's awake, she just cries. I try feeding her and she doesn't want to eat. Then she seems to cry when I pick her up or put her down. I don't know what I'm doing wrong!'

'I can give you some literature on caring for adoptive kids.'

'I've read the literature, it isn't helping. She's fine with my husband, it's me! I swear she doesn't like me!'

Beth couldn't help it; despite her efforts to appear fine, tears filled her eyes and she started to cry. She was so exhausted. So tired of trying to be brave, trying to care for this baby who felt like a burden. The healthcare assistant made sympathetic noises and passed her a tissue. Beth shook her head; she didn't want more pity.

140

After a few seconds, she sat up straight and put her smile back on.

'Are you OK?' The woman's face was kind, but Beth couldn't bear the way she made her feel: scrutinised, pitied, pathetic. She picked Cassie up again; her daughter immediately started to wail, as though Beth's embrace was causing her pain. Beth ignored the cries, putting Cassandra back into the pushchair and avoiding the other woman's gaze.

'Thank you,' she said mechanically and made her way out of the building, no longer able to sit and pretend to be fine.

She returned to the car, dismayed to see that she had a flat tyre. Could this day get any worse? She spent several minutes trying to get Cassie to sit in her car seat. Her daughter arched her back, struggling. Beth was overcome by a sudden desire to push the baby into the car seat using all her strength, but instead she picked her up and cuddled her, which just seemed to make matters worse. On the third try, Cassie seemed to finally accept that the car seat was the lesser of two evils. Beth pulled out her mobile phone. She had no idea how to change a tyre. Jeremy always did that sort of thing. She wandered to the back of the car and opened the boot.

'Are you OK, miss?' A voice came from behind her. She turned around and saw a man standing there; she didn't recognise him but he had obviously heard the commotion.

'Just a flat, I'm going to call for assistance.' She smiled nervously.

The man leaned into the boot of the car and pulled

out the spare tyre, smiling at her. 'Lucky you've got one of these, then. Your baby's a real cutie.'

She put the phone back in her pocket and smiled. She didn't usually accept help from other people, least of all strangers. But she was tired and frustrated; she wanted to get Cassandra home so that she could bathe her and feed her before Jeremy got back. She felt her eyes growing heavy as she watched the man change the tyre. She was desperate for sleep. Maybe she could drop Cassandra off with her neighbours for an hour or so, just to give her the chance to close her eyes for a moment. Their neighbours had always been good with Cassie. The wife, Andrea, had looked on with sympathy many times whenever Beth would open the front door with a crying Cassie in her arms.

Their neighbours were nice, yes, but Beth still wished they hadn't moved so far away from home in London, she wished they hadn't had to keep the adoption a secret. The plan was that they would go back in a couple of years, a happy family. No one would ever know that Beth had never actually been pregnant.

'All done.' The man was smiling at Beth, shaking her from her thoughts. He wiped his hands on his trousers.

'Thank you so much.' She smiled at him, suddenly overwhelmingly grateful.

'No problem, any time.' She watched him walk back to his own car a few spaces down, and waved at him as he pulled away.

For the first time in a while, Beth had managed to cook a proper meal. She had bathed and fed Cassie but it hadn't stopped her from crying, and so Beth had taken her for a walk, knowing full well what time her neighbour Andrea would be coming home from work. Beth had made sure to bump into her and then it was just a question of waiting for her to offer to help, as she always did. Beth jumped on the opportunity, handing Cassie over. She just wanted to make dinner and eat one meal without having to interrupt it and forgo her food because Cassie just wouldn't stop crying.

The table was laid and Beth had even lit a candle in the centre. She smiled to herself as she smoothed down her short white dress, no stains, no mystery marks or milky lesions. Maybe they would even have time for a little intimacy before she had to go pick Cassandra up. She looked up at Jeremy, sat across from her at the table, and could see he was visibly relieved that the baby wasn't home. She felt pangs of guilt as she thought of how she had badgered him into the adoption. Now that she had her, all she could think about was that maybe she wasn't meant to be a mother for a reason. The doorbell rang. Beth sighed. There wasn't going to be any intimacy tonight after all; Andrea must have had enough and brought Cassandra back.

'I'll get it,' Jeremy said, offering Beth a tired smile. He touched her shoulder and went out to answer the front door. She stood up to clear the table, trying not to cry. Back to the grindstone. She hated herself for regretting the adoption. There was no way she could tell Jeremy that she wasn't sure about it any more; it had cost them a lot of money and caused no end of arguments.

She heard a clatter from the hallway and turned to see Jeremy clutching the wall, his face ashen. Startled, she moved closer and to her horror saw that his trousers were darkening with blood. As she looked on, he dropped to the floor. Without having to go to him and check his pulse, Beth knew that he was dead. Panic and bile rose in her throat.

A man burst into the kitchen, holding a bloody knife. Beth screamed. He was wearing gloves, his face was menacing. Beth moved backwards, back against the table. She could see her husband's lifeless limbs in the hallway. The room felt as though it was closing in on her.

'Where's the child?' the man barked. Beth couldn't breathe. How did he know about Cassandra?

'Who are you? What do you want?' Suddenly as she stared at him, Beth realised – he was the man who had helped with her spare tyre earlier. Horror filled her bones.

'Your husband had it easy, lady. You should have answered the door yourself. Then he'd be the one I was about to torture. Looks like you drew the short straw.'

She backed away, moving a chair in front of her, using it like a shield.

'What do you want?'

'I want that baby. She doesn't belong to you.'

'She's not here.' Beth couldn't think of a lie to tell him that wouldn't get someone else in trouble or hurt. It suddenly occurred to her that she did have the maternal instinct after all; all she could think about was protecting Cassandra from this man. She wondered what he was to her daughter.

'Don't make this too hard on yourself. I'm not going to hurt the baby, just tell me where she is.' He moved forward, brandishing the knife. She was running out of space to back away from him. No one would hear her if she cried out again; it was over two hundred yards to the neighbours' and their own house was detached.

'She's with a childminder for the night. Please. I'll have to call her to bring her home.'

'Send a text.'

'No, she doesn't have a mobile phone, it's a landline. Her phone was stolen recently.' She was careful not to explain too much, she didn't want him to be suspicious. He picked up her mobile phone from the table and walked over. He handed it to her and put the knife up to her throat.

'Put it on speaker,' he said.

She looked for Andrea's home number and dialled, pressing the speakerphone symbol. She felt as though she was in a dream, a nightmare. She couldn't think about her husband, lying in a pool of blood in the hallway. She heard the phone ring. Tears threatened to fall down her cheeks but she bit down on her lip. She had to hold it together. She wasn't going to give this bastard the satisfaction of seeing her cry.

'Hello?' Andrea answered the phone. Beth could hear Cassandra grumbling in the background.

'Hi, it's Beth, Cassie's mum,' she said, careful not to let on how close Andrea was, reveal to the man that her baby was only next door. She fought to keep her voice normal.

'Oh, hey, she's been no bother, darling little thing,

makes me all broody again. I love having a little one in the house.'

Now was her chance. She couldn't let Andrea talk any more. She knew what she had to do, and could only pray that Andrea would know what to do too. In a sudden movement, Beth stomped on the man's foot with her stiletto; he dropped the knife and doubled over. She tried to get away from him but he grabbed her arm.

'Call the police!' she screamed, desperately hoping the speakerphone wouldn't blur her words. 'There's a man here, he's killed Jeremy, please keep my baby safe!'

'You fucking bitch!' the man said, pushing her to the ground and scrabbling around for the knife which had skidded across the parquet floor.

'I'm so sorry, tell her I love her!' She felt his boot connect with her ribs as he delivered a swift kick to her side. She dropped the phone and it slid under the large oak dresser.

'Should have just given me the fucking baby!' He punched her. She screamed an unearthly scream; it felt good; it felt appropriate. She clawed at his face, gouging the skin out of his cheek. She saw the knife come down and then the world became a hazy place, it was like going backwards on a train through a tunnel, she could see the world moving away from her, at speed. Hurtling backwards, further and further into what? She focused on his boots as his fists came down on her. She had been a good mother, in the end.

Chapter 19: A Boy and his Sister

Age 16

I'm nervous because I just finished my exams and I know I haven't done well. My mum won't be bothered, nothing bothers her, but my dad will be annoyed. He says school is a waste of time, but I know he doesn't like to think of me as a thicko, or at least he doesn't like people to think he's the father of a thicko. That's why he used to make me recite those passages for him. My teacher says I'm lying when I tell her about the books I've read, she says I'm showing off, but then I will quote a big chunk of text to shut her up. She doesn't like me.

My sister is sitting with my mother watching the television. They're holding hands, smiling at each other. Sometimes my mother will brush my sister's hair; she has beautiful long brown hair now. It reaches all the way down to her thighs but most of the time it's wrapped in a bun at the base of her skull. She lets me brush it sometimes. I wonder if my real sister, the one that died, would look like this now if she were with us and then I get a bit creeped out by the thought. My dad said I'm not going to university, I don't need to. He's got some jobs for me to do, wants me to work for a friend making deliveries on my bike. He said I look older than I am so I might even be able to help out in the club sometimes. It's only a year and a half until I turn eighteen anyway.

I think about Claire Hastings a lot, about all the ways I want her to suffer. I've been called a load of names at school since everyone saw my privates. Sometimes I'll just be walking down the high street and I'll hear someone shout 'maggot-dick' from somewhere that I can't see. Sometimes I'm with my dad when that happens and I just pretend I don't know what it's all about, but I fucking hate all of them. Claire's tried to talk to me a few times since it happened but she knows things aren't the same between us any more, she knows she can't take it back. We have the school end of year dance this weekend and I feel like that's the place I should get my revenge, in front of everyone. I could just chuck a load of acid in her face or something. But then I think I kind of want it to be between me and her, for her to know that I can destroy her whenever I want. I want to have power over her. Then another thought comes to me. That I could ruin her life and her never even know it was me. That thought is the most appealing of all.

She doesn't know, but I follow her home from school.

Sometimes I watch her in her bedroom. Sometimes I get to her house before she does and I hide under her bed. I put a key logger on her computer so now I know all of her passwords and I was thinking about putting a secret camera on the top of her shelves. My dad uses them all the time to keep an eye on those druggie bitches. When my dad first gets the girls, they act out a bit and he needs to make sure he knows who he can trust.

My dad has asked me to come with him tonight. It's one of the few runs I haven't been allowed to go on before; the trip to get new girls. I feel pretty good because this is the most secret part of what my dad does. If he gets caught he gets in serious trouble. I've heard him and his top man talking about it before, though, and I know that it's tonight. He doesn't know that I know. He thinks I'm really naïve, I think, but Mindy used to tell me about my dad's business all the time. She used to call me a sweet kid and say she'd like to run away with me. I think Mindy might have even been a little bit in love with me. I was sad when she overdosed on meth.

I woke up with her next to me and her face was blue. If Mindy hadn't been who she was then I think we would have got on really well. But without all of her problems she probably never would have looked at a boy like me. I've noticed that women always want something; with Dad's junkies it's drugs. The girls at school, they want more than that, they want everything from you. I feel sorry for the kids in my class who have the popular girlfriends, because they're completely controlled by the uptight bitches who won't sleep with them. The boys just have to be good enough at sports and have wealthy parents and then they're in with a shot. The girls have to prick tease because they instantly become a slut as soon as they start having sex, but up until that moment they have to be sexy enough to be wanted by the boys. It's like walking a tightrope. The stoner girls are different though. At some point all the boys have been caught getting a hand job from the scummy girls at the back of the school bus. There's a huge dramatic outcry from the bitchy uptight girlfriends but they always get back together, and the skanky girl is relentlessly bullied and made to feel like shit. That's the circle of life at my school.

We're sitting in my dad's van at the docks. I'm wearing all black because I know we have to be careful here. I'm in the backseat because Dad's friend Meathead has to sit in the front with him. I say friend, but he takes orders from my dad just as much as anyone else. The only person I've never seen take orders from Dad is his brother. I think my dad may even be a little bit scared of him. My uncle is really nice, well, he's always nice to me, anyway.

There's a torch flashing intermittently up ahead and Meathead gets out of the car to go investigate. My dad warns me to keep my mouth shut both now and later on. He does all the talking.

We're standing outside a shipping container and there's a man talking to us. He looks at me warily, obviously noticing how young I am, but I puff out my chest and stand taller until he looks away. He opens the shipping container and the first thing that hits me is the smell, it's like the men's toilets in the club. One of the men goes inside the container and comes out with a girl. She's not like Mindy at all, she looks scared and alert. She doesn't have that weird look in her eyes that doesn't change no matter what you do. The man is holding the girl's hair in a fist and she's all hunched up and covering herself. I can smell that she isn't very clean; I don't know how long they've been in that container. He shouts at her in a language I don't recognise and she starts to cry. He smacks her face and then pushes her to the floor and undoes his fly. His friend turns and talks to my dad some more while she does the first guy; she's still crying and the man smacks her on the head a couple of times. I'm a little bit uncomfortable watching it. That stuff should be private. My dad tells the man he wants five girls and the man asks if he wants to choose. My dad says no and sends Meathead in instead. Four girls practically fall out of the container and I can hear crying coming from inside. How many others are there? What's going to happen to them?

I have to sit in the back with the girls on the way home. They're huddled together and staring at me. I just watch them and wonder what they think I am. Are they scared of what I might do? I like the idea that they might be scared of me. We don't go home; we go to another building that I don't recognise. It's a house with all the windows closed up. Meathead goes in first, and comes out with some other men who slide open the back of the van. My dad tells them to wait and he turns to me and says I can pick one to replace Mindy. One of the girls looks a bit like Claire and so I choose her because I think that will make it more interesting. My dad and the other men go inside and I'm left with my new girl. I ask her name but she just cries a lot, it starts to get on my nerves. I don't think she speaks any English. I think about the TV shows I like and decide to call her Monica. It's been ages and my dad hasn't come back to the van. I start to get worried and so I get out, tie Monica to the bench, and pull the scariest face I can to make sure she doesn't try to escape. We would both be in a lot of trouble with my dad if that happened.

Inside the house I can hear shouting, my dad is shouting at someone. The house is a mess, there's plastic sheeting all over the place and the room in the front of the house that should be the lounge looks like it's still being built. There are lots of tools and things everywhere. The floor creaks as I move forward and I close my eyes, hoping that no one has heard me, but a man comes out and starts shouting. He holds up a gun and I just shout for my dad. My dad comes out and punches the man in the face, then kicks him when he's on the floor. I go to my dad and he takes me through to another room. Here in the back room there's a dead girl on a camp bed. She looks like Mindy did when she overdosed so I guess that's what happened to this girl as well. There are plastic sheets all over the place here and more tools. The man my dad punched is back, rubbing his face. There's another man in the room and he's been hit a few times too, he's kind of slumped in a chair. My dad grabs a hammer and hands it to me. He tells me to hit the man in the knee as hard as I can.

The man looks scared and I don't want to do it. My dad looks at me all disappointed. He goes and picks up a can of something from one of the many unclean surfaces in the room. He asks me if I would rather use the can and I ask what it is, but he won't tell me. He says if I don't do one or the other then he will punish me. I hand him the hammer back and he gives me the can. Both of the men look terrified and I can't help but like the feeling of power. My dad holds the man's shoulders and tells his friend to hold his mouth open. The man is crying now and I feel really weird. I walk over and take the lid off the can. It's got a nozzle like squirty cream. The man's head is tipped back and his mouth is wide open. My dad tells me to squirt the stuff in his mouth as far back as I can. I squirt it and the man splutters as it goes into his throat. Not much comes out of the can before the man throws up. My dad smacks him in the head and then we start again, the man more subdued this time. As I squirt the foam into his mouth, I notice the bits he spits out are getting bigger on the floor. He starts to judder and tries to suck in air through his swollen nose. His face is going purple and his eyes are bulging. I drop the can and back away. His neck is distended and I can see his Adam's apple pushing forward against the taut skin, it looks like it's going to burst through. The noise he was making is over and he jerks himself off the chair on to the floor. His head lands with a rock-solid thump and blood pours from his ears and eyes. I watch him until he stops moving completely. The other man rushes to the corner of the room and pukes in a bucket.

After we drop Monica off, we go home and I quickly shower and dress so that I can see my sister before I go out again. She tells me she's worried about Mum and that she wants me to make sure Dad takes her to a doctor. I promise that I will and then I brush my sister's hair and plait it before she goes to bed. We go down into her room and she shows me some of the drawings she did today. She did one of me and I guess it kind of looks like me, but I look really ugly so I rip it up. She cries but I get her to calm down and she goes to bed a bit early. I check in on my mother, who doesn't look well at all, she just stares into space and so I help her go to bed, too. I feel so alone in the house and it's weird because it's still light outside. I stroke my mother's forehead until she falls asleep. I look at the pills on her bedside table. I decide I want to go and see Claire. I've finally figured out what I need to do.

When I get to Claire's house, I can see her family is sitting down to dinner, so I climb up the trellis and drain-pipe on their back wall. I have to go in through her little brother's room, which is risky, but I know they're all downstairs at the moment. The key to being stealthy in these situations is just to own it, walk steady and don't piss about too much. I know the house pretty well by now so I don't knock into anything any more. I get to Claire's room, slide under the bed and wait. While I'm lying there I start to cry, I don't know why really, I guess it's been a long day. I can't stop seeing the face of that man and it occurs to me that I have killed someone. Which is a weird thing to have occur to you, at any time, let alone when you're lying under a girl's bed.

Claire has a nightly routine. She comes in and puts her stuff down, usually a book and a drink or something, then she grabs her nightclothes and goes to wash in the bathroom. When she comes back she puts some music on and reads her book, then turns the light out and goes to sleep. I don't think much of the music she likes. It's all really current and pretentious; slutty women who sing about being strong and independent or something while dressing like they're giving it away – it's all very confusing. Tonight is the same as any other night and as she takes herself off to the bathroom I get out from under the bed and pull out the little bottle of crushed and dissolved sleeping pills that I took from my mum. I checked all the dosages and stuff and three won't kill her, but she definitely won't wake up before morning, even if she only drinks half of it. I'm pretty good at chemistry, as it goes – it's probably the only exam I haven't failed.

I pour the liquid into the drink and stir it with the plastic spoon I brought with me. I had to make sure there were no bits and the only way to do that was with boiling water, so I just made a small concentrated amount of the solution and put it in a little plastic bottle. I quickly get back under the bed before Claire comes out of the bathroom.

By the time she falls asleep, it's dark. I slide out from under the bed again and look inside the cup that had her drink in it to check that she drank some. She almost finished the whole cup and so I lean down and blow on her face to test. She doesn't move at all. I panic, thinking she might be dead, wondering if maybe I've killed two people today. I check her pulse and she's alive, which is good. I would hate for her to get away with it after all.

I go and look down the hallway and see that the house is dark and silent. I take most of my clothes off and get in the bed next to Claire; she doesn't move and I watch her sleeping for a while. I put my hands on her body, it's not the same as it is with Mindy, Margot or Carla because she isn't touching me back, but I like touching her without her knowing. Her skin is nicer to touch than those other girls' was. It's warm and she smells nice. I can taste the toothpaste as I kiss her lips. I wonder if she has ever slept with anyone before. I laugh at my own joke as I tell her to say mercy before I begin.

Chapter 20: The Comedian

Plymouth, two years earlier

Imogen woke up on her mother's sofa with one of Irene's many cats chewing on her chin. They never came near her when she was awake, probably because they knew she would boot them across the room. She pushed the cat away and instinctively put her hand up to her chin to see if it was still there. She was not a cat person, she was beginning to think she wasn't an anything person. She liked animals even less than she liked people, much to her mother's horror. Although she blamed her mother entirely for both of these dislikes. When Imogen was a teenager, she'd once come home to find a homeless man asleep in her bedroom, and was relegated to the living room floor. It was only after her mother actually witnessed the man getting fresh with Imogen that she finally kicked him out.

Tonight Imogen was hiding, hiding from DCI Stanton.

She was so ashamed of herself for sleeping with a married man. Was she turning into her mother? It was something she promised herself she would never do. There were so many things about that notion that made Imogen cringe. She remembered finding letters written by her mother to her father, a man she could never have, a man Imogen wasn't even sure existed except for the fact that she was alive, proof of their union. Imogen didn't want to be the woman pining at home for the kind of man who could do that to a person he was supposed to love.

She didn't want to eat anything in her mother's apartment. Hygiene was definitely not on Irene's list of talents, and actually, she *was* talented. She was an artist, although it had been years since she had so much as put a pencil to paper. She would always be an artist to Imogen. Her mother's paintings were the one thing she had been proud of as a child. She still had her favourite piece hanging above the sofa in her own lounge. It was an abstract picture of their old garden; she could feel herself back there when she looked at the picture. Something about it reminded her of a different time, a time before they had even heard the terms 'manic depression' and 'bipolar disorder'. Sometimes she would look at the painting and cry involuntarily, tears of grief springing from her eyes. She was never sure if she was grieving for herself or for her mother. She did miss her mother; she had never known her father and so Irene was all she had. They were all each other had.

Irene was still asleep. Imogen slipped out to go to

work; she didn't want to risk an argument. She would bring a takeaway round later on tonight and they could watch repeats of game shows together. It might even be nice.

She walked into the police station to see a bunch of flowers on her desk. Her heart froze and she looked over at Stanton's office. He wasn't in yet. She took a deep breath and smiled at Sam, who was walking towards her sheepishly, carrying a cup of coffee from the Italian café down the road.

'You shouldn't have, Sammy.' She took the coffee from him.

'I was an ass. I'm sorry.'

'You were, and I accept your apology.'

'You don't have to go sending yourself flowers so I believe you about a boyfriend though. You were right; it was none of my business.'

'Those aren't from you?'

'No, I couldn't see a card. They are some pricey flowers though, somebody loves you.'

'Well, I sure as hell didn't send them to myself.'

She picked up the flowers and took them into the kitchen. She searched the cupboards for anything resembling a vase, found a plastic picnic jug and filled it with water. Unwrapping the flowers, the card fell out.

IMOGEN
ALWAYS HERE FOR YOU
D

She had avoided being alone with Stanton in the last few weeks, ever since the night they'd slept together. She'd been firmly sticking to business and keeping it strictly professional. As soon as the hint of a conversation outside of work seemed to be taking place, she would make her excuses and leave. Did he want more? Is that what the flowers were about? She couldn't go there again; she was already crippled with embarrassment. She was tempted to throw the flowers in the bin, but they really were beautiful and it wasn't their fault, so she left them on the kitchen table and went back to her desk.

'I have to go out for a second, Sam, you OK here?'

'I'll struggle through.' Sam smiled. He had the frustrated look of a man wading through the bureaucratic nightmare that was day-to-day paperwork.

Imogen hazarded a guess that Dean Kinkaid would be at Aphrodite's. She wanted to speak to him alone, without Sam's juvenile observations. For a nightclub, there seemed to be an awful lot of daytime activity. As she pushed the door open, she could hear music and laughter coming from inside. Four men were sitting around a poker table, surrounded by empty beer bottles. Dean wasn't one of them.

'A little early to be getting wasted, isn't it?' She held up her credentials as she walked across the dance floor towards the men.

'Well, hello, officer. It's a little early for a strip-o-gram, too,' one of the men called out, and they all laughed. He had an accent which she assumed was Greek.

'You should be a comedian,' she said dismissively.

'I am.' He laughed again, his eyes fixed firmly on her breasts.

'He actually is,' the dusty blonde-haired man closest to her said, without looking up.

The comedian stood up and walked over, adjusting his crotch as he got closer. The other men stopped and watched. The comedian reached forward and touched the seam of her blouse where the buttons were. Imogen slapped his hand away. The other men stood up quickly, all apart from the blonde guy.

'You mean, you really are police?' He smiled and took the badge from her hand, studying it. 'Wow, where were you the last time I got arrested? I had some sweaty bald guy's hands all over me. Would've much preferred yours.'

'I can see why you need to subsidise your income with gambling,' she said. The other men snickered and the comedian's sunny disposition took on a much darker tone.

'What do you want?'

'I'm looking for Dean Kinkaid.'

'He's not here.'

'I can see that.'

'Well then you can leave; you're kind of a buzzkill.' He turned his face into a fake frown.

'Can I see your ID, please? All of you,' she said and she heard the faintest of groans as the men pulled out their wallets. She looked at the comedian's ID; his name was Vasos Kanelos.

She walked over to the table and picked up the wallets one by one. Giannis Charalambos, Michalis Antonios and finally Elias Papas. She looked at the man with the dusty blonde hair. So he was the mysterious club owner who was supposedly out of the country.

'Mr Papas – you're a very hard man to get a hold of.'

'I didn't know anyone was looking for me.'

'We came by here a few times. We were informed you were visiting relatives back home.'

'I was. I came back yesterday, which is why I am catching up with my friends here.'

She looked down at the table; he had all the poker chips gathered in front of him. She wondered if he really was that good a poker player or if these men were just letting him think he was. He was a tall man, with pale hazel eyes. There was a classical look about him. With his curls and his tan, he looked like a man with money, a man who spent a lot of time on a boat. He had a windswept look in his eyes, eyes that had a kindness she wasn't expecting behind them. He even smelled of the beach. He wore a white linen shirt with the sleeves rolled up – he must have been at least fifty, but he looked good for it. Imogen noticed the Rolex on his wrist and knew instinctively that it wasn't a knockoff. He looked at the Rolex to check the time.

'Is there anything in particular you needed to talk to me about?' He put his hands in his pockets. 'Only I've been up all night and I'm very tired now.'

'I'm sure you are. There were a couple of questions pertaining to two deaths. Two young girls were found dead after each taking a massive overdose; they both had stamps for this club on their hands.'

She saw Elias' face flash with anger as he glared at the other men. All of them shifted their gaze and looked down. If there had been any doubt in Imogen's mind as to who was in charge before, there certainly wasn't now. They seemed afraid of him, even though every single one of them was significantly larger and younger.

'I'll look into this matter for you,' Elias said at last. 'Like I said, I've been away. I don't tolerate drug use or distribution on my premises. It seems as though someone may have been taking liberties in my absence.'

Unfortunately, she believed him, he looked like the kind of man who, if he was involved in anything shady, would certainly maintain a distance. She looked again around the bar. Was George the barman the dealer? Where was George now?

'Thank you for your cooperation, Mr Papas.'

'What's your name, Detective?'

'Imogen Grey,' she answered. Elias looked up at her. She was uncomfortable at the amount of time his eyes rested on hers, as though he were studying her face. He stood up and offered her his hand; she shook it, feeling that he was holding on for a little longer than was absolutely necessary. This man was someone who was used to authority.

'I'm afraid I really do have to go now, Ms Grey.' He left his chips on the table and walked out of the bar. He pulled his phone out as he was leaving and she heard him speaking Greek to whoever was on the other line.

'You play poker, Detective?' the comedian asked. He was obviously second in command; on the disappearance of Elias Papas they had all puffed out their chests a little more and tried to restore the upper hand, but she knew they would be getting seriously reprimanded when she was gone. They had evidently let things slip while the boss was away. He wasn't happy about it, that much was clear.

'I wouldn't want to take your money, boys,' she said.

The comedian reached forward again and touched her on the arm. Imogen went to slap his hand away but he grabbed her wrist with his other hand, squeezing it hard. Before she knew what was happening, one of the other men grabbed her free arm and twisted it behind her back. She struggled not to show the pain on her face. The younger man, Giannis, watched but did nothing. The comedian was a big man; a little more pressure and she thought he might break something. He kept his grip at an uncomfortable level, continuing to trace his fat fingers along the crease of her blouse. She could feel his hand moving downwards and she braced herself as he brandished a half smile, waiting for her to scream out or say something, waiting for her to crack. His hand reached her waist and he ran his fingers along the front of her waistband, following the line of her belt, then bringing it back again until it was central. She knew where this was going and for the first time today was grateful at least that her trousers were a little tight, he wouldn't get his fat fingers in there without a fight. He moved his fingers over the edge and then started trying to move his hand inside her trousers, down the front; she could feel his fingers brushing against the tip of her knickers. She was petrified.

164

'Hey, Vasos!' Dean Kinkaid's voice came from the club doorway. Imogen couldn't move.

'Deano. Why are you here? This is not a good time.' The comedian's hand remained between her thighs.

'I just got a call from Elias, he sent me to talk to you guys.'

'Well, we're a bit busy right now, come back later.'

'He made it clear that it had to be done now,' Dean said, his voice a little frostier.

She could hear him getting closer. She wasn't sure if this was about to get a whole lot worse for her or not. She looked at his face and watched as his eyes travelled down her body and rested on the comedian's hand. She saw his eyes flicker with anger.

The comedian took his eyes off Imogen and looked over to Dean.

'I said we're busy . . .' The comedian barely had time to get the sentence out before Dean had moved forward, grabbed his ear and twisted it.

'Let go of the lady,' Dean said. Vasos and his friend obliged immediately. Imogen gasped, wanting to cry with relief.

'What the fuck are you doing?' The comedian tried to maintain his balance but she could see blood coming from his ear as Dean continued to twist.

Imogen staggered back out of the way and watched as the skin began to rip. She should probably stop Dean but she found herself cheering him on silently. The comedian fell to his knees, wailing in agony, not once lifting a finger to fight back. The other men stood and watched as well, even though surely there was a possibility they would be next. This told her a lot about what kind of man Dean was. These men were afraid of him. He'd either done something bad to them in the past or they had watched him do it to someone else. Whatever it was, it had obviously scared them enough to know not to intervene.

'You messed up, Vasos. You need to apologise to the lady.'

'I'm sorry, I'm sorry, just stop it, OK?'

Dean let go of his ear. The comedian grabbed it and sobbed; it was half hanging from his head. Imogen could feel that she had gone as white as a sheet; she had never been very good with blood.

'Listen to me, and listen carefully.' Dean held out his hand to help the comedian up. 'This woman is out of bounds.'

The comedian looked at Dean's hand before reluctantly taking it with the same hand that had been in Imogen's trousers. Dean grabbed his arm by the wrist and slammed it on the table. He pulled a knife out of his pocket and flipped it open.

The comedian looked at Imogen, blood streaking his cheek, pleading with his eyes. He was pulling his hand back but not with any force, she could tell it was taking Dean very little effort to keep it there. She saw the knife hovering over his hand.

'This is happening, Vasos.' Dean leaned in and spoke quietly. 'I think the lovely detective has it in her power to decide. Imogen, should I cut off his little finger or his thumb? If I take his thumb, he can't half finish those stupid Sudoku puzzles he's no good at. He would have to learn how to write with his other hand. If I take his finger, however, life essentially continues as normal. Guess he'd just have a bit missing.'

'Do something!' the comedian screamed.

She should stop him, she knew she should. But instead, Imogen thought about Dean's offer, relishing the power he had given her over this oaf. She loved the fact that he was afraid of the next thing to come out of her mouth.

'I need a cigarette,' she said.

Vasos whimpered.

She still had time to stop Dean, but she didn't. As she walked towards the door, Imogen heard the serrated edge of the knife struggling against Vasos' flesh, splintering the bone as he cried out. The noise he made was inhuman, raw pain; he was screaming through his teeth. She wanted to look behind her but didn't. The comedian gurgled and sobbed. She liked that sound.

Outside the club, Imogen had a cigarette. She should feel ashamed of what she had just allowed to happen, but in reality, the only thing she regretted was that she had chickened out of watching. She could still hear arguing inside but she didn't want to know. To be honest, after what they'd done to her, she didn't care if they were all missing fingers and thumbs.

The door opened and Dean stepped outside. Imogen could see a little blood on the cuff of his sleeve. She offered him the pack and he ignored it, taking the lit cigarette from her mouth. She found her eyes drawn to his lips again, watching him inhale and then lick his lips as the smoke billowed out slowly. It wasn't until he put the cigarette back in her mouth that she realised she was holding her breath.

'Those guys won't bother you again; they know that if they do they'll have to answer to me.'

'So you're an enforcer, is that it? You do Elias's dirty work for him?'

'I have been told I have a natural aptitude for violence, yes. They say if you get a job doing something you love then it's like not working at all.' He grinned at her.

'Your parents must be proud.'

'I don't have any parents. Elias is the closest thing to a family that I have. Just admit it, Imogen, you were a little glad to see me today. Did you come to ask me to dinner?'

'No, I came here to bring you in for questioning, boss's orders.'

'I gave you my number, you could have called.'

'I thought it best to come in person. You lot have all been a bit slippery lately. I couldn't be sure you'd be here.'

'I'm always here for you.'

As the words registered, she thought back to the morning. The flowers on her desk. Had they been from Dean? She flushed.

'You sent the flowers?' She clenched her jaw to stop herself from smiling. She was glad the flowers weren't from Stanton.

'I figured you would have thrown them away.' He backed towards his car, parked in front of hers, without once breaking eye contact. 'I'll drive to the station immediately.'

'It's not really appropriate, you sending me flowers.'

She knew she didn't look as displeased as she should. She wished he would turn his eyes away for a moment so that she could break the eye contact. He was like a bloody hypnotist.

'And what would be appropriate?' he asked, before getting in his car and pulling away, leaving her standing outside the club, completely without an answer.

Imogen was sitting in Stanton's office, waiting for him to get back. She had been instructed not to go anywhere near Dean. Between Sam and Stanton, the testosterone brothers, she felt a bit sorry for Dean as they exercised their protective machismo over him. She looked through the glass over to her desk. Dean's flowers were next to the phone; she'd moved them back when she'd returned from the club, before she'd been strong-armed into staying out of the way.

Stanton stormed into the office, and by the look on his face, she could tell his efforts had been fruitless.

'Everything all right?' she asked, somewhat pointlessly. Obviously everything was not all right.

'He won't talk to anyone but you.'

'Does he even know anything?'

'I've been asking around, and to be honest with you, I don't know how this man stayed off our radar for so long.'

'What do you mean?'

'He's seriously bad news, I reckon, but somehow he's managed to avoid us. He has a sealed incident from when he was a teenager. Couple of speeding tickets. Also arrested on suspicion of murder when he was twenty. No further action was taken due to an unreliable witness statement.'

'Well, he might have been innocent.'

'Imogen, I asked around. I have my sources. He's the muscle, basically. A lot of violence. He's well known for being beyond crazy.'

'Like what sort of stuff?' She remembered the sound of Vasos pleading with Dean.

'Like stabbing, scalping, castration, witness tampering, amputation. He's basically the guy they bring in when things go wrong. He's independent.'

'Doesn't castration come under amputation? He hardly seems like a criminal mastermind.'

'Oh, he's not, but he's a good soldier, no questions, follows orders regardless of what those orders are. He doesn't discriminate by age or gender. Rumours are he makes people disappear.'

'Sounds a bit far-fetched,' she said. She found herself wanting to defend Dean, which was strange given that several hours earlier she had heard him cutting through someone's hand.

'You're up, Imogen. He knows something and you need to find out what.'

She headed through to the interrogation room. Dean's face cracked a smile as she walked in and pulled up the chair opposite him.

'Aren't you going to record this for posterity?'

'You're not under arrest; you're just helping us out.'

'Someone needs to tell the Brothers Grimm that.'

'We can record it for your safety, if you want. Make sure I don't put any words in your mouth.'

'I trust you.'

'So, what can you tell me about Elias, your employer?'

'Employer is a strong word,' he said. 'He's not a bad guy, just making a living.'

'I don't know about you, but I'm hungry, I'd like to go home and eat at some point today. I don't want to be here, you don't want to be here, and I specifically don't want to be here with you.'

'Are you always this hostile?'

Imogen leaned forward and placed a file on the desk, splaying out pictures of the first girl who had overdosed, the Jane Doe. Dean didn't even flinch. He glanced at them briefly and then looked straight back at Imogen.

'Do you know this girl?' she asked.

'I do know her.'

'I showed you her picture before and you said you didn't know her.'

'You showed me her face; you didn't show me these pictures.'

'You recognise her from something other than her face?'

'Look at that. That red mark on her shoulder.'

'It looks like a burn.'

'It's a laser scar; she used to have a tattoo there. I remember her from that. I remember because the tattoo was bad enough but she got ripped off on the removal, too.'

'Do you know her name?'

'I tried not to get involved with those girls. She used to be a hardcore regular, I think she had something going on with one of the staff.'

'Not George, by any chance?'

'I don't remember who it was.'

'I have to say, I was surprised to see Elias there today. I thought when you used the excuse "gone back to Greece" you were using a euphemism for something more sinister.'

'I'm not a killer, Imogen,' he said as he fiddled with the cuff of his shirt, still stained with Vasos' blood.

'I heard different.'

'People like to talk. Everyone likes a bogey-man story.'

'Is that what you are?'

'Come to dinner with me and I'll let you know exactly who I am, Imogen.'

'That's not going to happen.'

She liked the way he said her name, as though it were more than words, as though it was his way of touching her. He was getting to her. Dean leaned forward and put his fists on the desk. She looked at them: strong hands, with veins that protruded from under the thin layer of skin. He slowly moved his hands towards Imogen's. She wondered if Stanton was watching; she imagined he was, but he probably couldn't see where her hands were, he probably couldn't see that Dean's fingers were just millimetres away from her own.

'Are we being watched? Who's behind that glass, Imogen?' he said as though he could read her mind.

She wasn't sure if it was her own heat or his that she was feeling, but she wanted him to push further, she wanted his skin to touch hers. The door opened and she snatched her hands away. Dean smiled. She turned to see Stanton standing in the doorway.

'I think you've been useful enough for now, don't you?'

Dean stood up.

'Glad you liked the flowers, Imogen.' He smiled and walked out. He knew, he knew about her and Stanton. She could tell. If he had worked it out, then who else had? Was everyone in the precinct blind or was Dean just very clever? It was slightly alarming, considering they were supposed to be the detectives. She looked up at Stanton; he looked angry, or jealous, or both. She could see his chin subtly vibrating as he clenched his jaw and looked at her. Imogen stood up and pushed past him. She couldn't stand this kind of behaviour. He had no claim to her, no right to be jealous. She thought about his wife and hated herself for what she had done. There was no excuse for it. All the time she had spent judging her mother, and here she was making the same mistakes.

Chapter 21: The Forgotten

The present

Adrian banged on the door of Andrea's house. She never called him, she specifically never called him for help so when she'd rung him in tears an hour ago he had known something was seriously wrong. Andrea opened the door and threw her arms around Adrian. Yep, something was very wrong.

'Andrea. What the hell is going on?'

'I didn't know what to do, I was looking after my neighbour's baby and she phoned me, she was screaming and crying. There was a man there . . .' She sobbed uncontrollably into his chest. 'I think I heard them getting murdered.'

Adrian put an arm round her, feeling her body shake against his. 'Did you call the police?'

'I called you! I don't trust the police any more. I tried

to call Dominic but he wasn't answering.' She wiped her nose with a soggy tissue.

Adrian shook his head, unable to fully grasp the situation. He patted his ex on the back, looked across the room and saw a baby asleep in a pushchair. Truth was he was half disappointed that Andrea wasn't calling about Dominic's infidelity. If that was in fact what he had been up to.

'I'm going to call Fraser and tell him to send some people over. Is that OK?'

'OK.' She nodded.

'I'm also going to go over there and see.'

'You can't! What if the killer's still there?'

'I know what I'm doing. I'm a police officer, Andrea. Don't worry.'

'What if he comes here?'

'Is the place locked up?'

'Yes, totally.'

'I'll check the perimeter of your house. If he knew where you were he would have been here already. You're not in any danger, just lock the door behind me. Did she give any indication what he was after?'

'She told me to take care of the baby. I think it was about her, about Cassandra.'

'Why do you have her? Do you have her often?'

'Sometimes. I just feel sorry for Beth sometimes, she's always so exhausted and I like the company when the boys are both away. I don't do so well on my own.'

'I remember.'

They both looked over at the pushchair and Adrian kissed Andrea on the forehead.

'Lock the door behind me!'

'Be careful, Adrian!'

The neighbourhood was quieter than Adrian's, even more so at night. There was a contented feeling in the air; or maybe that was just the chip on Adrian's shoulder making him imagine things. It wouldn't be long before sirens shattered the cocoon of security that sheltered this affluent little haven. He walked towards the house and stopped at the gate; the lights were on and the door wide open. He pulled out his phone and dialled Imogen. He didn't like doing this kind of thing without her. They were a team.

'What is it?' she answered in her usual friendly and welcoming way.

'Are you busy? Only I'm about to walk into a possible murder scene.'

'Whose? Are you on duty? I thought you went home?'

'Andrea's neighbour. Couple called the Ackermans. Just get over here and we can catch up then.'

He put the phone back in his pocket and gently swung the gate open, the iron scraping along the path. He stuck to the hedge like glue as he walked across to the front door – watching the shadows for a glimmer of movement.

The garden was surrounded by a tall hedgerow that blocked out most of the streetlights. Adrian tried not to imagine someone standing in the shadows, watching him fumble his way to the house. He felt the crunch of glass under his feet, and realised it was the remnants of a motion activated light. It was possible that the couple knew the killer, but the fact that the bulb had been smashed made Adrian suspect otherwise – the killer wanted them to open the door and look outside, most people would if the light was broken and the doorbell rang. He switched the torch app of his phone on, shining it into the areas of the front garden that he couldn't see. No one was there.

There was definitely something wrong. From the outside porch, Adrian could see that there had been a disturbance inside the house. He ignored the sinister feeling that crept up his spine, shivering a little to shake it off. If someone broke into his house his neighbours would hear, they might not give a shit but they would hear it. Out here he didn't think sound even carried the same way as it did everywhere else. There was no false sense of security like this in Adrian's street. He could well imagine how safe these people all thought they were. He felt totally isolated as he moved to the side of the house and quickly surveyed the garden again before going inside.

Adrian moved forward cautiously. He took some gloves out of his pocket; he didn't want to inadvertently contaminate the crime scene. One thing you could never truly appreciate without experiencing it first hand was the smell of a large quantity of blood; metallic, not dissimilar to the smell of copper coins when you rubbed them together. He shortened his breath so he didn't fully breathe it in, or he might throw up. He carefully felt along the wall until he found a light switch and flicked it on.

There was a man on the floor at the end of the

hallway; streaks of red along the pristine white wall marked his final journey. Adrian heard the first whiff of disturbance as the sirens got closer.

'Miley?' It was Imogen, her voice coming from the garden outside.

Adrian breathed a sigh of relief that he wouldn't have to do this alone. Over the last couple of years, he'd seen some things that fundamentally changed his understanding of human nature. He wasn't sure how much more of that he could handle.

'In here!' he called out. Moments later Imogen was standing in the doorway.

'You got here quick.'

'I was in the car already.'

They walked towards the man's body. They couldn't see the woman, but there had obviously been a considerable struggle. There was a pool of blood underneath the body of the man; Adrian assumed he was the husband. Imogen knelt beside the body and looked it over, putting her fingers on his neck to check for a pulse. A formality only; it was obvious to anyone who had ever seen a dead body that this man was long gone. If for no other reason than the fact that he was lying in about four litres of his own blood. The red against the beige and white of the room was a stark contrast. Adrian was reminded of an article he had read in a magazine once. It said that if you were watching a movie and a scene came up that was overly white, you were about to see a lot of blood. Imogen stood up again, unaware that Adrian was waiting for her before he proceeded.

'Does this feel familiar to DS Reid's crime scene to you? Where is the husband's wound?' Adrian asked.

'You're right. It's his femoral artery. Like the blonde girl from the brothel, Dee. That can't be a coincidence – it's a pretty unusual way to kill someone.'

'Pretty effective.'

'We had a case back in Plymouth a few years ago with a femoral cut. We were told it took between thirty seconds and a minute for that one to bleed out.'

They continued through to the kitchen as the crime scene investigators entered the house. The walls were lined with pictures: graduation photos, wedding day pictures and finally baby photos. A perfect family. DCI Fraser was right behind them. Despite his eternally optimistic demeanour, Fraser had a stomach made of iron. Adrian had often noted how completely unfazed he was by even the most gruesome of crime scenes.

The woman – presumably Beth – was laid out on the kitchen floor. There was less blood than expected, considering the injuries, but Adrian still had to turn away to compose himself. He'd seen the family pictures but what was in front of him bore no resemblance whatsoever to the woman in the photographs. Her head was twice the size. The blood pooled in her injuries. There were thick dark black lines on her face where her eyes had been hit so hard and so many times that they had bled and swollen shut. Adrian felt the bile rising in his stomach as he imagined the beating it must have taken to make her look like this. Her features were distorted to an inhuman degree. She had dark dried blood coming from her mouth, nose, ears and eyes. Even her hair was wet and matted, partially stuck to her face. In amongst the mess on the floor Adrian thought he could see teeth. She had obviously suffered a massive head trauma.

Adrian looked up at Imogen. Her face was pale; sometimes you just couldn't hide the shock.

'You holding up, Grey?'

'I'm fine . . . it's just . . . fuck . . . look at that! Who does that?'

'It's horrible. You should go outside. You don't look so great.'

Fraser had placed his fingers on Beth's wrist.

'No pulse.' He shook his head.

'No? Thank God she's not alive. There's nothing left of her.'

Adrian backed out of the room, walked through the lounge and out of the front door into the front yard, Imogen following close behind.

'What is wrong with people?' Adrian shook his head, feeling a bit sick.

'Do you still think this is linked to DS Bridget Reid?' Imogen asked, pulling her cigarettes out of her shirt pocket. Adrian took one and went out of the gate.

'If it is we need to find out where Sam was when this happened. We both know he doesn't mind smacking a woman around.'

She shuddered. 'I'll go square things with Fraser and then I'll drop you home.'

'No, I'd better go check on Andrea again. You go home. I'll be fine. I'll have to wait with her until Child Protection comes for the baby.'

Adrian watched Imogen head back into the house before walking down to Andrea's, thankful for the fact that his ex-wife hadn't had to witness the horrors next door.

Chapter 22: The Connection

The present

Imogen walked into the station with a pounding headache yet again; another night without sleep. Oddly, not sleeping felt better than sleeping at the moment; she couldn't bear to lie down. Every time she did so she imagined her insides trying to escape. She was reminded of how lucky she was to be alive, after seeing the man's body lying in a pool of his own blood she'd felt really shaken. She knew that she wouldn't get away with another life-threatening injury. If she had been cut differently in Plymouth, if the knife had slipped – well, she would never have survived. Her headache was compounded when she saw Sam Brown in DCI Fraser's office. Another source of her insomnia. They were both looking very solemn indeed. She threw her bag on the desk, startling Adrian who was sitting at his desk.

'They want us in there,' he said as he looked up. Thank God he had stopped asking her if she was all right every time he saw her.

'What for? Any news on Bridget Reid?'

'I have no idea, on both counts.' Adrian stood up and sighed.

'How's Andrea?' Imogen asked. She knew that Miles still had a big thing for his ex; you could tell by the way he looked at her. She noted he had different clothes on to the night before, so he obviously hadn't stayed over. Imogen hoped he wasn't planning on making a move, because however he looked at Andrea, she definitely did not look at him in the same way.

'She's dealing with it.' He sighed again.

'So, no news at all on Reid? Any developments to catch me up on before we go in there?'

'Well, apart from the evidence that Bridget collected herself, we haven't got much. The phone records on Bridget's mobile show a few calls between her and Sam. They found the car with her bag in it, but all that does is corroborate what we already know. Anything pertaining to her original abduction has been gone over as much as possible and there's nothing. Now of course, there is the possibility that this new crime scene might have some answers.'

'What do we know for certain?' Imogen asked.

'We know she stole a car and dumped it. We know she got in the water and made it a ways down the river to the Double Locks pub. We know she got put in that RAV4 that seems to have disappeared off the planet.'

'Fake plates. What can you do? Common car, common

colour, no obvious stickers, dinks or scrapes. That lead is dead.'

'We know what time she was put in there. The description of the driver we got from Ben Vickers was pretty useless. Dark hair and stubble, average height and build, etcetera.'

'What about friends and family leads?' Imogen asked.

'Family haven't heard anything or been contacted by anyone strange. No demands – whoever has got her isn't in it for the money. As for friends, she didn't really have many she kept in contact with.'

'Come on, let's get this over with.'

They both walked over to the office and knocked. Fraser stood up and smoothed out his suit as if he were in trouble, or about to deliver some difficult news.

'Take a seat please, Imogen.'

This couldn't be good. 'Is this about DS Reid?'

'We got the bloods back from DS Miles' crime scene,' Fraser offered, obviously determined not to be derailed at this point.

'What? You could have told me!' Adrian seemed affronted.

'I'm informing you now, aren't I?' Fraser snapped uncharacteristically. 'We wanted to speak to you both at the same time.'

'We?' Imogen sneered, glancing sideways at Sam, who she could see was rolling his eyes at her immaturity.

'Well? Get on with it,' Adrian said.

'I was looking through your file, Detective Grey, and I noticed you don't have a father listed on your birth certificate.'

'That's right,' she said suspiciously. 'What's that got to do with anything?'

'The lady . . . Elizabeth Ackerman . . . the mother who got her face all bashed in,' Sam said.

'I know who you mean. Are you getting to any kind of point anytime soon?'

'She fought the attacker and managed to get some of his DNA, his blood, under her fingernails.'

'Right?'

Fraser took over. 'Because of the similarities to the murder at DS Reid's flat, we asked Gary to put a rush on the results. Anything that might help us get closer to finding out what happened to Bridget is a priority and will continue to be so until . . .' He trailed off, obviously not wanting to add *until we find a body* in front of Sam Brown.

'Basically,' Sam interjected, 'there are so many things going on here I don't know where to start. First off, there were prints recovered at the scene of both this scene and the attack at Bridget's place. They seemed to match, although we haven't been able to trace them. Couple that with the injury to the husband and we can assume, for now, that this is connected to Bridget's disappearance.'

'OK, so what's that got to do with me?' Imogen asked uncertainly.

'There was blood under the victim's fingernails, as we said. We ran it through all the databases, including the familial match.'

'Right,' she said, although she wasn't sure whether she'd actually said it out loud. Adrenaline was pumping around her body and she had a strange sense of dread. She wondered what Sam was going to say next. Adrian moved towards her protectively; he was pretty good at noticing when she was upset. She couldn't tell if this annoyed her or not. 'Get on with it, Sam.'

'Imogen, the DNA came up as a half-sibling, a brother to be exact. Your half-brother.'

'What?' Imogen reeled backwards. There was a buzzing in her ears. 'How can that even be possible? Would that show up?'

Could she be hearing right? She knew what they were going to ask her; she braced herself for the question.

'The DNA stuff is a bit beyond me, to be honest, Imogen,' Fraser said apologetically. 'But it's something to do with having no shared DNA on the X chromosome, only on the Y, which is how they know it's from your dad's side, not your mum's. I know you didn't know your father, but did you know that he had other kids?'

'I guess I never thought about it, I knew he was married . . .' She trailed off. From a young age her mother had explained that Daddy had another family and it wasn't possible for him to look after them both. Imogen had had to accept it.

'Can you speak to your mother? Find out who he is?'

'She won't say, she said she'd take it with her to the grave. I used to ask when I was younger. She even told me that if I was dying and needed a transplant she still wouldn't tell me, so there would never be any point asking her. After a while, I stopped.' Imogen could hear

186

the pitch of her voice was higher than usual. *Calm the fuck down.*

'Surely once you explain the gravity of the situation . . .'

'Stubborn wouldn't even begin to cover the kind of woman my mother is, Fraser.' She stood up and started to pace. 'I'm not kidding you, she would die before giving that name up.' She knew this wasn't the end of it.

'We can bring her in for questioning?'

Imogen shrugged and walked over to the door. 'Do what you have to do, but I'm telling you, you're wasting your time.' She put her hand on the door handle and went to pull it open.

'Wait!' Sam called out. She turned again, heckles up, ready to defend her position once more.

'There's more, much more,' Fraser said and smoothed his suit down again. More bad news.

'You mean that wasn't the bombshell?'

'No, it really wasn't,' Sam said. He looked bright eyed, almost excited. Fraser sighed deeply and looked down at his feet, preparing to speak.

'For fuck's sake, will you two just spit it out already!' Adrian hissed.

'Well, here's the thing, Imogen, and this is why we need your mother's cooperation on the matter. We got the baby's DNA back too. You know the baby was adopted, and the perp wanted the baby – so we wanted to check for a familial link there, see what was so special about it.'

'Don't tell me, she's my second cousin or something?' Imogen folded her arms, trying not to betray how she felt inside.

Fraser shook his head with foreboding, but he was clearly excited. She could feel Adrian's temper rising. The suspense was horrible.

'Well, the perp was the baby's biological father, that's been confirmed, but that's not the special bit. Wait for it. The baby is none other than the daughter of Isabelle Hobbs.'

'Who?' Imogen asked stupidly. She felt confused for a split second, then it hit her: Isabelle Hobbs was the little girl who was plastered all over the newspapers every six months, murdered by her parents who were on the twelfth year of a life sentence. The parents had always maintained their innocence, claiming their daughter was abducted, but the jury hadn't agreed. *Cassandra Ackerman was the daughter of Isabelle Hobbs?* Imogen felt her mouth go dry and she took a step forward, feeling Sam's excitement, but understanding the unbelievable shit-storm that was coming their way.

'Are you sure?' Adrian asked, the first to break the silence. Fraser nodded.

'Have you told anyone?' Imogen asked. 'Who else knows?'

'The head forensic tech came straight to me with it as it's such a high profile case,' Fraser answered apologetically. Adrian waved dismissively as if that hardly mattered at this point.

'Well, he spent all night checking and double checking, he couldn't understand any of it. I think he's gone home to have a nervous breakdown. He says he didn't tell anyone else. So at the moment, it's just us.' Sam smiled.

'I'm going to have to kick it upstairs, and when I do . . .' Fraser added.

'I know.' Imogen nodded. She would have to try and get the information out of her mother. For all Irene Grey's faults, she could keep a bloody secret.

'Whoever killed those people knew who that baby was, and quite possibly knows what happened to Isabelle. There also seems to be a connection to Bridget. We have a definite link with you, Imogen, and now we need to find out who your father is so that we can question his other kids.'

'You make it sound so simple, Fraser. Look, OK.' She sighed. 'OK, I'll try. I'll try to talk to my mother, but there's no way she will tell me anything about my father without a struggle.' Imogen knew her mother. 'Please give me a little time to deal with her. She has mental health issues and she won't respond well to being put under pressure.'

'Time is of the essence, but I do understand. I'll give you as much time as I can.' He looked at his watch, then back up at her hopefully. 'Any chance you could drop in on her now?'

Imogen stared at him.

'I can go with you, Grey,' Adrian offered softly.

'OK,' she said at last. 'OK. Let's go.'

She walked out of the office with Adrian in tow, still reeling from the barrage of bizarre news they had just received.

'Wow,' he said, stealing a sideways glance at her.

'Wow is right. I am not looking forward to this conversation.'

189

'I can try to talk to her too?'

'Best not, she hates cops.'

'But you're a cop.'

'Now you're getting it.' How to explain a life where your mother flitted between adulation and loathing, how to explain the back and forth Imogen had put up with over the years? It was impossible.

'I'll stay in the car then, but I'll drive you.'

'Is that wise? Last car you drove ended up at the bottom of a ravine.' Imogen noticed Adrian's eyes darken at the thought and instantly regretted her wise-crack. She sighed. 'OK then, Miley, come on. Let's go sign a car out.'

Chapter 23: The Question

The present

Adrian was sitting on her mother's sofa, sipping tea made with cold water that still had the tea bag in. It wasn't the best. They'd barely been able to make their way inside Irene Grey's house; the corridors were stuffed to the ceiling with books, old magazines, and newspapers going back about ten years. Imogen had felt the embarrassment on her face as she watched her partner push through the debris.

As Imogen had said in no uncertain terms, there was no persuading her mother to give away the identity of Imogen's father. Irene absolutely would not say, not even with the threat of prison.

'It's my right, isn't it, right to remain silent?'

'You're not under arrest, Mum, we just need to know.'

'What kind of a mother would I be if I allowed myself to be swayed by this when you've asked me so many times in the past? To just chuck it out there without a care as to what the revelation might do to you!'

'I'm a big girl, Mum, I can handle it.'

'I'm sorry, Imogen, but I swore that I wouldn't ever tell you.'

'You could tell me, though?' Adrian piped up, and the look he received was like a boot to the face.

'They're probably going to pull you in for questioning, Mum, again and again, and it won't stop until they find out what happened to that baby, and the little girl. It would be better if you just told us now,' Imogen said.

'And there's also the police officer who's disappeared,' Adrian added. 'This information really is vital, Mrs Grey.'

'Maybe if I contact your father, ask him about it for you?' Irene offered.

'You know where he is?' Imogen asked, surprised.

'He's in the same place he's always been. I'll call him.'

'What? When was the last time you had contact with him?' It was a question that she didn't necessarily want the answer to. It was one thing for them to have no contact with the man, but quite another for her mother to have been giving him updates. Imogen's skin flushed with anger.

'I spoke to him after your attack in Plymouth. He heard that you were in hospital and he called to see if there was anything he could do. So it's only been a year or so.'

'You know, in all this time, Mum, I always thought you were protecting me when you wouldn't tell me who he was, because he was indifferent and didn't give a shit. Which was fine, because I was indifferent and didn't give a shit either. But now you're telling me you guys stayed in contact the whole time. What's his reason for not meeting me?'

'You do look like him too, believe it or not,' her mother said wistfully, ignoring Imogen's question. A smile crept across her face as her eyes fixed on something beyond the window. 'He's the one who bought you Albie, the teddy, do you remember him?'

Of course she remembered him. She remembered spending nights clinging to the bear while her mother lay in a sleeping-pill-induced stupor. Albie was the one who would help her fight off the nightmares, because there was no way her mother was waking up. She searched her memory for the moment she was given Albie, but it seemed he had always been there, as far back as she could remember.

'Well, you call him then, Mum.' Imogen was losing her temper. 'Do what you want, but one way or another that information is coming out. You can either be in control of when it does, or not. The choice is yours!' She stood up and walked out of the house, resentment and hurt bubbling inside her. Adrian trailed awkwardly in her wake.

Chapter 24: Inside

The present

Bridget was struggling to keep track of the days. She almost wished she was taking the pills again, but she'd been crushing them all, blowing the dust away. She had worked out that the man keeping her here visited twice a day. He gave her the same food every time. She tried to act the same every time he came but it was getting more difficult. Still, she couldn't understand why she wasn't overcome with anger whenever she saw him. The anger would always come later, a few hours after he'd left.

She'd been trying to keep her physical strength up by doing chin ups on the bar that held the curtain around her toilet. After starting with barely two, in just a few days she could do ten. She did them several times a day. It was not like she had anything else to do. She knew that although her captor was bigger than her, he was not a strong man; he didn't have a particularly healthy body. If she kept working hard, maybe she could overpower him at some point. She was a small woman, and so she knew that she barely stood a chance right now. She had let herself go a little while she was working undercover, noting that the other girls in her block didn't do any physical exercise. She hadn't wanted to seem different to them, she'd wanted to fit in. So now, she would stand in her makeshift prison and practise her punches, so that she might at least be able to knock him out at some point, however unlikely the chance would be. She had to be ready, she couldn't just wait for him to lose interest in her and stop visiting altogether.

Bridget tried to remember the training she'd received in the police force. She stood in front of the wall with her legs about half a metre apart and dropped her hips to lower her centre of gravity. Slowly, she started to punch the wall, barely making contact at first. She stood there for hour after hour, repeating the same move over and over. The flat side of her fist hit the wall with a thud every third second. When the time came, she wanted it to be muscle memory and not a decision or a thought. Practise. As the hours morphed into days that never seemed to end, still she stood there. One, two, punch. One, two, punch. Twenty per minute. Twelve hundred per hour. Change fist. Each hour pushing a little harder, her knuckles starting to bleed. Two hours, then chin ups, then two more hours, followed by a visit, then two hours, chin ups and another two hours. When she was with him she would focus on what she would do when he left. Routine was everything right now. The repetition kept her sane, gave her purpose. Her mind was clearer without the pills.

At night in bed, Bridget thought about the TV shows she used to watch, wondering what her favourite characters might be doing now, trying to imagine scenarios in her head just to kill the time. Endless time. She knew sleep was important and so she lay still every night until she managed to drift off. Ready to wake up and start her regime again.

Ten days had passed since she'd stopped taking the pills. Ten days of working out. Already she could feel the skin on her fists getting tougher, she could feel her arms getting stronger. She had found a glimmer of hope.

Chapter 25: The Third Wheel

The present

Adrian was walking home, his mind spinning with what Fraser and Sam had told them, thoughts of Irene Grey spiralling through his mind. He wanted to talk to someone, wanted a friend. As he approached the corner shop at the end of his road, he saw the shop assistant Eva, busying herself with something in the window. She was a nice girl, they had become friends over the last few months. He popped into the shop a lot and they'd got chatting; sometimes he would just sit there for a bit and watch her work, comfortable in her easy company.

He stopped outside; the shop was closed but he could see Eva moving around inside now, tidying the shelves. She seemed to be always there, going through every can and packet, checking the dates, keeping things neat. Adrian tapped on the window; Eva turned with a start and then unlocked the door.

'All alone?' he said.

'Yes, Dimi has gone home already.' Eva looked nervous. 'Did you need something from the shop?'

'No, I was just going for a walk. Do you want to come with me?'

She considered it for a moment, looking at her watch.

'OK, I'll come.'

She disappeared back inside and returned with an oversized coat, obviously not her own. Adrian welcomed the cold breeze after being stuck in the station all day, going through video surveillance, phoning people who had called in sightings of Bridget Reid. None of which panned out. This had to be better for him than getting drunk again.

They walked towards the main road. As much as Adrian liked spending time with Eva, he realised he didn't know much about her. She didn't talk a lot. What did that say about him? Maybe that's what he liked. He didn't like to be alone, but he didn't want anything else right now. He just wanted something simple. A friend.

They weren't far from his house when it started to spit. Adrian took Eva by the hand and began walking faster as the droplets of rain got bigger. A few hundred metres later and they were almost running towards the railway arches. The rain fell heavy on the muddy grass around them as they sheltered. Eva's smile was wide and bright as she blinked away the beads of rain that lingered on her eyelashes.

'Sorry!' Adrian exclaimed. 'Shouldn't have suggested a walk with the clouds the way they were.'

'I like the rain.' She smiled, holding her hands out from under the eaves, trying to catch it.

'What else do you like?' He watched with interest. She was so different to other people he knew. So unaffected.

'I like to read books. I like to draw pictures sometimes.'

'What do you draw?'

'Faces, people I see in the shop mostly.'

'Did you ever draw me?'

'Before we were friends, I did.'

'We're friends?' Adrian smiled.

'I can't draw you any more, I know you now.'

'What do you know about me?'

'I know that you're a better person than you think you are.'

Through the rain, Adrian heard a muffled humming in the distance, the faintest vibration under his feet. He turned towards Eva. 'Here, give me your hand.' She held her wet hand towards him, it was cold and much smaller than his. He pulled her towards the wall and placed her palm on the red brick. He placed his hand by the side of hers. They waited and he smiled as the train surged over the tracks above their heads. Before the train had fully passed, Eva snatched her hand away; in her eyes he saw a shadow crossing her mind, a memory. Something about the vibration had distressed her. He didn't want to ask what it was.

'I should get back,' she said as she wrapped her arms around herself. 'I'm cold.'

They walked briskly back to the shop. Eva kept her

head down and hood up for most of the way. She didn't speak.

'Do you want to come in for a coffee?' she asked as she hurriedly unlocked the door.

'I'll just have some water.' He stepped in after her.

Adrian didn't want a drink, but he didn't want to leave her alone right now. Something had upset her, clearly. He felt bad. As he sat down on the shop stool he realised he wasn't so different from the afternoon drunks who frequented the alcohol section, the ones who spent all day telling Dimi their woes.

'Did you have to work today?' she asked.

'I did, but I'm not really allowed to talk about it. I never asked you why you stay here so late, Eva. Don't you get lonely?'

'I don't mind being on my own, sometimes your own company is the best company.'

'Oh . . . Do you want me to leave?' He stood up, and she laughed. Adrian felt a surge of relief; it was good to see her smile again.

'No, no, that's not what I meant. I just meant that sometimes being alone is better than being with someone . . .'

'Bad ex-boyfriend?'

'Yeah, that's why I'm here. He can't get to me here.'

Adrian had been to enough seminars on domestic violence and had enough first-hand experience from his own parents' relationship to know not to push any more. He sipped on his water and watched her work.

'I'm sorry to hear that. If you want to talk about it . . .'

She smiled and continued to tidy the shelves. The

rain was easing off now, and Adrian knew he was outstaying his welcome as Eva's thoughts had clearly taken her over. He grabbed his wet jacket off the counter and made his way to the door. Feeling altogether quite lost himself, he decided maybe he could use an early night.

Chapter 26: The Husband

The present

Gary Tunney was sitting in Adrian's chair when he arrived at work an hour earlier than expected the next morning.

'Comfortable?' he said to Tunney, who was reading through the papers Adrian had given him, his feet up on the desk.

'We need to talk.'

'About Dominic? What did you find?'

'Well, the good news is, he's not having an affair.' Was that good news? Adrian didn't think so.

'So what's with all the hotel bills and stuff?'

'I haven't quite figured it out yet, but whatever it is, it's illegal, and very, very bad.'

'You're kidding?'

'I wish I was, my friend!'

'So if you haven't figured it out, what makes you think he's up to something bad?'

'It's a gut feeling, with a tiny bit of evidence. But when there's money involved, there's always evidence somewhere, some kind of paper trail.'

'OK then, what do you have so far in the way of evidence?'

'Not enough is the short answer.'

'Are you being deliberately vague here, Tunney?'

'I think he might be a drug baron or something.'

'Dominic? Are you sure?'

'I'm not sure, no, but it's something I'm considering. The thing is, even though he moves his money around a lot, some of it seems to come from nowhere. Like if you add together all of the profit from all of his companies, subtract all of his expenditures and all of his bank accounts, none of it makes any sense. Not to mention the fact that three of his companies are in his wife's name.'

Adrian's ears pricked up at this.

'Say that again.'

'His wife, she's a director of three of these companies, although he is a proxy signatory. Her signature doesn't seem to be on any other paperwork, other than the original company application docs.'

'So she doesn't know about those companies?'

'Hard to guess, really. She might. She might not. It's probably just a tax dodge.'

'How much money are we talking here? Overall . . .' He hated to ask, but in the context of the situation, he thought he should know.

'Big millions, we're talking upper fifties overall. But sometimes a lot more, sometimes a lot less. Generally, it's a pretty healthy-looking balance. I say drug dealer the way the money moves makes it look like a regular cycle and that's pretty common when it's involving drugs. If you want, I can see if I can tie the patterns in his income with criminal activity in the county.'

'You can do that?'

'It's my own algorithm that I'm developing. I've been running it through old cases that are already solved to see if the program picks up on it. It takes into account location as well. Say, for example, you have a serial rapist who travels around – except you don't know that, but you catch a guy for something or other and then you put all the details through the system. The fact that women were raped in each place he visited at the time of visit would flag up on the program.' Tunney had the glint of a mad genius in his eye as he tried to explain his system to Adrian. 'I'm still perfecting the algorithm, but it's close to being marketable. There is other stuff like this out there, but I'm hoping this blows all of the other programs out of the water.'

'Sounds complicated . . . not for you obviously.' Adrian was the first to admit he was somewhat of a Luddite, and computers irritated the crap out of him. 'So, what about this money then? Where does it go?'

'Eventually back to him. The thing is, some of the amounts are really random, not round numbers. The same amounts appear over again, but split between other companies. So here is a pay-out of thirty-four thousand, six hundred pounds and then in these other two accounts on the same day is a pay-in that adds up to exactly that amount. He pays himself a wage and none of his bank accounts really show it in a clear-cut way. I'll get to the bottom of it though.'

'So do you really think his wife might not even know about it?' Adrian asked again.

'I don't think so, she seems to live within the limits of their personal accounts whereas he strays outside, obviously knowing full well that he has the funds to back it up. But that's just a guess.'

'So definitely no affair then?'

'No, definitely not.'

'Thanks, Tunney,' Adrian said, as his colleague gathered up his papers and stood up to go.

'Remember, you didn't hear it from me.' Tunney tapped his nose.

'I won't tell anyone. Wouldn't want you to get in trouble.'

'I'll figure it out though, Ade, just leave it with me,' Tunney smiled. 'Oh, Brown's coming in, by the way. I don't know if you want to warn Imogen. He wants an update on Bridget Reid.'

'Do we have any updates?'

'I've managed to improve the resolution of the tapes from the night of the murders somewhat but you still can't see the guys' faces, they keep them covered up. Still . . . maybe you'll spot something I haven't. I'm not the detective!'

'You're a better detective than me, mate.'

'Shhhh, someone will hear you.' Tunney laughed and walked off.

*

Imogen knew she was in for a grilling when Fraser saw her. She had managed to avoid him for most of the morning but she couldn't avoid him forever. She dialled her mother's number again, but it went straight to answerphone. She knew Irene didn't want to talk to her, didn't want to talk about her father. Even thinking that soon she might know the identity of the man who she had long since filed under 'as good as dead' made her stomach dip. Miles was in Fraser's office, along with Sam Brown. They were discussing the disappearance of Bridget Reid and how the case was coming along. The truth was, the case wasn't coming along and she didn't want to sit in a room with Sam while they explained that. Miles had the good sense to text her and let her know when it was safe to slip over to her desk unnoticed. She had also received a text from Gary Tunney, so she went to find him at his desk.

'So, what have you got?' she asked as he messed around with some footage on his set up.

'The murder at Reid's house.'

Imogen settled in and they watched the video from the start.

'Bridget looking out of the window, checking her phone. Her flatmate comes in and a conversation takes place. I'm working on the sound quality, I checked and the setting on the laptop was all wrong so she doesn't pick up much at all. OK, then here . . . Reid leaves the room and comes back with a man. The suit comes off and he's wearing a babygro. She goes and gets him a bottle and feeds him, until he falls asleep, then she leaves when her flatmate turns up – this is presumably when she went to have a shower.'

'And there's no footage of anywhere else in the house?'

'No. OK, here – the flatmate leaves and the blonde girl from upstairs comes in and looks through Reid's drawer. I think she takes some money from the bedside there and stuffs it in her bra before leaving. That guy stays asleep, sucking his thumb.'

'What was that?' A noise came through on the tape, a scream from outside the bedroom. The man on the bed stirred and sat up, still in character.

'I'm guessing that's blondie getting attacked. OK, so then this guy comes in, grabs that comb off the mantel there and jams it in that other guy's carotid – I mean, I know it looks easy in the movies, but this guy knows what he's doing. No hesitation, nothing, just straight in there.'

'And you can't get a better shot of his face?'

Imogen watched the man closely. His face was covered and he wore a hat, but still there was something familiar about him, something she couldn't figure out. In their line of work they ran into so many people; it was hard to pinpoint the source of the familiarity. As they watched the tape, the door to the bedroom burst open and another man walked in.

'This guy has obviously killed the chick in the bath, but I think they were definitely looking for Bridget. She wasn't in on it, no way. For a start, they clearly don't know about the camera.'

'Can you zoom in on him at all?'

Tunney clicked on the other man and paused the

tape. Imogen studied the image, it was clearer than before, and the two men together in the room were familiar to her too. She shook her head in frustration; the image wasn't clear enough.

'Hopefully I can clean the audio up even more. Look, he's on the phone there. Maybe we can get a clue on who he's speaking to, as well.'

'Great work, as ever, Tunney.'

The phone next to Tunney's workstation rang and he answered it. He passed it over to Imogen.

'Can you come to my office, please, Imogen?' Fraser said chirpily on the other end of the line. She hung up and looked at the screen again.

'When you get a better pic, can you print me off a copy of those guys, please?'

'Sure.'

Imogen walked into Fraser's office, ready to offer up apologies and to beg them again to let her deal with her mother. Instead, to her shock, she was faced with her former Plymouth boss, DCI Stanton. She fought to hide her reaction, glad that Adrian couldn't see the look on her face, because it would have completely betrayed her. She cringed as the memory of their one-night stand imposed itself on her.

'Sir . . . Hello,' she finally managed to say.

'DCI Stanton is here on the Isabelle Hobbs case. As you know, he headed up the investigation in Plymouth.'

'Yes.'

'We thought, seeing as you are so personally invested in the case, that maybe you could bring him up to speed.'

'Detective.' Stanton held his hand out and she reluctantly accepted his handshake. He held on a few seconds too long, and she snatched her hand away – she could hardly remember the time when she'd longed for his hands on her body. She flushed with embarrassment again.

'Of course.' She took a couple of steps backward.

'Any news on your mother?'

'She's contacting my father, that's all she would agree to do. DS Miles and I were going to go and see her again later on today. She isn't answering her phone.'

'We're giving her a lot of leeway here, Grey. I hope you appreciate how high profile this case is,' Stanton said. 'Any second the press are going to get a hold of it and then there will be no allowances whatsoever.'

'Of course, sir.'

'Come on then, I think you better tell me what you've been up to.'

She left the office, Stanton in tow, desperately trying to avoid eye contact with him. She took him over to her desk where she pulled out the files. She felt his hand running from her wrist up to her elbow, slowly, deliberately, and she moved away.

'My mother is a stubborn woman, but I'm hoping she'll come through for us.'

'This must be hard for you, Imogen.' He leaned in, she could feel him breathing in the scent of her hair and she wanted to pull away, but he had a grip on her elbow. 'Grey, you don't know how much I've missed you. I wish there was some way for us to be alone together. I wish things had happened differently.'

The scar on her stomach seemed to throb.

'I'm sorry, sir, that won't be possible.' She shook him off and walked to the other side of her chair. Stanton straightened up. Imogen could see Adrian watching him for a moment, trying to gauge what kind of a man Stanton was. She wondered how Adrian's opinion of her would change if he knew about her indiscretion with her boss. She hated the idea of him being disappointed in her. She threw the files in front of Stanton and sat down, folding her arms.

Chapter 27: The Waiting

Plymouth, two years earlier

Dean Kinkaid sat in his car, watching the entrance to Aphrodite's nightclub. The smell of nicotine had saturated the seats; he opened the window in a vain attempt to clear the air but it was too late for that. He had been sitting here for hours, ever since the club closed. He'd almost finished his second pack. He smoked because he was starving. He hadn't brought any food with him, forgetting that the kebab shop across the road had been shut down for numerous food hygiene violations. The sky was getting lighter, the sun threatening to come up.

A lot of Dean's time was spent watching and waiting. Waiting for someone to make a mistake that would hurt either him or Elias and now, of course, Imogen. There was only one way off Dean's shit list. He had grown up in foster care, struggling from one difficult situation to another. Compared to some of the other kids whose paths he crossed, he knew he'd had an OK time of it. It was crap, but it was better than most. Elias had taken him under his wing in what seemed like an act of complete altruism. Maybe Elias saw that Dean prided himself on his loyalty. Like a knight, Dean swore his loyalty from a young age. They looked out for each other. Their own families were both disappointing; they had found family in each other.

The guys still hadn't left. Dean guessed it was another poker night – how they had the energy he didn't know. He'd been asked by Elias to monitor who went in and out, tasked with finding George. There was no doubt that George had been the one dealing, and Dean was well aware that Imogen Grey thought he'd murdered him, even if she hadn't admitted it yet. The truth of the matter was that George had disappeared, and not in a bad way, in a 'Shit! They're on to me' kinda way. Dean had told Elias that George was trouble, with his Mediterranean Clark Kent good looks that all the girlies fell for. George was Michalis' cousin from Cyprus, and had been here a little over a year. Dean had been instructed for weeks now to be around whenever George was on duty. After Imogen's first visit, George had skipped out for a cigarette and never returned.

Finally the door opened and Vasos emerged, pulling his coat on. His hand was bandaged up from when Dean had cut his finger off. That's when he'd known he had her; he knew Imogen was his when she didn't stop him. Dean was a patient man; he could wait. At this point he decided not to follow Vasos, and to wait instead for Michalis to materialise. If anyone was going to lead them to George it would be him.

Two cigarettes later, Michalis finally surfaced. He looked shiftily over his shoulder as he climbed on his motorbike; Dean waited for him to get to the end of the road before starting the car engine.

The streets were dead, the only people out were the newspaper delivery truck drivers and the corner shop workers. The rest of the city was fast asleep. Dean kept a safe distance and although he knew where Michalis lived, he couldn't know for sure that he was going home until he turned on to his street. Dean followed him and pulled up a distance away. He watched as Michalis parked his bike, took his helmet off and looked around before going into a house. Dean figured surprise was his biggest advantage here so he walked around the back of the row of terraces and looked over the wall. He could see past the kids' trampoline and the lawn into the kitchen of the house. It was dark. Dean took his leather jacket off and put it over the edge of the crassly made glass barbs on the rim of the wall. He scaled the wall and jumped over on to the other side, letting the trampoline break his fall. He crept across the grass, his trousers getting wet from the dewy residue on the taller blades. He hid himself to the side of the kitchen, looking in. He could see a light in the hallway from the living room. The curtains had been drawn at the front. He tried the back door but it was locked. Locks had never really stopped Dean in the past. He pulled a lock-picking kit out of his wallet and started to work on the kitchen entrance. He waited for three clicks and then tried the handle: the door opened. It was always better to have the old-fashioned big key locks than a Yale lock, but people assumed the more recent invention was superior. Lucky for him.

As Dean stepped into the kitchen, he heard voices coming from the lounge. It sounded like the television was on, showing some sort of kids' programme. He could hear Michalis talking to his daughter, Stella, telling her that she should go back to bed. Then another voice interjected and Dean stiffened: it was unmistakably George. Dean listened for a few moments.

'I need to talk to Uncle George, honey, you need to go upstairs,' Michalis was saying.

Dean pushed the living room door open.

'Daddy's right, honey, you should go back to bed,' Dean said. George and Michalis stared at him, wide-eyed. Dean looked at Michalis and shook his head. 'Why don't you take her back to bed, Mike?'

'Not here, Dean. My fucking family is here.' Michalis looked scared. He swept Stella up in his arms and carried her quickly from the room.

'You brought the party here, not me,' Dean called out as Michalis disappeared up the stairs.

'What are you going to do?' George asked. His voice shook slightly. Dean could tell he was trying not to show his nerves.

'We're going to have a chat.'

'Are you going to kill me?'

'That's up to you, George. You need to tell me what you've been up to.'

'I thought I could make some money on the side,

that's all. I got hold of some product and I gave some of it to my girls.'

'You know, it's one thing when you give it to some junkie whose card is marked anyway, the police won't spend a whole bunch of time on that. But if you give it to some rich white schoolgirl, that's a whole other story.'

'I didn't give it to her, I swear, she must have found it.'

'Well, that's still your responsibility. Were you dealing out of the club?'

'Dean, I give you my word. I wasn't.'

'Your word is worth precisely shit at the moment, George. Elias told me to take care of you – what do you think he meant by that? He doesn't need that kind of scrutiny on him. You could get us all into trouble.'

'I didn't mean to mess up the other business. I thought the girl knew what she was doing, knew what she was taking. It's not like that skank had never taken a hit before.'

'Other business? What are you talking about?'

'You know, the girls.'

'What do you know about that?' Dean asked, pretending he had a clue what George was talking about. Dean really was a no questions asked kind of guy, but there was something that bugged him about his dealings with Elias. There was definitely a criminal air about him – you don't need a person like Dean around if you're clean. Elias always maintained it was to help control his brother. Dean could smell that a mile off, but there seemed to be no kind of illegal activity. At least, nothing big. He figured it was mostly from booze runs, bringing in dodgy knock-off alcohol that had no business in the country, let alone in anyone's body. This was the first he had heard of *the girls*.

'I don't know anything, I swear. I only saw them get off the truck one time, before they got handed over.'

'Handed over to who?'

'To Elias's brother, Antonis.'

'Get up,' Dean said.

'Come on, man. What are you going to do?'

'We're going for a ride.'

'Don't do this, Dean.'

'Relax, George, I'm not going to hurt you,' Dean said as he grabbed George's arm and led him out of the house.

Of course he was going to hurt him. Dean was a man of his word and he'd promised Elias that when he got his hands on George he'd take care of him. In this case though, he was just going to rough George up a bit. George was afraid of Dean and that meant he was useful. Dean's policy was that he only killed the ones he had no use for, the defiant ones, the ones who wouldn't give him what he wanted even when he beat them to within an inch of their lives. The ones who spit their broken teeth back in his face. Dean found that most people, when confronted with someone they knew was willing to kill, would do pretty much whatever was asked of them. Dean's reputation was an exaggerated version of the truth. He knew that fear was a powerful motivator, he knew that from the times he had been afraid, from the times he'd been on the receiving end, from the times he had been at the whim of someone else's power. From the times when he'd thought he was going to die and had done everything he could to stay alive. That was a lot to do with why Dean chose this line of work, because he refused to be afraid and there was something inside him that relished seeing that fear in others. As much as he'd used to despise that side of himself, he had now accepted it. He was looking forward to getting that reaction from George – George and his pretty face that made all the young girls drop their knickers. Well, he would see about that.

Chapter 28: The Lighthouse

Plymouth, two years earlier

Imogen stared at the photo of Nancy Baggott with her family. She looked dead already. She'd always thought that if you looked at photographs you could pick out the people who would die young, just from the look in their eyes. The eyes are the window to the soul, after all, and Imogen thought there was something about a life cut short that was projected through Nancy's dark pupils.

'Penny for your thoughts,' Sam said. He was sitting at his desk, watching her. She wondered how long he'd been staring for.

'Just thinking about this poor family. How do you get over shit like this?'

'You don't get over it, but you can put it to one side. You can train yourself to switch your feelings off, even if it's just to get on with everyday life.'

'I don't even know what to do next.'

'We need to check on George, see whether he ever did get on that flight to Greece like Dean says he did. I have a friend over in airport security; he's sending me the CCTV images we requested. They should be here any second.'

'In the meantime we just sit here with our thumbs up our backsides, do we?'

'Got them! They've just come through.' Sam fiddled with his computer and looked over at Imogen. She stood up and walked over to stand behind him, resting her hands on his shoulders. He was opening the picture file from the airport CCTV; the computers here were shockingly slow and low spec, it was amazing they got anything done. The picture file opened and they both leaned forward, staring at the screen. The man they saw wasn't George. Imogen knew it, and it was the best news she'd had all day. Wherever George was – he was probably still in the country.

'Do we need to go back to the club?' Sam looked hopeful.

Imogen swallowed, looking down at the desk. 'You go if you want; I don't see the point. They've obviously been lying to us.'

She avoided Sam's gaze, well aware that she was just making an excuse. She didn't want to go back to Aphrodite's, not after last time. She didn't want to see the comedian with his missing finger in case the guilt finally got to her. She didn't want to see Dean either. He kept popping up in her thoughts, the thought of him crawling under her skin. It was confusing. She thought about the flowers, the way he'd smiled at her. Was it all just a mind game or did he really like her? He was clearly a manipulative piece of shit, she knew that much – yet sometimes when she was with him she felt like it was the most honest interaction she had ever had. His affection for her felt pure, unwarranted, as though it had come from nowhere and yet somehow stuck.

'It seems like the drugs were coming from George directly, I think,' she said. 'There are no other links to the club, but I get a bad feeling from it anyway, don't you?'

'The presence of Dean Kinkaid certainly does not bode well,' Sam said. 'I've been looking into him further, asking all my contacts.'

'Yeah?' She feigned nonchalance; she wanted to know what Sam had found out. She had been reluctant to believe what Stanton had told her, even though she knew what Dean was capable of, she had seen it with her own eyes.

'He had a sealed record from when he was a teenager, but I know someone who knows someone. He set fire to some guy, one of the counsellors at the care home he grew up in. Kinkaid waited until he was asleep and poured scotch over the poor bugger. Then he lit the match.'

'How old was he? Why didn't he do time?'

'Oh, he did. He was thirteen, he stayed in kiddy-prison until he was eighteen, but they wouldn't transfer him to an adult facility. He got out.'

'Anything else?'

'He was charged with murder when he was twenty. But they couldn't prove it; he walked.'

'Maybe they couldn't prove it because he didn't do it?'

'Have you got a thing for this guy, Grey?'

'No! Of course not. Why would you say that?'

'Because you seem *really* interested. And you've got a funny look on your face.'

'Sam, I'm interested because of the case, I just want to know what we're dealing with. Anything about drugs?'

'Nothing, although his name pops up around known dealers, mainly for kicking the shit out of them. Few bar fights. Never any charges, statements always retracted, witnesses disappearing. People are afraid of this guy.'

'We need to find George.'

'If he's still alive. If he's not, I don't think we'll find him.'

'Grey!' Stanton's voice shot across the office, startling them both. It was his angry voice again. Imogen smiled ruefully at Sam and walked into the DCI's office.

'What is it?'

'That's no way to speak to your superior.'

'Sorry, sir.'

'I came by your place last night. Where were you?' His voice softened. She hated feeling like she'd upset him, like she'd let him down.

'I went to bed early. I've not been feeling so hot the last week or so.'

'I don't know when I can get away again. I really want to see you.'

'I'm sorry, I don't think we can. It's not a good idea. You're married.' She paused. 'It was a mistake. I'm sorry.' She really wanted to kiss him.

'Why the sudden attack of conscience?' he said.

'It's not that sudden. I won't be that woman, David. Frankly, I'm better than that.'

She could feel the pull of him even as she stood there. It was like gravity. She was trapped in his orbit. She knew people talked about magnetism but she had never really understood what it meant until she'd met Stanton. From the moment she'd started working in Plymouth, there'd been an undeniable chemistry between them. She'd always hung back, never once making a move, until eventually late one evening he had said something that made her realise he was attracted to her too.

Imogen stared at him across the desk. Maybe part of the attraction for her was that feeling, that feeling of always wanting more. When you're with someone who's married, you never get the whole person; you make excuses to yourself but in the end you are not their first choice. She knew deep down that she was just a way for him to unwind, or a way for him to generate some excitement. He already had the dutiful wife at home. Imogen had never wanted to be a bit on the side, but there was still something about him that made her want to be, made her want to disregard her morals and take whatever she could get. It wasn't like her to feel this attached to anyone.

Sleeping with a married man was now the only thing Imogen had in common with her mother. Her father had been a married man. To this day, Imogen didn't know his name; her mother had always sworn she would take it to her grave. If there was one sure-fire way to end up like her mother, alone and sad, then it was to continue down this path. No, thank you.

After several moments of just standing silently in each other's presence, looking into each other's eyes, Imogen inhaled sharply and made her way to Stanton's office door. She closed it behind her and didn't look back.

Sam intercepted her. 'Are we going to see Elias then?'

'OK, but let's cut out the middle-man. Let's go straight to his house,' Imogen said. That way she could avoid Aphrodite's, and avoid Dean. She didn't want Sam watching her every move, trying to figure out whether she had feelings for Dean or not. God help her, she did have feelings. And she had feelings for Stanton too.

Elias' house was not a house at all; it was a converted lighthouse. There was a pristine white schooner bound to a small jetty nearby. Imogen and Sam found Elias on the deck, watching three children playing on the lawn to the side of the building. He looked relaxed and happy, standing and smiling when he saw the pair of them approaching.

'Detectives!'

'Mr Papas.' Imogen smiled as they walked to the end of the jetty.

'Please, come aboard!'

He held out his hand to help her up. What the hell, she thought to herself, and took it, feeling his skin soft and smooth beneath hers. This wasn't a working man's hand. Sam clambered aboard behind her; she could hear him clumsily making his way on to the deck.

'Would you like a drink?'

'No, thank you, we're on duty.'

'So, what can I help you with?'

'Just wondering if you know the whereabouts of your barman George? We reviewed the airport CCTV footage and the man who boarded the plane to Greece was not the man we met in your bar.'

'We all look alike, no?' He bellowed with laughter; Imogen and Sam looked at each other curiously, unsure what the joke was.

The movement of the boat was making Imogen's stomach churn. She had never been particularly fond of the sea, or very good on boats. Even the slightest movement made her feel sick.

'Are you OK?' Sam asked, his hand on her shoulder. She must have looked as bad as she felt.

'Jimmy! Give that back to your sister!' Elias called out to the children as the little girl started screaming.

'Cute kids,' Sam said.

'My grandchildren. I know, I know, I don't look old enough.' He laughed again. He was a different man to the one Imogen had seen in the club. He seemed much nicer when he wasn't around his cronies.

'Actually, could I have some water?' Imogen asked. She could almost taste the bile trying to make its way to the surface.

Elias poured a glass of icy water from a jug standing on the boat's table, handing it to her with a smile. Imogen took a sip, then immediately rushed to the side of the boat. Her stomach heaved and she threw up over the side, straight into the sea. That would definitely cost her the upper hand – losing her breakfast when she was supposed to be questioning someone was not a good look.

'Jesus, Grey, are you OK?' Sam asked.

She threw up again.

'You're not made for the water, are you, Detective?' Elias laughed.

'I'm OK, I'm fine, sorry.'

'Sea-sickness? Or maybe it's something else?' Elias smiled and winked at Imogen. She stared back at him, her mind beginning to whirl.

'I need to get off this boat.' Imogen put the glass down and climbed over the side of the boat and back on to the jetty, Sam following behind her.

'I promise you, Detectives, I do not know the whereabouts of the man you are looking for, but if I find him, you will be notified.' Elias remained aboard the ship, raising one hand in the air by way of a goodbye.

'I'm sure we will. Thank you, Mr Papas,' Imogen managed to say, trying to ignore the stale taste in her mouth. She needed to get to her toothbrush. She had to get home.

Imogen walked towards the front door of her house, immediately sensing that something was off. The door was slightly open, only a sliver, but she most definitely had not left it that way. It was at times like this that she wished she had a gun, but instead she just had to push the door open and hope that whoever was inside wasn't standing directly on the other side of it. She moved slowly. The door opened fully and she stepped into the house. There was an overwhelming silence. Whoever had been here had left. Nothing had been disturbed. She walked through the hallway and peered into the kitchen, which was still the same mess she had left it in that morning. She headed towards the living room, grabbing a didgeridoo that her mother had bought her at a folk fair years ago; it was the closest thing she had to a weapon that was within her grasp. It wouldn't be the first time she had used it in that manner, and she knew it left one hell of a mark.

Imogen pushed open the living room door and gasped as the sight hit her. There was no doubt about it: Dean Kinkaid had been in her house. Like her mother's cats, he had left her a gift, an offering to show his affection. George the barman was strapped to her dining chair, gagged and wrapped in cling film up to his neck. His face was beaten and bloody, his eyes swollen shut. A present just for her.

Chapter 29: The Artist

The present

Elias Papas watched his brother, Antonis, as he scolded one of the barmaids. Antonis had always said Elias was the soft touch of the family, but the truth was, the way Antonis made people feel like shit was an art form. Who was Elias to take away the small pleasures he got in life? The petite blonde shrank into her skeleton as he barked at her, but Elias could see that there was still a hint of attraction in her eyes as she looked at Antonis. Elias shook his head. He would never understand women.

They worked as a team in their business ventures, but Elias was the public face, and he took care of the paperwork. Because of Antonis' history with the law, it was better that he wasn't on any of the documentation. The barmaid scuttled out of the office and Antonis laughed. They were twins, but you wouldn't know it. They had been identical at one point, but now that

Antonis was bloated and kept his head shaved, there was little resemblance. Antonis wanted to be feared, whereas Elias just wanted to make money. It worked well.

'You need to give her a break, brother.'

'Oh, I'll give her a break.' He winked at Elias.

'What does that even mean?'

'It means what it means! You know what it means.'

'We go through a lot of blondes; maybe you need to take it easy.'

'You know I can't resist the pretty white girls.'

'You are white, Antonis. I hate to break it to you.'

'You know what I mean, the English girls, they're different.'

'I don't want to know. Keep me out of it.'

'Don't tell me you've never looked, because I know you have.'

Elias was saved from answering by the sound of the bar landline ringing. He reached over and looked at the caller display screen, before quickly picking up the receiver. He hoped his brother hadn't noticed his cheeks flushing.

'Aphrodite's?'

After a brief pause he shot a look at his brother that suggested he leave the room. Antonis winked at him and left the office.

'To what do I owe the honour? I haven't heard from you in some time, my love . . . OK, we can meet. I will come to you. It's easier for me that way . . . Are you in the same place?' Elias heard a click, and was sure that Antonis had picked up the other line to listen in.

'Don't tell me now . . . let's talk when I see you, I'll come now.'

He put down the phone and walked into the club. Antonis was talking to Giannis, huddled together and whispering as usual, although Antonis did not look pleased. Elias was sure his brother had some other business dealings that he didn't know about, and the truth was he didn't *want* to know. Plausible deniability; he had needed it before with his brother and he had no doubt he would need it again. Elias was the favoured child, and Antonis had the complex to go with his inferiority. Always quick to anger and happy to dish out punishment, sometimes even finding a sadistic pleasure in hurting people. It was a part of his brother which Elias tried to ignore.

Not wishing to get involved in any heavy business debates at this time, Elias left the club and walked to his brand new Mercedes. He still got excited when he bought a new car, even though he bought them often. The smell of the white leather wafted out as he opened the door, the heat had made it even more pungent than usual. Elias smiled. He turned the air conditioning on to try to neutralise the air somewhat, switching the radio on to make the journey go faster. His excitement was undeniable; he was feeling a long-lost sense of anticipation, which until this moment he had thought was perhaps just a memory. It was the feeling he got when he went to see Irene.

Irene Grey was all of a fluster for the fifty-five minutes between speaking to Elias and the doorbell finally ringing. She had changed her dress four times and reapplied her lipstick in a desperate bid to remember the exact shade that used to drive Elias wild. They had met years before in an art gallery. Irene was fresh out of college and her work was being displayed. Elias had bought it all for twice the price. The electricity between them had never faded, even after all these years, but Irene knew that Elias could never truly be hers.

He had been forced into an arranged marriage, all of which he had explained at the time, whilst telling her that she was the true love of his life. When Irene had found out she was pregnant with Imogen, Elias had begged her not to have an abortion, convincing her that their daughter would always be a reminder of their love for each other. Sometimes Irene couldn't help but get angry with Imogen because even just her face reminded her of what she so desperately wanted, what she'd had to live her whole life without. But Elias had always provided for them, even though Irene had refused the money at first. She had never wanted anyone to ask any questions, and she didn't want to feel like the other woman – as far as she was concerned, his wife was the other woman. Eventually though, she started using a little here and a little there. She liked to collect things, and collections cost money. In the old days, Elias used to meet up with her once or twice a year for a stolen moment or two, but even that became too painful over time. Now, at last, she was going to see him again.

The doorbell finally rang and Irene breathed in sharply. Before she could change her mind, she pulled open the front door. Elias' eyes lit up at the sight of her. No one on this earth made her feel as special as he did.

'You never change, Elias.'

'Neither do you, my love.'

'Nonsense, I look like I could be your mother.'

'Please, don't say such things.' He laughed and she chuckled too, unable to stop herself from feeling like a giddy teenager around him. 'How is she, Irene? How is our daughter?'

'Sullen, as usual. Come inside.'

He followed her into the house and they sat down together on the sofa. It was strange having him in her home after all this time.

'Did you know that I met Imogen again recently?' he said softly.

'What?' She stared at him, shocked at the revelation. Having always been the conduit between father and daughter, it never occurred to her that they might meet without her knowledge.

'Don't worry, she had no idea who I was. It was a while ago, during one of her investigations.'

'She was investigating you?'

'No, one of my staff. Nothing came of it anyway, but she is a very beautiful girl.'

'That wasn't why she was attacked, was it?' Irene said, holding back the tears. She couldn't bear to think of her daughter as she had been, lying in hospital for weeks, unable to eat, unable to do much of anything at all.

'No, no one knows our secret. In fact—' He stopped.

'What?'

'I spoke to the hospital at the time, paid them to make her more comfortable.'

'I didn't think it worked like that?'

'It's amazing how things work when you have the funds.' He laughed. 'You called me for a reason, said it was very important, something to do with a baby?'

'There's a police officer missing, a woman. They've linked her disappearance to a murder that Imogen is investigating, a couple were killed and they left a baby behind.'

'OK, go on, what has this got to do with me?'

'The killer left behind some DNA and there was a sort of match or something, they told Imogen it was her half-brother . . .' Irene looked up and saw the colour drain from Elias' face.

'It can't be!'

'I know we don't talk about our families, but I know you have three sons, is there any way—'

'No, no way at all, they're not like that. They're good boys.'

'Then who?'

'I don't know. I need to speak to a lawyer, I think, see what this DNA business proves before I come forward.'

'Come forward? You can't!'

'My wife no longer cares and my children have all left home. I've been thinking about it more and more since I met Imogen. I want her to know who I am.'

'I have never told anyone, I promise you, you don't need to tell anyone now if you don't want to. I don't want you to get in trouble because of me.'

'This is not because of you. I will speak to a lawyer first though, please, let me tell Imogen.'

'Oh, Elias, if you're sure. I told them I would go to prison before I revealed you to them.'

He kissed her forehead. 'It's a different time now, my beauty. My father is long dead, there is no one to disapprove. There is even a chance for us now, where there was not one before. The world is opening up to me, Irene.' He said her name with a Greek intonation, *Irini* – meaning peace. If there was one thing that Irene had never felt, it was peace. He tilted her chin towards him and put his lips on hers. She felt like a young woman again – only he could do this to her; he was the one. People talk about the one as if they know what it means, but Irene knew falling in love wasn't a decision, it was a punishment. Yes, Elias was the one, and because of his circumstances they had not been able to be together. His family had fervently disagreed with mixed marriages. Elias, being the obliging son that he was, complied with their demands and married a wealthy young Greek debutante, most likely a virgin, with a dowry to boot. How could Irene ever compete with that? So she had sat by the sidelines and watched the man she loved marry and have three sons with another woman, followed by countless grandchildren. All the while, Irene remained virtually faithful to him, occasionally losing her mind over not being near him, not being able to look in his eyes for comfort. It was the main reason she would never totally move away from Plymouth; she wanted to be near him, she wanted to bump into him on the street and

233

feel that sudden rush of blood to her abdomen. She was and always had been homesick for Elias. The one place she felt like she belonged was here in his arms. He ran his hands over her body, making her feel alive as only he could. She took his hand and led him to the bedroom, because that's what they needed, to be together.

'I cannot stay long, my love, I have to get back to work. But I will return, my wife is away for the whole weekend. Let's go somewhere together. I will come back for you tomorrow. No one will be able to reach us; we can take my boat on to the water, get away from the world.'

'But the police?'

'I'll talk to them when we return. I will talk to Imogen too. We'll get this straightened out.'

'What about your sons?' she asked, not wishing to hear the answer.

'They were not responsible for this, and I know enough about DNA evidence to know that once you start looking outside the parents and direct siblings it gets complicated. I know they did not do it.'

'If you're sure?'

'I am. Now, you must pack.'

'You're coming back?' She tried not to sound too desperate.

'Give me until tomorrow, I need to set some things in motion. I will be here as soon as I can.' He kissed her hard on the lips, hard enough to make her recoil slightly before pushing into him. She watched him walk out of her apartment, not for the first time hoping he would turn around and drag her out with him, take her with him forever.

Early the next morning, Irene was packed and ready to go. She thought about Elias' boat, the clean blue water, the thought of escape. For the first time in years, she noticed the mess and filth around her, and felt embarrassed at letting him come here. She should have met him in a café or something.

She took in a sharp intake of breath as she heard the elevator doors open in the outer hallway. She looked at the clock. Maybe he had come early. She had almost been waiting for him ever since he'd left, tensed for the sound of the doorbell. It rang now and she stood up, hushing the butterflies in her stomach as she walked to the door, took a deep breath and turned the latch.

No sooner had she heard the click than the door burst open, throwing her to the ground. She looked up to see a man, not Elias, someone younger, with a smaller frame. His face was obscured with a bandana and a baseball cap. From the corner of her eye she saw something sparkle; her gaze travelled down his heavily tattooed arms and rested on the knife which he gripped firmly in his left hand.

'Wh . . . Who are you?' she sobbed, panic overtaking her. 'What do you want?'

'I'm sorry, lady,' the muffled voice answered, and he swung the knife at her face. She managed to scuttle back just in time.

'Get out!' she screamed. 'Help!' She cried out, knowing full well that no one would hear her or come to her aid. Irene was known as a bit of a nuisance in her neighbourhood, she was the very definition of the boy who cried wolf, always screaming and howling at something or someone, real or imagined. This time, however, it was very real.

She looked over at the side table next to the sofa where her phone was. She grasped at the air behind her until she came into contact with the cord from the lamp. She yanked the cord and the lamp fell next to her hand; she grabbed it and swung at the man. She missed but he dodged backwards and she was able to throw herself across the room to the phone.

'Don't make this any harder than it needs to be.' She sensed he was mocking her.

Bloody smartphones, she thought to herself as she tried to unlock it and dial the number before he got to her. He knocked the phone out of her hands and she felt his fist connect with her face. The picture frames fell to the floor beside her, a picture of Imogen's half-smiling face stared up at her. She remembered the day it was taken; it was the day that Imogen had been promoted to detective. Irene had made her stand on the docks holding a celebratory gin and tonic aloft, the sun shining in her eyes.

The room was blurry and her head was ringing. She had never taken a punch to the face before. She knew she was in grave danger. Elias wasn't due for a while and her neighbours wouldn't come. There was only one thing for it. She had to make sure she got some of his tissue or DNA, she had to cut him or hurt him somehow. She grabbed the glass from the picture frame in her hand and swished it blindly in front of her. Her vision had not yet returned. He was trying to grab her hand when she jammed the glass into his cheek.

'Son of a bitch!' he shouted, glass still protruding from his face. Irene's vision was clearing now and she could see the blood pouring from the wound, dripping on to the carpet.

'My daughter will find you, you piece of shit!' No sooner had she got the words out than he swung for her again, sweeping the knife across her breastbone. The adrenaline meant she couldn't feel the pain, could only watch in horror as her flesh parted to expose the bone. She figured she had one last good attempt at the bastard before he finished her off. She grabbed one of the sides of the picture frame that had come apart on the floor and thrust it towards him with all her might, jamming the raw corner into his eye. He let out an unearthly scream before slashing at her repeatedly. She could feel the skin ripping, she could see the red marks the blade left. And then she could see nothing at all.

Irene felt the blood leaving her and heard the man as he gasped; she assumed he was clutching his eye. The fact that he was still breathing meant that she hadn't driven the frame in deep enough, which was disappointing. In her last moments, Irene took solace in the fact that she had at the very least half-blinded this asshole for life, or what was left of his life. Imogen was going to be so pissed off about this.

Chapter 30: Best Laid Plans

Age 19

I feel so good every time I see Claire's stupid confused face as she pushes the pram round town. The only thing better than that is her boyfriend's even stupider face. I can imagine their whisperings about how on earth she got pregnant when all they did was dry hump each other through their clothes. Fucking idiots.

I watched her swell and felt the curve of her belly as I lay next to her at night in the months leading up to the birth. She cried a lot when it finally dawned on her. At first she thought she'd just put on weight, I know she did, but as the weight grew into a solid mass that writhed and wriggled under her skin, the truth became harder to deny. She deferred her A levels, she stopped coming to school. I saw her around the town; sometimes her disappointed parents would be with her and I could feel their tension too. Our baby mainly looks like her, it's a boy, but I think he has parts of me in him too. Not that she would ever even entertain the idea that the child was mine. She has no idea how well I know her body. I know every groove, every secret blemish.

After school I visit Monica. I want her to have my baby, too. I like the feeling that a part of myself will always be around. I guess that's the privilege of being a guy. I don't think I can tell Claire just yet that I am the father, although I definitely want her to know one day. Maybe I could even ask for custody or something. Not right now though. I'm too busy helping my dad to have time for a kid. At least if Monica has one I will be able to see it all the time and have it know I am the dad.

After Claire got pregnant I started to try with Monica. I love the way girls feel when they're pregnant, softer somehow. Monica was pregnant for a while but she put too much shit in her body and she lost it. I didn't know what was happening, one minute we were doing it and the next she was screaming, I had to call my dad's mate, because we aren't allowed to call ambulances for the girls. I thought it was my fault when I saw the blood, it was bright red. At first I thought she had pissed herself when I felt the warm liquid sticky against my thighs, that was until I looked down. So ever since then, I have been cleaning Monica up, she's stopped injecting and she only huffs when she's in a really bad way. She's promised me she won't fuck it up this time. We're going to keep trying for another baby.

It's my sister's thirteenth birthday today. It's a special occasion because she's going to be a teenager, just as I

239

am about to stop being one. I have to keep this a secret from Dad though. He doesn't even like looking at her any more. She has to be in bed before he gets home. I think maybe he is starting to feel guilty for what happened to my real sister, but it was an accident, we all knew that.

Hopefully my mum will be well enough that she can help out for my sister's party. They say my mum has Parkinson's and they keep giving her medications, but my dad won't let her take them, he thinks the drugs are what make her worse – he doesn't really agree with putting chemicals in your body. He says he's seen what it does to people. I still fill out the prescription every month and hold on to the pills. I'm going to try something with them, I think. I might try them out on Claire.

I give my sister a necklace for her birthday; Monica helped me choose it. It's an angel with a purple amethyst stone, because my sister loves the colour purple. She smiles and lifts her hair up while I put it on her. I ask her what she wants to do for her birthday and she says that all she wants to do is hang out with me, which is sweet. I know I've been neglecting her a lot lately, between working on Claire and the stuff with Monica. I'm out of the house a lot, and I think she gets lonely when I'm not there. We get a board game out and play together, it reminds me of when she first came to us and I see how much she has changed since then. I let her win, because she is both a terrible loser and a terrible winner. She gloats and tickles me – it doesn't really feel like anything but I pretend it does, because she likes it so much. I watch her erupt into giggles and I wonder

if I have ever laughed that hard in my life, at anything.
I give her a cupcake that I bought – I can't really cook
or I would have made one – with a pink case, white
frosting and sprinkles. I find a candle in one of the
drawers. She is so happy and she blows her candle out
in one go. I watch the concentration on her face as she
makes a wish and I wonder what she wished for. We
watch the creamy smoke drift up and disappear and
then she asks me if we can watch a movie together. I
can't remember the last time I sat down and watched
a movie, so I say yes. We watch an action film and she
snuggles into me and hides behind my arm when it
scares her. It's nice to be with a girl, just hanging out.
The only girlfriends I have ever had have been women
my dad employs and they always say what I want to
hear. Sometimes I say dumb shit to them just to see
what they will do, but it's always the same and it makes
me doubt everything about myself. With my sister,
though, I know that she likes me, she's not just
pretending we're friends.

She finally falls asleep and I carry her to the bedroom,
which is tricky because it's down the stairs in the basement – my real sister's old room. I tuck her in and close
the door. I don't lock her in this time. I just leave the
door shut.

I go to the club to meet my dad and Monica is already
there talking to one of the barmen. I'm not gay or
anything but I can tell he's good-looking. Good-looking
people just act different to people like me. Monica
doesn't notice me for a while, so I watch her talking
to him and it makes me angry. I know she has sex with

other men, she has to or my dad will get rid of her, but I don't like to think of her as enjoying it. I know it sounds awful, but I'm just being honest.

My dad and Meathead come out of the office and they both look annoyed. They always have that look after they've been speaking to my uncle. The club is different now, it's no longer full of the worker girls that my dad has, they are all strewn about in houses around the county. My uncle took over the club because the police were looking at my dad, and he made sure my dad cleaned it up so there were no more illegal things going on there, like, nothing at all. My dad doesn't like being told to change. He's been talking about us moving away from here, away from my uncle's judgmental eye. My uncle is the only person who can tell my dad what to do. I think he's kept him out of prison a few times.

Dad tells me we have to go somewhere together. I ask if we can bring Monica and he tells me it's up to me but that if she comes with us, she might not come back. Meathead laughs at this. I don't know what he means, but I think I will leave her here. My dad doesn't make empty threats and he doesn't say things just for effect either. We get into his car and he drives me out into the countryside. We seem to be driving forever, so I nod off for a bit. I'm not sure exactly where we are but I can't see any lights until we arrive at another house and get out of the car.

It's a large house, like something out of one of those Victorian TV shows my mum watches. There are lots of windows and they all seem to have candles in them. It's very dark out here. We go inside and there are a lot of men drinking and talking, probably about twenty of them. They're all wearing browns and greens, like that really expensive stuff the posh farmers wear. There are some other men there, in uniform. I stand with my father. He's talking to one of the uniformed men about me; apparently the man has a daughter who is fifteen. They show me a photo and the man asks me if I think she's pretty. She is pretty so I say yes. He tells me that when she is old enough he would like me to consider her for marriage. My dad looks at me and winks. He had told me this would happen, when people started to see me as a man I would be treated with more respect, people would want to be a part of my life. The man obviously wants my father as a business partner for something and so he is trying to force our families together. I don't really know what to say so I go and stand somewhere else and listen to the other men.

After a while of wandering around and mingling without actually taking part in any conversations, I get bored and decide to have a look around the house. Almost all of the doors are closed but I can hear noise coming from behind them. Every room is different. I try a couple of the doors but they're all locked. I come to another door and twist the knob, it opens and I slowly open a gap big enough to see through – I don't want the people inside to know I'm watching them. There's a naked girl strapped to a chair with a man standing behind her. She pleads with the man to do something. Over and over again she asks him, until eventually he puts a carrier bag over her face and starts to suffocate her. When she stops resisting, he pulls the plastic bag off her face and she is just completely limp. I wonder if she's dead, but then I see her suck in some air before bursting out laughing and then it begins again. She pleads with him and he obliges. I close the door. I don't understand people.

When I get back downstairs, my father has a strange look on his face. He is smiling but I know he is angry. Most of the people at this party think they are better than him, just because they went to posh universities or whatever. My dad never went to university, he worked from the age of fifteen because he had to. He says people who stay in school are afraid of real life.

A bell rings and then everyone starts to move towards the French doors and out on to the back terrace as a man opens them. A man walks in with some young men and they make their way towards the patio. The men are all standing in a row looking out over the trees. I realise now that the men are dressed for a hunt.

A van pulls out on to the side of the lawn just in front of the trees and a man gets out of the driver's seat. I recognise him as the one we got Monica from on the docks, and before he even opens the van I know what's inside. I look at the men around me, normal men, people you would see anywhere, and I don't know how they got here. How does this kind of thing come up in a conversation? How do these people find each other?

The man opens the van and pulls a girl out. She is weak and falls to the ground, crying. The party guests continue to talk to each other as if she isn't even there, as if she isn't real. The driver pulls the woman to her feet and whispers something to her, then she runs off into the woods. He does the same thing several times. I count six girls altogether. Six people who are completely disposable. The guests go over to a table that looks like a dessert trolley in a fancy restaurant, except that it's full of weapons. Several of the men choose a weapon, some have guns, some have other things, like knives, and one man even has an axe. It's a competition. I want to go home and be with my sister, but we have to stay until it's over. After a few minutes, the men follow the women into the woods and it's not long before we hear shots.

I'm walking behind my dad and Meathead. They're following one of the gunmen. He is crouched down as though he is stalking a big cat, like a tiger or something. From the corner of my eye I see a flash of red so I slink back a bit to investigate. I see someone huddled in amongst some foliage. I move towards the figure, hoping to God I don't get shot. I stay in the open so that there is no mistaking me for prey. When I finally reach my destination, I see the girl. She is startled to see me and I can tell that she has tried to hide herself under loose leaves, but even in this half-light her pale skin flashed with red is like a beacon in the darkness. Some part of her must know that there will be a count at the end, that there is no way she will be able to stay hidden forever.

I have a small flask of whisky in my jacket pocket. She sobs as I approach her and offer her the flask. I put my finger to my lips and she quietens down some-what. I see the red glistening against her bare skin and

I can see that she has been hurt, probably shot. Her thigh is practically torn open and she's bleeding really badly. I don't know how she got away, but I want to try and look after her. She takes the drink and nods me a thank you. I don't think she speaks any English at all. I reach out and pull the leaves away from the wound; the blood is still coming out in a steady flow. She needs a doctor and even though I know some of the men here are doctors, I don't think they would be in any hurry to help her. I take my jacket off and wrap it around her shoulders. She's shivering. I expect the shock is setting in or something.

Most of the hunters are further into the woods now and so she relaxes a little as the voices get more distant. I let her finish the drink. I think she does know that this is the end for her. I wish I could say something comforting at least. I ask her what her name is. She seems to understand that one and she tells me her name is Natasha. She leans in to me and I put my arm around her, stroking her hair and singing in a whisper into her ear. Every so often we hear a shot in the distance until finally the shooting stops and then we hear the sound of the men returning. She looks up at me with her green eyes and I know what I must do. She is giving me permission. I draw my arm up around her neck until her throat is locked under my elbow. She doesn't struggle or fight back, and within moments her body goes limp in my arms. I let her head fall into my lap and light a cigarette before I get up and walk away.

One by one, the bodies are brought back to the house and laid on the front lawn until all of the girls are back.

The sun is fully up now and the bodies look so other-worldly in the sunlight, the blood so bright against the white skin and perfect green of the lawn. I see Natasha in amongst them. She looks like an angel and her face is different to the others. Maybe I gave her some peace. Maybe I did help. I don't ever want to forget this. I don't ever want to be like my father, but I don't know how to get away from him.

As soon as I get home I throw up. I'm confused because I don't think it's right to treat people like that, no matter who they are. I wonder if my dad thinks people are any different to animals; he doesn't seem to.

I still think about Mindy sometimes, about her dead body. I mean I really think about it. I am glad I saw her die, because slipping away after an overdose looks like a much better death than what those women went through. Then I think about Margot and wonder whether this is how she died. I imagine it was. After I have been sick, I go and have a shower. When I'm done I dry myself off and put my clothes on. I go to my sister's room and lie on the bed next to her. She's still asleep. My back is to her and I stare at the wall, searching for the face of God in the wallpaper, but I can't see him any more. I whisper some words I remember from the book my father made me recite.

Now let Earth be my witness, with the broad Sky
   above,
and the falling waters of the Styx
that I harbour no secret plans against you.

247

I realise my eyes are wet and before long I am crying. I miss my sister, my real one. I feel bad for the girl next to me. It's only just dawned on me that we should never have taken her and I should have protected her from my dad. Just like I should have protected my other sister. I don't think my dad likes women very much. He's violent towards everyone, but it's always inhuman when it involves a woman, when it's something like what he did to those girls.

I feel my sister's hand in my hair. She is comforting me the way I used to comfort her when she would cry. I continue to cry as she strokes me and eventually I fall asleep. When I wake up, her arm is around me and it feels nice. I decide in this moment that I'm not going to let my dad hurt my sister. She's a teenager now, she's starting to look like a woman and I worry that my dad will put her to work in one of the houses that he runs. I know my uncle would stop him if he knew, but it's difficult to stop my dad. He's got friends in the police. One of the guys has been my dad's friend for years, he works in organised crime or something, specifically so that he can give my dad information. My dad pays him like ten per cent of the revenue. He says they all call him Hitchcock, so that no one ever finds out his real identity. He says they keep each other safe.

I notice that my sister is singing softly, but I don't recognise the song. I ask her what it is and she says her mum used to sing it to her. I have to stop myself from telling her the truth. That we took her and her parents didn't know. That they didn't give her to us to keep her safe; that they searched for her until the media turned on them and they ended up in prison for her murder. I read the newspaper reports at the time and they found a bloody dress under her bed which the parents said was from a nosebleed. At first people believed them, but the problem was that no one saw anything, no one saw us on the street. So then they blamed the parents. A neighbour said he'd seen the girl's mother telling her off, and the newspapers ran with the story. Isabelle. That was her name, before we gave her a new one. I don't even know if she remembers her real name.

Chapter 31: Sweet Air

The present

There was something Bridget was missing. She had prepared herself to make a move over and over again, but when the time came for action, she didn't want to do it. Was there something in the food? She checked it as best she could but there didn't seem to be anything wrong with it. No grittiness, no suspicious flavours. Her captor always waited until she'd finished her food before he left, so she couldn't not eat it. As soon as he had gone she would drink as much water as she could and stick her fingers in her throat, but that meant she was constantly hungry and it seemed to make very little difference.

She wanted to ask him for a book or a pen and paper, but she didn't want to appear to change her behaviour too much in case he realised she was no longer ingesting the pills. He never ate or drank anything when he was with her, so she couldn't even save the pills and drug him. There was definitely something she was missing. What was it? *How was he doing this to her?* She tried to think of what her training would tell her to do in this situation, but memories of life on the outside were fading. She struggled to remember if it had been real at all. He never used her name, and so these days she was unsure if she had just imagined who she used to be. She would often close her eyes and try to picture Sam's face. If she was feeling particularly confused, she would cry, but it wasn't a luxury she afforded herself very often. She had to stay detached or she would go crazy. If she wasn't crazy already. It felt like months since she'd got here. *Would she ever escape?*

She had mentioned going for a walk on more than one occasion, but the man had told her it was too dangerous, that people wanted to kill her, that she should trust him. She wondered if anyone had spoken to her parents. Her ex-boyfriends? Old friends and long-lost family members? She knew that it had been far longer than seventy-two hours, after which point the search for her would have been scaled down a little. With every passing day, her disappearance would become less and less important as more people succumbed to the notion that she was most likely dead anyway.

Did Sam think she was dead?

Growing up, Bridget had wanted to be a pop star, like every other girl in her class. Now, while she worked out in the basement room, she sang. The rhythm of her punches had become second nature to her; she no longer needed to count along, so instead she would sing, replacing real words for nonsense here and there where the memories had faded. Maybe she could ask her captor for a radio. Her knuckles were used to the dull thump against the brick wall now; she wasn't afraid of the pain. All she cared about was getting out of there before she ceased to exist even in her own mind.

One thing Bridget had begun to notice was that there was a delay between the sound of her captor entering the house and his arrival in her room. She began to wonder: was he doing something between those times that could affect her?

She waited for his next visit, listening hard. There was a slight clunking sound after he came through the door upstairs and before he arrived at her room. As she listened, she could feel her mood changing. She could feel herself beginning to lose interest, starting not to care, but despite that, she forced herself to put her ear to the wall. She could hear something else. Something faint. She was determined to fight this bizarre mood that was starting to take her over. As she moved along the wall the sound got a little louder. It was a hiss. There was only one explanation for it; he was pumping something into the room somehow. Bridget's thoughts crystallised, her time in the police force flashing in her head like a tape on fast forward. *Hiss.* She knew what he was doing. She knew what that sound meant. He was filling the room with nitrous.

Chapter 32: The Face

The present

Imogen was watching Gary Tunney giving a demonstration of facial-reconstruction software to the team that were working on the reopened Isabelle Hobbs case. DCI Stanton was standing by his side. It was still a shock having him here in Exeter; he belonged in Plymouth, with her past, with the horrific memories that she fought to keep at bay. Imogen's worlds were colliding, and she didn't like it.

'Any news from your mother?' Fraser approached.

'No, I've been calling but she hasn't answered. To be honest, that's not unusual, sir.'

Fraser frowned and waved his hand whenever she called him sir; he still wasn't used to his position as acting DCI, and Imogen knew he couldn't wait to be replaced.

'Well then, we have to bring her in for questioning.

We need to find DS Reid! I'm sorry, but there's nothing else we can do. I should have brought her in already. If anyone finds out about this . . .'

'I understand, and I really appreciate your letting me handle this so far, sir.'

'As soon as Adrian gets back from lunch you can take a car over there and see if you can get her to talk to you . . . Speak of the devil.'

Imogen looked up to see Adrian in front of them. He was even less shaven than usual and there was an air of sleeplessness about him. Imogen thought he looked slightly manic.

'Everything OK, partner?'

'Yep, sorry I'm late.' He rubbed a hand over his face. Imogen smiled.

'Late night?'

He ignored her question. 'What's Tunney doing?'

'They're going to be doing an aged reconstruction of Isabelle Hobbs so we can see what she looks like now, it'll be broadcast later on. He's just showing off his new software program or something. The circus is about to begin, the tip lines will be full of a load of nonsense that we're going to have to investigate. Fraser wants us to go see my mum again, and if she won't cooperate then we need to bring her in.'

'Are you sure we shouldn't let someone else handle it?'

'Let's just get it over with, yeah?'

Imogen could hear the phone ringing on the other side of her mother's door, but there was no one answering.

She put her mobile in her pocket and took a step backwards.

'What are you doing?' Adrian asked.

'I'm going to kick the fucking door in.' Her mood switched between anger and worry as she wondered why her mother hadn't answered the phone.

'Don't you have a key?'

'No, not for this lock. Mum's paranoid. She changes the locks every other week.'

'At least let me do it.'

'Fine, but hurry up about it.' She started to pace and Adrian took a deep breath before slamming his foot into the door. The frame rattled but the wood didn't break, so he did it again. This time there was a crack. Immediately, Imogen sensed it. A feeling of foreboding came over her. There was something wrong. Adrian looked at her and she nodded, he nodded back and gave the door one more almighty kick, at which point it gave way. He stumbled forward and grabbed hold of the door frame. Quickly he turned around and looked at her.

'OK?' His face said it all.

'OK.' She nodded again and gripped her fists tight, concentrating on her breathing.

Adrian went ahead of her, but it was only seconds before his shout bounced out of the apartment.

'Imogen! Call an ambulance!'

Before he had even finished the sentence, Imogen knew her mum was inside. He only ever called her Imogen when there was something wrong; the rest of the time she was Grey. She ran into the apartment and was struck by two things. The first was that her mother had a packed suitcase by the front door, and the second was that there was a *lot* of blood. The worst thing about the scene was the colour of the blood: it was brown and dried; it wasn't fresh. She wondered how long Irene had been lying there. She stood over her mother's mutilated body in horror. Adrian had already taken his phone out and was dialling for an ambulance; his other hand was on Irene's neck, desperately feeling for a pulse.

It seemed like forever as they waited for the ambulance to turn up. Adrian was speaking to Irene, telling her they were there, that they were going to make sure she was OK. He put Irene's limp hand in Imogen's and looked at her. She wondered what he must think of her lack of reaction, but she couldn't feel anything, just confusion. The paramedics swept in, lifting her mother on to a stretcher, hooking her up to machines and drips and placing an oxygen mask on her bloodied face.

Imogen wasn't sure if she was remembering to breathe. She was still alive so she guessed she must have. Thank God for muscle memory; she seemed to have forgotten everything else.

'How long was your mother lying there?' The paramedic's voice broke through her thoughts.

'I don't know!' she managed to say.

'When was the last time you spoke to her?'

'Yesterday, I think, I'm not sure.'

'She's lost a lot of blood, but her pulse is still regular, even if it's faint. Do you have any idea who could have done this?'

'I'm sorry, I don't. I don't know.' But even as she said the words, Imogen realised that she did know, or at least she knew something – she knew it was to do with her father. Was he a cold-blooded killer? Is that why she wasn't allowed to know him? Was this about the baby, Cassandra? Given the timing, she thought that perhaps it was. She made a decision. She wanted to know the deal, and she wanted to know who her father was, right now.

Adrian had left Imogen at the hospital and headed over to Andrea's to explain why he couldn't have Tom today. She would take it better if he was standing there; she always thought he was lying when he called with an excuse. His heart jumped a bit as he approached her house. Maybe he was kidding himself, he thought, perhaps he was just looking for an excuse to be near her. He wished she didn't still have such an effect on him.

Whenever he was in the same room as Andrea and Dominic lately, Adrian felt as though somehow her husband was jealous of him. He wondered how much it stung that Andrea had refused to have any more children. That her one and only child should be with him, a lowly police officer. Of course, Dominic had adopted Tom as his own and raised him without complaint. Adrian had always assumed it was Andrea who had kept him away from Tom growing up, but as he'd become close to Andrea again he'd realised that maybe this wasn't the case. Maybe it was Dominic after all. Adrian got the impression that Dominic was a man who was used to getting what he wanted.

He knocked on the door of the house. Andrea opened it and stood there, dressed all in white. The muslin dress made her burnished skin glow all the more. She leaned her hip against the door. He wasn't sure if she was trying to draw his attention to it. Had it been a game, he would have lost, for his eyes rested a second too long on the shapes underneath the fine cloth.

'Adrian?'

'I'm really sorry to spring this on you right now, but would it be OK if I had Tom next weekend instead of this one?' He couldn't help but look behind her. Inside, the house was still apart from a muffled noise coming from Tom's room upstairs.

'Oh, yeah? What's her name?' Andrea said snarkily, making Adrian feel like crap.

'No, it's not like that. It's Imogen, my police partner, we've just found her mum all cut up at her place. I've left her at the hospital to come explain to you in person. She was barely alive when we found her. I'd like to stay with her, until her mum's in the clear at least, and I don't know how long that's going to take.'

'Jesus Christ.' Andrea put her hand over her mouth. 'So you'll explain to Tom?'

'I will.' Andrea looked at her feet and then back at Adrian. 'We're having a party next week for Tom's fourteenth, so actually, it would be better if he was here with us next weekend . . . but I know it would mean a lot to him if you were here, too.'

'Oh, right.' Whatever Adrian had expected, it wasn't this.

'Bring Imogen, or, you know, whoever else you want to.'

'I'll think about it. Thanks for understanding, Andrea. I better get going.'

Every time he saw Andrea, Adrian still felt that primal attraction. It never went away. He opened the car door and turned his head, just to see if she was still there, standing in the doorway as he imagined. She was. He smiled to himself as he got in the car and drove away, looking through the rear-view mirror all the while, wanting to see how long it would take her to actually close the door.

He had a firm rule when it came to relationships, what little experience he had of any that lasted over a month. When it's over, it's over. You should never go back. Andrea was part of the reason he had made that rule in the first place. He had pined after her until it made him crazy, and he still felt now as though it wasn't quite over. He hated how powerless she made him feel. They had been so young though, childhood sweethearts. When Andrea had married Dominic, she had only just turned nineteen and he was well into his forties, but he had the money and she had the looks. Now she was older and virtually unrecognisable as the girl she used to be, except when she was with Adrian. As for Dominic, the silver glints in his hair had all but taken over and his skin was a rich walnut colour, leathery but well moisturised, the traces of pitted skin still evident, like a used tea bag. Adrian still looked young for his age, and he was only thirty-two. He wondered whether Andrea ever regretted the decisions she'd made. He was glad that the worst of the animosity between them had gone, but couldn't help wondering whether if he were to turn on the charm, she might one day fall for it. But maybe he was just kidding himself. Maybe there really was nothing left but friendship.

Adrian walked back into the hospital to find that Irene was still in surgery. Imogen sat in a room on her own, her head in her hands. She looked up as Adrian walked through the door, a mixture of grief and guilt written all over her face. He sat down next to her and folded his arms. Neither of them spoke for a few minutes, until Imogen finally broke the silence.

'What was your dad like?' she asked, out of nowhere. It was not something they'd ever discussed before. It certainly wasn't a welcome topic for Adrian.

'He wasn't a good person.'

'In my head, my father was a prince, or a noble man who absolutely couldn't be with us because of some insurmountable obstacle. Over the years I built him up in my mind as something bigger than human, as some kind of spirit. I don't know what to make of all this. I can't imagine that the person I had in my head would do something so utterly heinous to my mum.'

'There'll be an explanation, Grey, and we will find it. But you can't think about that right now.'

'I saw your face when you watched Sam hitting Bridget on that video tape. I got the impression you'd seen shit like that before.'

'You're not wrong. My dad was always pretty generous with his discipline.'

'Do you think you would've been happier without a father?'

'There were plenty of times when I wished he was dead, but no. I think it's better to have known him than always wondered.'

'Better the devil you know than the devil you don't,' she said before standing up and running her hands through her hair. Her actions were quick, almost manic. 'I don't even know how to find him without her. I mean, I know my mum was unstable, but all these years she's talked about this man like he was the bloody second coming.'

'When she wakes up we'll see what she has to say, yeah?' Adrian offered. Imogen wasn't one to ponder the 'what ifs' and 'could have beens' – this was a new side to her that he hadn't witnessed before.

'You mean *if* she wakes up?'

'I think it would be naïve to assume this isn't connected to the baby, Grey, but that doesn't mean it was him, right? The crime scene techs are at your mother's place now. You know if there is any evidence there they will find it.'

'I always thought she was indestructible. She's done so many crazy things over the years and been fine. I just can't believe this has happened.'

'Now come on, Grey, it's not like you to give up. We'll get to the bottom of this. I'm going to put the TV on and then I'll go see if I can find anything out for you, OK?'

'Adrian, when I left Plymouth I never thought I would trust anyone again. But I trust you.'

Adrian smiled, unsure how to respond, and patted her on the back before reaching for the remote. He flicked through all five of the channels, but as the screen flickered into life, it became clear that everything had been interrupted for a special broadcast. Both detectives sat forward on the hard hospital chairs.

On the screen flashed footage of Isabelle Hobbs' parents, sitting together on a couch, imploring the public for any news on their daughter. A banner ran across the bottom of the image: HOBBS' PARENTS CLEARED OF ISABELLE'S MURDER.

'Jesus,' Adrian said. 'They had to clear them after finding Cassandra. Those poor people.'

The strain of the years in prison was evident on both of them, but they held hands tightly and even without the volume turned up, Adrian knew what they were saying. The desperation was written all over their faces. They were currently trying to get custody of their grand-daughter – cue shot of the adorable little girl. Adrian shook his head. This little girl seemed to be the key; she was connected to Imogen, and she was most likely the reason Irene lay in surgery as they watched TV in the next room.

He glanced over at Imogen, who looked distraught and exhausted. It seemed there was no way of escaping the case, not even for a moment. Adrian was just about to turn the TV off and suggest a coffee when the aged reconstruction of Isabelle Hobbs appeared on the screen. The image had been released to the press. Adrian had forgotten about it amidst all the chaos surrounding the attack on Irene. He always thought these computer programs were just to make the public think you were doing something rather than sitting on your hands. It was rare to find anyone who had gone missing after forty-eight hours, let alone more than twelve years. They showed the face of the girl they were looking for. Adrian's stomach dropped.

'What is it, Adrian? You look like you've seen a ghost,' Imogen said, but Adrian couldn't answer, he could barely even breathe.

Chapter 33: The Girl

The present

Adrian couldn't tear his eyes away from the screen. There she was. Isabelle Hobbs. He felt his throat closing and his Adam's apple triple in weight as he tried to swallow. Her long black hair and big brown eyes were unmistakable. It was Eva, his Eva. The girl from the shop on his road, the girl he'd taken to visiting. His friend.

'Well?' Imogen's voice surprised him, reminding him that he wasn't in fact alone in the room. He debated whether to tell her or not, but the words spilled out. He raised his hand and pointed at the screen, at the image of Eva with the phone number underneath it.

'I know her! I fucking know her! Jesus, Grey! How could I have been so stupid?' His breathlessness had turned to panting now and he could feel the adrenaline coursing through his veins. 'I can't believe this. I've stared at her face so many times and I've always felt there was something familiar about it, but I just ignored it and carried on.'

'Oh my God, Miley, you didn't sleep with her, did you?'

'No.' He paused, feeling sick. He remembered them running in the rain, her hand in his. Shame washed over him. How had he been so blind? Why hadn't she said something? He saw Imogen's eyes open wide with incredulity as if she thought he was lying. 'No. I swear to God I haven't.'

'Do you know where she is now?' Imogen asked him.

'Yes, I think I do.'

'I'm calling this in. Where is she?'

'Literally round the corner from my house. She lives in the corner shop.'

'She lives in the shop? You didn't think that was weird?'

'Can we argue about this later? I need to go get her . . .'

'Oh, I'm coming with you.'

'But your mum needs you.'

'She won't be out of surgery for a few hours and you shouldn't be alone when we pick her up. You're in enough shit as it is. If anyone finds out you knew her whereabouts . . .'

'I swear I had no idea it was her.'

'I believe you, Miley, but you need to think about how to play this, because if anyone gets wind of this then your career is over. The second they realise you've been speaking to her for weeks there will be all kinds of theories on what your involvement is. The media will fucking crucify you.' She opened the door and pushed Adrian out into the hallway. She looked around, presumably to check nobody was listening to them.

Adrian knew she was right. He followed her. 'I don't even know what I'm going to say when they ask me about it. Maybe I should phone in an anonymous tip.'

'No way, we need to stick to the truth as much as we can,' she said. He could hear her brain ticking over as she spoke. 'We need someone who's good at lying.'

'Who do you have in mind?'

'Walk and talk, Miley.'

Adrian braced himself as Grey pummelled her foot on the brake, stopping the car outside the corner shop. He slammed his hands on the dashboard and just about managed to stop himself going through the windscreen. It was dark, and the shop looked empty, but then it always did.

'What do we do now?'

'We wait for Sam, he's on his way. We need a witness and he'll know the right thing to say.'

'I suck at lying, Grey.'

'You don't have to lie. You just have to word things carefully.' She looked at her watch. 'Are you completely sure it's her?'

'I'm sure. It's not just the picture. When you meet her, you'll see it. I don't know why I didn't realise before.'

'Come on! Why would you? Everyone thought she was dead.' She pulled out her cigarettes and offered one to Adrian; he took it, lit it and got out of the car. He couldn't stay sitting there while they waited for Sam, so he walked over to the shop and cupped his hands over the glass to look inside. Nothing. The windows were dark.

He concentrated on the cigarette. Imogen was right; he couldn't just go bursting in there. For the first time since he'd realised who Eva was, he really thought about what this meant. He thought about Eva and the life she must have led. His heart felt heavy as he wondered whose child she'd had, and how old she must have been if the child they had found was hers – she must have been around sixteen. He felt like this was his mess. Why did he feel so responsible? Because he knew, had always known that something about Eva wasn't quite right. The way she stayed so late in the shop. The nerves that were apparent whenever they spoke. The way she talked about a bad ex-boyfriend, the look she got when she mentioned the owner Dimi.

Adrian had always told himself that she had the keys to the shop and could leave whenever she wanted to. He'd convinced himself that she chose to stay there. He shook his head. Anyone who had ever dealt with a case of extreme abuse would have known that it's not that simple. Maybe it had been pure selfishness on his part, because he'd liked spending time alone with her and hadn't wanted anything to change that. He had heard of cases like this before, where long-term imprisonment had led to obedience from the captive. He thought about Dimi, the pushy old man who could sell ice to an Eskimo – was he behind this? A car horn beeped and Adrian turned round to see Sam Brown pull in with DCI Fraser. Imogen got out of the car, looking annoyed.

'What the hell, Sam?'

'Hi,' Fraser said, almost apologetically.

'I brought Fraser because we all need to be straight,' Sam said. 'As soon as we get this girl back, we aren't going to get a chance to talk.'

'Can I knock on the door now?' Adrian's stomach was twisted with nerves.

'Look, Miles, we just need to tell the truth here,' Sam said. 'You were working undercover on a human trafficking case and you were trying to get information on the operation for us. That's not a lie, it just doesn't necessarily relate to this – but the press don't know that. Anything else, you just say it's an ongoing investigation and you don't have clearance to discuss it. OK?'

'We've got your back, Adrian,' Fraser offered.

Adrian stubbed his cigarette out and knocked on the glass door. No movement. He hoped to God she was still there. He knocked harder this time, and saw a shadow move towards the glass. Eva appeared in the door frame. She looked taken aback when she saw the others standing behind him, but he just nodded for her to let him in.

'Adrian?' The other officers hovered behind him. Eva's eyes were wide.

'Eva, I need to ask you something, OK?'

'OK. Who are these people?'

'They're people I work with, don't worry.'

'Hi,' Imogen said, and Eva's face softened. She sucked

in a deep breath. She obviously understood the serious-
ness of the situation.

There was no easy way to say this. Adrian took a
deep breath.

'Is your real name Isabelle Hobbs?'

As the name left his mouth he saw the tears forming
in her eyes; they spilled over her cheeks and she let out
a sob of emotion, bursting forward out of the shop and
into Adrian's arms. He felt the weight of her sink into
him, and put his arms around her carefully, aware of
his colleagues watching. She was crying hard. Adrian
settled his arms more tightly around her and caught
Imogen's eye. Her expression was that of shock, and
for once, she seemed stuck for anything sarcastic to say.

Chapter 34: The Player

The present

After heavy questioning and an interrogation that made Adrian's skin crawl, he headed back to the hospital to find Imogen, who after finding Isabelle had gone back to see Irene.

He felt awful; disappointed in himself, disgusted at his very nature. Deep down he had known that Eva was someone in trouble, but because he'd wanted to keep her to himself he had buried his misgivings. He was selfish. He had ignored her situation entirely because it didn't benefit him to pay attention to it. The anchor in his stomach pulled him down, the physical feeling of his insides making their revulsion known. Surplus energy ran through his veins with a dull pulse.

'Whatever you're thinking, Adrian, stop it!'

'Huh?' Adrian looked up to see that Imogen had found him first. 'How's your mum?'

'Still in surgery. She's not going to be ready for visitors for a while. I don't know if I can just sit here and wait. What's the news on your friend?'

'She's getting a full check-up and they need to conduct some interviews before I'm allowed to see her again. My rep says it's a better idea if I don't have any contact until all the smoke blows over. It may be some time.'

'It's for the best, Miley, you need to be cleared so you can get back on the case.'

'We can stay here, I don't mind waiting with you. It's not like I'm getting any sleep tonight, well, what's left of tonight, anyway.' He could feel her eyes on him; he wasn't sure if it was pity but at the very least it was some kind of sympathy, which didn't make him feel any less pathetic.

'Nah. Come on, Miley, you're a mess. I don't know about you but I need a drink!'

'I don't need a babysitter, Grey.'

'No, but maybe I do. I don't really want to be alone right now, and I don't want to stay here.'

Self-absorbed, narcissistic. The world doesn't revolve around you. At times like this Adrian's father's voice was clear in his head, reminding him exactly where he belonged, exactly what he was. Nothing.

They drove home from the hospital together. Adrian flung the door to his house open and headed straight for the bottle of whisky standing on the kitchen counter. Right now, what he needed was to get drunk. Imogen shut the door behind them and Adrian immediately handed her a tumbler, full almost to the brim.

'Have you got any beer instead?' Imogen asked.

'In the fridge,' he said and gulped down the contents of the whisky glass for her, welcoming the warm dry honey. He put her empty glass down and then started on his own. He finished that one as quickly as the first, making sure he had time to pour himself another before Imogen turned back from the fridge. He went through to the living room and slumped on to the sofa, kicking his shoes off as he did so.

He could feel the anger building inside of him; whisky did that, turned his self-loathing into anger, made him more comfortable. He thought of Eva in the hospital, alone. Until they had conducted the preliminary investigation, he wasn't allowed any details on where she was. They needed to know if he was involved, if he had trafficked her. The thought of it made him sick. He'd explained what had happened and, thanks to DI Brown corroborating his story, he'd so far managed to avoid any official action. They asked him all of the questions he would have asked himself if he were conducting an interview, even the unpleasant ones.

He was uncomfortable at the thought of the psychologists probing Eva, finding out exactly how damaged she was. It was difficult to think of her as Isabelle. He thought about her parents, how they must be feeling at the news. He wanted to be with her when she met them, hold her hand and make sure she was OK. He could at least try to make it easier for her. He couldn't even bring himself to think about how long she might have been kept in the corner shop, stuck under the rule of Dimi or whoever was controlling him. He wondered if she would be reunited with her baby. Would she even want to be?

'You need to stop torturing yourself.' Imogen touched him on the arm.

'Are you sure about that?'

'You didn't know, Miley, and downing a bottle of whisky won't change that.'

'It's better than thinking about her. Why didn't she say anything?'

'When did you meet her?'

'Last year, in the shop, and then she was nice to me a few times after that. Now I sometimes go and see her when I know she's alone.'

'And you didn't . . . do anything?'

'No. I did kiss her once though. God, I feel like such a twat!'

'Well, I won't argue with you there, Miley . . . but you did save her, just focus on that.'

'I wish it were that simple.'

'It is.' Imogen clinked her bottle against his tumbler. 'Thanks to you she can rebuild her life, meet her baby and finally be with her parents.'

He knocked back the drink; another step towards at least temporary oblivion. He wanted his brain to switch off; for the guilt to dissipate. Imogen poured him another then finished her beer. She got up and walked to the kitchen. Adrian called after her.

'How are you holding up, anyway?'

'My mum is a nightmare, but I love her. It was always just me and her and the idea of her not being there any more . . .' Her voice cracked and Adrian got up as she re-entered the room and walked to her, putting his hand on her shoulder, then moving down her arm and holding on to her hand. She shook the tears away and lost the sad expression almost immediately. She wiped her cheek with the back of her free hand.

Adrian moved a strand of hair gently out of her eyes. For a moment, they looked at each other, and he saw her eyes flick fleetingly to his mouth. Quickly, Adrian kissed her on the forehead, then moved back to the sofa before anyone did anything stupid. He cleared his throat.

'She's going to pull through. From what I saw and from what you've said, your mum is one tough cookie. She's a survivor.'

'You're right.'

'Do you want me to make you something to eat? It might make you feel better.'

'I have a better idea.' Imogen reached for the Xbox racing game on the coffee table. 'I think thrashing you at this might cheer me up nicely.'

He picked up the controller and tried to push all thoughts of Eva out of his mind.

Chapter 35: The Victim

Plymouth, two years earlier

It wasn't an interrogation room, but it would have to do. Imogen and Sam sat at George's bedside waiting for him to wake up. After finding him in her house, Imogen had called the ambulance, unable to live with the man's death on her conscience. Plus, she wanted to question him good and proper.

George's head was still a state and apparently he had several breaks to the actual infrastructure of his skull, so it would be very painful for him to talk. He was hooked up to a morphine drip and handcuffed to the bed, although from what Imogen could see, he wouldn't be running anywhere anytime soon. His legs were bruised and his ribs were cracked. Dean had really done a number on him.

George swallowed hard and looked at Imogen. 'I gave the girls the drugs, but I just had them for personal use. I'm not a dealer.' His voice was slurred.

'Where did you get the drugs?'

'I want a lawyer.'

'There's a brief on his way, but for right now, we need to get that crap off the streets. You know, you don't look like a junkie.'

'There's no more of it anyway. I only used it when I liked to party, with girls, you know.'

'How many girls?' Imogen leaned forward.

'That stuff wasn't even mine. I didn't give it to Nancy! She just took it!'

'What about the other girl?'

'Monica?'

'Monica? Is that the girl's name?' Imogen asked. She could see George kicking himself; clearly that was a piece of information he wasn't meant to have let slip.

'Yes,' he said, clenching his jaw, wincing in pain.

'Where was she from? What was her surname?'

'She had an accent, but I don't know. Told me to call her Monica, but she said it wasn't her real name. When we were alone I was allowed to call her Binky, she was Binkowicz or something, I don't know, something foreign. Eastern European, maybe. She's the one who gave me the drugs.'

'Where did you meet her?'

'Please, I don't know anything else.' He started to wheeze and cough, and a doctor swiftly appeared.

'I'm afraid you'll have to go now, Detectives, he needs to rest,' the doctor said.

'You know this scumbag is responsible for the death of two teenage girls?' Imogen snapped at him.

'First do no harm.' The doctor smiled falsely at Imogen, recusing himself from any responsibility.

As they walked out of the hospital, Imogen turned to Sam.

'Do you think we have enough to get a warrant for the club? He's admitted to giving them the stuff, they both had the stamps and he worked there, so we know they were in Aphrodite's at some point.'

'If we get the right judge we can get a warrant. I know who to go to. I'll meet you back at the station. You go clear it with Stanton.'

DCI Stanton was on the phone when Imogen returned to work. He still had that stern look about him. She knocked on his office door and waited as he finished his call before ushering her in.

'Sam's getting a warrant for us to search Aphrodite's. I just wanted to let you know.'

Stanton stared at her. 'What's going on with you, Imogen?'

'Nothing, what do you mean?'

'I mean, I'm sensing something off between us, and you're like a dog with a bone on this case. Is it this Kinkaid character? Did you fuck him?'

'What? No!' She was shocked to hear the words come out of his mouth; they were never usually that forthright with each other. In all the years she had worked for him, she'd never seen him jealous like this. He was practically spitting at her.

'I made Nancy Baggott's parents a promise, David, that's all. I said I would catch whichever bastard did this. George is no criminal mastermind, the drugs had to come from somewhere and he's not giving us anything to go on. I don't know what the deal is with this Elias character, but he's got money all right. His house, his boat, everything about him screams criminal, and yet on paper he seems to be squeaky clean. I know he's doing something bad, and if it's the drugs then I need to know so that I can give the Baggott family some kind of closure, because I can't give them their daughter back.'

Imogen didn't even notice the tears streaking down her cheeks until she'd finished speaking. She saw Stanton's hard face change to that of comfort and sympathy.

'Imogen, you look tired, you should get some rest. Sam doesn't need you there for the raid on the club, and you clearly need some sleep. Promise me you'll rest.'

'OK, thank you. I don't know why this case is getting to me so much.'

'Go home, yeah?'

She wasn't lying; she didn't know why she was so emotional. She got in the car and started the engine. Really, she wanted to go and meet Sam at the club but the way she was feeling right now, she wasn't sure if she could trust herself to carry out a raid.

Imogen remembered the sensation of being on the boat, the sickness, the sight of Elias winking at her after she threw up. Her thoughts were spinning. A thought had been nagging at her, and she couldn't ignore it any longer.

Could she be pregnant? Is that what these weird

feelings were? It would help explain the sickness, and help explain why she felt as though everything inside her was slightly tilted, off, not working as normal. Stanton's face flashed into her mind, the memory of him pushing her back against the bookcase that night. She couldn't remember if she was late or not, but Imogen knew she had to get a pregnancy test. She had to face up to this now.

She drove straight to the chemist's and pulled up outside, even though it was a no parking zone. She dashed in and grabbed as many tests as she could carry, from the most expensive one to the cheapest; she didn't care, she just wanted to be sure. In her heart she felt as though she already knew, she knew she was pregnant. It was as if the answer had been staring at her all along, and it wasn't until now that she was finally acknowledging it to herself.

At home, Imogen went straight to the bathroom, threw the bag with the tests on to the floor and pulled her trousers off. She was desperate for the toilet anyway. She ripped open four of the boxes and pulled out the sticks, sat down and peed on them before lining them up on the side of the bath. She tried to remember how long it had been since her last period. It felt like a while; they had always been erratic and she never paid much attention. She pulled her shirt off and looked in the mirror. She stood to the side but saw no change. The minutes passed. Imogen lowered her gaze to the row of tests, a strange sense of calm enveloping her. They all said what she already knew: she was pregnant.

Tears formed in her eyes. She was the same age as her mother had been when she'd fallen pregnant with Imogen; she was finally becoming Irene. Imogen had never wanted kids, had always had a horror of becoming her mother: bitter, crazy and alone. But then there was Stanton. If she had this baby, she would always have a part of him, she could make sure that he always had to be in her life. Well aware that she was thinking like a lunatic, she threw all of the tests in the bin and went to bed.

Imogen awoke to the sound of the doorbell. She grabbed her dressing gown and went downstairs. It was dark out so she looked at the clock; she had been asleep for five hours. She opened the door to find Sam standing there. Surprised, she pulled her dressing gown a little closer together.

'Sam?'

'I thought I'd bring you the good news myself.'

'You found something?'

'No, I was being sarcastic: there is no good news.'

'Oh, OK then.'

'I brought you a burger.' He handed her a crumpled brown paper bag. She knew what had happened, he had bought himself three or four burgers on the way over and then felt guilty and saved her one. She didn't care though; she really wanted a damn burger. She took the burger out and took a big bite; it suddenly felt like the best thing she had ever tasted.

'You're my hero.'

'What's going on with you, Grey? You're all over the place.'

'You really want to know?' Fuck it, she was just going to tell him. 'I'm pregnant.'

'No shit?'

'No shit. Don't tell anyone, and I mean anyone,' she said as she shoved the burger hungrily into her mouth.

'You don't hang around, do you? I only just found out you weren't available any more and now you tell me you're in the family way. Way to let a guy down gently.'

'Oh God, don't say it that way, it sounds so . . . well, wrong.'

'The idea of being with me that bad?' He stared at her; she tried to ignore the genuine look of hurt on his face.

'Stop being silly.' She wiped her mouth on her sleeve. 'So how was the raid?'

'The place wasn't even dusty. Nothing whatsoever out of place. Forensics checked the bathrooms and there wasn't even the usual trace on the cisterns. Nothing, zero, nada, zip.'

'You think they were tipped off?'

'I expect they knew it was coming, yes. The Baggott family have been making a lot of noise in the media and they must have known George was the only lead we really had.'

'Did you go back and see him?'

'Yeah, he's going to cut a deal, but he wants some kind of assurance that he'll be protected, he's terrified of someone. My guess is it's your boyfriend.'

'What?'

'Kinkaid. He worked him over nicely.'

'Oh, yeah. Probably. He's pretty terrifying.' Imogen rolled her eyes, chewing the last bite of burger. She was still hungry. 'He's also not my boyfriend.'

'So what now? Got any other ideas?'

'I should talk to Kinkaid again, see if he knows who George's supplier is.'

'Any excuse, huh?'

'You want some pizza?' She grabbed the phone and started dialling. At least with a baby inside her she could justify eating for two.

Chapter 36: The Club

Plymouth, two years earlier

Morning sickness was no joke. Since Imogen had confirmed the news, the only time she could stop thinking about puking was when she was actually being sick. She finally got her head out of the toilet at about ten, and only then because she'd booked an appointment at a private clinic to talk through her options and didn't want to miss it. She wasn't sure what difference it would make, but she felt as though she ought to see someone professional before things got too far along.

Should she explore the idea of an abortion? It wasn't something she thought she'd be able to go through with, but if she considered the different options she'd at least be able to tell Stanton that she'd done so. God, would she even tell him? She hadn't decided. She sat in the waiting room of the clinic until someone came to get her. It felt as though it had been hours, but further examination of the clock showed it to have been less than twenty minutes.

'Ms Brown,' the nurse called out. Imogen grimaced at the sound of it, but Brown was the only name she'd been able to think of on the spot.

She was led into an ultrasound room. The nurse gestured to the narrow blue bed; Imogen lay down and the woman unceremoniously lifted up her top. She pushed Imogen's stomach a few times before squeezing what felt like liquid nitrogen on to her abdomen. Imogen shivered; it was so cold.

The nurse smiled and put a handheld scanner on to Imogen's stomach. She moved it around until Imogen could see a flickering blob of white noise on the screen.

'There he is!'

'He?'

'Figure of speech, dear. Is this your first one?'

'Can you tell me how long I've been pregnant?'

'I would say you're roughly seven weeks along. The baby is about the size of a blueberry now. You're a healthy-looking girl. Everything looks and sounds normal.'

Imogen began to cry.

'Sorry,' she sniffled.

'Don't worry, dear, it's all good.' The nurse handed her a tissue from the box on the table; she obviously got a lot of criers in here.

When Imogen left the clinic, the crying got worse. Was this her hormones stepping up a gear? This whole

284

situation was so new that she wasn't sure how she felt. There was a part of her, a tiny part, that felt elated. If she was honest with herself, she had hoped for this on some level, hoped that something would happen to force Stanton's hand. She would find out how much she really meant to him at last.

She decided to drive past the club on the off-chance Dean was there. She felt a strong need to speak to him. Was it to thank him for bringing her George? As broken and bloody as he was, it was still one of the best gifts she had ever received. It sure as hell beat a bunch of flowers or a box of chocolates. As she approached the turning to Aphrodite's she noticed Sam's car, parked on a side road; he must have had the same idea she had. She pulled up just past the club and got out of the car. Just as she did so, she heard raucous laughter and turned to see Sam coming out of the club, Vasos' arm firmly around his shoulder. She stared at them in shock, then dashed quickly into the club's car park, hiding behind a parked van to see if she could hear the tail end of their conversation.

'Thank you for letting me know about George, Detective. I didn't think he was stupid enough to talk. What about that other matter?' Vasos' voice sounded jovial, familiar.

'Don't worry about her, I'll take care of her,' Sam replied. 'I can make her go away, shut that case down. You'll be in the clear. But I might need something in return.'

What the hell did that mean? Sam was obviously talking about her. *Take care of her* how?

'If you don't, Detective, then I'll have to speak to someone with a little more influence, if you know what I'm saying. She's become a very big problem.'

'She's not going to be a problem, Vasos. Leave her to me. She seems to have developed some kind of friendship with your mate Kinkaid though; he's a bit of a wild card here.'

'Kinkaid isn't going to be a problem for much longer. After the business with George, we've decided to part ways.'

'What's going to happen to George?'

'Don't you worry about that, Detective. Disloyalty is not something my boss takes lightly. If you can really make sure the spotlight moves away from me, away from the club, then we will direct you towards some solid evidence that links the drugs back to both Michalis and George. They'll go to jail without argument, or else they'll suffer the consequences. Let's just say I'll be taking care of two birds with one stone, maybe even three.' He laughed.

Imogen leaned in to hear more, accidentally triggering the alarm on the van. The sound was deafening and she hoped to God Sam didn't notice her car parked on the road. She heard the club door close, and when she looked again Sam was walking back down the side street. Her head was spinning. This was not happening. *Vasos and Sam? And Michalis was behind the drugs?*

Imogen waited a few moments to make sure they weren't coming back then slowly edged out from behind the van. She realised as she looked down that she'd been clenching her fists. Getting back into the car, she drove straight to the hospital to check on George. When she arrived, the nurses were floundering at his bedside. She snuck a peek into the room and took a quick step back, her hand to her mouth. George was covered in blood, his body slashed open. He was gargling and convulsing and the machines were going haywire as the nurses and doctors hurried around him in futility. As the familiar sound of a long, slow, continuous beep penetrated the atmosphere, Imogen approached one of the nurses; she was white as a sheet.

'What the hell happened?'

'No one saw anything . . . someone must have got into his room.'

'Do you have cameras?'

'Not in this part of the hospital.'

'How long ago did this happen?'

'It was only two minutes between the alarms and the call. I don't see how anyone could survive a wound like that, even if we were standing right here. He was cut in both the carotid and femoral arteries.'

'I'm guessing that's twice as bad as just one artery?'

'Your heart pumps blood out through the arteries, if one is cut then your heart is basically pushing all of the blood out of your body. It's killing you.'

Suspecting she was too late, Imogen ran through the corridors and to the nearest exit. She felt like she had to do something. She pulled out her mobile phone and called Stanton. Thirty minutes earlier she would have called Sam in this situation, but now she knew she couldn't trust him.

'I'm at the hospital. George the barman is dead.'

'Was it Kinkaid?' Stanton replied coolly.

Imogen remembered Vasos' comment to Sam about killing two birds with one stone. Whether it was Dean or not, she had a feeling he would be taking the fall for this one. Her mind worked quickly; Dean was in danger and some part of her wanted to protect him, even though he was more than capable of looking out for himself. She felt as though she owed him one after the horrible incident in the club. She had to go find him.

'David, I need you to give me Kinkaid's address.'

She rushed to her car and pulled out as fast as she could without killing any of the smokers who were gathered in the corner of the parking lot with their wheelchairs and their drips. An old man with an oxygen tube running across his nose attached to a canister sucked joylessly on a cigarette. She wondered if he knew how flammable pure oxygen was. She wondered if he cared.

Dean's house was not what she expected. It was a Victorian-style house with a nicely kept front lawn and garden gnomes dotted about in what looked like a very organised, deliberate design.

She knocked on the door and rang the doorbell impatiently. It was quiet in this part of town, too quiet. There were no cars on the street, no people walking around. It felt like a ghost town. She was expecting the police sirens at any moment. The blinds were drawn but the lights were on, the TV was blaring loudly. She banged harder on the door and saw the outline of someone walking towards it through the toughened glass. The door opened, but the figure standing there wasn't Dean. Before Imogen had time to react, the world went black.

Chapter 37: The Blade

Plymouth, two years earlier

Imogen's head was splitting, her arms hurt and her eyes struggled to adjust to the half-light. She wanted to rub the sleep from her eyes but she was bound, her hands suspended above her head. She could hear laughter and realised it was the television. She looked down and saw she was on her knees in her underwear, on the floor of Dean's house. A sinking feeling hit her. She wondered how long she had been out, what they had done while she was unconscious. Finally, she adjusted to the light and saw Dean sitting opposite her. At first, she wondered why he wasn't moving but then she saw the blood and the ropes. His head was lolling to one side. Vasos the comedian was behind him, pulling at some of the knots. He looked over and noticed Imogen looking at them.

'Don't worry, it's not his blood.' A younger man

appeared from the corner of the room: Giannis. He had been in Aphrodite's the day Dean had cut off Vasos' finger, but Imogen hadn't noticed him here today. There was an awkwardness about him, a strain to his voice that made him sound vulnerable, somehow. She looked at his hand. He was holding a knife.

'Are you going to kill us?' Imogen said.

'You sound a bit hoarse, Detective. Can I get you a drink?' Vasos smiled and grabbed a glass filled with clear liquid from the table. It was standing next to a vodka bottle.

Imogen was so thirsty; she longed for water. But the liquid that touched her lips was straight vodka, sharp and strong. Vasos grabbed her nose and held it as he forced her to drink the whole glass. She choked it down and felt the liquid immediately rising to the surface again. Vasos grabbed the vodka bottle and poured some over Dean's head. Dean coughed and woke up.

'Imogen,' he said, struggling to find his voice. He was badly beaten. 'I'm so sorry.'

She heard the sound of a phone beeping and saw Vasos checking his messages.

'We need to get going.' Giannis sounded nervous.

'Why is Elias doing this?' Imogen asked.

'I'm not taking my orders from Elias today,' Vasos said. He held out his hand, and Giannis handed him the knife. The steel blade already had blood on it; she guessed it was probably George's. Vasos was wearing latex gloves; she saw the slack in the rubber where his finger was missing.

'Come on, we have to go!' Giannis said.

'Help me with her then.' Vasos jerked his head at Imogen.

'What are you going to do?' Dean asked.

'We're going to frame you for the detective's murder.'

'Wait, no, don't hurt her!' Dean said. 'I'll do whatever you want. Please.'

Imogen saw Dean's teeth clench as he said it. There was something in his voice, something that sounded a lot like acquiescence. His chest heaved as he struggled against his ropes, desperate to get free.

'That's real sweet, but we have our orders, Deano. She's toast.'

'If you do this, you're dead. Now I know you're not allowed to kill me, I have contingencies set in place in the event of my death. So with me alive, if you do this, if you kill her, I'm coming for you.'

'Big talk for a man who's about to go down for double murder.'

'Vasos, I have more friends in fucking prison than you do full stop. You think I'm going to be doing any kind of hard time? No. I'm going to be the fucking king in there; they all owe me, or they know someone who owes me. I'm a very popular guy.'

Vasos looked exasperated. He huffed and looked at Giannis.

'I have my orders.'

'Orders, my backside. She stays alive, or you die. Don't you understand, I can get to you! Prison doesn't change that!'

'Are you the baby-daddy?' Vasos laughed. 'Are you the one that knocked the pretty detective up?' Imogen

292

felt sick. How could he know? *Sam*. He was the only one she had told.

She could see the anger flash across Dean's face. Was he angry that she was pregnant? Or was he angry at how they were treating her?

Imogen looked up at Vasos. Her heart was hammering. She pictured Sam walking with Vasos, heard their laughter in her ears. Betrayed didn't even cover what she was feeling right now.

'Vasos, have you cleared this with Elias? You need to put that fucking knife down,' Dean said in a very calm voice. It was chilling. He didn't sound like a man who was in the weaker position, he sounded like the man with all the power. She couldn't imagine how his performance could possibly work; they were planning on killing her anyway. Vasos picked up the bottle again and held her nose as he poured the liquid in. It burned her throat and she felt it hit her stomach, desperate to make its way out again. She thought of the baby inside, the tiny foetus fighting for life. Vasos was laughing.

She realised for the first time that she trusted Dean. Staring at him, she felt a rush of what felt like love. He was looking back at her just as intensely.

'You're right, Deano, I might hurt myself. I should put the knife somewhere safe . . . out of harm's way.' Vasos put the blade against Imogen's skin and moved the knife downwards until he could slide it between her legs, she could feel the hilt of the black handle rubbing against her. He was moving it faster and faster, as though they were lovers and this was some kind of foreplay.

She spat in his face.

'Maybe you'd prefer it if I use my fingers?'

'All three of them?' She smirked at him, determined not to give him the satisfaction of tears. He grabbed the vodka and poured it down her throat again. She spluttered and coughed but welcomed the dizziness it brought. She looked at the knife resting on the carpet next to her legs. If only she could free her hands.

'Come on, that vodka must be loosening you up some, pretty girl.' He slid his hand inside her knickers. His fingers were cold, rough.

'Fuck off,' she hissed.

'I think he likes to watch,' Vasos nodded at Dean. He leaned forward and whispered in Imogen's ear. She could feel his repulsive hot breath on her. He smelled of cooked meats and cigarettes. She tried to ignore the sensation of his hands rubbing her, disgusted at the way her body was betraying her. She tried to think about anything else but what he was doing, embarrassed that she was responding to his touch. She looked over at Dean and saw his anger as he watched Vasos' hand buried between her thighs, deep inside her underwear. Dean saw her looking, he held her gaze for a moment as she tried not to cry and suddenly his expression changed, as though he had come to some sort of decision in his mind.

'You're so dead,' Dean said slowly. 'I should have cut off your whole fucking hand.'

'Shut your mouth, my friend,' Vasos hissed, a smile plastered across his face.

'That's what I'm going to do, you know, I'm going

294

to cut off that fucking hand and shove it down your throat . . . and any other part of you that touches her.'

Imogen allowed herself to sigh with relief as Vasos removed his hand, but the feeling was short-lived when she saw what he was doing now. He reached for his buckle and deftly undid it with one hand, ignoring Dean's words. She had suspected from the moment she met him that he was capable of something like this; sometimes you just got a feeling about people. She could practically hear the vein in Dean's forehead throbbing as he watched helplessly, obviously deciding whether to speak or not. What would make things better? What would make things worse?

Vasos loosened his trousers and smiled at them both. 'I'll give you a choice, pretty girl. You can either have this inside you.' He pushed his hand inside his sagging grey boxers, she could see the form of his semi erection and her stomach lurched. 'Or this.' He held up the knife, right on cue the light hit the bevelled ridges of the blade and it glinted. Not much of a choice, she thought.

'Don't you fucking touch her.' Dean struggled against his bindings some more, still trying to break free.

'I should probably take the knife, at least I'll be able to feel it,' she challenged him.

Before she knew what was happening, the knife was in her stomach. The pain came a few seconds later. Her mother had always said that one day her sarcasm was going to get her into real trouble, but still, Imogen doubted Irene had envisioned a scenario quite like this one. She was surprised at how clean it looked; there were no spurts of blood. The knife was just nestled in the fat of her stomach as though the handle were glued to her. She could hear the distant sound of Dean screaming something but the words were unrecognisable, they seemed so far away.

'Take him out the back,' Vasos instructed Giannis. 'Just so I don't have to hear his stupid voice any more.'

Giannis punched Dean hard in the face before dragging him out of the room.

Vasos pulled the knife out and the blood started to trickle out, slowly at first, then faster. She was wearing pale white underwear; the blood spread slowly across the fabric as she watched helplessly. Vasos grabbed the vodka and poured it in her mouth again. This time she drank. Her vision was starting to blur. She watched him pick the knife up again. She longed for more alcohol as she saw the tip of the blade travel up her body. She heard the clunk of the front door closing before everything went black.

Chapter 38: The Host

The present

Adrian was at Tom's birthday party, well into his fourth Pimm's by the time Andrea came and said hello. There wasn't a colour in existence that didn't make her look like some kind of goddess, she wore an electric-blue summer dress and yet somehow the vibrant silk looked dull against her skin. His phone buzzed in his pocket again; he knew it was Gary, this was the second message he had left unread. He couldn't look at it now: Andrea was approaching.

'It means a lot that you could come.'

'Thanks for inviting me.'

'Have you seen Tom yet?'

'No, where is he?'

'In his room. Go up if you want, he's got his mates up there, they're all on the Xbox, killing stuff no doubt.'

'Which is his room?'

'Oh.' Andrea looked somewhat embarrassed, obviously realising that Adrian had never been upstairs in this house before. 'It's the last door on the right, got a skull and crossbones poster on it.'

'I'll just go up then?' Adrian checked, not wanting to misunderstand the situation here. He didn't need it thrown back in his face at a later date.

'Tell him we're doing the cake soon, would you?'

Adrian looked around the house as he walked up the curved staircase on to the mezzanine landing, noting the pretentious abstract art and wondering how much each piece was worth. In terms of investments, he was almost certain some of his nerdy toys from when he was a kid were a sounder acquisition. He found the door to Tom's room and knocked before going in to find Tom and his friends sitting around a massive TV screen with controllers in their hands.

'Happy birthday, mate!' Adrian said.

Tom looked up and smiled when he saw his dad, instantly dropping the controller. He hugged Adrian and then pushed him out of the room on to the landing.

'Did you find anything out? About Dominic, I mean?'

'Not yet, although it doesn't look like he was having an affair.'

'Oh.' Tom was visibly relieved.

'Yeah, well, something's up, we just haven't figured out what it is yet. Most likely some creative accounting to avoid taxes or something, a lot of people do it. You shouldn't worry about it.'

'I got hold of this for you.' Tom reached into his

pocket and pulled out a key. 'It's the key to his office. No one's ever allowed in there, not even the cleaner.'

'You guys have a cleaner?'

'Yup. But listen; Mum's not allowed in there either. No one is.'

'Where is it?'

Tom pointed at a door on the other side of the landing before slipping back into his bedroom. Adrian's curiosity wasn't going to allow him to walk away without having a look. He wouldn't stay too long and he wouldn't pick any locks, just have a poke around in the obvious places. He knew it was a betrayal of Andrea's new-found trust for him, but this affected his son. If Dominic was into anything dodgy then he needed to know. He'd already run Dominic's name through the police database systems, but nothing had come up. Whatever Dominic was, he wasn't stupid.

The door opened with ease and, considering the room wasn't visited by a cleaner, Adrian was struck by how sparse it was. It looked almost unused. There was, however, a thin layer of dust on every surface, apart from the desk which looked pretty clean.

Something was off about the room. Adrian couldn't figure out what at first, until he put his hand on the wall. It was carpeted. Why would Dominic need a soundproof office? He looked at the door again and saw that it was solid metal, with just a wooden fascia to match the rest of the house. This was almost a panic room. Adrian walked over to the filing cabinet and tried to open it. It was locked. He reached his hand down the side and felt along the back; sure enough, the key was hanging on a hook attached to the unit. He took the key out and unlocked the cabinet. The first drawer was empty, with a pile of suspension files bunched together at the back. He thumbed through them but there wasn't one piece of paper there. He closed the drawer and opened the second one. Same again. Why lock a cupboard with nothing in it? The third and fourth drawers were the same. This was confusing. He opened each drawer again and looked both inside and out. He realised that the drawers were deeper on the outside. Feeling around inside the top one, his fingers caught on something and he tapped. The drawer had a false bottom. He pulled out the sheet of steel and fumbled around underneath it.

Papers. Papers relating to Andrea's neighbours' adoption. What did Dominic have to do with that? Adrian got his phone out and took pictures of the papers one by one, quickly, before putting them back in the drawer. He opened the next drawer, it had the hidden compartment but nothing inside it. The third drawer was the same. He opened the final drawer and lifted up the lid to reveal the secret space. Inside was a leather washbag. He picked it up. It was heavy.

Before his hand even touched the zipper, Adrian knew what was inside. He could feel the shape and the weight through the leather. He took a deep breath and unzipped the bag. He recognised the gun as a Browning Hi-Power, he had come across one or two before. He put the gun back in the cupboard and locked it up before leaving the room.

Downstairs, his son was cutting into his cake as

everyone whooped and cheered. Dominic was standing behind Tom with his hand on his shoulder. Tom rushed over to Adrian when he saw him and Adrian slipped the key back in his hand.

'Find anything?' Tom's voice was low.

'No, but stay out of there, it's not right to go through his stuff.' Adrian didn't want Tom to accidentally find the gun.

'So you think it's just a tax thing, then?'

'Probably. You just enjoy yourself. Whatever it is, it's nothing major. Look, I just got a call from DS Grey, so I need to go. Happy birthday, mate.' The lie came easily.

Dominic walked over with the confident air of someone with a lot of money and a hot wife. He held out his hand and Adrian had to shake it. Dominic was almost a foot taller than Adrian, which was annoying enough in itself, and he always wore that shit-eating grin, exposing his unnaturally white teeth. Add to that the fact that Adrian hated men who wore smart jackets with quirky t-shirts, especially if they were over twenty. He looked like an extra for *Miami Vice*, right down to his tasselled moccasin brogues. Andrea appeared at his side and Dominic immediately put his hand on her shoulder. *My property*. The message was clear.

'Adrian, I want you to meet the Carters.' Andrea smiled at him and nodded to a couple standing a few feet away. Adrian recognised them, they'd appeared in various news articles about their charity work all over the county.

'Stefan!' Dominic called, and the couple smiled. They walked over.

'This is Tom's bio-dad, Adrian.'

'Ah, the police officer! We've heard a lot about you.'

'Detective,' Adrian corrected as he held out his hand. Stefan Carter shook it enthusiastically. Was this just an excuse to parade their semi-famous friends in front of Adrian?

'I'm Felicity Carter. Great to meet you. We heard all about your heroics.'

Adrian blushed. She was very attractive, mid-forties he estimated. She was dressed in beige, with tanned skin and blonde hair, a general golden tone to her from head to toe. He realised he was the one being paraded.

'Just doing my job. Speaking of which . . .'

'Are you off, Adrian?' Dominic said, almost a little too quickly.

'Yes, sorry, I wish I could stay but I have to get back.'

Saying his goodbyes, Adrian walked out of the house and got on his bike. The streets were empty as he cycled home. He couldn't stop thinking about the gun and how to deal with it. So far everything he had done with regards to Dominic was illegal, so he couldn't explain how he'd come across the gun, and he couldn't say that he'd been looking into Dominic's finances either. Aside from anything else, no one would believe he was capable of the technical finesse it would take to get all of that information. He didn't want to get Tunney in trouble. He pulled over on his bike and called him.

'Adrian? What is it?'

'You weren't asleep, were you, Tunney?'

'No, I was playing *Warcraft*.'

'Ha, good stuff. Well listen, I got some more stuff

from Dominic's place. Just photos on my camera, not sure what the resolution is or anything but I did my best.'

'Email them over then. I'll take a look.'

'Thanks, mate, you're a star.'

'I know, I know,' Tunney said, and the phone went dead.

Chapter 39: Loose Threads

Age 23

I am in deep shit. There are so many ways that I'm in trouble that I don't even know where to start.

It all began with Monica, that stupid bitch. I told her to be careful but when my dad found out she was pregnant, he took her away until she had the baby and was made to give it to someone else. I will have to be more careful next time. Dad told me that I should know all about protection by now and not to trust those cunts when they say they are on birth control, and how I should always use rubber because these aren't even his high-end girls and they do some crazy shit with some crazy people. My fists clench when I hear him talk about Monica like that.

My dad gave me some stuff to deliver to one of his contacts, he said it was important that I take it straight there and not fuck around with it, because if I got caught I would go to prison. The thing is though, I went to see Monica first and now I can't find it, or her. I know she took it. If I don't get it back before my father finds out then he'll kill her, he might even kill me.

I go to the club and see if she's there. She isn't, but she was. My uncle brought this guy Kinkaid in to make sure that the club stays on the up and up and he tells me that the pretty boy barman got a call from some girl and then took the afternoon off. I know it was Monica, I just know it. She's always had a thing for George. I hate the way she looks at him; she makes me feel like nothing because she never looks at me that way. I don't like being reminded that she is owned by my father, that she has to do what I say.

The back rooms in the club have been absorbed into the main area now to make more floor space; no more secret fumbles with the girls behind closed doors. My uncle wouldn't allow it. Pretty boy left several hours ago now and I have to take a deep breath to stay calm. I ask Kinkaid if he knows where they went and he said he heard George say they were going to go down to get an education. I know what this means. There's a derelict building in Plymouth that used to be an all-girls' school. It's a huge big grey thing, looks like an old castle or something. It's been shut down for a couple of decades now, you wouldn't think a building could get so fucked up so fast, but it's basically a giant public toilet. The shit of the city go there now to shoot up. Girls get turned over and illegal deals go down, although not so much any more because the cops have a handle on it, but you still get a couple of lowlife stragglers just looking for a place to hang out and fuck. I bet Pretty boy isn't paying for her fucking time, my fucking time.

I get in my car and drive down to the school. I know the way in and I look around for Monica. The place is completely falling apart and it's so big that I don't even know where to start. I don't call out her name because I don't want to warn her I am coming. I'm really angry with her for taking the drugs, and a part of me just wants to leave her to get caught by my dad, but I know I would miss her if she went. She's the only person apart from my sister who is nice to me. I hear a clatter from one of the dormitory rooms followed by the sound of running. I follow the origin of the sound and when I get to the room I find Monica. Her eyes are rolled into the back of her head and she has that strange colour that only dead people have; maybe it's not a colour but an absence of it, dull somehow. I check for a pulse even though I know there's no need. She is dead. I look around for the stuff but she doesn't have it with her. I leave her on the floor and get out. There's nothing I can do for her now. My dad has strictly forbidden me from messing with anything that my uncle deals with and so I can't go after the pretty boy either. I make a mental note that I will deal with him at a later date.

When I get home I'm really tense. My father isn't home yet but it won't be that long until he asks me what's happened to his stuff, he will know already that I didn't take it to where it was supposed to go. I'm so stupid for trusting Monica.

I go to my sister's room because it relaxes me. She asks me if we can go outside, so I take her into the garden. We lie on the red and yellow concrete slabs and look at the sky together. The weather isn't particularly great but I can see this makes her happy. She asks me about the shed and I tell her it's where all the junk is kept. We go inside and look around; there is an old chandelier with all the droplets smashed on the floor beneath it. She picks up some of the crystals and hooks them on her ears, then adds a few more in her hair. She grabs a blue velvet curtain and wraps it over her shoulder. She pretends she is the queen and I am her servant and she orders me around in between laughing. I love her laugh.

She makes the sofa look like a throne with the giant gold sunburst mirror tucked behind it. The gold paint is charred, bubbled and split where it was caught in a fire, but behind Eva's head it looks like a radiant halo. She reminds me of an old painting with her long dark hair trailing down. I call her 'milady', and she laughs even harder. She grabs an old broom and knights me with it as I bow my head at her feet. I look up and the glow from the sunset lights up the mirror behind her in a flash of orange. With the blue of the curtain and the black of her hair she looks like a high priestess, like the God I searched for in the wallpaper. The smile is gone from her face and she leans over to kiss me on the forehead but I lift my head and our lips touch. I know she is not my real sister and so I don't feel so bad. I am more worried that my father may appear at the door. We lie together on the sofa and she lets me touch her under her shirt. I remind myself that she is almost seventeen and so I'm not doing anything wrong. We kiss some more and then we have sex; it's awkward but beautiful. It feels nice. I ask her if she is OK afterwards, because she seems a bit upset. I tell her we have to go inside before my dad gets home, but she won't stop crying. Chances are my dad won't look in her room and so I tell her I will have to lock her in the shed and come back for her later if she doesn't move now. I don't know why she's being so dramatic. She just lies there and so I go inside.

When Dad does finally get home a few hours later, he is angry and I know he's found out that I lost his stuff. He tells me that I had better find it because if anyone takes it they won't last very long. Apparently it needs to be cut down even further because the guy who made it messed up the quantities, which is why my dad got it so cheap. He wanted me to take it to his guy to see what he could do with it. My dad is pretty new at selling drugs, he doesn't really know what he's doing. He says moving girls is getting too dangerous and drugs are a lot easier to hide if something goes wrong. I tell him a lie, I tell him that I left them in a jacket at a friend's house and he believes me, or at least I think he does.

My dad sits in the living room watching TV and tells me to sit with him and watch the boxing that's on later, so there is no chance to go back outside. I know Eva won't make a sound, because she is more afraid of my father than she is of me, but it starts to rain and I feel bad as I think of the noise inside the shed. With its corrugated metal roof it must be loud, and she probably won't get much sleep. At least she has the velvet curtain to keep her warm.

The police are sniffing around the club because they found Monica's body. I managed to get most of the stuff back; George had it in his pocket at work. If I told my dad that, he would be so mad at me. I have to leave it for now. I don't forgive and I don't forget though. George thinks I don't know he was with Monica. I will make sure that he knows I know before I kill him.

My dad has scaled down all of his business dealings while the investigation is happening; his brother is more suspicious than ever and my dad knows Uncle Elias will only give him so many more chances. Forgiveness is rarely unconditional. Uncle Elias has forbidden us from messing with the police. Dad says his police friend has assured us he will make Monica's death go away, he just needs someone to take the fall. It seems obvious to me that George should take the heat but my dad seems to think Kinkaid is a better option. Kinkaid is another person who isn't scared of my father and so my father doesn't trust him. My father doesn't trust anyone he can't manipulate, which is ironic when you think about it, really.

Meathead doesn't like my uncle and so he ignores him about the police, he tries it on with the lady cop and then Kinkaid turns up and cuts his finger off. I have never seen Meathead so scared; I find it quite amusing. At this point Meathead gets a real bee in his *bonnet about the woman and tells my dad that she needs to go and so does Kinkaid. All these men running round with secrets about each other seems a bit juvenile. No one is going to know my secrets but me.*

Chapter 40: The Transfer

Plymouth, two years earlier

Dean Kinkaid sat in his cell, waiting to see his lawyer. His whole body hurt from the beating he had taken from both the Greeks and then the police when they had discovered Detective Imogen Grey bleeding to death on his living room floor. He hadn't so much as had a drink of water for hours, he wasn't sure how long he had been in here. It was amazing how time warped and twisted when you were locked in a room alone. He didn't even know if Imogen was all right. The anger inside him was overwhelming; the helplessness, the complete lack of control. This was the first time he had been in a position where he had something to lose. It had been a long time since he'd last felt this way, which was exactly why he never had relationships. For him, relationships were a sign of weakness.

He cursed himself for being concerned, for caring

about Imogen. His feelings for her had been thrust upon him without warning, and he had become acclimatised to them within an alarmingly short amount of time. He felt unravelled by them. He'd always known his feelings would get him into trouble, and now they had. He should have just stayed as a stone-cold killer.

The lock clicked and the door opened. He followed the constable into an interrogation room. As they walked through, he saw Detective Brown, Imogen's partner, sitting helplessly at his desk staring at the phone.

'Detective Brown!' he called out. 'Is she OK? Did they kill her?'

'Get him out of here!' The big boss, DCI Stanton, called out to the constable angrily.

Detective Brown looked at Dean with hatred, disgust and contempt. Dean knew what he was thinking: that Dean was going inside for what had happened to Imogen, for what had happened to George. Typical that after all of these years, he was going to be put away for something that wasn't actually his fault.

He hadn't lied to Vasos when he'd said that one day, Vasos would cease to exist because Dean would have finally caught up to him. He also hadn't lied about how popular he would be in prison. He had a lot of friends on the inside, a lot of people who owed him. Dean had always known he would end up back in prison, it was only a matter of time, so he made sure he was available to people on the inside, people who needed things done, a beating here, an accident there. There was no reason why time in prison had to be hard time; you just had to be smart about it. Dean liked to plan ahead. He hadn't lied about the contingency plans he had in place either. He was a lot of things, but he wasn't a liar.

'I'd like a moment alone with my client.' His lawyer was already in the interview room, sitting at the table. Brian Jenkins had been his lawyer for years; he was an old friend who had had Dean's back through thick and thin. He didn't have to sugarcoat things for Brian.

'Hey, Brian,' Dean said as he pulled out a chair.

'Dean. Tell me what I need to know.'

'In my house, I have cameras. Everything will be on tape, but the police won't have found any of it.'

'How can you be sure?'

'Because I own the houses to either side of it too, the cameras are literally pinhole cameras and none of the recording equipment is kept on the premises.'

'Smart move.'

'I'm a smart man, Brian.' He stopped smiling and put his hand on Brian's arm. 'Tell me about Detective Grey, how is she?'

'Well, you dodged a bullet there, sunshine, she is actually, rather miraculously, going to make a full recovery. She probably won't be eating steak for a while but all in all, I'd say she's had a narrow escape.'

'Thank God.' Dean put his head in his hands, a sense of relief washing over him.

'There's something else you should know.'

'What?'

'She woke up, briefly, but she gave a statement. She wanted to make sure everyone knew that you were in no way involved with what happened to her.'

'She said that?'

'Yes, and she was rather insistent apparently that someone write it down and pass it on. She also said the men who attacked her actually confessed to framing you for George's murder in front of her.'

'That's my girl!' Dean could hardly believe his ears. She had come through for him! If he could just keep proving himself to her, she would eventually see that underneath it all they weren't so different. One day she would realise she loved him, too.

'However, it's not all rainbows and butterflies.'

'What is it? What's the problem?'

'They can pin George the barman's assault on you; some witness came forward and identified you from the photo sheets.'

'Well, that's a bullshit way to get done.'

'It's a three-year sentence, tops. You can do it standing on your head.'

'I'd rather not do it at all.'

'The police are angry, they see you as at least partially responsible for what happened to the detective. Elias thinks that for the time being at least, you're better off inside. You can reconnect with some of your old acquaintances. If Elias's brother, Antonis, is behind this then you're both going to need all the help you can get. He's crazy.'

'God, I hate it when you make sense.'

'Plead guilty to the assault, do the time and by then everyone will be over it.'

'OK, make the deal.'

'You will do a year of it at the most.'

'I said do it!'

'What about the tapes?'

'Let's keep them a secret; I might need them for a rainy day. For now, no one needs to know what actually happened in there. I'll just say I was unconscious.'

'Don't tell me any more.'

'Thanks, Brian. I need you to do me a favour though.'

'Name it.'

'I need you to speak to Elias, I need you to tell him to be patient, that I will do my time and when I get out, I will take care of this. He doesn't need to worry.'

'OK, brother.' Brian stood up and they shook hands.

It was a weight off Dean's shoulders, knowing both that Imogen was making a recovery, and that she'd actually spoken up to help him. He had her now; he knew where he stood.

A few days after Vasos' attack, Imogen could sit up in the hospital bed and carefully drink small sips of water. It was amazing how bored her mouth had felt; she hadn't been allowed to eat and there had been nobody to talk to. The latter was her own fault; she'd specifically said no visitors. Her stomach throbbed. Lifting up the covers she saw the bandages covering the fresh scar that bisected her, the scar that'd been stitched up before she lost any more blood. She winced. Marked for life.

There was a constable stationed outside her door. She wasn't sure why. She didn't know what was going on. Stanton had called in, of course, and Sam had tried to call in. Today she had agreed to let her friend Gary Tunney visit, he was a sweet man who had an aura of goodness about him. She kicked herself for even thinking about hippy nonsense like auras; she guessed that was her mother's influence again. As she grew older, Imogen became more and more grateful that her name hadn't been 'Rainbow' or 'Waterfall'. Over the years her mother had been involved in several scams, all through psychics, spiritual healers, mediums and the like. She would drag a teenage Imogen along to the shows and watch the medium pick sad-looking people out of the crowd to tell them what they wanted to hear. She often found herself cringing as they talked, but always left feeling a little disappointed that there had been no revelations for her, no messages from beyond.

The door opened a sliver and Tunney popped his head round, smiling. He walked in holding a bunch of carnations and a pack of cards.

'Hey, stranger,' he said. He was trying to seem like his normal upbeat self, but from the look in his eyes she could tell she was probably a complete state.

'Good to see you, Tunney.'

'I thought you might be bored, thought we could play a couple of games.' He shook the cards in the air at her; she smiled, trying to contain her enthusiasm.

She didn't realise until Tunney walked into the room how much she missed everyone, how much she just wanted to get out of this bed and go back to normal. She knew nothing would be the same though, there was no going back now. At least in here she could pretend that nothing had changed. She knew full well that when she eventually did leave the hospital she wouldn't be able to work in the Plymouth precinct again. She wouldn't be able to look Stanton in the eye, not now she had lost his baby. Not because he would have cared, but because it was too big a thing for a casual affair. She couldn't tell him; she couldn't not tell him. It was just ruined. As for Sam, without evidence that he was up to no good she would have to keep working with him. She didn't think she could handle pretending not to want to punch his lights out every second of every day. She remembered the night he'd brought her the burger, the night she'd made the mistake of telling him she was pregnant. The image came to her of him with his arm around Vasos. She shuddered and pushed the thoughts away, trying to focus on Tunney.

'So tell me what I've missed?' She was suddenly longing for an update.

'Well, you caused a massive shit storm. They haven't found the guys who did . . . this . . . to you.'

'OK, well, they're probably visiting the motherland at the moment.' She rolled her eyes.

'Excuse me?'

'Never mind. What else?'

'Well, Sam got a promotion, he pulled in a massive haul, managed to find the dealers who were distributing that nasty stuff, *before* it hit mass market. Guy called Michalis was dealing pretty heavily, along with that George guy – who clearly isn't a problem any more. Sam brought Michalis in. He had a shit ton of the drugs ready to go, they were just rebranding it and waiting for the investigation to die down. They thought when you were out of the picture it would be OK to move it out. That's when Sam swooped in and nailed him.'

'Lucky Sam,' she scoffed. How could she tell Gary

that Sam was no big hero? That he'd been tipped off by Vasos, and that he'd probably taken in just enough of a haul to get the police investigators off his back?

'Mayor found out and a few local MPs wanted to make some kind of public statement about drug intolerance. It was a big deal, so Sam got the DI gig.'

'What about Dean Kinkaid? They got my statement, right? They know he didn't have anything to do with what happened to me or George?'

'They got it, yeah, but he was picked up for the barman's assault, someone saw him beating the shit out of him.'

'And? What's happened to him? Spit it out!'

'Well, he's inside. He's doing time in Exeter prison.' Tunney looked sheepish; she figured it was because she had raised her voice. She hadn't even noticed she was doing it. What was it about Dean Kinkaid that made her fiercely protective?

'Sorry for snapping.'

'Hey, no. It's OK.'

'I can't wait to get out of here and get back to some kind of normality.' She sighed. 'I'm going fucking crazy. If I have to watch one more episode of *Deal or No Deal* . . .' She noticed Tunney look away as the words left her mouth. Something was up. 'What is it?'

'I'm not supposed to tell you.'

'You know you have to tell me now, right?'

'Well, it's just a rumour at the moment, but Stanton did some rehiring, and, well, your position isn't – isn't there any more.'

'What?'

'The teams are all filled up again. I don't think you're coming back, Grey.'

'How can they do that?' She looked down at the bedsheets, trying to keep calm. After all her work, this is how they repaid her?

'I don't know how or why, I don't even know if it's true . . .'

'Oh, I'm sure it's true,' she said.

She pulled her blankets off and ripped the drip out of her arm, slowly lowering her legs out of the bed.

'What the hell are you doing?'

'I need you to get me a wheelchair, Gary. We're going for a ride.'

Imogen felt all eyes on her as she rolled into the station. Tunney obediently pushed her through the desks to DCI Stanton's office. Sam saw her and immediately jumped to his feet, rushing over.

'Imogen, what the hell are you doing here?'

'Yeah, sorry to inform you, but I pulled through.'

'What?'

'We don't talk any more, Sam, we are not friends.' She lowered her voice. 'I don't ever want to speak to you again.'

'What? What are you talking about? Are you mad at me about something?'

She put her hand up, signalling for Tunney to stop pushing. He stopped and stepped back, out of earshot. She then motioned to Sam to come closer and spoke in the smallest voice she could.

'I know what you did, Sam. I know it was you who

ordered them to cut me up. I know you're dirty.' She felt her voice breaking as she spoke, almost choking on the betrayal. She wanted to kill him, she didn't want him to exist after what he had done to her and her baby.

'You got this all wrong, Imogen.'

'We don't talk again. You hear me? We're done.'

She waved her hand and Tunney took the handles of the wheelchair again. Imogen was weak; her anger was the only thing fuelling her at this point in time. Stanton opened the door and Tunney pushed Imogen inside.

'Just shout when you want me to take you out of here, OK?' he said before closing the door behind her. She glanced back through the window and saw Sam walk over and speak to Tunney and then Tunney shrugging in turn. She hadn't told him her suspicions, so there was nothing he could tell Sam. She'd decided in the hospital that there was no one she could trust, not any more.

Stanton just stared at her, a mixture of pity and concern on his face. She suddenly regretted her decision to come here; it had all made sense in the hospital.

'This is a surprise. Should you be here, Grey? When I spoke to the doctor he said you had a long way to go still.'

'I'm feeling much better than I did,' she lied.

'Well, you look better than I expected, considering.'

'I'm not sure if that was a compliment or not.'

'You've lost weight.'

'Really?' She was annoyed at the stock compliment people threw at a woman. Of course, it was less of a

320

compliment when you'd had half of your stomach removed after it was turned to pulp by some psycho-pathic chauvinist.

Stanton lowered his voice. 'The doctor told me.'

'Told you what?'

'About the baby, Imogen. Why didn't you come to me? I would never have let you go to that dickhead's house on your own.'

'Let me? Do me a favour. It wasn't him anyway, he didn't do anything wrong.'

'Have you got some kind of Stockholm syndrome?' Stanton's anger was brimming under the surface; she could hear him trying to suppress it. 'He was bad news, everyone told you he was.'

'Was? He's not dead.'

'As good as. He's got a lot of enemies. The boys up top aren't very happy about the way this went down, about what happened to you. You should never have gone there alone, you broke the rules and you made the whole department look stupid. The fact is, Imogen, the local papers had a field day with your story, and in-house your name is an embarrassment.'

'Jesus, tell it like it is, why don't you? So I'm a laughing stock?'

'Well, there's always medical retirement.'

'Fuck off, David, I'm not retiring.'

'Well, either way, they want you out of the field for a while, when you come back off sick leave, until everyone forgets about this. We managed to get an injunction to stop your name being publicised, but to be honest it was already out there. Even after Sam's big haul, we're struggling to recover. You made us look weak. Thank God you didn't die or there would have been a media frenzy.'

'I want a transfer.'

'What?'

'When I'm recovered, I can't come back here. If I'm really that much of an embarrassment, no one's going to want to work with me, are they?'

'Where would you go?'

'Well, I have to stay close to my mother, so I can't go too far.'

'You've thought about this already?'

'I want to go to Exeter.'

'If they don't agree?'

'Then you make them agree, David. It was fun while it lasted but the thing between me and you was seriously against the rules, and you don't want that coming out, do you? What would your wife say?'

'Are you threatening me?'

'No, I'm just saying that we need some distance after what's happened. I can't be around you. After losing the baby – your baby . . .'

'And you going to Exeter has nothing to do with that filth Kinkaid, I suppose? Were you sleeping with him? Was it even my kid, Imogen?'

'If that's what you think then you can go fuck yourself, David. There was never anyone but you. But that's over now.'

The truth was that Dean *was* a factor in her decision. He had proven time and time again that he would be there for her, and she felt obligated to him, she felt duty-bound to protect him. She could tell that, like her, he had had to fight his way through life, that things had never been easy for him and that's why he'd ended up as the person he was today. She saw that instinct in him to survive, no matter what. She used to have that, but she had grown softer as she'd allowed other people in. Well, no more. She needed a clean break where no one knew who she was.

'Fine.' He sat down at his desk, indicating that he was done talking. 'I'll see what I can do.'

She turned her wheelchair around and banged on the glass. Tunney shot over to the door and opened it. She wheeled herself towards the exit and he took over. Sam was sitting at his desk watching as they left. She wished she had the courage to call him out in front of everyone. The fact was, and as crazy as it sounded, she didn't get any points for being hurt out in the field. If anything, she had made more enemies inside the department. No one wanted to be reminded of how vulnerable they were, least of all her colleagues. Never mind that she was a woman and her attack had highlighted the plight of female police officers all over the country. Her being hospitalised was a win for the bad guys, because it continued the cycle of fear in the public eye and spread the idea that the police were not in control.

She knew as she left the room that this would be the last time she was in here, as an employee, anyway. No one looked at her; no one wanted to see her in the chair, to remember that they'd failed her, to remember that the same thing could happen to them. Any day could be the day when they themselves were stabbed, or strangled or shot. She was sad to be going, sad that her years of service didn't really mean much.

Tunney wheeled her outside and she looked back at the building. She didn't know when she would be returning to work – even walking right now was excruciating. But she felt determined. She was going to fight, she was going to get better and then she was going to move on and put all of this behind her. Who knew what the future would bring? All she knew was there would be no more Mrs Nice Guy.

Chapter 41: The Admission

The present

Adrian had left God knows how many messages for Imogen, but had no response. He phoned the hospital and found that her mother was in a medically induced coma until some of the swelling had gone down, but that it was still touch and go.

Since the night Imogen had come over he hadn't heard anything, not even a whisper. She had even taken a couple of days of compassionate leave. He'd had a call from Fraser telling him that he was cleared to come back to work for now, and so here he was. Isabelle had corroborated everything he'd said, obviously. He wondered if she'd mentioned the kissing. He guessed not, as no one had asked him about it. Yet.

Inside, the precinct was awash with pictures of Isabelle and the inside of the newsagents. There was a big photo of Dimi the proprietor, who had vanished without a trace. There was a whole notice board dedicated to the basement beneath the shop where Isabelle had lived. It made Adrian cringe. At least he knew forensics would clear him of any wrongdoing in there. To his surprise, Imogen was sitting at her desk, frosty faced and filling out paperwork.

'How's your mum?'

'Brilliant, thanks.' She stood up and walked over to Fraser's office. Adrian stared after her retreating back.

'This came for you.' Denise Ferguson popped up beside him, handing him a box of paperwork. 'It's a detailed list of all Irene Grey's financials. I take it Imogen doesn't know about this?'

'No, she doesn't. I'd appreciate it if you don't say anything.'

'Well you know I can keep a secret.' She winked and walked away. Adrian grimaced. The two of them had had an on-off relationship in the past; a relationship that was very much off at the moment. He may be a prick, but he wasn't about to string her along. He guessed that Denise was letting him know she was available if he needed a shoulder to cry on, or something else. It wasn't something he was in the mood for at this moment in time.

Adrian sat at his desk and looked through the file. There were statements going back several years. Irene Grey liked a drink, and she habitually subscribed to a variety of magazines. She bought a lot of crap she didn't need. From lamps to bird food to exercise machines; there seemed to be no rhyme or reason to it. Adrian had been in her flat so this came as no surprise to him.

326

There was one consistency throughout the statements, and that was that she had money coming from somewhere else. No one could afford a hoarding habit like Irene Grey's without means.

Imogen had told him how his mother habitually gave her possessions away. How bizarre. Clearly, there was thousands of pounds' worth of goods being bought and no discernible way for Irene Grey to have been able to afford it. Did she buy stuff then sell it? Then Adrian saw a transfer account that popped up fairly regularly, clearing overdue debts, paying bills and putting her back in credit. He circled a few figures. It looked like Irene Grey had a wealthy benefactor.

He picked up the papers and went to find his partner. He couldn't reasonably keep this from her any longer and she would want to know. She had come out of Fraser's office, taken her papers and gone to one of the other desks, presumably to be away from Adrian. He knew this awkwardness would pass eventually but at this precise moment it was pissing him off.

'Grey?' he said.

'What is it?'

'I've got your mother's financials.' No use beating around the bush.

'You've got what?' She clenched her teeth as she looked at him.

'There's an account here that's not based in the UK, your mum has received a fair bit of money from it.'

'You looked through my mother's financials without telling me?'

'We need to find your father. I don't have time to

pander to your emotional bullshit at the moment.' Her head snapped back as the verbal slap landed on target. This was a murder investigation and more to the point, it was a missing persons case. So much was riding on finding out who Imogen's father was now; it had stopped being about her the moment Isabelle Hobbs' name was brought into the frame. Bridget Reid hadn't just vanished into thin air. They owed it to themselves to find her.

He could see Imogen fighting back the urge to tear him a new one, but as the seconds passed he saw her face resign itself. She knew he was right. Time to get on with some work.

Imogen looked over the paperwork that Adrian had been going through. He was right, there was a mysterious bank account that bailed her mother out over and over again. Could it be her father?

She was almost relieved to see that the great love her mother had spoken of for the entirety of her life wasn't a figment of her overactive imagination. She had to remind herself that Adrian was on her side. He had come to her with this. It wasn't like it was in Plymouth. Everyone had made her feel like a drama queen in her last job, as though Sam's unwanted attention was a minor irritation at best; they didn't understand how utterly betrayed he had made her feel. They didn't understand how scared she was of him. She had allowed Sam to make her feel vulnerable and she had promised herself once before that would never happen again.

'Are we OK?' Adrian said, as though he could tell what she was thinking about.

'Just let it go, Miley. We're fine. I'm just worried about my mum . . . and this is all doing my head in a bit.' She half smiled at him and looked up to see Denise walking across the room with a man. She couldn't place him at first. There was something about seeing someone out of context; her mind struggled to place him. Suddenly it clicked: it was Elias Papas.

'Someone here to see you,' Denise said to Imogen.

'Hello, Detective.' He smiled at her, offering his hand.

'Mr Papas? What are you doing here?' She looked at his hand but didn't take it. He put it back in his pocket. Despite the cold temperatures outside, he still looked like he was straight off a boat, with his navy blue jacket and ivory chinos.

'Is there somewhere we can talk? I have some information that pertains to your investigation.'

'Um, sure, Interview One if you want to make a statement. Follow me.'

'This is personal.'

'Oh – right. Come to the liaison room then.' She wondered fleetingly how it could pertain to her investigation if it was personal.

She dismissed Adrian's concerned look and took Elias with her to the liaison room, shutting the door behind them. She folded her arms and stared at him, waiting.

'Can we sit down?' He sat on the sofa but she didn't move. He'd had a disconcerting smile on his face when she had greeted him, but in this room his face had changed, he looked sombre. 'Please.'

She huffed and sat down in the chair next to him.

'I'm sorry to hear about your mother.' He turned towards her and took her hand. She couldn't pull away.

'You heard about that? Have you been following me?'

'In a manner of speaking, I have.' He put his other hand over hers, it was weirdly comforting but strange, tight, like he didn't want to let go. 'There is no easy way to say this, Imogen, so I'm afraid I'm just going to come out with it. I'm your father.'

'Excuse me?' This time she did pull her hand away. She pulled it away because she knew he wasn't lying, she knew instinctively that he was telling the truth. She saw herself in his face. All the missing pieces fell into place. She clutched her hand to her chest. 'What the hell is going on?'

'I know this is a shock to you. Your mother told me about the child and I was going to come forward, but then . . .'

'Then you decided to have her killed instead?'

'What? No!' He looked genuinely surprised at the accusation.

'One of your sons murdered Beth and Jeremy Ackerman and you're afraid they'll go to prison? Is that why you attacked my mother?'

'Your mother is the love of my life, Imogen. I swear to God I would never hurt her. My family and I were at a wedding, in a place with cameras if you want to check, on the day of your mother's attack.' He reached into his pocket and pulled out a flash drive. 'I came back for your mother and she didn't answer. I banged on the door. I had asked her to come away with me – I just figured she had changed her mind. I never expected that Irene would hang around all these years and wait for me . . .'

Imogen wanted to hate him but she could see the pain, she could hear it in his voice as it cracked when he said her mother's name. She watched as his chest rose and fell. He was distraught but trying not to lose his composure.

'They found DNA at the scene, a half-brother they said. So it must be one of your kids. Did you know about Isabelle Hobbs? Did you know where she was?'

'I swear I didn't. I would never do anything like that. I don't understand why the results say that. I have done my own investigations and there is just no way my sons were involved. You understand I had to make sure before I came to you. I also consulted a DNA specialist who told me that half-brother is not a clear-cut result, it just means a second-generation male from the father's side of the family.'

'Do you know someone else who would have a reason to hurt my mum?'

'I think I do.'

'So let's go take your statement.' She stood up.

'My brief is on her way. There is one thing I want your people to do for me before I talk.'

'It doesn't really work like that.'

'I'm going to be giving you a lot of information. If I am right then both you and I will be in danger from the moment I make the statement, and so I need protection if I'm going to be completely honest with you.'

'We can protect you.' She realised she didn't know what to call him. Was he still Mr Papas? She noted the irony that his last name actually meant father.

'You can't protect me from these people.' He smiled and leaned forward, lowering his voice. 'You should find a way to accommodate my request.'

'Fine, I'll see what I can do. What's the request?'

'I want Dean Kinkaid released from prison.'

Chapter 42: Resolutions

Age 24

I am sick of people leaving me. They either leave or they die. It's always just me. Me on my own. My father doesn't come home much at all any more, not now my mother has passed and he got rid of my sister. I knew he would take her away as soon as she became a woman, and nothing says woman like a pregnancy. He has taken so many people from me that I despise him.

I'm not afraid of him any more. I know how to hurt him. I could just go to the police, but I will bide my time. He will pay for everything he's taken from me. He will pay.

Today I am at the club because my dad doesn't know where Meathead is and so I have to do his dirty work for him. I can feel my father's disappointment in every word he says to me, if he speaks at all. My uncle has been spending a lot more time in the club over the last year, my father says it's because his marriage is falling apart and he can't admit it to himself. I wish I had been his son instead. He is always nice to me.

My sister has been gone for over a year. We made plans together but when my father found out she was pregnant he went crazy. I have been looking for my child, my sister's daughter for the last year and I finally think I may have found her. I have tracked her down. My father said that he had to give her away after she was born, because my sister died in childbirth. I hate him for that. I miss my sister, we became very close and I was going to ask her to marry me, but when I told my father that he said he would never let it happen and that I was sick for wanting to marry my sister. He said I wouldn't be a good father and he knew someone else who could take care of the child. So again, it's just me, always just me.

He got a call from his police friend the other day. Apparently he has recognised a girl in one of our houses as a police officer, so we need to go and sort her out. I haven't been to this house before and neither has Meathead. My dad is so angry and he whispers something that I can't hear but Meathead gets a look on his face that I have seen before. We arrive at the house and the first thing I see is a man dressed as a baby: I have no idea what that's all about. People are confusing.

I am left to deal with him and so I just do it quickly. I don't like doing this kind of stuff for my dad. I can hear a girl screaming in the bathroom as Meathead does his thing and as I walk out into the hall I see a woman trying to leave and so I slice her in her thigh. I don't like killing women, but this is one of the quickest ways. I feel bad about it because she's all dressed up nice, like she was going somewhere special and now she's nothing. It's funny how everyone disappears in that one second between life and death. I often find myself thinking about whether other people think as much as me. I feel like I think about everything.

I can't imagine other people thinking and feeling like I do but I know when I used to speak to my sister she would tell me things about what she would want to do when she was older. I found it strange that she thought about things like that at all, I thought I was the only one. I watch as the blood pools around the blonde and Meathead tells me to make sure there is no one else here. I can hear the girl in the bathroom sputtering and I don't want to imagine what he is doing to her. The police girl we are looking for isn't here. Meathead comes out of the bathroom and calls my father, he looks under the beds but there is no one else there. We're told to drive around the places she might be, but really, that could be anywhere.

We go down by the river and look around, I know what he is going to do when he finds her and I feel a bit bad about it. She's not the same as the girls my dad employs.

As we look around the riverbank, I see movement in the park. Meathead is moving towards it and so I call him, coax him back to me. He hasn't seen her in the park yet. I don't want him to get her but at the same time I don't want to get my dad put in prison, *because I want to deal with him myself. He comes back towards me and I watch as the girl slips into the river. After a small argument we decide to try somewhere else. I convince him that we should head towards the police station, as that seems like the most likely place she would go. We drive around for hours until eventually we give up because the city is completely dead. Everything is so still, it almost feels unreal, like a photograph.*

As the sun comes up I find myself alone again and I drive down to the river to see if I can see anything. The world is washed in orange as the noises of the day start. There is nothing by the water and so I drive as far along the bank as I can; it's mostly pedestrianised. I drive back on to the road and try to find a way to a clearing in the river further up. Then I see her: she is lying on the grass and her eyes are closed. I know what I have to do. I look around; nothing is moving, but the world is waking up and so I know it is now or never.

I grab the girl. She's shivering and muttering something under her breath. She calls me Sam as I put her into the car and buckle her in. She slumps against the window when I close the door and get in, checking for spectators before I drive away. There is no one around; I decide it's unlikely that anyone saw me. If they had, I would have just taken her to the hospital, but instead I take her home with me.

When we get home, I carry her into my sister's room and lay her on the bed. She is very pretty. I see a spot of blood on the blanket and see that she has hurt her knee quite badly; there is glass sticking out of it. I tend to the wound and her eyes start to open; she begins to scream. I try to explain that I saved her life but she won't stop screaming. I explain that I found her by the river and she seems to calm down. She asks me if I saw the people who were looking for her and I tell her I did, she tells me she needs a phone to call her boyfriend and I explain that I don't have one but I will go out and get one. I don't want her to freak out again. I ask her if she is hungry and she says she is. She explains what happened with a panicked look on her face. I like her. She asks me where we are and I tell her that she will be safe here until I bring her a phone. She lies down again and starts to sob. I explain that I will get her some food first then go for the phone; she seems OK with this idea.

In the kitchen I try and think of ways to keep her here. I don't want her to go. I forgot how lonely I was until I saw her. I make her some food and a drink and put it on a tray. It makes me think of my sister. I look in the cupboard and find my mum's old medications. I tried some of these on Monica; she didn't really care what she put in her body. I take some of the Zolpidem and crush it up, putting it inside the sandwich I have made her. It's a sleeping pill and it's pretty strong stuff. Then I get some of my mum's other pills, they make people really confused and if you take enough of them they give you hallucinations, but they used to stop her shaking.

I'm assuming the girl has got a lower tolerance than the girls from the club, but I think I'm going to have to start out quite strong anyway. I'm sure it will be fine, but I need something else too if I'm going to keep her here. I make a mental note to get hold of some nitrous. My dad has an illegal store of it. When they first get the girls, they pump it into the containers on the docks before opening the door. I can rig it up to the vent that goes into my sister's room. It's not dangerous at all, but it does make people happier and relaxed. Sometimes I had it when me and Monica were together, it kind of takes you out of your own head and makes everything feel good. You forget the things that stress you out and you just want to stay like that forever. It's like a kind of pretend happiness.

Today I am going to go and get my daughter. I know the registration of her parents' car. I believe I will know the baby when I see her. Just like I can see my face in the Hastings boy. I still think about telling Claire the truth sometimes, but it will have to wait for now.

I drive to where I believe my daughter lives. I see a woman at the end of her rope struggling with a baby, my baby. I follow them for a bit, and then I help the woman change her tyre. I see the baby and I know for certain that she is mine. There are too many people around, but I have to get this done today because my father has a job for me tomorrow. I go back round to my daughter's house later on but she isn't there. I watch through the window and see her fake parents sitting at the table, eating their dinner together. It makes me angry. I knock on the door, and when the man answers, I cut the femoral artery in his thigh. He falls instantly. The stupid bitch who lives here won't tell me where my daughter is, but I find out that she is called Cassandra. I like that name. It's a good name for my little girl.

I was planning on leaving the woman alive, but she just pisses me off too much. She warns the person who is looking after the baby that I'm here and tells her to call the police, so I have no choice. I can't have her telling them what I look like. She doesn't struggle much. Afterwards, I manage to get away.

Yet again, I find myself on the wrong side of my father's temper. The murder of the family is on the news and now my father knows what I did. I know he knows, I can tell by the way he looks at me. The man my dad works for isn't happy, and now my dad is in trouble.

The missing persons case surrounding my sister's disappearance has been reopened. The case against her parents has been reopened too, and to be honest with you, I am glad about that. It never felt right them being in prison all that time, called child killers and stuff just because my dad did what he did. What we did. He tells me that I have jeopardised everything and he just wants me to understand the shit storm I have created. I'm suspicious because when he refers to my sister, he always hesitates, as if there's something he is hiding. I don't trust him, I never have done and to be honest I am not afraid of him any more. I have lost everything because of him.

We are at the club and my father comes out of the office and tells me I have to do a job for him. I know what he means; he wants me to kill someone. The police are asking too many questions about my sister, *apparently. The man my dad is so scared of wants someone dealt with or he's going to kill my dad. They have a witness who could lead them back to us. Of course he means lead them back to him. I am quite sure he doesn't give a shit about me. He would normally ask Meathead to do this type of job, but I'm the only one here and apparently it's something that needs to be taken care of immediately. I have to go and kill someone's mother.*

I go to the old lady's house and it's a mess. She has so much stuff, random junk piled up everywhere. She is waiting for someone, her suitcase is packed by the door. My father didn't give me any details, just that I have to do this and not fuck it up. I get a few hits in but she's a fighter and she hurts me really badly. I start to lose my vision as the blood pours from my face. I wish Meathead were here because he would know what to do. I can feel myself getting faint and I know I have to leave before I lose consciousness.

I stagger out to the car and manage to drive home. I'm so angry with my father, he has messed everything up. When I get home he is there and he asks me if I have done what he asks. I tell him I have but when I tell him I need to go and see a doctor he calls me a pussy and lets me know what a disappointment I am to him. He screams repeatedly in my face about how much I have messed up, how I always mess things up. He has no idea who I am, no idea what I am capable of. I think it's time I showed him. I think it's time I stood up for myself. My father doesn't deserve to live.

Chapter 43: Locked and Loaded

The present

Bridget awoke to the sound of the key in the lock. She kept her eyes closed until he was in the room. She was ready to make her move. She had found the hole the nitrous was being pumped through, and blocked it with a torn rag from her sheet. Usually he would pump it in for a few minutes before he entered the room – once she had figured that out she knew when he was coming. She heard him panting as he pulled on the handle. There was a clatter as he fell through and on to the floor.

'Help,' she heard him mutter. She sat up and watched as the door clicked closed. Impulsively she rushed over to him. He was covered in blood. His face was split open in several places on one side and his eye was swollen shut, even though part of the flesh seemed to be missing. His shirt was saturated; she couldn't imagine how he had managed to drive here in this state.

'What happened?'

'The door . . . the key,' he mumbled. It took a few seconds before she realised what he was saying. The door had closed and the keys were on the other side.

'Do you have a phone? I can call an ambulance.'

Or the police.

'No ambulance, no phone.' He moved his head from side to side very slowly. He was ebbing fast. She could see that he was weak. She patted him down and looked through his pockets but the only thing in there was a stupid e-cigarette and some pills. She thumped him in the chest.

'Don't you fucking die!' He wasn't listening, or couldn't hear. He just lay there. She felt for a pulse; it was very weak. She wasn't strong enough to carry him to the bed. His fingertips were frozen and the little flesh on his lips that wasn't bloody had a grey-blue tinge to it. She pulled off the blankets, covering him and curling up beside him, attempting to give him some of her heat. She tried desperately to remember her first aid training but it wasn't coming back to her. Nothing was. All she could think about was how she was trapped. She wondered who had hurt this man. Were the police on to him? Were they any closer to finding him?

She had a sudden desire to take the pills, remembering how safe and happy they had made her feel. She could use some of that feeling right now. Anything would be better than this overwhelming feeling of dread. The inability to admit to herself what was happening.

She clutched him to her and sang to him softly, her mouth close to his ear. She ignored the rapidly decreasing temperature of his body and the ever-slowing thump of his pulse against her skin.

The dreams were holding on to Bridget. Somewhere in her subconscious they knew not to allow her to wake up. She was fighting consciousness, fighting the outside world, but eventually she couldn't hold on any longer and her eyes opened. She knew she was alone in the room before she even felt for a pulse.

The body next to her was cold as dough; soft and rigid at the same time. As soon as she had accepted the fact that her captor was no longer alive, she scooted backwards. She left the top sheet but pulled the rest of the blankets away from him. She covered his face; the blood that had pooled in his eye socket crept through the white cotton, as though he were still watching her. If he had actually left the keys in the door before it shut then there was no way out. She had tried too many times to break out; she knew there was no other way. She had even tried screaming, but it had been pointless.

She suspected that he'd lied about the people who knew she was there. She didn't think anyone knew she was there. She had never wanted to accept that before because she didn't want to think about a scenario like this one. Her thoughts became desperate. Maybe there was someone who would miss him? Maybe someone would come looking for him, someone who knew about this place? After all, someone had done that to his face.

She had no idea how long she had been in the basement now. It could have been weeks, months, or even years. With no way of knowing the time, days merged into nights, and then there was the time before she had stopped taking the pills. She didn't know how long her hazy state had lasted for. For all she knew, they had given up looking for her weeks ago, assumed she was dead. In fact, for all she knew, she *was* dead and this, right now, was hell.

She had running water, but that was it. No food, and she wasn't about to cannibalise her friend here. So the way she saw it, she had three weeks until she died of starvation. Of course, only a small amount of that time would be at full strength. She looked around the room at the things she could use. Now she knew he wasn't going to burst in at any given moment, she could get to work.

She used some of the spare change he had in his pocket to dismantle the bed, using the coins in place of a screwdriver. Once she had removed the metal slats, she used them to attack the hinges on the door. She knew she would never break the lock, but hinges were generally weaker. Nothing happened.

It was two days before the effects of the hunger really kicked in. Add to that the smell of the rotting corpse on the floor, and Bridget was feeling weak. Every now and then, she laboriously tried the door hinges again to no avail. The dead body on the floor haunted her; it was awful sharing a room with that smell.

She smoked the last of his e-cigarette, just to ease the hunger. Now all she had left was water. Each day her skin felt looser on her body, hollows appearing where they had not been before. Her muscles were wasting away – faster than she'd thought possible.

Bridget had a decision to make. Did she continue to wait indefinitely? What was the brave thing to do here? Was it better to take action now? She looked at his pill bottle again. Every day she looked at the bottle, again and again, at shorter and shorter intervals. How long would she wait before she took the easy way out? How long before the smell became unbearable? How long before she became too weak to physically put the pills in her mouth and swallow?

The idea that she would somehow die just moments before help came crashing through the door in a rescue attempt was becoming more and more unlikely, but it had played on her mind long enough. The idea tortured her. She finally had to concede that no one was coming. She would die of hunger before anyone turned up.

Bridget was getting closer to death now, just filling her bladder to feel full, and then emptying it moments later. It wasn't long before the only thing that really mattered was the bottle of pills. They were all she could think about. She would catch them out of the corner of her eye and they would whisper, softly at first, but soon they were shouting. Could she hold out for this death? Could she wait for this slow agonising hunger to envelop her? If she was lucky, starvation would take her before the putrefied body's noxious gasses invaded her lungs completely.

As she held the pill bottle in her hand, Bridget felt like a coward. She emptied the pills into her palm and swallowed them one by one, leaving a minute or so between each one to make sure that they stayed down. She continued until she no longer had the strength. Her body was desperate to reject them, but she held them down, sobbing as her gut convulsed under the alien feeling of substance. She stared at the door, waiting for the crash, waiting for the rescue. It never came.

Chapter 44: The Convict

The present

Imogen waited by Exeter prison gates, Adrian at her side. She was unable to bring herself to go through them; it didn't seem right to go in now, not when she hadn't visited him the whole time he had been there, though she had driven past at least once a week. She hadn't quite figured out how to explain Dean to Adrian. Given that Dean Kinkaid had served well over half of his sentence and had no black marks against him, the process of getting him released had taken less time than Imogen had expected. Dean was instructed on the terms of his probation, and they had been informed that he would be out within the hour.

'So this Kinkaid guy, you know him?'

'I do. I know him from when I worked in Plymouth, two years ago. He's been serving his sentence.'

'I looked at his file: a lot of accusations but not a

lot sticks to him. In and out of care, sealed juvie report. He's a career criminal. But he doesn't seem to do any real time.'

'Apparently not.'

'But he's bad news though? I mean, is this the right thing we're doing here? Are you sure he has the information we need?'

'Don't worry about Dean Kinkaid, I can handle him.' Just saying his name out loud felt good. She was doing her best to look professional, but she kept her eyes trained on the exit, waiting for the moment she would see Dean again. She wondered if he would look the same. She wondered if he would feel the same way about her.

Finally, the large metal door opened and Dean stepped out into the light, shielding his eyes before walking down the path. She could hardly breathe as he walked towards them; his head was down and he hadn't noticed her yet. She got out of the car and walked around to the bonnet. Dean looked up. His eyes flickered with surprise and then something else. *Yes,* she thought, he still feels the same.

She had to hold her breath for a moment to steady herself. He walked straight up to her, stopping only inches away. She wanted him to plant his lips on hers and she could see he was thinking exactly the same thing. She should have insisted she come alone. Adrian got out of the car and leaned on the door. Dean took a step back to maintain the air of decency.

'They told me I would be getting a lift to the station,' Dean said, not once taking his eyes off Imogen.

Imogen wanted to respond, but felt all the unsaid words stick in her throat. She thought of all the conversations she had wanted to have with him while he had been in prison, the things she had imagined when she was alone in bed.

'Get in then,' Adrian said eventually. Dean stepped around Imogen, eyes fixed on her, and sat behind her in the car.

Adrian started the car and pulled out into the rush-hour traffic. Imogen still couldn't think of anything to say and was well aware that her silence had transcended into oddness. She focused on her breathing and stared at the side mirror. She could see Dean's reflection as he leaned against the window, looking out on to the Exeter streets. He appeared tired and worn out. His eyes connected with hers in the mirror and she attempted a smile. He shuffled in the seat behind her and sat up. She felt something brushing against her thigh and she looked down to see that he had slipped his hand round the side of the seat and was touching her, caressing her thigh and running his hand up her torso. She slid her hand down by her side, hoping that Adrian wouldn't notice. Fortunately, he was more preoccupied with driving. She took Dean's hand in hers and squeezed it. He squeezed back.

As Adrian shifted his focus from the street, Dean let go and leaned back in the seat, folding his arms and staring out of the window. She closed her hand into a fist as though she could somehow keep the feeling of him in there.

At the station, Imogen opened the door for Dean to

get out of the car and he followed them into the precinct, where Elias Papas was waiting. He stood up and threw his arms around Dean. They hugged with genuine affection. She noticed Elias whisper something in Dean's ear as they moved apart. Dean nodded at him.

'DCI Fraser is going to take your statement now, Mr Papas,' Imogen said.

'Please, call me Elias at least.'

'OK, Elias.' It didn't feel right; she had known it wouldn't. She still hadn't quite got her head around the fact that he was her father. She wasn't sure if she would ever get used to it. What she found the most strange was that she had investigated him before, looked at his history and spoken to him and yet the thought of the family connection had never occurred to her. She watched Fraser lead Elias into an interrogation room and close the door.

For the second time today, Imogen stood awkwardly with Adrian and Dean.

'Is there somewhere I can go and wait for Elias?' Dean asked.

'Sure, I'll take you to one of the waiting rooms,' Adrian said. He looked Dean up and down and Imogen wondered what he made of him. So far, her partner hadn't seemed to notice Imogen's strange behaviour, or if he had, he must have attributed it to the recent revelations about her father.

Dean glanced at Imogen again before following Adrian. Imogen went into the observation room to watch the interview with Elias Papas.

*

350

'And you know nothing about how the child came to be adopted?' DCI Fraser's voice was clear and clipped.

'I don't. But I think my nephew, Giannis, may be the father.'

'Your nephew? Not your son?'

'I spoke to a specialist when Irene told me about the child and the DNA, and he said there is a possibility it's not actually my son. Because of the way it works, it could also be a nephew or a cousin. My brother and I are identical twins.'

'Where is your nephew right now?'

'I don't know, but I suspect he's also the one who hurt Irene. He is a troubled boy.'

'Troubled? You can say that again! Why would he hurt Irene Grey?'

'The same reason he does anything. My brother told him to.'

'Antonis?'

'That's right. He is protecting himself, his business. He thinks I don't know. You can't change some people – I put a stop to all of his criminal dealings in Plymouth but he just relocated them here. There's always money in sex and drugs.'

Adrian came into the observation room and stood next to Imogen.

'This must be weird for you, huh?'

'You think?'

'You don't have to stay if you don't want to.'

'Where else am I going to go?'

He switched off the sound from the room next door and turned to Imogen. She couldn't look at him, worried

351

that her face might betray her emotions. She had been feeling like a raw nerve for weeks now, what with Sam back on the scene and now Elias and Dean. The world seemed to be revolving around her at the moment.

'Any news on your mother?'

She shook her head. Adrian reached up and rubbed her arm. The truth was, Imogen wasn't even thinking about her mother. Occasionally she would remember that Irene was lying in hospital and feel guilty that she wasn't by her side, but there was nothing she could do there and so there was no point going, not with everything else that was going on here. She was thinking about this man, her father. He had a reputation for being bad, but maybe that wasn't the case, maybe it was all his brother. She didn't know what to think any more.

Everything about her had changed. And then there was Dean, somewhere in the station, alone, probably thinking about her. She had to see him.

'I need the loo.' She walked abruptly out of the room and went to where Dean was most likely to be, but he wasn't there. She opened another door and that room was empty too. Her pace quickened and she tried to think where else Adrian would have put him; it wasn't like there was an abundance of free space in a police station. He wouldn't have left, would he? She walked along at increasing speed, starting to feel sick. She turned the corner for the bathroom and smacked straight into someone coming the other way. It was Dean. He quickly looked around and then slid his hand under her hair to cradle her head and pulled her in, kissing her hard and fast before anyone saw. The sickness subsided and she pulled away.

'I've been waiting nearly two years to do that.' He smiled as she stood there, suddenly breathless. 'You realise you haven't said a word to me yet?'

'Sorry,' she said instinctively.

'It's OK, I can tell you're happy to see me.' He brushed his thumb across her face, his hand still cradling her head.

'I'm sorry I didn't come to visit you.'

'Why would you?' he said. She could tell he was trying to be his light, confident self but he was clenching his jaw. He still had his defences up.

'I wanted to,' she said, but she didn't really know how to explain the reason why she hadn't. 'Why does Elias want you out?'

'To protect you.'

'Me?'

'Put it this way, there's a good way to hurt Elias now that his brother knows you're his daughter.'

'You knew?' She was taken aback by his matter-of-factness.

'I knew.' He ran his hand down her arm and held her hand. 'He told me straight after he met you.'

'So that time in the club? You knew before you cut Vasos?'

'I knew.'

'You and Elias are close then?'

'He's like a father to me, he saved my life.'

'Do you know his nephew?'

'Giannis? Yes, he was in the club that day, too.'

'I don't remember him.'

'He's quiet, shy. Young. He was at my house as well
. . . when you . . .'

'Oh, I do remember,' she interrupted before he could
finish the sentence. She didn't want to hear whatever
words he might use to describe what had happened on
that day.

'He's not right, in the head I mean. Never has been.
But he never really stood a chance.'

'And you believe Elias had nothing to do with any
of this?'

'He didn't, he wouldn't. He had been trying to get
Antonis straight for years. Elias didn't want anything
to do with the other stuff his brother was into. He
didn't even know half of it. When you were investigating
two years ago in Plymouth, Elias had no idea how much
shit was going on. Antonis was running it all. He was
controlling Dimi, the guy who held Isabelle in the newsagents. He had girls everywhere. Drugs everywhere. And
Giannis did his dirty work.'

Imogen's head felt fuzzy. 'I have to get back.'

'I'm not going anywhere.' He kissed her on the lips
again. She wasn't as surprised this time. His hand
brushed hers again before she turned back to watch
the rest of Elias' interview.

Adrian was transfixed on the interview when Imogen
re-entered the observation room.

'Do you have any idea what your brother would
want with Isabelle Hobbs?' Fraser was leaning forward
across the table, the tape recorder whirring next to him.

'I remember when she went missing, the photos were

354

everywhere. She looked just like his daughter, my niece who died.'

'Do you think that's why he took her?'

'Yes. She must have been at his house. I feel horrible when I think about it.'

'So you never saw her there?'

'I didn't go to their house very often, as little as I could, in fact. There was always a bad feeling there.'

'How did your actual niece die?'

'She drowned. They were all on holiday when it happened.'

'An accident?'

'There was some speculation within the family that Giannis had maybe done it, never any proof though. Their world revolved around that little girl, so everything changed after she died. Losing a child is not something anyone should have to live through,' Elias said as he looked at the mirror. Imogen flinched involuntarily. Was he talking about losing her or was he referring to the baby that she'd lost?

'These names that you have given me are all the people involved in your brother's operations?'

'Probably not all of them. I only saw a fraction of it; he knew I would shut it down. When we were in the club together he would run prostitutes out of the back rooms and I put a stop to it.'

'And the accounts you gave us?'

'I don't know if that's all there is, but that's all I could find.'

'Why are you doing this? Why now?'

'Because he went too far when he hurt Irene, he

proved there is no blood feeling between us. I'm reciprocating with the destruction of his life.'

'So this is revenge? You're not just doing the right thing?'

'It is the right thing, so what does it matter what my motivations are?'

'And what about the police officer you say helped your brother evade any kind of prosecution?'

'Yes, I told you I only met him once, he was very careful. DCI David Stanton would alert my brother to any problems coming his way.'

Sucker-punched, Imogen recoiled at the sound of Stanton's name. Elias must be lying.

'Grey?' Adrian was holding on to her. She had stumbled backwards, almost falling.

'It's OK, Miley.'

'Stanton, he was your old boss, right?'

'Yeah, he was. Fuck!' Imogen felt as though the world was tipping. She clutched her stomach. *Stanton*. Not after everything. It couldn't be.

'You should sit down, Grey. Let me get you some water.' Adrian's words were the last thing she heard before she sank down on to her knees.

Chapter 45: The Guest

The present

Imogen opened the front door and let Dean into her house. All things considered, she didn't want to be on her own. The night before, she had laid in bed with the knowledge that Dean would be out of jail the next day. She'd got up early this morning to clean the house, just in case he happened to find his way there. She hoped it wasn't obvious.

'I've made the spare room up for you,' she made a point of saying. She didn't want him to think it was a done deal. He took her meaning and nodded.

'I don't actually have any things.'

'I'm sure you can pick some stuff up tomorrow.' She struggled for words, not knowing how to say what was really in her head. 'Can I get you a drink? Do you want a beer?'

'Beer sounds like a great idea.'

She led him through to the kitchen, grabbed a beer from the fridge and handed it to him. He took it from her and put it on the table. Slowly, he lifted his eyes to meet hers and she knew the small talk was over. He moved closer and took her face in his hands.

'Just let me look at you for a while. I can't believe you're really here.'

'It's my house.'

'I'm sorry,' he said, his eyes full of sadness and remorse. She looked into them. The moment felt endless.

She knew what he was talking about – he was sorry for that awful night, the last time they'd seen each other. The night she'd been attacked. The night she'd got her scar.

'Dean . . . don't,' she said, and a smile spread across his face.

'You know, I don't think I ever heard you say my name before.'

'Dean,' she said again flirtatiously, and he kissed her before pulling her into an embrace.

'I've been waiting so long to do this.' He stroked her hair and Imogen began to cry; she didn't want to but she couldn't keep it in any longer. There was just too much going on at the moment and she was completely overwhelmed. She felt like a bitch for not visiting Dean, and even more of a bitch for not visiting her comatose mother. She pulled away and wiped her face with the back of her hand.

'I'm being stupid, ignore me.' She grabbed the beer and smacked the top off on the counter before leaving the kitchen and going into the lounge. She put the beer on the table and sank into the sofa. Dean followed soon after. He had taken his jacket off and she could see his forearms; there were recent bruises on his wrists. He sat next to her.

'I'm going to get them, Imogen – just like I said I would.'

'It's better if you don't tell me. I won't lie for you if it comes down to it.'

'I don't care if I go back to prison. Some days the only thing that kept me going was the thought of killing those fuckers.' He sighed and looked down at his hands, wringing his fingers nervously. 'As soon as they turned out the lights at night all I could think about was what they did to you. I saw it over and over again. I couldn't stop them then, but I can stop them now.'

'Don't you see? I'm the one who should have known better. I let my guard down.'

'They blindsided you! They blindsided me! That's pretty hard to do!'

'I thought they were going to kill you.' She wiped her face again.

'So did I, for a minute there.'

'I'm glad they didn't.' She took his hand in hers.

'What he did to you . . . I wasn't lying when I said I was going to cut his hand off.' He stroked her fingers. 'I should have been able to protect you, but I couldn't even think, I was so angry.'

'Don't say that. Not to me.'

'I'm going to kill him, Imogen.'

'No, you aren't. We're going to catch him and put him inside.'

'Not if I get to him first.'

'Promise me you won't. This – me and you – only happens because you've served your time and the slate is clean as far as I am concerned. You can't go back to who you were before.'

'There is no who I was before, there is just who I am now.'

'I don't want you to avenge me, I don't need you to. Just help me find Vasos and let me put him away,' Imogen implored. She attempted to push down the feeling that was trying so hard not to be ignored: the feeling that perhaps the fantasy she had of Dean was better inside her head.

'After what he did?' Dean's teeth clenched together as he forced the words from his mouth.

'It's probably nothing less than I deserved.' She thought about Stanton and how she'd let him pull the wool over her eyes for so long.

'You don't mean that.'

'I should have got free! I should have done something! I feel so stupid whenever I think about it. You know, I haven't let anyone touch me since then? I just can't! Do you want to see my scar?' She started to unbutton her plaid shirt.

'You need to stop being so hard on yourself.'

'So that's a no then?'

'I don't give a shit about your scar. It's not going to change anything. I'm still going to feel what I feel and I'm still going to find Vasos and put him in a fucking hole!' Dean was angry – Imogen could see his chest heaving, his jaw clenching hard.

'Even though it's my own stupid fault?'

Without warning Dean stood up and started pacing, he rolled his sleeves up to the elbow and turned back to Imogen, quickly reaching out and putting his hand around her throat.

'What are you doing?' She clawed at his hand, but he was gripping her tightly. It hurt.

He kept his hand there and pulled her leg sharply with his free hand so that she was flat on her back. He leaned over her. Her eyes widened with shock and she scratched at his arms. Dean's eyes stayed focused on hers, full of malicious intent. He ripped her shirt open and she started to punch him.

'Come on, Imogen! You know you want this or you wouldn't have brought me here.' He didn't even look at her scar, but instead kept his eyes on hers, a slight smile lingering at the edge of his lips.

'What the fuck? Get the fuck off me!' She was starting to panic now. His hand was still clamped tight around her throat and she was struggling to draw breath as he deftly undid her trousers with his other hand, pulling at them hard until they were loose around her hips.

'I've been locked up, Imogen, I need this.'

'Dean! Stop it! You fucking prick, get off me!' She started to cry as she looked down and saw him undoing his belt. She punched him as hard as she could, but it didn't make any difference; he didn't even flinch. Tears streamed down her cheeks and she was about to try to spit in his face when, just as abruptly as the attack had begun, Dean let go. He stood up, did up his belt and moved away from her, pacing the floor like a caged tiger.

'What the fuck's wrong with you!' Imogen screamed and jumped up, pulling her trousers up. She punched him repeatedly in the back. 'Motherfucker!'

Dean spun round and grabbed her by the shoulders.

'Don't you see, Imogen? If someone wants something that bad, they can just take it. There were two of them and they had weapons; they caught you by surprise! There was nothing you could have done! Nothing! I just wanted to show you.'

'You bastard!' She thumped his chest with her fists again, still sobbing. 'You scared the shit out of me!'

'I would never hurt you, you have to know that.' He kissed her as she continued to hit him. He kept kissing until she stopped and put her arms around him. All the guilt and shame she had felt after the attack somehow abated; he had made it go away. He had made her understand that it wasn't her fault. He had shown her that there was nothing she could have done. An oddly comforting thought, given the circumstances. She started to pull at his top until she found the opening to lift it over his head. She took her open shirt off and Dean dropped to his knees, kissing her stomach and running his hands up her back.

'Come on.' She moved back and slipped her shoes off. He sat on his knees, watching as she pulled off her jeans and undid her bra, still moving back until the dining table stopped her. Standing in her underpants, she stared intently into his eyes, daring him to come and get her. 'Your turn.'

He stood and kicked off his boots, removing his jeans once again. He had a Celtic tribal tattoo running from his chest up across his shoulder. He moved towards her until she was looking up at him. He brushed her hair back and leaned down to kiss her shoulder and neck. It tickled; she had to resist the urge to snap her shoulder up so he would stop.

'I missed you,' he said, running his thumb across the tender scar on her torso.

She had missed him too. Even though they had never done this before, it felt like the most natural progression in the world. It was as if their imagination over the last year had fostered the relationship into being, and all of this was inescapable and somehow preordained. She was torn between her frenzied need to be with him and the unbearable anticipation of every single move. Restraint was never a quality she'd possessed, but she balled her fists by her sides and let him kiss her gently, relishing every touch.

'This is such a bad idea,' she whispered as she watched him kissing her shoulder.

'Do you have any better ones?' He looked up at her and a faint smile appeared for a split second, dismissing her misgivings. Even through the smile, his eyes burned with lust.

He kissed his way to her mouth and as he put his lips on hers, she had no choice but to lean back with the sheer force of his upper body. She placed her hands on the table to steady herself but he just kept pushing until she was bowed right back. Kissing her neck again, he moved his attention to her breasts; she inhaled sharply as the wetness of his tongue and the cold air made her skin contract. His mouth travelled down her body, his fingers drifting the faintest touch over her skin. It had been so long since she had felt like this; in fact, she wasn't sure whether she had ever felt this way before. She was electric, she was alive.

If Dean's time in prison had been anything like her time on the outside, he must have lain awake at night thinking of her, thinking of touching her like this. She had spent plenty of nights lying on her bed, feeling connected to him while she was alone in the dark, pretending her hands were not her own. Now the dreams were becoming reality.

He grabbed her backside and hoisted her on to the table before climbing up, his knee between her legs. She could feel the full weight of his body as he pushed against her, so she slid backwards further; forced to recline almost entirely until she was staring up at his face. She looked on as he placed his bruised arm directly next to her head. She kissed his wrist and he ran his other hand slowly down from her neck, between her breasts and over her scar, only pausing when he reached the thin layer of black lace that was between them. She saw the question in his eyes and answered by lifting her hips and moving her body into his hand, grinding herself against him.

She raised her head until she could feel his jagged breath on her face as he slid his hand under the hem and edged her underwear down. Shifting the weight of his body on to his other knee, together they completely removed the last barrier between them. She pushed up further on to her arm and their lips parted. He moved his gaze from her eyes to her mouth, his own eyes cloudy with longing. He tilted his head before kissing her firmly, breathing her in as he slid his hand between her thighs. She made an involuntary noise when his fingers found their way inside her. She fell back again and he lowered himself on to her, running her hand across his waist and down his back.

'Are you sure about this?' he asked.

'Yes, I'm sure.' It was a half-truth, but in this moment she had managed to squash the niggling voice in her head that told her Dean couldn't change. In this moment, she didn't care.

He kissed her neck again and she found her impatience growing. She reached down and touched him, taking him in her hands. She had thought about it so many times before tonight that she needed to feel him between her fingers. He groaned as she made contact; her touch was obviously unexpected. She guided him inside her. His breath fractured with every inch of him that entered her. He moved slowly and his face was so full of concentration that she had to stop herself from cracking a smile.

'Been a long time, huh?' she said teasingly.

'Oh God!' he mumbled as she moved her hips into him. It had been a long time for her, too.

'It's OK . . . Dean,' she whispered in his ear, using his name to weaken him further.

He started to move a little faster, the impact driving Imogen back with each thrust. She grabbed on to the sides of the table as he pulled his body up. She watched his face as he looked through the space between them, past her scar to where their bodies crashed together.

He groaned at the sight of himself moving in and out. He kissed her hard again, not stopping for breath, just devouring her until she found it hard to keep a grip on the table. She ignored the pain in her fingers and moved against him, doubling the impact of the collision between them.

She watched his face, the face that was usually so full of control. His guard was down. She realised the ever-increasing moaning she could hear was in fact her own voice. It had snuck up on her but now it was here, it was happening and she wanted him to feel it, too. She bit into his shoulder and cried out through her teeth. He understood and she felt his body language change as though he were finally allowing himself to be here in the moment, and in that same moment he lost all control. Her body was aglow with sensation when he finally succumbed to himself and collapsed on her in a breathy heap.

She lay there for a moment, still in that place where she couldn't really think straight. After a few minutes, she found the present pulling her back from the midst of disorientation.

'You're heavier than you look,' she said, pushing at his shoulders. He lifted himself up and she shifted as he left her body, feeling empty again. He climbed off her and stood, looking across her naked form. She sat up and looked him up and down before sliding off the table. He leaned down and kissed her, the urgency gone.

'There were moments, when I was inside . . .' He put his arms around her and held her close. 'Moments when you didn't come to see me, and you were all I could think about. I thought this might never happen . . . it nearly killed me.'

'I should have visited you. I wanted to.'

'When I saw you standing outside the prison waiting for me . . . I've never been so happy.'

'I wish I had come alone . . . I almost didn't come at all.'

'Tell me the truth now, Imogen. I promise I won't repeat it.'

'What?' She pulled away and looked up at his face.

'Do you want me to kill Vasos?'

She picked her shirt up, quickly putting it on and buttoning it.

'Why do you need it to be my decision? He hurt you, too.'

'It's not the same and you know it. I don't want to just go ahead and do it, I don't want to take it away from you.'

'I wouldn't kill him, I'm a police officer. I don't do that . . .'

'I know . . . look, Imogen, I've been there before and I felt like the revenge belonged to me and no one else. So, however you choose to deal with that scumbag, just tell me and if I can help I will.'

'As much I would like him wiped off the face of the earth – because of what he did to *both* of us – I still think we need him. We might need him to get to Stanton, to get to Antonis.' She shuddered at the mention of Stanton's name.

Chapter 46: The Boyfriend

The present

Adrian stared at his phone and watched as the screen went back to the clock. His call to Imogen went straight to answerphone. Things had changed between them and he wasn't sure if it was because of something he did or didn't do. She had withdrawn from him, and it was not like she'd been particularly in his face before. That was the best thing about his partnership with her: no judgements. Adrian liked boundaries; he liked it when he knew what he had done wrong. With Imogen at the moment it was anyone's guess; her behaviour was erratic and unpredictable. Granted, she had a lot on her plate, but he didn't feel like he was on the inside any more. She was pushing him away and he had to get back in or something was going to go horribly wrong – he could feel it. Maybe he had been trapped in his own selfish ways for too long. He was used to everything being about him, his fuck-ups and his indiscretions. Perhaps that was why he was struggling right now – because he had to give a shit about someone else.

There was something else that bothered him. The way that Kinkaid guy looked at Imogen. He'd spotted the tension between them. When he'd seen him gazing at her, it had reminded Adrian of the way he looked at Andrea. Could they actually be together? Imogen had never seemed the impulsive type, but still . . .

He had never asked her much about her time in Plymouth – she'd always found it very difficult to talk about. He knew there'd been an attack, he knew she'd sustained a brutal scar, he knew Dean was somehow involved and he knew she had a real problem with Sam, but she'd always clammed up when he'd tried to find out more. Now though, it seemed as though old issues were worming their way to the surface and he was getting sucked into her old life. It was high time they talked.

He arrived at her place and banged on the door. Kinkaid opened it. He was fully dressed but he had that *look* about him.

'Imogen isn't here,' Kinkaid said. Adrian pushed past.

'Where is she?'

'She went for a run.'

'Oh, yeah. I forgot she does that.'

'Thanks for picking me up from the prison the other day.' Dean held his hand out to Adrian. They shook hands, both men maintaining eye contact, trying to read each other. Adrian let go first.

369

'Look, Detective,' Dean broke the silence. 'Imogen says I can trust you.'

'You can. Can *I* trust *you*?'

'Aside from the fact that I'm not stupid enough to assume that anything I say will make a difference, I'm after the same people that you are.'

'You didn't know those people were up to no good?'

'In my experience, everyone is up to no good somehow. It just depends on whose standards you judge them by.'

'I guess by your standards?'

'I didn't know most of it. It wasn't my concern until Imogen became involved. You don't get to be where I am by poking your nose where it doesn't belong.'

'Do you know where they are now?'

'In all honesty, Detective, I have no idea.'

'And Bridget Reid?'

'I know nothing about that. I told Imogen I'd see what I could find out though. Giannis isn't that smart, I doubt she's very well hidden.'

'Elias?'

'What about him?'

'Is he involved?'

'No way. Elias is a good man.'

'What's your connection to him? How did you meet?'

'He caught me trying to steal from him. I was around twelve years old and constantly in trouble in one way or another; detention centres, foster care and boarding houses.'

'Must have been tough.'

'I didn't know any different. When I met Elias, he

looked out for me. He made sure I didn't go into an adult prison. Eventually, he gave me a job.'

'What kind of job?'

'The legitimate kind. I would just keep an eye on people for him. I'm a wily sort, Detective. Elias realised my talents lay in non-conventional employment.'

'So you never worked for his brother?'

'No. His brother is a sadistic man. I knew well enough to stay clear of him. Elias told Antonis I was off limits and that was that.'

'What about this Vasos character?'

'I've had a lot of dealings with him before. He is to Antonis what I am to Elias, but dumber and softer.'

'And what's that?'

'There isn't a name for it. If someone gives Elias trouble then I'm the one who makes them see sense. In Vasos' case, I would say there's very little he wouldn't do. He's not a thinker; he just does what he's told.'

'How come he doesn't have a record, if he's so dumb? I mean . . . you're in the system . . .'

'Sometimes that's the best place to be. Vasos is in a lot of trouble.'

'With Elias?'

'With me,' Dean smiled.

'Because of what he did to Grey?'

'Yes,' Dean said. He looked like he was trying to work something out before he spoke again. He was staring at Adrian and attempting to read his expression. What had Adrian said to elicit such a reaction?

'Are you and Grey . . .?' Adrian asked.

'Don't ask questions you don't want the answers to.

The relationship I have with Imogen is a complicated one. I'm sorry if my presence is disrupting anything between the two of you.'

'Us? God, no! We're just partners. It's just that in my time working with her she's never seemed very . . . I can't even think of the right word . . . she just didn't seem like relationships were very high on her list of things to do.'

A schoolboy smile spread across Dean's face at this revelation. Against his better judgement, Adrian was actually warming to the man.

'Did you know about Stanton?' Adrian asked.

'I didn't know his name; I knew of him though.'

'But Elias did? He's the one who gave him up.'

'When I was taken in for questioning, I saw him. He came in when Imogen was interviewing me. I knew his face then and so I told Elias and he did some checking with his brother.'

'Did you know about him and Imogen?'

'I saw the way he looked at her, like she was everything and nothing at the same time; like she was his possession. I guessed the rest. To be completely honest, that's part of the reason I checked him out. Have you met him?'

'Yes, since we found the baby and it was connected to Isabelle Hobbs, which was his case back in Plymouth.'

'I can't believe that I'm connected to that mess. That poor kid. Her poor parents.' Dean shook his head and looked at his hands for a moment before taking a deep breath and looking at Adrian again. 'I suspect Stanton might have been behind the attack on me and Imogen.'

'Not Sam Brown?'

'No, he wasn't anything to do with it, we checked. He seemed like such an obvious narc to me.'

'What happened that night?'

'If Imogen hasn't told you, then I'm not going to betray her confidence.'

'I'm going to guess that some stuff was left out of the report. I can see you're a man who holds a grudge. I just need to know if I'm the man who helps you, or the man who gets in the way.'

'What they did . . . they will pay for. No one has heard from Giannis in a while, so I suspect he may not be a problem any more.'

'Maybe he's hiding?'

'Like I said before, Detective, he's not that smart.'

'And Vasos?'

'I know where to find him,' he said with a stony clarity.

'Where?'

'It might be better if I deal with Vasos. He is a dangerous man; you should probably stay off his radar.'

'You never answered my question.'

'It's probably best if one of us keeps a level head about this.'

'What's that supposed to mean?'

The door opened and Imogen burst in. She was sweating and breathless but there was something else, a look about her that Adrian had never seen before. Both himself and Dean stared at her as she undid her trainers, waiting for her to look up and see them sitting together.

'I can see you both watching me,' she said, her eyes still to the ground. 'I'm sure you've lots to say, but right now, I'm going for a shower.'

Imogen disappeared and they were left alone together again. After a few moments Dean spoke.

'Look, I'm going to lay it all out for you, Detective. I can see you care about Imogen, and I can see that she trusts you. If I find Vasos first, I'm going to kill him. I told him I would as soon as he put his hands on her. Whatever I do to him is on my conscience and not on yours or hers. If you have to come after me for it, then that's fair enough, but I promise you he deserves it; if not for touching Imogen then for a million other things. Imogen doesn't care about him; she wants to get Stanton. I'll see what I can find on him, but he's not my biggest problem. As for Antonis . . . I can't touch him, I won't touch him. He's Elias' brother and I don't want that to be a thing between us.'

'What about Sam Brown?'

'What about him?'

'I'm sure Grey wouldn't want me to tell you this, but I feel like my hands are tied on this particular matter. I promised I wouldn't do anything.'

'What did he do?' Dean's eyes narrowed.

'He broke into her place, more than once.'

'Did he touch her?'

'She says no. Still, I think he needs a little scare.'

'Just a little one?'

'Yeah. He's not afraid of me, but you . . .' Adrian stood up to leave. 'Did Vasos touch her?'

'Yes, he did.' Dean looked up at Adrian. His jaw was

clenched so tight that Adrian could see his pulse. He took a deep breath and looked back down at his hands. 'He tied her up and assaulted her in front of me before sticking a knife in her and leaving her for dead. I watched the whole thing while tied to a fucking chair and there was nothing I could do.'

'Then when you do catch up to him, do me a favour and don't leave any evidence.' Adrian put his hand on Dean's shoulder and squeezed. 'I'm going to do my best to look for him, and if I get to him before you do then he'll be processed, just like any other criminal. I'll bring him and any of his scumbag friends in too. So don't get in my way and I won't get in yours. This conversation never happened.' He held his hand out and Dean shook it. 'Tell Imogen I'm waiting by the car.'

'Goodbye, Detective . . . and good luck.'

'Thanks.' Adrian made his way to the front door. 'Oh, one more thing.' He paused, standing in the doorway. 'Have you ever heard of someone called Dominic Shaw?'

'Should I have?'

'He's a friend of a friend. His name came up but I don't know if he's connected to this or not.'

'Want me to ask around?'

'No, it's fine for now, I'm sure he isn't. Just putting it out there.' Adrian nodded to Dean and left just as the sound of the shower came to a stop.

It was ten minutes before Imogen finally emerged from her place, hair dripping wet and cheeks flushed. Her shirt was on inside out. Adrian forced back a smirk.

So she was human after all. Maybe even more human than him.

'Shut up and drive, Miley.' She smiled and shook her head.

'I didn't say anything! He seems nice . . . you know . . . considering,' Adrian said as he pulled away. 'You know, Grey, we need to find Vasos before your boyfriend does. Unless . . .'

'No. I'm with you on this. We do need to find him before Dean. I want to know what he knows.'

'If you're sure . . .'

'I'm sure.' She paused for a second. 'He's a nasty piece of work, but at least he doesn't pretend to be anything else.'

'Who? Dean?' he joked.

'Vasos. He's only ever done what he's been told to do.'

'Told by Antonis Papas?'

'Maybe . . . maybe not.' She sighed. 'All in all, the last few weeks have done my bloody head in.'

'Not surprised. So I don't suppose Dean told you how we find Vasos?'

'No, but I know a few places to try. We need to go to Plymouth.'

Chapter 47: The Deal

The present

Dean Kinkaid made himself a strong coffee in the unfamiliar kitchen. He was still adjusting to life outside the prison. The first major adjustment was Imogen – the memory of her waiting for him at the gate kept playing in his head, bringing a smile to his face every time. He had all but given up on her. During the time he'd spent inside, he had waited for her to visit, but the only person who ever came was his legal advisor, Brian. Over time, Dean had trained himself to stop caring, to stop thinking about her. When he saw her standing there though, he realised at once that all his feelings were still there.

The back door to the kitchen opened and DI Brown walked in. Dean watched him put his meal for one in the microwave before making his presence known.

'Hello, Detective,' Dean finally said. Sam Brown nearly jumped out of his skin.

'Jesus fucking Christ!' Sam said. His eyes moved to the table and past the empty mug before resting on the large kitchen knife that lay next to Dean's hand.

'Long time no see.'

'What the fuck are you doing here? How did you get in? This is my house!'

'Same way you got into Imogen's place before, I expect.'

'Now listen, you have no right to . . .' Sam started to protest when the microwave beeped. Dean smiled at him and stabbed the table with the knife.

'Let's just skip the chit chat, shall we? You know who I am . . . what I'm capable of. If you don't, I can give you a demonstration.' Dean stood up.

'Is this about Imogen? I don't know what she's told you but I had nothing to do with what happened to her in Plymouth.'

'Do you have a thing for her, Brown, is that it? Do you honestly think a woman like that would want anything to do with someone like you?' He smiled.

'Someone like me? What the fuck does that mean?'

'You know what it means.'

'Are you threatening me?'

'No. Just some friendly advice. I believe that you weren't involved in the assault at my place but I want you to tell me what you remember about that night.'

'I was trying to find Imogen; she wasn't answering when I called her.'

'She said she heard you talking to Vasos outside the club – saying you would take care of her.'

'I was working undercover, Kinkaid. I was getting

close to Vasos so that I could find out more about the trafficking – I had to make him trust me. I phoned Stanton that day to find out where Imogen was, that's when I told him she was pregnant. Because I was concerned. That must be how they knew. Stupid, because I knew someone was feeding whoever was in charge the information; it just never occurred to me it would be him. He always seemed like such a straight shooter.'

'What did you find out about the trafficking?' Dean paused for a moment, knowing the answer to the question he was about to ask but still feeling the overwhelming urge to ask it anyway. 'Was Elias involved in all that?'

Sam shook his head. 'There's no direct evidence of that. Antonis on the other hand is up to his neck in it, but even he doesn't account for the kind of movement and money we've been seeing. There's someone else above him.'

'Detective, I'm sure that on some level you're not an asshole, but when it comes to Imogen you need to take a wide berth. You make her uncomfortable, and I can't have that. It's only out of respect for her that I'm not kicking seven shades of shit out of you right now. I'm asking you nicely – leave her alone.'

'OK, but I can't control what happens inside work.'

'That's fine. But if anything does happen, I *will* hear about it.'

Dean left the knife sticking out of Brown's table and walked out to his car. He had to go and find Vasos now that that particular detour was over. It felt good to be in control again.

*

Adrian arrived at Antonis' house in Plymouth. Imogen had headed towards Aphrodite's, both agreeing to call each other if they found anything. Adrian had made her promise not to go in alone, to ring him if she saw anything suspicious. He looked up at the house – he knew this was where Isabelle had been kept as a child, even though she had failed to identify either of the men who had held her captive. He wondered if that were some kind of misplaced loyalty; he rather expected so. The police were still trying to get enough physical evidence to push for a search of the place, yet two judges had so far refused to sign the orders. Given what Adrian knew about Antonis so far, he imagined he had some people in high places buying him some time.

Just looking at the building gave Adrian a bad feeling. It was a cold, miserable-looking place, certainly not what you'd expect for someone with the kind of income that Elias had claimed Antonis was pulling in. The house had a wooden door that looked split and swollen through lack of care, and the painted brick walls were cracked and peeling. The only discerning features were two square windows that were thick with dust from the passing traffic. Squinting at them, Adrian could see a glimpse of heavily patterned, nicotine-stained net curtains that blocked the rooms from view.

Adrian walked through the grubby alleyway that led to the back of the house and climbed over the wall. The back yard was devoid of sunlight, he found seventies stonework, chequerboard pink and yellow garden slabs and a shed at the end. He tried the back door; it was open.

Adrian walked through the door as quietly as he could. He could hear a TV or a radio playing somewhere in the house, but he wasn't sure where. The kitchen floor stuck to his shoes as he tried to move across the room quietly. There was a smell in the house, not just any smell but *that* smell, that sweet putrid smell of rotting meat. He was glad he'd left the door open.

In the hall Adrian found a baseball bat resting against the wall. He picked it up and moved towards the lounge. The noise got louder. It was the TV after all; he could see the light reflecting against the walls. His eyes adjusted to the dimly lit room, everything was a yellowy grey, almost like the sky just before the sun came up.

The good news was that Adrian had found Antonis; the bad news was that he was either dead or in a really deep sleep. Someone had obviously made an attempt at saving Antonis' life, judging by the amount of dried bloody bandages on and around the body. Adrian's eyes moved to the coffee table, it was littered with wrappers and cans. There was another smell mingling in the air; Adrian couldn't put his finger on it at first, but then he saw the ashtray. There was the faintest hint of smoke rising up from the cigarillo perched on the edge. Someone else was here. Adrian backed himself up against the wall and tried to keep silent. He wasn't sure if the person who was there knew he was inside the house or not. He would work on the assumption that they did.

At first glance, there was nowhere to hide in this room and so Adrian conceded that whoever it was probably wasn't in the lounge, and he definitely hadn't been in the kitchen. That only left upstairs. At that exact moment, Adrian heard a toilet flush. Whoever was there perhaps didn't know about him after all. He stood out of view at the bottom of the staircase and waited. Heavy steps sounded upstairs; Adrian heard a zipper being done up and then he saw him. Vasos was almost at the bottom of the stairs; he was much heavier than Adrian and so the element of surprise was probably the most he had going for him. Adrian rushed towards him as he entered his line of sight, taking him out at the knees.

'Who the fuck are you?' Vasos shouted.

'Police.'

Vasos put his hands up and didn't fight back, the gesture going against everything Adrian had heard about him.

'I turn myself in. I want protection.' Vasos' voice was clear.

'Did you kill Antonis Papas?'

'No, I didn't. He was almost dead when I got here, he'd been attacked by his son. I tried to save him but he wouldn't let me call anyone. It was Giannis that did it. Little bastard finally grew some balls.' Adrian released his hold on Vasos, who got to his feet laboriously and propped himself up against the wall with his hands in the air, fully surrendered.

'Where is Giannis now?'

'I have no idea. Antonis said he was hurt when he attacked him. Asked me to find him and make sure he is OK.'

'Did you?' Adrian pulled out his phone and started

to dial, holding his finger up to shush Vasos while he spoke. 'Just calling this in.'

'Who are you calling?'

'My partner.' Adrian kept his finger held in the air. 'Hi . . . yes . . . I found him, we're at Antonis' house, yes, in Plymouth . . . No problem, we'll wait here . . . the back door's open. Later.'

Adrian hung up and put his hand down, nodding for Vasos to speak. 'So did you find Giannis?'

'No, I stayed here – without Antonis' protection I'm as good as dead.'

'What about Bridget Reid? What happened there? Why did you go after her?'

'Antonis got a call from DCI Stanton, he was at the house she worked from and he bumped into her. He said he recognised her as a cop and so we had to go and deal with her.'

'Will you testify to that?'

'Anything you want, but you have to protect me, give me a new ID or whatever it is you do.'

'Who are you afraid of? Dean Kinkaid?'

'Kinkaid? No, I can take that fucker whenever I want. I could have had him finished off in prison.'

'Then who?'

'The man in charge, the main guy.'

'There's someone else? Why didn't Elias mention him?'

'Elias didn't know anything about it. If I tell you, they'll kill me, and maybe even you.'

'They? You're not making any sense!'

'The man, I never knew his name – no one does –

but he's fucked up. I saw him rip a guy's head open by pulling his mouth and jaws apart once.' He shook his head. 'It was crazy.'

'What does he look like, this mysterious guy with no name?'

'Tall, older than you, with kind of long grey hair . . . but polished, very polished.'

'White? Black? What?'

'White but tan, like an Italian model or something. Long coat, some kind of necklace . . . silver or white gold, with like a medallion on it.'

'Medallion?'

'Like a St Christopher, I think. But with a weird pattern in black or blue stones, about the size of a ten pence piece. It looks pretty expensive. He's obviously got money.'

'How come this is the first we're hearing about this man?'

'I only met him maybe twice. Antonis was very private about him, even with me. As soon as all this crazy shit about the girl and the baby started happening, Antonis got very scared.'

'Scared, why?'

'Because he was told he had to kill that girl, that one that went missing, but he couldn't do it and so he told me to hide her in the corner shop with Dimi. He cared about her. He wasn't a total monster.'

'What about you? Are you a total monster? Give me one good reason why I shouldn't just hand you over to Kinkaid after what you did to my partner.'

'I was ordered to do that because she was snooping

around too much. Plus we needed Kinkaid out of the way. Without him, Elias didn't have the same kind of power. We got the all clear from her boss.' Vasos shrugged.

'Kinkaid wants to kill you for that. I told him I was taking you in though.'

'Well, thank you, officer.' Vasos grinned.

'Trouble is, then I saw you and all I could think about was your hands on my partner, so I kind of changed my mind.'

'But you called this in now? I'm under police protection . . . right?' Vasos didn't seem concerned.

'I hope I'm not interrupting anything.'

Adrian and Vasos turned around to see Dean in the kitchen doorway.

'What the hell is this? How did he know I was here?' Vasos' face had gone white.

'I may not be a rocket scientist, Vasos, but realistically, where else were you going to go?'

'You can't let him have me! I surrendered!'

'I dunno, mate. If Kinkaid wants you, I'm not sure I could put up much of a fight.' Adrian and Dean nodded at each other in solidarity. Vasos' complacent expression had changed into one of obvious concern.

'Looks like Antonis got what was coming to him. Karma is one righteous bitch.' Dean ran his eyes over the dead body on the sofa.

'So you didn't call your partner?' Vasos was staring at Adrian.

'If I were you, I wouldn't talk about her,' Dean said, his voice as cold as ice.

'I actually did call her. She'll be here any minute. You two had better get going.' Adrian watched as Vasos' eyes darted around the room, obviously searching for an exit. Adrian could almost see the cogs turning in his mind: if he made a break for it, he'd have to go through both of them, and that wasn't going to happen. Maybe he could take down Adrian, but Dean Kinkaid as well? He didn't fancy the man's chances. Especially not when Dean had just spent the last eighteen months in jail, dreaming about the moment he'd have Vasos to himself.

Adrian knew it was wrong to leave Vasos to be killed, but all he could think about was Eva, or Isabelle as he was trying to force himself to call her. He thought of her scared face, her kindness in the corner shop, and what Antonis and Vasos must have put her through for all these years. He thought too about Imogen, imagined the knife plunging into her stomach, Vasos knowing full well that she was pregnant. Surely the world would be a better place without him?

'Face or stomach, Vasos?' Adrian looked at Dean – it seemed like the decision to deal with Vasos had been decided for him. The man looked like he was going to be sick as Dean stared at him. Adrian felt his morality slipping away. It seemed to dislodge itself a little more with every case. Where would it end? He used to respect the process but now he was confused. He thought about Stanton – he couldn't even trust the people in the process any more. Dean was smiling. Adrian looked the other way as he launched himself at Vasos. The sounds of their struggle filled his ears. He swallowed hard, forcing himself not to act, letting Dean's actions run their course.

He heard the sound of Dean dragging Vasos from the house, followed by the slam of the front door. It was no more than Vasos deserved.

'Miley! What happened?'

Imogen was standing in front of him, staring down at Antonis' dead body.

'Grey. You made it.'

'Fraser's called the medics to come check you out. Where's Vasos?'

'Last thing I saw was his fist,' Adrian lied. He rubbed at his cheek.

'You're lucky he didn't kill you! Did he kill Antonis?'

'No, apparently Giannis did that. I don't need a medic, cancel them.'

'Without Vasos we can't get Stanton, he'll get a free pass. Elias has no physical evidence, but I bet Vasos would.'

'Now we know about Stanton, we can look into him properly. We can—'

'We got something!' Fraser's voice interrupted Adrian. He was calling from inside the kitchen. The detectives followed the sound of his voice. The DCI was pushing on a doorway behind a defunct-looking dishwasher. With a scraping sound, the lock gave, leading to a set of stairs. Without speaking, all three of them squeezed through the gap and made their way down, down into the depths of the house. The smell that Adrian had assumed was just Antonis was getting stronger by the second.

A gruesome scene confronted them at the bottom.

Adrian's stomach swam. He could tell he wasn't going to forget this in a hurry. Bridget Reid lay emaciated on the ground, her cheeks hollow and sunken, her skin grey. Fraser leaned down and pulled up a blood-stained sheet to reveal Giannis' corpse. Everyone in the room recoiled involuntarily. Adrian looked over at Imogen, whose eyes were fixed firmly on Bridget Reid's face.

She seemed unusually focused, almost mesmerised. 'Are you OK? Grey?'

Imogen bent down to look at the body more closely, he watched as she slowly reached her hand out and placed her fingers on Bridget's neck. He put his hand on Imogen's shoulder. He was certain Bridget was dead.

'When's that medic getting here?' Imogen's voice was breathless as she looked up at Adrian, her eyes glassy and wet. 'I can feel a pulse!'

'What? Are you sure?' Adrian broke the silence as everyone stared at Bridget Reid. She couldn't have looked more dead. Adrian leaned down and put his hand next to Imogen's; she moved her fingers away so he could feel it too. 'Jesus Christ. She's right. There's a pulse.'

Fraser sprang into action, running back upstairs and pulling out his phone. They heard him shouting into it, telling the paramedics to get a bloody move on. Imogen sank to her knees.

'I can't believe we've found her.' She put a hand out to Bridget and began to stroke her hair. She was filthy, her skin encrusted with dirt and Giannis' blood.

'It's OK, Bridget, we found you; you're going to be

OK. The doctor is on his way.' She looked up at Adrian again. 'Call Sam.'

It hadn't even occurred to Adrian to call Sam Brown. He wasn't relishing the idea of talking to him, but Imogen was right; it had to be done. He pulled out his phone and dialled.

'What is it?' Sam answered in a less than enthusiastic manner.

'We found Bridget.'

'Oh my God! Is she OK? Where is she?'

'She'll be going to hospital. I'm not going to lie to you, Sam . . . she might not make it.'

'But she's alive?'

'She's got a pulse . . . a very weak one . . . but yes, she's alive.' Adrian hated doing this kind of thing at the best of times, but over the phone, to a fellow police officer, it felt even worse.

'Text me with the details. I'm on my way to the hospital.'

Three paramedics burst into the basement. The air in the room added to the feeling of urgency; they all wanted out as quickly as possible. The medics put the oxygen mask over Bridget's face carefully, barking questions at Imogen and Adrian. Bridget looked so fragile, her skin the white grey gloss of a porcelain doll. They moved her on to the stretcher and attached her to a mobile saline drip before transporting her upstairs and into the ambulance.

'You should go home,' Fraser said to Adrian. 'We can talk about what happened here tomorrow. Not here, at the station. You know what I mean.'

'I'm not going to argue, I've got a splitting headache.' He turned to Imogen. 'Are you OK if I go?'

'Go, it's fine. I'll fill you in tomorrow.'

Adrian walked out before they could ask him any more about Vasos, before either of them could begin to question whether he'd seen him, and if so, how he'd managed to get away. Luckily the discovery of Bridget Reid had diverted the focus away from him, at least momentarily. He felt like a shit for thinking that, but then he seemed to have less and less control over the thoughts that popped into his head these days.

Adrian got in the car and drove. He needed a beer, or ten. He needed to stop thinking about what Kinkaid was doing to Vasos right at this moment. He needed to forget that he'd just broken the law. Again.

Chapter 48: The Hand

The present

Dean could still smell the aroma of Imogen's coconut shampoo. He had just picked her up from Antonis' house and dropped her off at the hospital. It was good having his old car back, he'd missed it. Missed the feel of his hands on a steering wheel, the sensation of freedom at his fingertips. He thought about Imogen and wished that things were different, he wished he didn't have to lie to her. He promised himself that as soon as he had dealt with Vasos this would be the end – he wouldn't do anything like this again. He wanted to be the man she could depend on and he knew how important trust and honesty were to that equation. He parked his car and took a deep breath. Time to get to work.

Inside the house it was damp; the windows hadn't been opened in years. It was an old terraced building that Dean had bought years ago, one of three small properties he'd purchased next to each other. He lived in the middle one and used the other two for storage. It also meant he didn't have to constantly second-guess his neighbours or worry about what they could or couldn't hear through his walls. He had pinhole cameras fitted through the walls on both sides so that nothing happened in this house without being carefully documented.

He rarely brought business home, but sometimes it was unavoidable. He looked through the archives for the date when he and Imogen were attacked and watched the camera footage back, his jaw clenched tightly throughout. Memory is a funny thing. Perspective is another. Dean watched himself take a beating and then he watched Imogen arrive. He watched Vasos and Giannis strip her to her underwear as he was slumped unconscious in a dining chair facing her, unaware of what was happening. During his time in prison, Dean had wondered whether he'd exaggerated the horror of the night; he had never trusted his memories and knew his mind played tricks on him at times. Watching this video confirmed that he hadn't been delusional – the night had been every bit as horrific as he remembered it. The one thing he hadn't seen before was the moment Vasos actually cut Imogen. He'd seen him stick the knife in, but not the part where he dragged the knife up her torso as she lolled helplessly. Dean took the clip and put it on a memory stick.

He walked through into what would have been the lounge, had the house been in any way decorated or even fit for living in. There was tarpaulin everywhere. Vasos was taped to the wooden skeleton of the wall, clawing at the tape that Dean had wrapped around his neck after dragging him back here from Antonis' house. Vasos' neck was bleeding.

Dean held out a bottle of water to Vasos.

'Mi casa, su casa,' he said. 'You must be getting thirsty. You've been here a while now – I had a couple of errands to run, you see.'

'I'm going to break your fucking neck when I get free.' Vasos smacked the water out of his hands.

'I see your hand is totally healed now.'

'Just get on with it, you piece of shit!'

'I've been waiting for this a long time, mate. Just let me savour the moment.'

Dean went to the corner of the room to the trestle table. On it were a bunch of power tools. In the unlikely event that anyone would find Vasos' body when he was done with it, Dean wanted to be sure that the cuts and marks on his skin were made by common and generic items that could be found in any household. He had bought the most popular model of drill several years earlier, as well as the most commonly sold saw; in fact, Dean used to go to car boot sales and buy anything that could be used as a weapon. He had a storage room in an unregistered lock-up that wasn't connected to him or anyone he knew. If anyone searched it, all they would find was a load of second-hand crap that was in no way illegal to own. Dean knew that you didn't need an army-issue hunting knife to kill a person, you just needed something pointy. His deep-rooted survival instinct had made him see every item as a possible weapon and look for the escape route in every room.

Dean picked up the nail gun. He walked over to Vasos and stared at him.

'What are you planning on doing with that?'

Dean fired a nail into Vasos' knee. He screamed.

'Realistically, there isn't enough pain in this world for you, Vasos, and so I think for my own sake I'm going to make this pretty quick. That's not to say you won't suffer, you will, but my main desire is for you not to exist. I'm done thinking about you.'

'I just did what I was told! It wasn't personal!'

'You can either whine like a bitch or you can accept that this is happening. Makes no difference to me. You're the last stop: everyone else is dead or else they ran as fast as they could – away from you and that psycho you work for.'

Vasos' eyes were bulging. 'Can I have a cigarette at least?'

Dean pulled a packet of cigarettes from his pocket and held it out to Vasos, taunting him with the just out of reach packet. Vasos swung his leg out and kicked Dean in the thigh. Dean barely felt the force; there was no real leverage behind it given that the man's neck was strapped to the wall. The cigarettes fell to the floor. Dean smiled and walked towards his prisoner, firing another nail into his body. Straight through the kneecap. Vasos sagged a little and grabbed at his leg, trying in vain to get the nail out. Dean fired three more shots into Vasos' hand, nailing it to his thigh. Now the only hand Vasos had left was the one with three fingers, the one Dean had promised to cut off. He wondered if Vasos remembered the threats that Dean made as clearly as he did. He grabbed that hand and held it against the post next to Vasos' head; with one quick movement he nailed it to the wood.

Dean moved back over to the table and put the nail gun down, ignoring Vasos' cries of pain. The sobs were satisfying. Dean picked up the circular saw and started the motor. He walked over to Vasos again and held it up.

'I told you this was coming.' He moved the blade towards Vasos' hand and leaned back as the jagged metal ripped through the skin and bone as if it weren't there. The hand remained in place, nailed to the wall, while the arm fell limp, blood pumping from the wound and pooling at Vasos' feet.

'I'm not going to beg you, Kinkaid. You've won!' he screamed.

Dean was disappointed that he wasn't enjoying it as much as he thought he would. He almost felt like he was betraying Imogen by doing this. If she ever found out, he didn't know if she would give him a second chance. It was time to make Vasos disappear; he hadn't been lying when he'd said he wanted to make this quick. For his own sanity, if nothing else. He moved the blade through the other wrist and straight through Vasos' leg; the blood pumped furiously and Vasos' arm sprang out, spraying Dean's shirt with warm red liquid. He was going into shock, his face ashen and eyes tearing with a mixture of pain and fear. Dean turned the saw off and dropped it on the floor, reaching for the flat chisel.

'You're lucky I'm feeling generous,' he said as he thrust the chisel into Vasos, moving the blade between his ribs in an upwards motion. A dissatisfying gurgle leaked from Vasos' mouth before he slumped forward completely. It was over.

Peeling his shirt away from his chest, the deep red liquid acting as an adhesive, Dean stripped down and left his clothes on the floor. He would burn them later. He felt his skin tighten as Vasos' blood started to dry on him. He stood and watched as the life literally drained from the body, listening to the syncopated thuds as the blood hit the plastic.

Dean had made a promise and he'd kept it. Gradually, the sound of the dripping blood slowed until the only disturbance in the room was Dean's breathing. He would deal with the body later, but right now he needed to go and shower. By the end of the day he would remove all traces of Vasos. His body would never be found, and Imogen would never know.

Chapter 49: The Hunter

The present

Adrian was half naked and half asleep on the couch when he heard the key turn in the lock. The last few days had mainly been spent sleeping, trying to shake off the memory of leaving Vasos in Dean's hands. Imogen had been round to see him once, and the pair of them had sat for hours, discussing the ins and outs of the case. Bridget was still in hospital, but it looked as though she was going to make it. A silver cloud in a truly fucked-up case.

He sat up at the sound of the key in the door, expecting to see Tom. Instead, he was confronted with Dominic Shaw. He was wearing a floor-length navy wool coat, and what Adrian assumed was a cashmere scarf. He looked out of place in Adrian's front room; he was actively avoiding making eye contact with any of the plastic spacemen in boxes whose gaze followed you around the room.

'I borrowed Tom's key. He's just gone to the corner shop. I see it's under new management,' he said as Adrian shot to his feet, grabbing at the waist of his unbuttoned jeans to stop them from falling down. 'I figured it was time we had a chat.'

'This is bang out of order, Dominic, and you know it!'

'Maybe. What I also know is that you've been sticking your nose where it doesn't belong.'

'What are you talking about?'

'It's been a long time, Adrian. You need to get over the fact that Andrea is with me now.'

'This isn't about Andrea, but as long as you bring her up, she's married to your wallet, not you.'

'You know I saw you snooping around my office at the party. I'm guessing you got the key from Tom.'

'He was worried about his mother.'

'Listen, mate, I tolerate you in Tom's life because you're his biological father. That's it. Andrea doesn't want you around any more than I do.'

'Are you sure about that?' Adrian smiled. If there was one thing he knew for sure it was that Dominic was a jealous man; possibly even intimidated, and if there was one thing Adrian was good at it was making other guys feel insecure about themselves when it came to women. He had discovered this entirely by accident, but over the years he had cultivated this skill to his advantage. He felt a shiver run down his spine as Dominic's eyes travelled over him and rested on the line of hair that ran down from his belly button.

Adrian narrowed his eyes and grinned at Dominic.

If he didn't know better he would say he could see a hint of attraction in the older man's eyes. Was Dominic *into* him? An interesting turn of events if he was.

'You need to leave my family alone,' Dominic finally said.

'Your family?' Adrian wasn't sure if he was reading Dominic right, but if he was, he felt he had no option but to poke the bear. He moved closer to him, eyes fixed on his, daring Dominic to look anywhere but his face. Dominic's gaze shifted down for a split second and Adrian smiled.

'I could make life very difficult for you, Adrian. I could convince Andrea that you had done something bad. You know?'

'You can't stop me from seeing Tom any more. He's pretty much old enough to decide for himself where he goes. If you try to mess with my relationship with him, do you really think you will win? How do you think Andrea will feel if he chooses me?'

Dominic snorted. 'I couldn't give a shit about Tom. I wanted Andrea – Tom was just part of that deal.'

Adrian saw a flicker of something between Dominic's lapels, a silver disc. He felt his throat dry as he finally saw the medallion hanging just under his scarf. Dominic followed his eyes and pulled out the pendant.

'What's that pattern?' Adrian pointed at the configuration of sapphires.

'It's Orion; the constellation,' Dominic said.

'Where did you get it?'

'It was a gift from Andrea actually, she designed it and had it made for me.'

'So I couldn't just go out and buy one?'

'It's platinum and sapphire, Adrian, so I highly doubt it.'

Adrian wanted to sit down again, his legs weren't feeling that strong as he remembered the description Vasos had given him of the man in charge, the one Antonis was scared of. The man trafficking all the women.

'Hi, Dad.' Tom walked in and Adrian felt the pressure lift immediately. Tom chucked his bag on the floor and thumped up the stairs.

'Thanks for bringing him round.' Adrian needed Dominic out of his house so he could think. He'd have to play nice.

'I just hope we understand each other now. You need to back off.'

'I will, I promise.'

Dominic stepped forward, lowering his voice. 'I know you think she still wants you, but she doesn't. You should hear the things she's said about you over the years.'

'I guess I just thought now that we were talking again that maybe I was in with a shot . . . I get the message. I'll back off.' Adrian said the words through gritted teeth, trying to appear sincere. He couldn't let Dominic know what he was thinking, couldn't reveal that he knew about the pendant, and what it might signify.

'Good.' Dominic threw Adrian the key and walked out.

Adrian sat down. Was Dominic a human trafficker? Is that where he got his money from? One thing he knew for sure was that Tom wasn't safe there any more. If Dominic thought Adrian was on to him, that house wasn't safe for his son.

Tom bounded into the room again.

'Have you got any food?'

'There's some pizza you can reheat in the fridge. Tom, I need to ask you something.'

'OK?'

'You're fourteen now. We have a great time together. I want you to come and live with me for a bit.'

Tom looked surprised. 'I couldn't do that to Mum. She's on her own most of the time as it is.'

'I know, but even just for a few months . . .'

'I'd rather stay at home, Dad. I'm sorry.'

'I'll talk to your mum. She might be OK with it. Would that change your mind?'

'What's this really about, Dad? Did you find something out about Dominic? You're being weird.'

'I don't trust him, that's all.'

'Me neither . . . that's why I have to stay. Keep an eye on him.'

Adrian sighed. 'Just be careful, OK? Don't go snooping around. If you see anything suspicious at all, you tell me but no one else, OK?'

'Relax Dad. I won't do anything, I promise.' Tom disappeared into the kitchen.

Adrian would have to tread carefully from now on, but he swore to himself that he'd find out what Dominic was, and he'd have him put away. Tom was his main concern.

He wanted to kick himself for not looking into

Dominic before, not properly, anyway, dismissing himself as the pathetic jealous ex and not trusting his own instincts. He grabbed the file he had on Dominic's financials from the bottom drawer of the dresser and spread the pages out on the floor. He started to organise all of the things he knew about Dominic's life.

He had to make sure he didn't arouse any suspicion. People were afraid of Dominic. Bad people. He had to assume that Dominic was dangerous. There was one thing Adrian knew for sure; he would get to the bottom of this or die trying.

Acknowledgements

Since writing my debut novel *The Teacher* on my own in the basement, things have changed so much. I have so many people to thank and it's unlikely I will remember everyone by name, so if you think you deserve a thank you from me, you probably do. Take it, it's yours.

First of all I would like to say a huge thank you to Diane Banks, my agent, for taking a chance on me in the first place and thank you also to everyone at Diane Banks Associates. I'd also like to thank everyone I have worked with at Avon, it's been a real pleasure to be in your safe hands – I can't possibly name you all!

A special shout out to Eleanor Dryden, the commissioning editor who took *The Teacher* on!

Thanks to my mum and stepdad who are always there for me. Thanks to both of my sisters for their support, too. Also the rest of my huge extended family – far too many of you to name.

Thanks as well to Scheherazade Pesante, Karen Bellamy and all the lovely ladies at the Ramsgate women's writing group, where I started writing *The Teacher*. Thanks also to Jane Wenham-Jones and the judges at *Ramsgate's Got Writing Talent* for giving me the confidence to pursue my dream.

A big thank you as well to my fellow crime writers who have been nothing if not supportive – you know who you are – you know what you've done.

Lastly I would like to say thanks to my husband, my son and my daughter – or as we like to call ourselves, 'The just-us league' – you rock.

Before *The Secret*, there was
The Teacher...

You think you know who to trust?
You think you know the difference
between good and evil?
You're wrong . . .

Discover how it all started.